PA.

UNN.

They were now right in the thick of the stampede as the city streets funnelled the animals into the bottleneck of Regent Street, towards Oxford Circus. Despite the alien nature of their surroundings, some of the dinosaurs were reverting to their natural instinctive behaviour. Apatasaurs charged past startled shoppers, crushing the unwary beneath their elephantine feet, running in fear of the pursuing carnivores.

Still some way ahead of Nimrod and Genevieve, the Megasaurus Rex turned into a packed Piccadilly Circus. A startled omnibus driver spun his steering wheel to avoid the prehistoric obstacle. The bus lurched violently to one side and into the path of a steam-belching hansom cab. The two vehicles collided with a dreadful inevitability, the bus toppling onto its side. The Megasaur put a huge clawed foot on top of the stricken omnibus, as though claiming its kill, and snapped the driver from his cab.

An Abaddon Books™ Publication
www.abaddonbooks.com
abaddon@rebellion.co.uk

First published in 2007 by Abaddon Books™, Rebellion Intellectual
Property Limited, The Studio, Brewer Street, Oxford, OX1 1QN, UK.

Distributed in the US and Canada by SCB Distributors, 15608 South
Century New Drive, Gardena, CA 90248, USA.

10 9 8 7 6 5 4 3 2 1

Editor: Jonathan Oliver
Cover: Mark Harrison
Design: Simon Parr
Series Advisor: Andy Boot
Marketing and PR: Keith Richardson
Creative Director and CEO: Jason Kingsley
Chief Technical Officer: Chris Kingsley
Pax Britannia™ created by Jonathan Green and Andy Boot

ISBN 13: 978-1-905437-10-8
ISBN 10: 1-905437-10-2
A CIP record for this book is available from the British Library

Printed in the UK by Bookmarque, Surrey

PAX BRITANNIA

UNNATURAL
HISTORY

Jonathan Green

Abaddon
Books

WWW.ABADDONBOOKS.COM

For Mattie –
for being late

PROLOGUE

The jangling of the doorbell rang through the echoing space of the entrance hall. It rang through rooms of shrouded furniture and echoed from marble and alabaster columns. It rebounded from ancient family heirlooms and antique vases. It did nothing to disturb the eternal sleep of the ancestors who were depicted in the portraits adorning the dark, papered walls. Eventually the sound was lost along the tiled passageway leading to the kitchen and the servants' quarters, no longer an echo but merely the memory of one.

Peace returned again to the London town house, the only sound in the otherwise silent rooms the regular mechanical ticking of the grandfather clock standing in the hollow of the stairwell. It was unshrouded, the motto 'Tempus Fugit' clearly visible on its peeling face. The gentle ticking marking time in a house where time no longer had any meaning.

A tapping joined the steady count of the clock; that of leather soles on glazed white tiles. The house's guardian strode purposefully, and yet unhurriedly, towards the front door. He passed along the corridor from his retreat beyond the kitchen, back straight, head upright, the aquiline features of his face cold and unsmiling as he stared straight ahead of him with piercing sapphire eyes.

The portraits watched him with their impassive canvas eyes as he passed. Electric light bathed everything in its yellow luminescence.

He walked past a huge gilt-framed mirror that dominated one wall but did not even glance at his reflection to check the starched collar, the knot of his cravat or the set of his grey hair, swept back from a widow's peak.

The bell rang again as he put his hand to the doorknob and pulled the front door of the London town house open. The shorter, stouter man waiting impatiently on the step physically jerked back, startled by the suddenness of the manservant's appearance.

The stout man looked up at the servant looming over him and into the flinty eyes glaring down from beneath darkly shadowed brows. Breaking eye contact, uncomfortable beneath the piercing stare, he looked the butler up and down, taking in the rest of his intimidating figure. The butler was a man of indiscernible age although he could not be younger than forty-five and could even be into his sixties. His expression of aloof disdain and his chiselled features gave him an aristocratic air. However, the butler's nose had clearly been broken on more than one occasion. It gave him the look of an aging prize-fighter carried off with the bearing of a gentleman's loyal retainer.

"Ah, Nimrod."

"Mr Screwtape, sir," the manservant replied. His accent was as polished and refined as his collar was starched crisp and white. "You are expected. Please come in."

There was nothing in Nimrod's tone and his impassive expression that suggested the lawyer was welcome. In fact the invitation made Screwtape feel as if he were trespassing.

"Mr Quicksilver awaits you in the study."

The butler stepped to one side and then shut the door on the chill of the night outside. Screwtape removed his bowler hat with one hand – a briefcase held in the other – revealing his feeble attempts to brush his thinning, obviously dyed black hair over the balding dome of his head. Small piggy eyes, set amidst flabby features, peered out from the lenses of a pair of pince-nez spectacles beneath which nestled a short, bushy moustache.

"May I take your coat, sir?"

"N-No, it's all right. I'll keep it with me." Nimrod was making him feel nervous.

"Very well, sir." Nimrod's tone was almost wearisome. "If you would care to follow me."

The butler led the lawyer through rooms of dust sheet shrouded furniture and glowering ancestral portraits, through a musty-smelling formal library and to a single oak-panelled door. There he stopped and gave the door a gentle knock.

"Come in," came an aristocratic voice from beyond. The butler opened the door, allowing the visitor to enter before him.

Screwtape found himself in a spacious study. The walls were lined with cases of books and, where the paisley-print wallpaper still showed, there were walnut-framed aquatints and spectrum-tinted photographs of exotic locations from around the globe. There were also curious artefacts no doubt collected from those self-same destinations. Amongst them Screwtape could see a Masai warrior's spear and antelope-hide shield, a Burmese demon-mask and, most disturbing of all, a dark, stained human skull stuck with flints and the plumage of a bird of paradise. The lawyer had no idea where that particular item had come from, nor did he want to.

Several pieces of furniture were well accommodated within the study also. A large mahogany desk stood before him, behind it a rich leather chair. There was also another chair and a chaise longue. In one corner an effort had been made at horticulture where a potted aspidistra stood on a turned ebony plant-stand.

The room was finished in mahogany and wine-dark velvet. Behind the desk heavy drapes concealed tall windows and above the black iron mantle of a fireplace was the imposing portrait of a grey haired and moustachioed man. The subject of the painting was dressed in a tweed jacket, mustard-yellow waistcoat and hunting britches, looking every part the English country gent out enjoying an afternoon's grousing. He even had a rifle in his right hand; only the scene behind him was that of the African savannah and one booted foot rested on the carcass of a savage lion.

Screwtape looked from the heroic portrait to the young man standing beneath it. The family resemblance was remarkable.

Covering much of the scuffed green leather of the desk were clippings from *The Times*. A number of articles were of particular interest to the young man, which he was re-reading whilst he swirled the contents of a cut crystal glass in his right hand. As the lawyer peered through his pince-nez at the papers he saw from the larger print of the headlines that they appeared to concern the same matter. One headline read, 'Millionaire Playboy Missing over Himalayas', another, 'Hot Air Balloon Adventure Ends in Tragedy'. The most recent report carried the banner, 'Quicksilver Missing, Presumed Dead'. The date on this newspaper read 3rd April 1996.

The ornate ormolu clock on the mantelpiece chimed ten. Seconds later the echoing chime of the grandfather clock sounded elsewhere in the house. There was something clandestine about the timing of this meeting and, along with Nimrod's lingering presence, it made Screwtape feel uncomfortable. Why meet at such an hour to seal the deal if there were not something nefarious about this venture? The hours of darkness were when the criminal fraternity went about their unlawful business. Not that such things would have normally bothered the lawyer. Every day it was his job to work with the law, around the law, to bend the rules, counteract conventions, confuse and bewilder with clauses, quoting obscure sub-articles. The firm of Mephisto, Fanshaw and Screwtape had been in the employ of the Quicksilver family for the last five generations, since the time of the Crimean War. They had a long-shared history and heritage.

"Screwtape, do have a seat won't you?" the young man said, gesturing to the padded leather chair.

The lawyer regarded the armchair uncomfortably, playing the rim of his bowler hat through his restless hands as he did so.

"No, it's all right. I'd prefer to stand."

The younger man cast his eyes towards the chair for the first time since the lawyer had entered the study. A distant, wistful look misted his eyes. "Yes, I know what you mean."

The empty seat seemed to exude an unsettling dominance.

"A drink then?" Quicksilver said, raising his glass as if in a toast.

"Yes, very well then," the lawyer said with some relief. A stiff drink was just what he needed. "Whisky."

"It'll have to be cognac I'm afraid. My brother's drinks cabinet appears to be a little poorly stocked of late." He cast a withering glance at the manservant, who still stood in the open doorway of the study, and handed Screwtape a brandy glass. Placing his hat and briefcase carefully on the desk, Screwtape took the proffered drink.

"The future," Quicksilver suddenly announced, chinking glasses.

The young man downed the contents of his glass in one gulp. Screwtape merely sipped at his. The warm fumes of the cognac filled his mouth and coursed down his throat to soothe his knotted stomach. "Indeed," he muttered.

"So, the papers?"

"Y-yes, of course," the lawyer said dragging his eyes away from the empty chair with some effort. "I have them here."

After some fumbling with catches, the lawyer eventually managed to extract the precious documents from his case. He passed them across the desk and Quicksilver grasped them eagerly. But Screwtape did not let go.

"Once these papers are signed," he said, his voice suddenly calm and laden with the gravitas of the moment, "your elder brother Ulysses will be declared legally dead. All this will be yours," he took in the study, and by inference the rest of the house with one sweeping gesture of his hand. "You will inherit everything as your brother's sole heir. You do understand that, don't you?"

"Yes. Of course I understand," Quicksilver said tugging at the papers. Screwtape at last relaxed his grip. "Much as it saddens me to do this," the young man said, without any hint of genuine emotion, "my brother has been missing for over a year. There has been no word from him since he set out on that fateful adventure. The wreckage of his balloon has been found on the lower slopes of Mount Manaslu. At those altitudes, even if he survived the crash, a man could not last more than a night in those sub-zero temperatures. I am sorry to say that those icy slopes must now be his final resting place."

Silence hung in the air between the two men, heavy with a dozen uncomforting thoughts.

The doorbell clanged again, its jangling shattering the tense atmosphere. Both the lawyer and heir looked to the open door of the study and the shadows of the furniture-haunted library beyond.

"Who can be calling at this time of night?" Screwtape said, half to himself.

"Who indeed?" Quicksilver wondered, casting a suspicious eye in the lawyer's direction.

"If you will excuse me, sirs, I shall endeavour to find out," the butler said, the rich baritone of his voice unencumbered by the inflection of any emotion.

"Gladly," Quicksilver said, ushering him on his way with a wave of his empty glass, his eyes now fixed on the paperwork.

The lawyer's gaze returned to the pictures and curious paraphernalia that adorned the walls, the personal effects of a man they were about to condemn to the grave. Screwtape was drawn to a number of framed photographs. The same man could be seen in many of them; the only one who appeared more than once in any of the captured images, in fact. Moments of history preserved for posterity.

Here he stood with a half-naked tribe of pygmies from equatorial Africa, there he was shaking hands with a turbaned maharajah and in another he was dressed in the attire of an American frontiersman, standing arm-in-arm with an exuberantly over-dressed peacock of a woman at a poker table on board a Mississippi paddle steamer. This was not the same great white hunter depicted in the portrait over the fireplace – it was a younger man – but he bore more than a passing resemblance to the lawyer's client.

"He certainly travelled the world, your brother," the lawyer commented.

"Yes," the other replied, "and look where it got him."

Quicksilver continued to scan the tightly typed pages of sub-clauses and legal jargon that, in no uncertain terms, stated that on declaration of the death of Ulysses Lucian Quicksilver everything in the family estate would pass to him.

"These artefacts," the lawyer said, taking in the curios, "they must be worth something to a collector."

"Mementos, bric-a-brac, nothing more. I'll bequeath them to the Pitt Rivers Museum in Oxford. Why not? It's the house that's the only real asset my brother has left me."

"And what will you do with the proceeds of the sale?"

"Move to one of the lunar cities. I have grown tired of London and I feel that London has grown rather tired of me. There is nothing to keep me here now."

"I hear that Tranquillity is nice," Screwtape offered, "or Luna Prime. That is supposed to have a pleasant atmosphere."

"Look, Screwtape, I think we have exchanged enough niceties so let's just get on with the matter in hand, shall we?"

A minute later and Quicksilver had completed his assessment of the documentation. "So, I sign here and here," he indicated with a finger, "and the deed is done?"

"Yes, sir. Done indeed," the lawyer said wearily.

"You do not approve?"

"You mean of what you do, Mr Quicksilver?"

"Oh you have played your part fully and with a complete understanding of the consequences, Screwtape. Don't tell me you've developed a conscience. That's hardly healthy for a man in your profession."

"Your brother was well respected. So is your family name and has been for many years. I would not wish it to become otherwise."

"Oh, neither do I, Screwtape. Neither do I. You speak of it as if it were not *my* family name."

"I-I mean no disrespect, Mr Quicksilver, I assure you."

"And I assure you that my precious family's name and

that of my brother will be remembered for many years to come. I promise you that once we are done here, the first thing I shall do in the morning is commission a headstone to be raised in the family tomb at Highgate Cemetery and arrange for a memorial service to be held in his honour at St Paul's Cathedral."

"St Paul's, eh? Very grand. And what have I done to deserve such a display of public mourning?" asked a voice as rich as claret and as cutting as a rapier's blade.

Quicksilver looked up from the mess of newspaper clippings and legal documentation, the colour draining from his cheeks as he stared in stunned horror at the figure standing at the threshold of the study. Screwtape turned to face the new arrival, his mouth agape. The sound of glass smashing on the polished oak floorboards of the study shattered the silence as the solicitor's cognac slipped from his sweaty fingers.

"U-Ulysses?" The young man was supporting himself with one hand against the desk. He looked like he was going to be sick. "Ulysses... Thank God, you're safe and well! M-my prayers have been answered."

"I didn't realise that you and the Good Lord were on such amicable terms, Barty."

The man now standing in the doorway had the appearance of a taller and more strongly built version of the young man propping himself up against the large, mahogany desk. From his well-defined jaw-line to his thick head of hair, greying at the temples, and the sparkling glint in his deep brown eyes he was also the more handsome of the two. He looked every part the debonair gent, wearing a brown velvet frock coat, a paisley-patterned waistcoat with an emphasis on autumnal colours and moleskin trousers of the latest cut. A silk mustard-yellow cravat was set with a diamond pin at his neck and he was leaning jauntily on a black cane, set with a bloodstone at its hilt.

The manservant stood at his shoulder, his lined face still a cold mask of indifference, but now with a rumour of a smile about his eyes.

"This would seem to be rather a late hour for a meeting with the family solicitor, brother," Ulysses Quicksilver remarked.

"Ulysses, I still can't believe it's you," Bartholomew Quicksilver spluttered, colour returning to his cheeks in a flush of red-faced embarrassment.

"And what's this?" Ulysses said, striding over to the desk and snatching the papers from Bartholomew's hands. A wry smile on his lips, he began casually flicking through them. "So, the two of you were about to have me declared legally dead? Looks like I arrived just in the nick of time, as ever."

Ulysses calmly paced his way around the desk and lent against the mantelpiece, he glanced once at the painting of his father on the wall above him and then tossed the papers casually into the fire. The solicitor gasped and Bartholomew took a sudden step forward and then remembered himself.

"Well, I'm still alive and that's that. This residence is still the property of Ulysses Lucian Quicksilver, until I deem otherwise, and if I choose to leave it to the Cat Protection League in my will for when I really am dead and gone then that is my business."

Bartholomew opened his mouth as if to speak.

"And if you want to keep your allowance from our late father's estate, Barty," Ulysses said, silencing him with a glare, "then I suggest you don't say another word. Understood?" The younger man nodded, a look of defeat on his sallow face. "Nimrod, my brother will be leaving now. If you would kindly find him his coat?"

"At once, sir." The manservant bowed his head and then with an outstretched hand motioned Bartholomew Quicksilver to leave.

"Mr Screwtape will also be leaving now," Ulysses added, scowling darkly.

"M-Mr Quicksilver," Screwtape said, finding his voice at last, "you understand that I was working to help the Quicksilver family to the best of my ability and that if I had known..."

"Known what? That I was still alive?"

"Why, yes, sir. If I had but had word..."

"What are you trying to say, Screwtape? If you had known I was still alive you would have acted more quickly to bring this nefarious scheme to its conclusion for the benefit of my brother and yourself?"

"No, sir. Not at all."

"Nimrod?"

"Yes sir?" the manservant said, still waiting in the shadows at the threshold of the study.

"It has been a long day and I have travelled far. I am going to retire for the night very soon. If you would be so kind as to bring me up a nightcap – cognac, I think – once you have escorted my brother and our *ex*-family solicitor from my property."

"With pleasure, sir." Nimrod now ushered both Bartholomew and Screwtape from the room.

"Mr Quicksilver, I must *protest*," the lawyer persisted in foolish desperation.

"Yes, Mr Screwtape, so it would seem. But I insist, and I can be *very* insistent, as can Nimrod here, so I suggest you just go before my goodwill runs out. Do not think for one second that I would extend to you the same clemency as I do towards my wayward brother, which he has earned by dint of being my blood relative, heaven help me. So, I say again, *goodnight*, Mr Screwtape."

"Good night, Mr Quicksilver," the lawyer managed to bluster before a strong hand on his arm encouraged him to exit the study, leaving Ulysses Quicksilver alone, at last, for the first time since he had left over a year before to venture into the Himalayas and beyond on an endeavour that had nearly cost him his life.

Laying his cane on the desk Ulysses eased himself into the padded leather chair behind it and smiled as his eyes alighted on the same cuttings his brother Barty had been perusing earlier. 'Himalayan Adventure Ends In Double Death' one read. Certainly it had cost Davenport his life, the poor wretch. 'Search For Missing Millionaire Suspended' read another and 'Quicksilver: the Quick or the Dead?'

Well, the question had been answered now. Ulysses Quicksilver was back and tomorrow London would be reminded of what it had been missing.

ACT ONE
THE DARWIN CODE
APRIL 1997

CHAPTER ONE

On the Origin of Species

The night Alfred Wentwhistle died began just like any other.

The cold orb of the moon shone through the arched windows of the museum, bathing the myriad display cases in its wan blue light. The electric street lamps on Cromwell Road were a mere flicker of orange beyond the windows.

Alfred Wentwhistle, night watchman at the museum for the last thirty-six years, swept the polished cabinets with the beam of his spotlight. Gleaming eyes, hooked beaks and outstretched wings materialised momentarily under the harsh white attentions of its light. The beam's path was a familiar one, the repeated motions of a never-ending ballet of strobing light. The winding path Alfred took through the miles of corridors, halls and galleries was a familiar one also, the same route taken every night for the last thirty-six years. It was the course Shuttleworth had taught him when he was a boy of barely sixteen and when old Shuttleworth had just two months to retirement, having trod the same path himself for fifty-four years.

There was never any need to change the route. Night watchman of the Natural History Museum at South Kensington was not a demanding role. Alfred carried his truncheon and torch every night but he had never had need of the former in all his years in the post, and he no longer really needed the latter either. He could have found his way around the galleries on a moonless night in the middle of a blackout with his eyes closed, as he used to like to tell Mrs Wentwhistle with a chuckle. He simply carried the torch through force of habit. There had not been one break-in in all his thirty-six years at the museum. And apart from the infrequent change of the odd cabinet here and there or the moving of an artefact every once in a while, the familiar layout of the museum had changed little in any significant way since the arrival of the *Diplodocus carnegii*, ninety-two years before in 1905.

Alfred Wentwhistle enjoyed his job. He delighted in spending hours amongst the exhibits of stuffed beasts and dinosaur bones. Of course, you could experience the real thing now with the opening of the Challenger Enclosure at London Zoo, but there was something timeless and magical about the fossil casts of creatures that amateur archaeologists, who had effectively been the first palaeontologists, had taken to be evidence of the existence of the leviathans of legend such as the dragon or the Cyclops.

Every now and then, undisturbed by the presence of the public, Alfred took pleasure from reading the hand-written labels explaining what any particular item was, where it had been collected, who had recovered it and any other pertinent information the creator of the exhibit had seen fit to share. After thirty-six years there were not many labels that Alfred had not read.

He took great satisfaction from knowing that he was playing his part to keep secure the nation's – and by extension the Empire's and hence, in effect, the world's – greatest museum of natural history. Even though there had been no challenge to its peaceful guardianship of Mother Nature's myriad treasures since he took up his tenure, Alfred Wentwhistle was there, every night of the year – save Christmas Night itself – just in case the museum should ever need him.

Every now and again he would come upon one of the museum's research scientists working late into the night. They would exchange pleasantries and perhaps offer him a warming drink. They all knew old, reliable Alfred and he knew all of them by name. Over the years Alfred had seen professors come and go – botanists, zoologists, naturalists and crypto zoologists – but some things stayed the same, like the Waterhouse building itself and its night-time guardian. Alfred knew his place. The scientists were highly intelligent and erudite luminaries of the museum foundation and he was merely a night watchman. It was enough for him that he was allowed to spend hours enjoying the exhibits on display within. 'Nature's Treasure House' was what they called it; Sir Richard Owen's lasting legacy to the world.

Alfred's slow steady steps inexorably brought him back into the central hall and to the museum entrance. He paused beneath the outstretched head of the skeletal diplodocus to shine his torch on the face of his pocket watch. Five minutes past, just like every other night; regular as clockwork.

He looked up, shining the beam of his torch into the hollow orbits of the giant's eye sockets. It stared ahead impassively at the entrance to the museum and saw 20,000 visitors pass beneath its archways practically every day.

Alfred heard the tap of metal against metal, caught the glimmer of light on glass out of the corner of his eye, and it was then that he realised one of the doors was open.

There was no doubt in his mind that the door had been locked. It was the first thing he did when he came on duty. Should any of the scientists or cataloguers be working late and need to leave after this time, Alfred himself had to let them out and then he would always lock the door again after them.

No, there was no doubt in his mind that something was awry. Pacing towards the doors he could see where the lock had been forced.

The sound of breaking glass echoed through the halls of the museum from an upper gallery.

There was something most definitely awry. For the first time in thirty-six years his museum needed him.

Turning from the main doors the night watchman jogged across the central hall, his shambling steps marking the full eighty-five foot length of the diplodocus to the foot of the main staircase.

Once there he glanced back over his shoulder and up at the grand arch of the first floor staircase. Above him carved monkeys scampered up the curving arches of the roof into the darkness, amidst the leaf-scrolled iron span-beams. The sound had definitely come from the gallery where the museum staff's private offices were located.

Putting a hand to the polished stone balustrade and taking a deep breath, Alfred Wentwhistle started to take the steps two at a time. At the first landing, where the staircase split beneath the austere bronze-eyed gaze of Sir Richard Owen, he turned right. Hurrying along the gallery overlooking the central hall and running parallel to it, past stuffed sloths and the mounted skeletons of prehistoric marine reptiles, brought him to the second flight of stairs.

Here he paused, out of breath and ears straining, as he tried to work out more precisely where the sound had come from. In the comparative quiet of the sleeping museum he heard a crash, like the sound of a table being overturned. The noise had come from somewhere on this floor, away to his right, from within the western Darwin wing.

Alfred turned into this series of galleries, passing beneath the carved archway that read 'The Ascent of Man'. He quickened his pace as he came into a moonlit gallery of cases containing wax replicas of man's ancestors. They stood frozen in time, in various hunched poses, every kind of hominid from *Australopithecus* to *Homo neanderthalensis*. His sweeping beam shone from bared, snarling teeth, glass eyes and the black-edged blades of flint tools.

On any other night Alfred would have paused to examine the specimens and their accompanying explanations, telling of the evolution of Man from primitive ape. He would have been just as fascinated and amazed as he had been the first time he had read *The Origin of Species* and learnt of the incredible story of the human race's rise to become the most powerful and widely proliferated species on Earth, and beyond.

When Charles Darwin had first proposed his hypothesis of the origin of species, natural selection and the survival of the fittest, he had been derided by the greatest scientific minds of his day and denounced as a charlatan and a heretic. For he had spoken out against the worldwide Christian Church and its core belief that God had created all life on the planet in its final form from the beginning of time.

With the rediscovery of the lost worlds hidden within the jungles of the Congo, atop the mesa-plateaus of the South American interior and on lost islands within the Indian Ocean, others – many of them churchmen – had come forward to challenge Darwin's claims again, vociferously supporting the supposition that because dinosaurs and other prehistoric creatures still existed on the Earth in the present day, the idea of one species evolving into another was ludicrous. And the debate still raged in some persistent, unremitting quarters.

But over a hundred years after his death, Darwin had been posthumously exonerated of all accusations of bestial heresy and scientific idiocy to the point where he was practically idolised as the father of the new branch of science of Evolutionary Biology, and had an entire wing of the Natural History Museum dedicated to the advances made since he first proposed his radical ideas in 1859. In fact there were scientists working within that field now; men like Professors Galapagos and Crichton.

On many previous occasions Alfred Wentwhistle had found himself wiling away time gazing into the faces of his evolutionary ancestors, his reflection in the glass of the cabinets overlaid on top of the pronounced brows and sunken eyes beneath. On such occasions he had wondered upon Darwin's legacy for the human race and what implications such an accepted theory might have for Her Majesty Queen Victoria, in that it presumed that the British monarch was descended from the apes of aeons past.

The familiar smell of camphor and floor polish assailed Alfred's nostrils. Moonlight bathed the gallery with its monochrome light. He found himself in a gallery displaying mammalia, reptilia and amphibia ordered so as to clearly show the evolutionary path Man had followed. From the moment his Palaeozoic ancestors had first crawled out of the primeval swamps to the present day when he bestrode the globe like a colossus, the human race covering the Earth and the nearer planets of the solar system.

It was off this gallery that some of the scientists had their private workspaces. A number of doors on either side stretched away from Alfred bearing the brass name plaques of the great and the good.

Alfred could hear clear sounds of a struggle now. In the beam of his torch fragments of glass glittered on the floor before one of the doors, looking like a diamond frost on the first morning of winter. The flickering glow of an electric lamp cast its light into the gallery from inside the office before suddenly going out. There was a violent crash of more breaking glass and furniture being overturned.

He would certainly have a dramatic tale to tell Mrs Wentwhistle over bacon and eggs the next morning, Alfred suddenly, incongruously, found himself thinking.

As the watchman neared the invaded office he noticed wisps of smoke or some sort of gas seeping under the door and a new smell – like aniseed, with an unpleasant undertone of rotten meat – that made his nose wrinkle.

The door suddenly burst open, sending more shards of glass spinning into the gallery, clattering against the display cases. The figure of a man burst out of the office and collided with the ageing night watchman. Alfred reeled backwards as the man barged past him. He couldn't stop himself from stumbling into a case containing a family of Neanderthal waxworks posed around an inanimate fire. The torch fell from Alfred's hand and its bulb died.

"Here, what do you think you're doing?" Alfred managed, calling after the intruder as he sprinted from the gallery. He was holding something about the shape and size of a packing box in his arms. But the thief did not stop and before Alfred had even managed to regain his balance, he was gone.

Alfred's heart was racing, beating a tattoo of nervous excitement against his ribs. In all his thirty-six years he had never known anything like it. Adrenalin flooded his system and he was about to give chase when something reminded him that the thief had not been alone in the office. Alfred had heard more than one voice raised in anger as he had approached and there had been definite signs of a struggle.

Cautiously, he approached the doorway of the office. The rancid mist was beginning to dissipate. The soles of his boots crunched on the fractured diamonds of glass.

Inside the pitch black office-cum-laboratory he could hear a ragged breathing that reminded him of an animal snuffling. Then, suddenly, there was silence.

Alfred took another step forward.

"What the devil?" was all he could manage as, in an explosion of glass and splintered wood something burst out of the office, ripping the door from its sundered frame. The night watchman barely had time to yelp out in pain as slivers of glass sliced his face and hands as he raised them to protect himself, before a hulking shadow of solid black muscle was on top of him.

Alfred had a momentary impression of thick, matted hair, a sharp bestial odour – a rank animal smell mixed in with the aniseed and rancid meat – broad shoulders and a blunt-nosed head slung low between them. There was a flash of silver as the moonlight caught something swinging from around the thing's neck.

He had never known anything like it, never in thirty-six years.

And then, teeth bared in an animal scream, its hollering cry deafening in his ears, fists flailing like sledgehammers, the ape-like creature attacked. Feebly Alfred put up his arms to defend himself but there was nothing he could do against the brute animal strength of his assailant.

It grabbed Alfred's head by the hair so violently he could feel clumps of it being ripped from his scalp. Then, in one savage action, the enraged beast smashed his skull into display case. With the second blow the glass of the cabinet shattered and Alfred Wentwhistle's world exploded into dark oblivion.

CHAPTER TWO

The Inferno Club

Ulysses Quicksilver woke with the midday sun streaming in through the crack in the heavy velvet drapes of his bedchamber. The warm light reached his sleeping form, bringing to an end a night of vivid, almost feverish, dreaming. It banished the transitory memories of unsettling dreams and replaced them with physical reminders of a host of old injuries, his worn body aching.

He stretched beneath the crisp sheets of the grand four-poster and immediately regretted doing so. There was the sharp twinge in his right shoulder, the stab of cramp in his left leg and the dull throb in his left side.

He had slept long and deeply, his dreams overflowing with half-real recollections of the events of the past eighteen months. There was the rapid descent through the freezing fog above the snow-clad peaks, the violent lurch of collision as the gondola broke up on contact with the pitiless rocks. Then he was lying in the snow, teeth chattering hard enough to break, Davenport's body lying there next to his, his blood freezing black in the sub-zero hell.

Then his sleep had been filled with the sonorous chanting that had filled the monastery, the sensation of returning warmth, air thick with the smell of tallow fat and jasmine flowers. In another moment he had found himself training again with the masters of the temple, his still-healing body being subjected to a beating with bamboo poles and blunt wooden weapons. There had also been the mental challenges as he strove to acquire mastery over his body through strength of will alone. Then there had been the final test, the duel with the snow beast, his body suspended in the air above the arena before he had brought physical form and mind back as one and, incredibly, bested the creature.

His memories of what had followed since that time had been replayed in his sleeping mind in a time-lapsed blur, a hallucinatory haze of images. The journey back from Xigaze to Bombay, traversing the continents by train until, at last, Brunel's Trans-Channel tunnel had brought him back to England, London and home.

And now here he was lying in a bed in which he had not slept in over a year.

But was it really home for him anymore, he found himself wondering as he stared at the cracks criss-crossing the plaster of the ceiling above him. He kept telling himself that he was pleased to be back but for all the comfort of the goose-down pillows behind his head and the sprung mattress beneath him, part of him hankered for his hard wooden pallet back at the monastery and the ridged feel of the bamboo canes against his back.

A discreet tap at the door roused Ulysses from his reverie.

"Enter," he replied.

The handle turned and the door swung open as Nimrod entered the room. His manservant looked immaculate as ever, dressed in his grey butler's attire, not a hair out of place. Balanced perfectly on the splayed fingers of one hand was a silver tray. There was a starched linen cloth draped carefully over his other arm.

"Good afternoon, sir."

"Good afternoon Nimrod."

"It being past noon I took the liberty of asking Mrs Prufrock to prepare you some breakfast."

"Why, thank you, Nimrod."

"Not at all, sir," his manservant replied, placing the tray across Ulysses' lap and laying the white linen napkin open in front of him.

As well as a silver dish cover there was a slim cut crystal vase containing a single crimson carnation, a cafetiére of hot coffee and accompanying coffee cup, a silver toast rack, containing four triangles of both white and brown toasted bread and a copy of the day's edition of *The Times*.

Nimrod lifted the platter's cover with a flourish. Ulysses' nostrils were assailed by a bloom of steam smelling richly of the griddled eggs, smoked back bacon, Cumberland sausage, black pudding, grilled tomatoes, sautéed mushrooms and hash browns.

"I thought you must be hungry after your journey last night."

Ulysses heartily tucked into the meal in front of him. Eschewing good manners, through a half-chewed mouthful of sausage he spluttered, "Give Mrs Prufrock my compliments on what is, I think, the most wonderful meal I have ever eaten."

"With pleasure, sir."

Ulysses felt a warm glow well up within him and knew that it wasn't merely from having hot home-cooked food in his belly again. This was what it meant to be home, to be surrounded by those people who mattered to you and to whom you mattered also. It was all suddenly very familiar and he found that comforting.

"It's good to be back, Nimrod."

"And, if I might say so sir, it is good to have you back. If you will excuse me?" And with that he left, pulling the door to carefully behind him.

As he tucked into his breakfast, Ulysses spread out *The Times* on the bedspread beside him. It was time to get back up to speed with what was happening in the so-called civilised world. The copies of *The Times* he had been able to get hold of on the Orient Express had been woefully out of date by as much as a week in most cases.

The headline on this edition, however – dated April 16th 1997, the paper still warm from where Nimrod had pressed the pages with an iron – was very topical indeed. It read 'Buckingham Palace Confirms Jubilee Celebrations' and concerned the celebrations planned to mark the 160th year of Queen Victoria's reign. The occasion was to be marked by the unveiling of a colossal statue of Britannia in Hyde Park, outside Paxton's glorious construction of the second Crystal Palace. All this was to occur on the twenty-third of June, in a little over two months time. The politicians, toadies, toffs and royal historians were calling it the most glorious time in the British Empire's entire history.

Indeed it had been a most incredible century and a half, during which time man had risen from the dawn of the industrial age and the inventive uses of steam power to tame much of the world around him and even conquer the stars. Space travel, now an everyday occurrence, was once the preserve of science-fiction, conjured up by the writings of authors such as H. G. Wells and Jules Verne. With interplanetary travel mastered, and with regular launches from the space terminus at Gatwick south of the capital carrying all classes of citizen to Her Majesty's Imperial colonies on the moon and the nearer planets, there was now talk in certain secretive circles of attempts to break the only frontier remaining to mankind – time travel. What once had seemed preposterous was now the everyday, the impossible simply tomorrow's breakthrough.

There had been unparalleled advances made in the medical sciences, difference engines and the newer field of cybernetics. The empire of Magna Britannia – once rather apologetically known simply as Great Britain – would not be what it was without the advances made in those areas. The Widow of Windsor would not be where she was without them and the nation was now policed thanks in part to the quantum developments made in clockwork-cybernetics, since Charles Babbage had accomplished the astonishing achievement of constructing the first fully automated analytical engine.

But whilst much of the world had moved on, as mankind's achievements had exploded exponentially, so the more shameful aspects of Imperial life had continued to deteriorate. At this time London's slums were darker, dirtier and more over-crowded than even the visionary Charles Dickens could have imagined in his most despairing hour, its streets filled with the dissolute and the destitute, the gin-sodden inheritors of the darkest days of the Empire.

Many were slaves to the machine, forced to work tirelessly in the great gothic factories built by their suffering ancestors, or had become passed over by the machine, robot-drudges taking their place in those same industrial workshops.

The consequences of being the 'Workshop of the World' had come at a high price too. Great swathes of the British Isles were now nothing but blighted wasteland, its flora and fauna mutated or destroyed by the pollution vomited out of its many thousands of factories.

While the great and the good enjoyed the benefits of electric light, automobiles and the thinking machines that were Babbage's legacy, dreadfully high infant-mortality, prostitution, malnutrition, cholera and syphilis still blighted the lives of the poor underclass that riddled London's streets.

As Ulysses laid his knife and fork across a practically polished plate, there was another tap at the door. At his beckoning Nimrod entered once again.

"Sir, when you are ready there is a cab waiting to take you to the Inferno Club."

"Really?" Ulysses commented. "Already? It didn't take long for Wormwood to find out that I was back in town, did it?"

"No, sir."

"I suppose he'll be wanting a debrief. I'd best not keep him waiting," Ulysses said with a sigh, running a hand through his sleep-ruffled hair, "it only makes him irritable. Spending any period of time with him is a chore at best, and when he's irritable it only makes it ten times worse. Some warning would have been nice though; perhaps a welcome home card, or a bouquet of chrysanthemums."

Within half an hour Ulysses Quicksilver had made his ablutions, dressed and, cane in hand, was on his way to the Inferno Club in the back of the jolting hansom cab, enduring the worldly banter of the cabbie. The cab turned into St James's Square and pulled up outside number 16A, next door to the East India club and its pillared frontage. Number 16A itself was an otherwise unassuming Regency period façade that did nothing to belie what lay beyond its closed doors.

Somewhat disgruntled at not only having been disturbed so soon on his first day back in the capital but also finding that the cab had not already been paid for, Ulysses ascended the steps to the rosewood doors as the smoke-belching hansom chugged away. He rapped on the door with the head of his cane three times.

The door opened a crack. Standing behind it was a squat, liveried doorman with a face like a battle-tested mastiff and who, even with the added height of his top hat, still only came up to Ulysses' shoulder. Thanks in part to his diminutive size many a roustabout had misjudged Max Grendel, former carnival performer known as 'Grendel the Man-Monster, The Strongest Dwarf in the World'.

"Good afternoon, Mr Quicksilver, sir," the doorman said, his accent distinctly that of the lower classes; there was no hiding the fact that he had been born within the sound of Bow Bells. He gave Ulysses a broad, broken smile full of missing teeth. "It's been a long time."

"Hello, Max, old chap. How are you?"

"Oh, mustn't grumble. You here for business or pleasure today, sir?"

"Most definitely business. If I was after the latter I'd be asking you for a recommendation, wouldn't I Max?"

The doorman chuckled filthily. "Right you are, sir. If you'd like to step this way then?"

Ulysses passed the doorman half a crown and proceeded through a second set of double doors. Above these, carved into the doorframe and picked out in gold leaf, was Dante's doom-laden motto *Lasciate ogni speranza voi ch'entrate,* the original Italian seeming incongruously out of place in this bastion of Englishness.

Uriah Wormwood was seated in one of two huge leather armchairs set before a crackling fire in the Quartermain Room. Despite the time of year and his proximity to the fire, the thin rake of a man still looked pinched with cold, his long hands and fingers pale, the blue network of veins visible through his porcelain skin. The hair on his head was thin and greying, swept back from the top of his balding pate and hanging down to his shoulders in greasy lank cords. In his dated frock-tailed black suit, starched white shirt and unassuming black silk cravat he looked every part the elder statesman.

Standing behind him was a silent, unsmiling aide, who looked as capable of handling himself in a fight as Max Grendel.

Ulysses took the seat opposite Wormwood. The older man fixed him with a needling stare. "I'd heard you were dead," he said.

"Well as you can see, minister, reports of my death have been greatly exaggerated."

A starched footman appeared and delivered a glass of whisky to Wormwood. "Sir?" he asked turning to Ulysses.

"A brandy – cognac," he said and Wormwood waved the flunky away imperiously.

Ulysses took a moment to take in his surroundings. It had been some time since he had been here last but in all those months nothing appeared to have really changed.

The room was enveloped in a fug of blue smoke from the many pipes and cigars being enjoyed by the club's members. To the casual observer it would appear that this place was nothing more than a club full of aging peers, retired officers of Her Majesty's Armed Forces and directors of the board of a whole host of multinational companies. There was also a sprinkling of younger men thrown in, taking on the affectations of their elders, ready to take up the reigns of power when they were offered.

Ulysses Quicksilver knew that such bastions of English misogyny – and the Inferno Club more truly and more covertly than any other – was where the real power lay. This was where the really important decisions were made, those that influenced the fates of nations, where the agents of all manner of organisations made their deals, were given their frequently unpalatable orders and reported back to their shadowy masters. Ulysses Quicksilver knew this better than most for he was such a man.

"So," Wormwood said, peering at Ulysses over steepling fingers, "niceties done with... your report. What happened? Do you have the artefact?"

"There's really no better way of putting this," Ulysses said taking his brandy from the footman. "No."

"As I suspected," Wormwood said witheringly, that one simple phrase dripping with disdain.

"And our Oriental... friend? What of him?"

"His vessel went down along with mine," Ulysses recalled, images of their terrible, dramatic, and near-fatal, descent flashing behind his eyes as he did so. "He tried to board our gondola. We fought. He fell. I have not seen him, or the green-eyed monkey god of Sumatra, since."

"You should have informed us of your return."

"It was too risky. I still hoped to track down the Black Mamba myself. I take it that none of your other agents have reported his reappearance at any of his usual haunts?"

"No. We can only hope that he is lying there still on the southern slopes of Mount Manaslu, frozen like some relic of the ice age. But somehow I doubt it. And besides, the matter is out of your hands."

"What?" Ulysses said, taken aback.

"There is another more pressing matter I wish you to deal with."

"And what precisely is this new undertaking?"

"There was a break-in at the Natural History Museum last night."

"On Cromwell Road?"

"You know of another? A night watchman was killed. A lab was ransacked. You are to... investigate."

Ulysses took another casual swig from his glass. "Surely burglary and murder is the province of Scotland Yard."

"And your province is to serve your Queen and country as the representatives of Her Majesty's government see fit. Besides, there may well be more to this than there at first appears. You will, of course, be paid your usual retainer."

"Welcome home, Ulysses," the younger man muttered under his breath as he downed the rest of his drink.

"Is there a problem?"

"It's just that some things never change, do they, minister?"

Ulysses' governmental contact glowered at him, his knife-edge features becoming even sharper, even more threatening.

"I do not like you, Quicksilver, but then in my line of work I don't have to. I am, however, an... admirer of what you do and you are most accomplished, most of the time. But there are all manner of things afoot in the world. We are scant years away from a new millennium and Magna Britannia has never been in a stronger position. And neither have her enemies ever been more eager to see her fall so that they might feast richly upon the spoils.

"The Chinese Empire is an ever-increasing threat, looking to space to solve its own overpopulation problem. We can no longer rely on Russia being the surety it once was, even if it is still a princeling state of Britain. There is talk of ancient bloodlines asserting their self-professed ancestral rights in Eastern Europe. And then there are the unruly ambitions of the Germans and their National Socialist masters.

"There are even those within the empire who have their reasons for destabilising Her Majesty's most glorious realm, as well you know. Then there is the ongoing situation on Mars. The separatist-secessionist movement is gaining in strength and popularity daily.

"Of themselves, none of these are major threats to our stability or the stability of Her Majesty's throne. But together? The sharks are circling, Quicksilver, and there are precious few of us able to do anything about it. Mark my words. The sharks are circling... and they are hungry."

"Come on in, the water's lovely."

"What?" Wormwood asked sharply.

"Nothing minister," Ulysses replied with a sigh.

"What are you waiting for then? Be on your way."

"What indeed? The scene of the crime awaits and the game is surely afoot."

CHAPTER THREE

The Scene of the Crime

The cab turned onto Cromwell Road and pulled up outside the grand frontage of the Natural History Museum. The building's gothic façade was an awesomely impressive sight, although it was now dwarfed by other more recent edifices and the sprawling network of the Overground that filled the sky above it. The great pillar of the South Kensington stop rose from the right-hand corner of the Museum's grounds. The architectural design and execution of the Museum – that was Sir Richard Owen's cathedral to nature and his legacy to naturalists the world over – still took Ulysses' breath away every time he saw it, even after all the wonders and all the horrors he had witnessed in his life as an agent of the throne. Stone-locked monsters of a bygone age, pterosaurs, coelacanths, cats and primates gazed down at him through the sooty grime that sullied the face of the otherwise beautiful building.

Crossing the road Ulysses made his way up the steps that led into the Museum. There were already signs of the police presence that he would find inside. An automaton constable was tapping his truncheon rhythmically into the palm of his artificially manufactured hand. Passing through the main doors Ulysses entered the central hall of the museum to find a bustle of concerned staff, Scotland Yard's finest incompetents and bewildered museum visitors milling around beneath the impassive stare of the diplodocus skeleton that dominated the vaulted nave-like space.

Considering what had come to pass there the previous night it was amazing that the museum was even open to the public, Ulysses mused as he made his way up the central staircase, heading for the Darwin Wing. He hoped that once there it would reveal its secrets to him, such as why he had been sent to investigate a break-in and murder at the Natural History Museum in the first place.

Ulysses could see that the police had been there before him, marching in and trampling all over the crime scene. They had marked the entire Darwin Wing as theirs with strips of yellow and black tape bearing the legend, 'Crime Scene – Do Not Cross'.

Two constables stood either side of the entrance, their black bodies gleaming dully in the light cascading from the high windows. Ulysses approached the nearest of the Peeler-drones. The constable turned at his approach. "I am sorry, sir. This area is closed to the public," its voice crackled from somewhere behind its chestplate in an imitation of a cockney accent.

Ulysses deftly put a hand inside a jacket pocket and pulled out a leather cardholder with a flourish, flipping the case open. "I'm not the public," he said, the wry smile curling the corners of his mouth, "Constable Palmerston," he added, reading the badge plate on the automaton's breast. There was a curious habit amongst the Metropolitan Police of naming their cybernetic officers after the famous dead. Was there something that Scotland Yard's cyberneticists knew that the rest of the world didn't?

The constable scanned the card revealed inside the wallet with its visual receptors, the red glow behind its eye-visor panning from left to right. "I am sorry, sir," the drone apologised. "What can I do for you, Mr Quicksilver?"

"I wish to inspect the scene of the crime."

"Certainly, sir."

The constable unhooked the tape, allowing Ulysses into the wing.

"This way, sir. If there is anything else I can do to help..." the robot began.

"I'll be sure to find you," Ulysses interrupted, finishing the constable's sentence.

In the main hall of the wing Ulysses found more policemen – both mechanical and human – as well as other men not in uniform. A team of these, dressed in starched white lab coats, were dusting various cabinets and wooden benches.

Ulysses ignored them and made for the entrance to one of the secondary galleries, again flanked by automata-constables, through which a steady stream of forensics staff were flowing. Mote-shot beams of afternoon sunlight entered through skylights high in the ceiling. Ulysses took in the display cases, the doors to offices and workspaces beyond and the cluster of men working in the centre of the room. He could just make out a figure, lying awkwardly within the ruins of a glass cabinet.

"Oi! Stop right there!" came a shout from behind him.

Ulysses turned to see a look of shock seize the approaching man's face.

"Bloody hell! I thought you were dead."

"And I've missed you too," Ulysses said, regarding the pale-faced, weasel of a man before him, his ginger mop of hair an unruly riot as always. "You shouldn't believe everything you read in the papers, Inspector," he added with a smile.

For a moment the trench-coated policeman said nothing. The human sergeant accompanying him looked from his superior to the dandy in bewilderment.

"Inspector Allardyce, shall I have this man removed?"

"W-what?" the inspector managed. "Yes. No. Not yet," he snapped, never taking his eyes off Ulysses. "What are you doing here Quicksilver?"

"Oh, you know how it is. I've not been in town for a while and someone said that I simply must see the Ascent of Man exhibit in the Darwin Wing at the Natural History Museum."

"Don't give me that bullshit!" Allardyce snarled. "What are you *really* doing here?"

"I'm here to investigate a murder," Ulysses said darkly, his face suddenly an impassive mask. "What are you doing here?"

"Oh, ha ha, very funny. And what the hell do you think you're doing investigating *my* murder?"

"*Your* murder? Oh, I'm sorry, no one told me. My commiserations. Where shall I send the flowers?"

"You know what I mean you arrogant bastard."

"You know how it is. Orders are orders."

"Well you're too late. We've practically finished here. You want to try getting up before midday occasionally. There's nothing for you here."

"I think I'll be the judge of that if you don't mind."

"Well I do mind. The forensics boys have already been over the place with a fine-toothed comb," Inspector Allardyce sneered. "If there's anything to find, they'll have found it. I doubt there's anything you can add. Like I said, there's *nothing* for you here."

"Yes, and we all know how thorough your lads can be, don't we, Allardyce?"

The policeman flashed Ulysses a look of volcanic anger. "I don't like your tone! I could have you arrested for wasting police time, you know that?"

"I thought it was *you* who was wasting *my* time," Ulysses goaded.

"Look, Quicksilver, do I have to remind you that I am an Inspector of Her Majesty's Metropolitan police force? I won't be spoken to like this!"

"And do I have to remind you of whose authority I am here under?" Ulysses said reaching inside his jacket again. He pulled out the leather wallet for a second time and flipped it open. "My card. It certainly impressed your constable enough to let me in here in the first place."

"Yes, all right. You can put that away. You've got five minutes, then I want you out of here, never mind who pulls the strings."

"That should be more than enough time," Ulysses said, and strode past the inspector leaving the policeman grumbling to his sergeant.

Ulysses approached the men clustered around the body. The corpse was that of a man who had been enjoying portly middle age until the events of the previous night had resulted in his untimely death. He lay sprawled amidst the ruin of a shattered display case. The waxwork reconstructions that had been housed inside the cabinet had been removed and were now leaning against a gallery wall, baring their plaster teeth at anyone approaching the crime scene.

"Excuse me please, gentlemen," Ulysses said as he nudged his way between the white-coated men, waving his open cardholder casually at them. In the face of such superiority and upper class confidence the forensic technicians moved aside.

Blood, most of it dried, covered the jagged glass shards beneath the dead man's head and Ulysses could see that the victim's hair and scalp were matted with it too. Tiny slivers of glass, some of which were still embedded in the clay-like flesh, had cut the dead man's face and hands. But worse than the blood and mess of gore oozing from the back of his head, was the expression on his face. The night watchman had died in utter terror. His rigor-frozen features were a mask of dread, his lips pulled back from his teeth, his mouth open in horror.

"How did he die?" Ulysses asked, already suspecting the answer.

"A blow to the head; several in fact," one of the white coats said.

"Indeed," Ulysses mused.

But who, or what, had killed him? Ulysses wondered. What could have caused the poor wretch to die with such an expression of horror on his face?

"What time did he die?"

"From the onset of rigor mortis I would say... sometime around midnight," the pathologist examining the body replied. "Probably just after."

"Was anything taken from the body?"

"No," another technician said. "It doesn't appear so."

Ulysses stepped back, leaving the white coats to finish their work. He had his murder victim but Wormwood had said that there had been a burglary as well. So what had been taken?

Behind him a ransacked office gaped open, the shattered door wrenched from its frame. Policemen were busying themselves around the area. With cautious steps Ulysses approached, crunching tiny pieces of glass beneath the soles of his shoes. He paused at the entrance to look more closely at the splintered mess of the door frame. Then, in the muted sunlight spilling into the gallery Ulysses caught sight of no more than a thread of something, something all of Inspector Allardyce's forensic team had missed. Snagged in the splintered wood were three reddish-brown hairs. At first glance they made Ulysses think of coarse animal hairs. They certainly hadn't belonged to the murdered night watchman; they were the wrong colour.

The policemen and scientists around him were so caught up in their own work that none of them paid any heed as Ulysses took a small evidence bag from a jacket pocket, a pair of tweezers from another and, without touching them with his bare hands, extracted the hairs from the door frame, sealing them safely within the bag before returning it to his pocket. Then he entered the office-lab itself.

The place was a mess. The level of destruction suggested that more than a mere robbery had taken place here. There had been a struggle as well.

From the detritus now filling the office space and covering the floor, Ulysses was able to build a picture in his mind of what the laboratory had looked like before it had been invaded. There had been bookcases and shelves containing all manner of scientific journals and reference books, which now littered the floor, and tables covered with distillation apparatus, that was now just so much broken glass. One of these tables had been overturned and a leg broken off it. A framed print of a classic cartoon from *Punch* magazine disparaging Darwin hung lopsidedly. There were stains across some of the furniture and even the walls, suggesting a vessel containing water or some other liquid had been smashed, spraying the room with its contents.

To Ulysses' trained eyes, amidst all this chaotic mess it was quite clear that something was indeed missing. Careful not to lose his footing on any of the detritus covering the floor he made his way to the far corner of the room. Here there was a desk, a jar of upended ink, its blue-black contents covering most of the papers spilled across the top. Amongst the mess of papers there was a curiously clear space, as if something had been resting on the desk and had only been removed after the papers had fallen into disarray. Ulysses moved the papers out of the way altogether. There, in the green cracked leather of the desktop was a clear indentation, where something square and relatively heavy had sat. And there was more evidence on the wall itself, a discoloration of the paint, suggesting something hot had marked it over time. Ulysses considered the size and position of the marks. Something hot, something box-shaped; something like a small difference engine. That was what the mysterious thief had claimed from this sanctuary of peaceful scientific enquiry.

Ulysses glanced around the room one more time but he was certain he had seen enough. Besides he wanted to get a private opinion about the contents of his pocket. He began to pick his way carefully across the office-lab again.

But there was something else, gnawing away at the edge of his conscious mind. It was not something seen but something he had smelt, a rancid odour that caught at the back of his throat and which left his mind buzzing with more questions. Ulysses sniffed and caught for a moment the trace of a smell like beef and fennel stew past its best. That was it – aniseed and spoiled meat; a truly unsavoury and unusual combination, certainly not the usual aroma of a musty old museum.

Ulysses paused in the doorway and looked more closely at the broken door, now propped against the wall. Its brass plaque was still attached. It read, 'Professor Ignatius Galapagos' and underneath, 'Evolutionary Biology Department'.

Leaving Scotland Yard's finest to it, Ulysses made his way out of the gallery. He was pretty certain that there was nothing else for him to see. It was time he pursued his investigation elsewhere.

Inspector Allardyce was at the entrance to the gallery talking to an anxious-looking member of the museum staff. There was no way Ulysses could avoid him.

"I thought I said you had five minutes. I make that seven," he said looking at his pocket watch.

"I'm sorry if I've outstayed my welcome."

"You always outstay your welcome. As soon as you turn up you've outstayed your welcome. So, what do you make of it all then, Quicksilver? Do you have anything new to shed on the case?"

"Oh, I'm sure you already have a theory or two of your own. You don't need me complicating matters."

"Indeed I do, and I certainly don't," Allardyce confirmed. "It's actually very straightforward if you know what you're looking for and how to read the signs."

"Really?" Ulysses said. He had been ready to leave but the opportunity to provoke the pompous inspector again – having had so few opportunities in the last year or so – was just too tempting. "Would you care to elaborate?"

Inspector Allardyce could not resist the opportunity to expound on his masterly skills of deduction and chalk one up against the aristocratic know-it-all.

"It's very simple really. All the evidence is there for those who have eyes to see it." *Indeed*, thought Ulysses. "Our thief was disturbed by the night watchman and then killed the poor bugger so he could make his getaway."

"And do you know what was taken?"

"Not yet, but we will do, once we have tracked down Professor Gapalago and got a complete inventory of the room from him."

"Galapagos," the museum staffer corrected.

"What?"

"It's Professor Galapagos."

"Does it matter?" Allardyce bit back.

"Yes, I rather think it does," Ulysses muttered under his breath. And then, so that Allardyce could hear him quite clearly, "If you don't have a full inventory of the contents of the room, how do you know that anything's been taken at all?"

"Isn't it obvious?" Allardyce asked incredulously. "Why else would someone break in here? It obviously wasn't to bump off that poor bastard lying over there with his head smashed in."

"Indeed," said Ulysses, "which brings me to another point. The injuries sustained by the victim look like the result of a frenzied attack. Why would a thief stop to make such a brutal job of doing away with one, aging, overweight security guard? And what of this Professor *Galapagos*," – he made a point of annunciating the name with added emphasis – "the man whose office was broken into?"

"Look, I told you, he's not turned up yet. You know what these academic types are like."

"Better than you, I'll warrant."

"Are you lecturing me on bloody police procedure?" Allardyce challenged, stabbing his index finger at Ulysses' chest. "Because that's exactly how things got out of hand last time."

"Heaven forbid, Inspector."

"I'll get round to this Gapalogo soon enough. But it's quite clear what happened here last night. I told you there was nothing to see here, Quicksilver," he spat, his voice dripping with undisguised contempt. "Unless you've got any other amazing insights to offer then I rather think you're done here, don't you?"

Ulysses paused. Should he share his own theory with Allardyce, that be thought the inspector should be looking for two culprits, connected certainly but not as he might at first suspect? It was tempting, if only to see the look of exasperation on Allardyce's red face. But as long as the police were following up red herrings of their own making it would at least keep them out of the way while he continued his investigation and allow him to get to bottom of things, such as why Wormwood had set him on this case in the first place. And, Ulysses had to admit, he was hooked. There was far more to this mystery than merely a break-in and incidental murder. There was something else afoot, he was sure of it.

"I couldn't agree more, Inspector. Good day."

"And don't come snooping around my murder scene again, you hear?"

"*Your* murder scene?"

"Look, just piss off!"

"With pleasure."

As he made his way out of the gallery, Ulysses halted again. He felt someone's eyes on him. He looked around and then the feeling was gone.

Putting it from his mind Ulysses made his way out of the museum, cane in hand, evidence in his pocket. He would need to pay Methuselah a call but he decided that it could wait until after he had dined. It had been too long since he had last visited the Ritz.

Another thought distracted Ulysses as he exited the museum and hailed a hansom. There were many unexplained mysteries in the world – such as who built the giant heads of Easter Island and the mystery of the Whitby mermaid – and Ulysses had even solved some of them in his time, but how Maurice Allardyce had ever made it to inspector he would never know.

From a dark recess behind a roof strut, unseen eyes watched the exchange between the fair-skinned red-haired man and the taller, more confident interloper. The watcher had found sanctuary here in the darkened, elevated tunnels of the museum's ventilation system following the events of the previous night. After the attack it had become confused. Its mind was a fractured collection of half-recalled memories that made less and less sense as instinct gradually overtook rational thought.

It had wanted to flee but there had been something familiar and safe about the vaulted, hallowed halls that had made it stay. It felt curiously comfortable here. Besides, there were too many people around at the moment. There would only be more upset if it revealed itself now, more shouting, more panic, more fear.

No, the watcher would wait. It was safe here. It was secure. This was its home.

CHAPTER FOUR

An Unexpected Visitor

Having enjoyed an exquisitely prepared dinner of roast pheasant, seasonal vegetables and dauphinoise potatoes, all washed down with a half bottle of finest claret, Ulysses Quicksilver exited the Ritz, fully intending to hail a cab to convey him back to his house in Mayfair. Outside the hotel the gas lamps and sodium lights were glowing into life, the buildings of Piccadilly were dark monoliths against the russet and mauve sky.

Ulysses took a deep breath. The full-bodied scents of the fruity aftertaste of that last glass of claret mixed with the fumy air of the city, the bitter reek of the gas lamps and the smell of horse manure. London might have had combustion-driven automobiles for the last ninety years or so, and trams and trains for even longer than that, but there were still companies and private individuals who employed horses to carry them to and fro.

Cane in hand he paused for a moment as he savoured the familiar – even comforting – smells of the city and listened to the endless background noise that told him London was as alive as it had ever been. There were the unintelligible cries of the newspaper vendors, trying to shift the last of the late editions and the shouts of street sellers. There was the clatter of hooves and wheels on cobbles and the rumbling of petrol engines. There was the clamour of bells and whistles of the Overground as the trains rumbled past overhead, the cross-town railway network a black spider's web of seemingly infinite complexity with London ensnared beneath it.

Turning left out of the Ritz, rather than hail a cab,

Ulysses followed the railings that delineated the boundary of Green Park as he made his way past the thinning crowds making their way along Piccadilly in the dusky half-light. It felt good to have the London streets beneath his feet again. It reminded him of where home was and what it meant.

It was that curious time after the sun had set and the working day, for most, had come to an end but the revelries of the night were yet to truly begin. It would not be long, though, before others claimed the city as theirs. Not so very long ago Ulysses would have been one of them. He briefly considered returning to the Inferno Club to while away the evening over port and cigars but almost as quickly thought better of it. His body still ached and he suddenly found himself stifling a yawn. It would still take him some time to fully recover from his journey back to civilisation and, besides, his mind was awhirl with questions. Keeping his own company over dinner had only allowed him to go over and over all that he had seen at the Natural History Museum and ponder the nature of the crimes that had been committed there.

There were a number of questions that demanded answering. Why would a disturbed thief do away with the night watchman so brutally, using only his bare hands? And what would such a savage killer want with a laboratory difference engine belonging to a professor of evolutionary biology?

The more he thought about it, the more convinced he became that he had been sent to investigate two different crimes committed by two different culprits. But who were they and where were they hiding? Were they acting in league with one another? And what of Professor Ignatius Galapagos? What part did he have to play in all this? And where was he anyway?

His mind a jumble of questions and unsettling thoughts, Ulysses found himself at the top of the steps before the front door of his own house. He knocked and was admitted by the ever-faithful Nimrod.

"A good afternoon, sir?" the manservant enquired politely.

"Intriguing is the word I would use, Nimrod."

"Am I to take it that you are working again, sir?"

"Indeed. A most curious case."

"And how was Mr Wormwood?"

"Acidic as ever," Ulysses admitted. "And then, to top it all, I had a run-in with Inspector Allardyce of Scotland Yard."

"How unpleasant for you, sir."

"Indeed."

"Shall I ask Mrs Prufrock to prepare you a light supper? I believe that there is a hock of ham or some smoked salmon in the larder."

"No thank you, Nimrod, I've already eaten. You can let Mrs Prufrock go for the night," he added, only then realising that he had not been to see his cook and housekeeper since his return. But then he hadn't been back twenty-four hours yet, after having been away for over a year. Right now what he really wanted was a moment to himself with a glass of warming brandy in the familiar surroundings of his study to consider what he had discovered so far.

"Very good, sir. Then I should inform you that you have a visitor waiting to see you."

"Really, Nimrod?" Ulysses did a double take, giving the butler a look of genuine surprise. Who else knew he was back so soon? Once the news got out of his return he had expected the information to travel like wildfire but who would have come calling so openly, so early? "It's rather late to be having visitors call isn't it?"

"Precisely what I thought, sir. I suggested she return in the morning but she was adamant that she had to see you this evening, even if it meant waiting."

"She?"

"A Miss Genevieve Galapagos," Nimrod said, his haughty expression having never looked more unimpressed. From his manservant's tone Ulysses could tell that his female visitor was probably young and certainly attractive. What London's most eligible bachelor got up to with the ladies was his own affair – or more usually several ongoing affairs – but it was one area that the otherwise ever-faithful and accepting butler did not welcome being so openly flaunted within the Quicksilver family seat.

"Galapagos?"

"An unusual name certainly, sir."

"And one I have already come across today in another context. How long has she been waiting?"

"I believe it has been about half an hour, sir."

"Then let us not keep Miss Galapagos waiting any longer."

"I took the liberty of asking her to wait in the drawing room, sir."

"Very good, Nimrod."

With that, Ulysses made his way through the dustsheet-shrouded rooms to the sterile, forced informality of the drawing room. Other than the familiar space of his study, and possibly his bedroom, the house still didn't seem fully like home yet. He had been away for too long and in that time too much had happened. It would still take him some time to adjust and the best way for that to happen was for him to throw himself back into London life and involve himself in a mystery he could really get his teeth into. And it appeared that Wormwood had given him just what he needed.

Sweeping into the room in his frock coat, cane in hand, Ulysses startled the young lady who was perched uncomfortably on the edge of the one unshrouded chair, a teacup held in her lap.

There was no doubting that Ulysses Quicksilver knew how to make an entrance. Last night had proved that. It disarmed his enemies and potential allies alike and put him in control of almost any situation.

"Miss Galapagos, I presume," he said, his voice like velvet, and put out a hand.

"You must be Mr Quicksilver," she regarded him shyly through the veil of her fringe. Her expression made it look like she had the weight of the world resting on her shoulders, worry creasing her otherwise flawless features.

She was certainly attractive, still in the prime of her youth – Ulysses judged still in her early twenties. Her ivory features were clearly defined, her almond eyes large and a rich russet. Her rosebud lips were pursed. What little make-up she had applied – a little powder around her eyes, a little rouge on her cheeks and a touch of gloss on her lips – merely enhanced her natural beauty. Her hair was long and a rich auburn that caught the light from the electric chandelier, returning it as a shimmering golden sheen. Her apparel was striking too. She was wearing a tweed suit of the latest cut, the trousers plus fours that ended at the knee, where well-cut suede leather boots that accentuated the toned curve of her calves began, the jacket open enough to reveal the frill collars of the white blouse she wore beneath. Even though she was seated, it was clear that the suit was cut to accentuate the curve of her hips and the swell of her bosom, even though her figure was carefully covered up. The whole was finished with a crimson scarf tied loosely around her neck.

"At your service and please, call me Ulysses. All my friends do."

The young woman broke eye contact, looking down at the cup in her lap, the red of her rouged cheeks deepening and the rumours of a smile curling the corners of her mouth. Ulysses thought he heard a tut of disapproval from Nimrod behind him.

"I am not sure that would be appropriate, Mr Quicksilver," she said coyly.

"Oh, but I insist."

Cautiously his unexpected visitor took his hand. "Then you must call me Genevieve," she said, returning her gaze to his. For a moment Ulysses was lost in those depthless orbs that swam with colour like precious tiger's eye stones.

"Very well, Genevieve. It is an absolute pleasure to make your acquaintance."

"Likewise, Ulysses."

She was his now, he was sure of it.

"Now, Genevieve, what can I do for you at this late hour?"

The young woman's face was suddenly serious again. "I do not believe in beating about the bush so I will come straight to the point, Mr Quicksilver," she said nervously. "I mean, Ulysses."

She paused. It seemed to Ulysses that her eyes were glistening with barely suppressed tears. "Go on," he said.

"It's my father. I am dreadfully worried about him. I heard today that there had been an attack at the Natural History Museum."

"And your father is Professor Galapagos?" Ulysses offered. "Professor Ignatius Galapagos?"

"That's right," Genevieve said, surprise replacing concern. "Do you know him, Mr Quicksilver?"

"Ulysses, please," he chided gently. "I have come across his name in my... work. He is a member of staff at the museum?"

"Yes. He works in the Evolutionary Biology department. He often works late, sometimes well into the night, even the early hours of the morning. On occasion he has been known to spend the entire night at the museum."

"He is dedicated to his work then."

"Yes, like no other. It is his passion."

So where was he today? If he was so passionate about his work why not turn up for work on this particular day?

"And was he working late there last night?"

"He was and I haven't seen him since." At that admission Genevieve's shoulders sagged and she returned her tearful gaze to the empty teacup in her lap.

"But, if you will beg my pardon, Miss Galapagos – I mean, Genevieve – you have just said yourself that it is not unheard of for him to spend the whole night in his office."

"Yes, but I eventually went to look for him there today and was turned away by the police. The museum staff said that there had been no sign of him all day – not since the police were alerted to the attack on the night watchman – and then someone told me that it was his office that had been broken into..."

She broke off again, as grief and anxiety overwhelmed her. Ulysses put a comforting hand on her arm.

"I am worried that my father may have been abducted!" Genevieve sobbed.

"Did you relay your concerns to the police?"

"I tried to, but they weren't interested." That sounded

about right. "There was an Inspector Alla... Allardiss?"

"Allardyce."

"Yes, that was it. You know him?"

"You could say that."

"I thought so. He said that I should wait twenty-four hours before filing a missing persons report. The inspector mentioned your name though." Genevieve suddenly seemed tense, flexing her shoulders and shifting uncomfortably in the chair.

"Go on, you can say what you like. I won't be offended; not if it's what Allardyce told you."

"Well," Genevieve went on, still struggling with both anxiety and embarrassment, "he was rather... disparaging. But I didn't really like what I saw of him so I decided that if he didn't like you, you might actually be more willing to listen and help me. I understand that I can hire your services, for a suitable fee. I have some money saved..."

"Don't worry about recompense just at the moment," Ulysses said, interrupting her.

She suddenly smiled through the tears. Genevieve took both Ulysses' hands in hers and he was suddenly aware of the heady scent of jasmine flowers as she moved.

"Oh, Ulysses! You will help me then?"

Maybe it was something about being a Quicksilver, but Ulysses simply couldn't resist a pretty face, and when that pretty face belonged to a damsel in distress it made any attempt at resistance even more futile.

"I will do what I can."

"When can you start?"

"Well, as the saying goes, there's no time like the present." Ulysses turned to his manservant. "Nimrod, we're going out."

"You would like me to fire up the Phantom, sir?"

"Yes, I think our guest deserves better than a hansom at

this time of night, don't you?"

"Will Miss Galapagos be joining us, sir?"

Ulysses looked to Genevieve. She smiled at him weakly, looking at him from beneath long luscious lashes. She nodded almost imperceptibly.

"Yes, she will."

As he guided Genevieve from the room, Ulysses turned to his dour-faced manservant and gave him a manic grin. "The game is afoot, Nimrod."

"So it would seem, sir."

"Oh yes, the game is most definitely afoot. It feels good to be a player again. This is just what my life has been missing."

CHAPTER FIVE

Galapagos

The automobile purred through the sodium-lit streets, passing flickering broadcast screens on every street corner and the massive advertising hoardings of the mega-corporations. The spider's web of the Overground was black against the smog-laden velvet blue of the night above them. The vehicle passed chugging hansoms, its sleek silvered chassis glittering with the reflected lights of the city. Its engine running almost soundlessly, the car turned into Queen's Gate gliding past the wrought-iron railings that enclosed the Royal College of Music, the bold beams of its headlamps washing over the beggars and streetwalkers that lined the road before sweeping past them.

There was little traffic at this time of night. It would get busier again when the night owls were done with their revels. Nimrod turned the Mark IV Silver Phantom onto Cromwell Road. Ulysses looked out of the window at the cathedral-like towers of the museum, a shadow cut-out of the backdrop of South Kensington behind it.

The car pulled up smoothly outside the main gates and Nimrod turned off the engine. Ulysses opened his door and stepped out before helping Genevieve from the car, taking her hand gently in his. He could not help but take a lingering look at her legs as she climbed gracefully out of the Silver Phantom.

Genevieve looked up at him and, for a moment, their eyes met. He smiled confidently. The smile she returned was somewhat more demure and a moment later, she was the one to break eye contact.

As Genevieve adjusted her jacket Ulysses bent down through the open car door to speak to his manservant. "Nimrod, I want you to wait here just in case our investigation flushes something out."

"You think the killer could still be inside?"

"It's just a hunch – a feeling I have."

"Are you sure this is a good idea, sir?"

"Nimrod, you sound like someone's dear old nanny," Ulysses chided. "We'll be all right. I'm carrying protection," he added, patting the breast of his frock coat. "And besides, Her Majesty's finest Metropolitan Police will be able to keep an eye on us too."

Two robot-bobbies stood before the entrance. Nimrod looked at Ulysses, saying nothing but raising an eyebrow in undisguised disdain.

"Stop fussing, old chap," Ulysses said with a smile. "If I can survive the horrors of Kathmandu and the slopes of Mount Manaslu then I think there's little the Natural History Museum of South Kensington can throw at me that I won't be able to deal with."

"Is there a problem, Mr Quicksilver?" His new client was at his shoulder.

"No not at all, Miss Galapagos," he said, turning away from the driver's window with a dramatic swirl of his coat tails. "And please, call me Ulysses. I insist."

"Of course. Is there a problem then, Ulysses?"

"You know how it is, you just can't get the staff," he said, guiding her towards the entrance.

As they climbed the slope that led to the stepped entrance Genevieve suddenly hung back. "What are we doing here, at this hour?" she asked.

"What?" Ulysses asked, genuinely taken by surprise. "I thought it was because you had just hired me to find your missing father. And seeing as how you say he was last seen here it seemed like the logical place to begin our investigation. As to why at this late hour, it also seemed pertinent to be about our search straightaway."

Genevieve looked at him. There was a glistening sheen in her eyes, the rumour of tears. "That's not what I meant."

Ulysses stopped and took both her hands in his. "If anyone can find your father, I can. I assure you."

"That's what I'm afraid of."

"You have come here to find the truth," he said quietly, his words heavy with meaning.

"Yes, I have," Genevieve agreed.

"Then just remember that the truth is not always the same as what is good or for the best."

Genevieve squeezed Ulysses' fingers tightly.

"It will be all right."

"Will it?" she challenged.

Now it was Ulysses who said nothing.

Genevieve smiled at him, her eyes still wet. "Thank you," she said.

"For what?"

"For trying to spare my emotions."

"Come on," he said, "the truth awaits."

Ulysses mounted the steps at a jog, whipping his cardholder out of his jacket even as one of the automata-peelers initiated its own challenge with the words, "'Ello, 'ello, 'ello. What can I do for you sir? The museum is closed to the public for the night."

In the ambient light of the street lamps Ulysses' sharp eyes could make out the drone's nameplate quite clearly, as the robot scanned the card revealed inside the small leather wallet. "Ah, Constable Palmerston. We meet again."

The second drone – one Constable Disraeli – said nothing, but merely kept its ruby gaze fixed on Genevieve who stood a step or two below Ulysses.

"Indeed we do Mr Quicksilver, sir."

"And I think you will be able to recall from your memory-records your words to me at that juncture."

"Why, of course, sir," Constable Palmerston said in his synthesised voice. "I said that if there was anything else I could do to help..."

"And I said that I would be sure to find you. Well, here I am."

"What can I do to help, Mr Quicksilver?"

"My guest and I would like to examine the scene of the crime again."

"Inspector Allardyce ordered that you are not to be readmitted, sir," the constable reported without emotion.

For a moment Ulysses was taken aback. Genevieve looked at him anxiously. "Did he now?"

"Yes, sir."

"You scanned my card, constable. Then you will recognise whose authority I am here under."

"Yes, sir."

"Then you won't try to stop me if I enter this museum and examine the crime scene again, will you?"

"No, sir."

"Very good, constable. Keep up the good work," Ulysses said jovially as he marched past the two drones and pushed open the door. Genevieve followed, casting nervous glances at the two towering automata as she hurried after him. "Don't worry, they're ultimately on our side," Ulysses said, smiling darkly.

He might sound jovial, but inside he was fuming. How dare that little oik, Allardyce, try to stop him coming back here! What was he trying to hide?

Ulysses' steps rang on the polished stone floor of the entrance hall. Ahead of him the fossilised diplodocus gazed back across the millennia with its eyeless stare.

What *was* Allardyce trying to hide? Probably nothing. He didn't have the wits to. By now he would have decided that the wretched night watchman had been killed by his disturbed burglar and would have practically put the case to bed. Besides, in Allardyce's opinion, what could possibly have been worth stealing from an evolutionary biologist? Nothing that was worth him wasting any more police time over, that was for sure.

Passing the skeletal leviathan Ulysses climbed the grand staircase to the first floor and made his way to the Darwin Wing once again.

The place was deserted. There was no lingering police presence. There were no lights on anywhere in the museum either. Ulysses rather suspected that after the death of the watchman and the possible disappearance of one of their own, any other scientist who was in the habit of working late had decided that an early night was in order. Not that he needed any artificial light to see by. Here in the gallery, the monochrome light of the moon and the orange glow of the city's lights filtering in through the tall windows were quite enough.

Ulysses led the way into the gallery. The body of the night watchman had been removed by the police but dried blood still stained the floor beside the shattered display case. He stopped on reaching the ransacked office.

"This is your father's office, I believe," he said.

Genevieve gasped and put a hand to her mouth.

Allardyce's men had made little effort to secure the crime scene. The mangled door remained propped against the wall and a piece of black and yellow tape had been casually strung across the entrance. Ulysses took hold of the tape and tugged it free with a disdainful snarl.

"Should you be doing that?" Genevieve asked anxiously.

"Should the Metropolitan Police be sitting on their arses when your father has been reported missing?"

Taking out a flashlight from an inside pocket of his coat, Ulysses directed its hard white beam into the office. Light shone back at them from broken glass. Forensics must have been done with the place as some attempt had been made to clear the detritus that had littered the floor. Glass and smashed pieces of furniture had been swept into piles in either corner of the room.

Ulysses carefully stepped into Professor Galapagos' wrecked home away from home. There was still a lingering memory of an odour like aniseed and spoiled steak.

Genevieve paused at the threshold, her breathing rapid and shallow.

"It's all right," Ulysses said. "It'll be all right. Trust me."

Ulysses shone his torch into the far corner of the laboratory. He could still see where the professor's difference engine was missing from its place on the desk. It looked like someone had made some effort to tidy the papers that had been strewn across the work surface. Had any of them been taken away by the police for closer scrutiny? What secrets might they reveal?

But more importantly, what information had been stored on the Babbage machine?

"Your father used a difference engine in his work?" Ulysses asked, meticulously inspecting the walls and space around the desk.

"I believe so," Genevieve replied. "Doesn't everyone?"

"Indeed."

The sweeping beam struck upon several small, fractured

display cases, each one holding a stuffed creature, preserved forever by the taxidermist's art. There was a coelacanth, a kaymen and some manner of small primate, its face frozen in either an aggressive or terrified teeth-baring shriek.

"Can you tell if my father was taken from here?" Genevieve asked.

"There are signs of a scuffle, that's for sure. But are they also signs of an abduction?"

Had the professor been abducted from this place at the same time as the thief was stealing away his difference engine? If so, there must have been more than one miscreant, and one of them prepared to kill to ensure their getaway as well as to take a hostage. What manner of men was he dealing with?

The lack of any inkling from his unerring sixth sense was informing him that there was nothing more that Galapagos' quarters could tell him. There were too many distractions there anyway; the mess of papers hinting at greater unsolved mysteries of the scientific world, the glassy-eyed specimens in their broken glass cases, Genevieve...

"Where is the answer? What am I missing here?" Ulysses was becoming frustrated. Was there really nothing more that he could deduce from this mess? The measure of a crime could always be traced back from the wreckage of evidence it left behind it. A crime always left its mark, a criminal his fingerprint even if those investigating the crime could not always see it. What was it that Ulysses was missing?

With a snarl of frustration he suddenly turned on his heel and strode out of the wrecked office again.

"Ulysses?" Genevieve's anxious voice followed him out of the room.

Then he felt it; an uncomfortable prickling sensation that made his skin goose pimple and the hairs on the back of his neck stand up. It was that unerring sixth sense of his. His hand tightened around his cane, his knuckles whitening.

It was the same sensation he had felt earlier when he had first visited the scene of the crime; the feeling of someone's eyes upon him, only intensified now in the silence and emptiness of the museum. Like fingernails scraping at the inside of his skull.

Was it the killer? Had he returned? Or had Ulysses' suspicions been right all along and had the killer never left?

"Ulysses, what is it?" He was staring blankly ahead of him, his flashlight held at his side, pointing at the floor. Genevieve was at his shoulder.

"Stay close," he whispered.

"There's someone else here, isn't there?"

"I rather think there is."

Dark eyes watched as the two figures explored the gallery beyond the ruins of the ransacked room, the torch beam flicking into the darkened recesses of alcoves and behind glittering display cases. The watcher recognised the man; tall, confident, his stride purposeful, as if he owned the gallery and the museum. It remembered him from earlier that day.

It did not recognise the smaller female scurrying anxiously at his side. She smelt of fear and something else – something hidden.

The watcher pulled itself back behind a cast iron roof beam. It sensed, in its primitive way, that itself was what they were searching for, and the interloper was persistent.

He would not rest until he had found what he was looking for, until he had hunted the watcher down. It was only a matter of time before the sweeping beam uncovered its hiding place.

It was getting frustrated by its confinement in the museum. It was changing all the time. It wanted to stretch its limbs, test its new body, discover what it was capable of.

And its mind was changing too. It was no longer happy to watch whilst others trespassed within its territory. The desire was growing inside it to drive the interlopers from the gallery, to show them which was the dominant species here.

Lips pulled back from clenched teeth and a low growl issued from its altered throat.

Shadows flickered and writhed against the wall. Ulysses' sweeping torch beam suddenly picked out teeth bared in an angry snarl, eyes staring in open defiance. Genevieve gasped. The face that appeared in the cold white light was barely human, the expression contorting it one of bestial rage.

Ulysses leaned closer, pointing his torch directly into the subhuman's glassy-eyed stare. The creature didn't even blink.

"It's all right," he said. "*Homo neanderthalensis*, resident of the middle Paleolithic. Thought to have died out around 29,000 years ago until that inbred colony was found in the Urals in sixty-nine."

A hand on Ulysses' shoulder, Genevieve peered past him at the motionless figure in front of them. The waxwork replica of the Neanderthal, moved from its smashed display case earlier that day to lie propped against the wall of the gallery, continued to stare back, one arm raised, an antler held threateningly in its hand.

"This one isn't going to cause us any trouble." Ulysses said.

Awareness suddenly flared in his brain like a firework. Ulysses spun round, pushing Genevieve out of the way as something large swung out of the darkness and barrelled into him.

Ulysses was sent crashing to the ground, even as he reached inside his jacket for his pistol. His torch fell from his hand and went out. The wind was knocked from his lungs as the creature landed on top of him. He twisted, trying to free himself from the weight of the thing. As he did so he tugged his pistol free and aimed it at the shadow looming over him. A club-like fist smashed into his outstretched arm. In unexpected shock the muscles in his hand spasmed, releasing the weapon which skittered away across the floor of the gallery.

The beast let out a victorious roar. Genevieve screamed.

Disarmed, Ulysses would have to try a different approach.

In the eerie moonlit glow of the gallery the creature appeared as a ragged shadow above him. Ulysses could see nothing more than the glistening points of its eyes and the gleam of its bared fangs. The stench of its rancid breath made him gag as it came in hot gusts against his face.

He was suddenly back in Tibet as recollections of his struggle with the snow beast in the hidden monastery poured from his subconscious. He had survived that encounter and he would survive this one, thanks in part to the martial arts he had learned in the company of the Tibetan monks.

Ulysses kicked upwards sharply with his right leg. The toe of his shoe connected with the back of the creature's neck. The thing howled and arched its back, releasing Ulysses from the weight pressing down on his pelvis.

His leg swinging back down again he pendulummed his body forwards, raising his torso from the ground. As his arms came free he thrust them forwards, palms together. He struck the thing squarely in the sternum, the force of his blow pushing the creature from him.

But in a moment the creature was crouched on its haunches, ready to pounce again. Rising up on its muscular legs it towered over Ulysses, its hairy arms raised ready to pound him into the polished marble floor of the gallery. It bellowed its anger and beat its chest with its fists, declaring its claim to this place as its territory.

Without a moment's hesitation the creature sprang at Ulysses again. But this time Ulysses was ready. As the ape-like creature landed, grasping at him with leathery paws, he seized hold of the thing, grasping great tufts of hair in his fists as he let himself fall backwards beneath the creature's assault, pushing a foot into its midriff as he did so. He landed on his back again on the cold stone but this time the creature came with him, unbalanced by the change in its centre of gravity. As he felt the full weight of the thing above him Ulysses brought both his feet together and pushed upwards with all the strength in his legs, at the same time pulling the beast forward.

The creature sailed over Ulysses' head. He heard it howl in protest and then there was an almighty crash. Ulysses quickly got to his feet and turned, preparing to face his attacker again.

Shards of glass sparkled in the monochrome light bathing the hall. Unable to stop itself, the creature had smashed into one of the gallery's display cases. Snorting in annoyance the beast was trying to extricate itself from the shattered remains of the cabinet. Ulysses surmised that it must have been injured in the collision but whatever injuries it might have sustained did not seem to be slowing it down.

The creature was caught in the spotlight of his torch beam, pupils contracting against the sudden illumination. In that split second Ulysses saw his attacker clearly for the first time.

It was an apeman, dressed in a suit of ill-fitting clothes. What Ulysses could see of the creature beneath its curious garb was covered in reddish-brown hair, apart from its hands, feet and blunt-nosed face. The tweed jacket and trousers had torn where the beast's form was too large to be contained. A white shirt had popped its buttons, as had a formal paisley-patterned waistcoat.

Ulysses briefly wondered how anyone had managed to dress this savage in such a way, as he caught the glint of a silver chain hanging around its neck, until the only logical answer presented itself to him.

Ulysses pulled himself upright. Picking up his cane he took hold of the bloodstone at its end and gave it a twist. With one smooth movement Ulysses pulled a rapier thin blade from the middle of his cane. As the apeman's laboured breathing turned into a guttural growl Ulysses assumed the stance of an accomplished fencer. "En garde," he said with quiet purpose.

As the creature climbed free of the wreckage of the display case, Ulysses noted that its lumbering gait and low-slung head spoke of a kinship with the lower orders of primates. The semi-human features of the creature devolved into a bestial snarl and it knuckled forwards, using its forelimbs like another pair of legs, shrieking horribly. Rapier blade in hand, Ulysses prepared to meet its furious charge.

The shot rang out through the gallery like a cannon blast, the report of the pistol amplified by the acoustics of the hall. The apeman was suddenly hurled backwards, a welter of blood spraying from its left shoulder and a whimper of pain escaping its malformed lips. Then, as the blue pistol smoke cleared, the creature was back on its feet only now it was running to escape, rather than charging to attack.

Ulysses spun round. Genevieve stood behind him, the torch in one hand, his gun held rigidly in the other. "Nice shot," he said, the rumour of a smile inching itself onto his face, "but I had the situation fully under control."

Genevieve lowered the gun. "I thought that... thing was going to kill you."

"Your concern is touching, really it is," Ulysses said, sheathing his sword-cane and setting off at a run, back through the gallery, Genevieve trotting to keep up, "but I would rather we took that throwback alive."

They turned left into the main gallery of the Darwin Wing. In the dull monochrome light of the moon Ulysses could see black spots of blood speckling the polished floor, leaving them an obvious trail.

"Do you think that thing had anything to do with my father's disappearance?" Genevieve said.

They passed beneath the stone arch above which the words 'The Ascent of Man' were carved, Ulysses' shoes sliding on the polished stone floor. The slap of the ape-thing's leathery hands and feet could be heard ahead of them. "I would bet money on it. Which is why we can't let it get away."

Ulysses put on a turn of speed and, leaving Genevieve behind, sprinted onto the cloister-gallery that ran around the main entrance hall of the museum. Then he saw it, loping along on all fours like a dog. He swore sharply under his breath. He could have delivered a crippling shot to the creature, had Genevieve not still got his gun. He would have to try something else to halt the apeman's escape.

"Constable Palmerston!" he yelled at the top of his voice. "Constable Palmerston, if ever there was a time I needed your help that time is now! Palmerston!"

The apeman suddenly turned, its feet slipping momentarily on the polished stone and then it leapt onto the ledge of the colonnaded walkway. Ulysses could see the chain around its neck more clearly now. Hanging from it was what looked like a silver locket.

The beast glanced momentarily at Ulysses, its eyes burning with animal fear and malign hatred, and then the creature hurled itself into empty space.

"Palmerston!" Ulysses screamed.

The apeman landed with a rattling crash on the spine of the diplodocus skeleton as the museum doors burst open and the two Peeler-drones marched into the building.

"Stop, in the name of the law!" Ulysses heard the Palmerston unit pronounce in its synthesised voice.

But the creature had no intention of stopping, in the name of the law or anything else. The diplodocus swayed precariously as the apeman bounded across it, grabbing at ribs and vertebrae to aid its flight across the hall.

Another shot rang out through the museum and a prehistoric shoulder blade exploded in a cloud of dust and bone fragments.

"We want to take it alive!" Ulysses shouted.

The two constables were beneath the diplodocus now, the apeman scrambling across the skeleton above them. Grabbing hold of the fossil's neck with one hand it swung over the heads of the automatons and launched itself at the main doors. It hit the floor as the cables holding the relic's head and neck gave way and the dinosaur's skull crashed to the ground, its jaw shattering on the hard stone floor.

In one bound the apeman was through the doors. A moment later Ulysses barged past the bewildered droids as he hurtled through the doors after the creature, only to see it swinging away into the night, using street lamps as a monkey would have swung through a jungle canopy. With a squeal of tyres the Silver Phantom sped off after the creature, swerving to avoid a crawling omnibus as Nimrod gave chase.

"Did we get it?" Genevieve gasped. She stood with her hands on her knees, panting for breath. There was a manic gleam in her eye that was so unlike the demure young woman he had met only a matter of an hour or so earlier.

"You certainly got it," Ulysses said in an almost disapproving tone.

"Yes, but where is it now?"

"What's going on 'ere then?" The two robot policemen had joined them at the top of the steps.

"I think we just spooked your murderer," Ulysses muttered.

There was the crackle of static as the Peeler unit used its internal radio to report the escape to its controllers back at Scotland Yard.

There was the sound of a horn and the Silver Phantom pulled up again outside the museum railings. Ulysses was halfway down the incline from the museum building by the time Nimrod had emerged from the car.

"I do apologise, sir, but I am afraid I lost the monkey."

Ulysses sighed. His first major lead in this case had just

evaded him. But, he reminded himself, patting the pocket of his jacket, it wasn't his only lead.

"Don't worry, Nimrod old chap," he said. Genevieve had joined them, the drones following close on her heels. "Did you happen to see what that thing was wearing around its neck, along with the rest of its incongruous wardrobe?" Ulysses asked her.

"Why yes," she said, obviously somewhat shaken, the manic look gone from her eyes to be replaced by wide-eyed shock. "It was my locket."

"Your locket?"

"Well, I mean, it's my father's locket, but I gave it to him. It was a gift. That thing must have taken it from him. It must have had something to do with his disappearance."

Ulysses looked at Genevieve gravely and took her hands in his again. "Genevieve," he said, "I can't think of any other way to put this to you, but I don't believe that thing took the locket from your father. In fact I don't believe that your father has been abducted."

"What d-do mean? You're not saying that you think he's d..." She broke off, overcome with emotion. Her eyes were imploring him now, desperately wanting him to tell her anything that might help her make sense of what had happened.

"Don't ask me to explain how but I think that thing *is* – or rather, *was* – your father."

CHAPTER SIX

A Meeting with Methuselah

The partially rusted pull grated as Ulysses tugged on it and a moment later, somewhere deep within the house, he heard the clattering of an ancient bell. Then he waited. The old man didn't keep any servants; he preferred not to be disturbed even by domestic help while he worked, and his work was his life.

The debacle at the museum the previous night had prevented Ulysses from pursuing the most direct course of action regarding Professor Galapagos' disappearance. Despite taking off after the fleeing apeman in Ulysses' Silver Phantom, following the altered beast as it had swung from lamp post to lamp post down the Cromwell Road, Nimrod had had to give up the chase when the creature had scrambled up the side of a building and taken to the rooftops. There was no way he could have abandoned the car and still kept up with the apeman on foot.

After Ulysses had broken the tragic news to Genevieve Galapagos that her father had somehow become some kind of degenerate apeman, the girl had gone to pieces. She had refused the offer of something to eat, and a bed, at the Quicksilver residence – seemingly placing a portion of the blame for what had happened to her father at Ulysses' door – but Ulysses had insisted that Nimrod drive her home. He promised that he would contact her as soon as he knew anything more.

So it was that as the smog-laden sky over London began to lighten with the coming dawn, Ulysses found himself at the house of Dr Methuselah.

Although he was currently seen to be pursuing the Galapagos case, at the same time the mystery of the professor's transformation was inextricably linked to the mission that had been forced upon him by Uriah Wormwood. The more Ulysses could discover about what had happened to Professor Ignatius Galapagos, the more likely he was to find out what had really happened regarding the theft from the Natural History Museum. It seemed highly unlikely that the ape-like Galapagos – if it was truly he – would have had the wits to take his own difference engine, for some unfathomable reason. There had to be another felon involved, and somehow the two of them were connected. If he could track the errant professor down Ulysses Quicksilver was sure that he would eventually find his thief.

A clattering of bolts being drawn back and keys being turned stirred Ulysses from his reverie. The heavy black door creaked opened a crack. It was still secured by a chain, and a wizened bespectacled face looked up at Ulysses.

"What do you want?" the old man snapped in a voice that was high-pitched and cracked with age.

"Dr Methuselah, it is so good to see you again," Ulysses said, smiling broadly.

"Is it?" Dr Methuselah blinked at him myopically from behind bottle-bottom lenses.

"It's me, doctor, Ulysses. Ulysses Quicksilver?"

The hunched figure looked Ulysses up and down, his face twisted into a scowl.

"I thought you were dead."

"Yes, I get that a lot."

"So, if you're not dead, what do you want?"

"Your help, doctor, as ever."

This request solicited the same response it always did.

"You don't get something for nothing in this world. You can pay?"

"You can do this for me right away?"

"If you can pay me right now I can."

"You know I'm good for the cash," Ulysses said, feigning hurt. "At least I hope you do."

"You'd better come in then. You're letting in a draught."

The door closed, there was the rattle of the chain being unhooked, and then it opened fully to admit Ulysses to the house. Once he was over the threshold the stooped Dr Methuselah ushered him inside and shut the door behind him.

"Do you know what time it is?"

"I didn't think you kept conventional working hours."

"I don't, but that's not the point," the old man grumbled, and set off down the mahogany-panelled hallway. The musty smell of the place and the decaying décor all added to the character of the house.

As the ageing doctor shuffled down the corridor, Ulysses was better able to take in his appearance. Nothing had changed since the last time he had visited. Methuselah's clothes were filthy, covered in all manner of curious chemical stains. He had several days' growth of white stubble speckling his bony chin and hollow cheeks. He seemed to be permanently stooped and an unwashed odour hung about him like a mantle.

Ulysses followed Methuselah through the darkened house and into the back room that served as the curmudgeon's laboratory. Not that it looked or smelt like one. Floor to ceiling bookcases covered almost every available wall space, stuffed with yellowed tomes and rolls of parchment. More books were piled in tottering towers on the floor. There was no natural light in the room. Any windows that there might once have been were now barricaded by bookcases or covered by cork pinboards on which the doctor's meticulously ink-drawn autopsy studies were displayed. The air was thick with the unpleasant combination of formaldehyde, mothballs and tobacco smoke.

Along the length of the room was a timber-top workspace. All manner of curious, scientific or medical equipment cluttered its surface. There were jars with unnaturally shaped things floating in brackish liquid and Ulysses saw a half-dissected creature pinned out on a slab that might have been a deformed toad or could equally have been, even more horribly, a deformed human foetus. Another table was covered with a mess of electrical gadgetry.

"So what do you want me to look at?" the doctor asked.

Ulysses reached into the pocket of his frock coat and took out the evidence bag containing the sample he had taken from Galapagos' office. "I want you to take a look at this."

"Very well." Methuselah took the bag and peered at the reddish-brown hairs inside through his thick-lensed spectacles. Ulysses couldn't help noticing that the doctor's fingernails were black with grime.

Having scrabbled around within the clutter of his workspace to find a pair of tweezers, the doctor placed the hairs on a slide, which he then inserted beneath the rotating lenses of a brass microscope. Methuselah put one lens of his glasses to the viewing piece and, with no small amount of huffing and puffing and unintelligible muttering, twiddled a variety of brass wheels to focus the device and magnify what he saw.

The doctor paused while he pulled up a stool, so that he might continue his study of the specimen in relative comfort.

Ulysses looked for a seat himself, but there were no more available. It wasn't that there wasn't any furniture in the room it was just that every available surface was covered with the paraphernalia of the doctor's work. Instead he leant over the doctor's shoulder to watch what Methuselah was doing. The doctor's malingering body odour assailed Ulysses' nostrils, catching in the back of his throat. Ulysses pulled back before the festering smell made him gag. He occupied himself instead by distractedly poking at piles of papers with his cane, examining some of the titles on Methuselah's bookshelves and taking a closer look at some of his Da Vinci-like anatomical drawings.

"Darwin's eyes!" the old man suddenly exclaimed.

"What is it, Dr Methuselah?" Despite the poor state of the old man's personal hygiene, Ulysses was back at his side again.

The doctor of forensics looked round sharply. "No, I'm not ready to present my findings yet," he snapped cantankerously.

"Very well, doctor," his client said soothingly, "take as long as you need."

With that the doctor went back to his work, which was now accompanied by him noisily sucking his teeth. He extracted a cogitator keypad from somewhere on his desk and it was only then that Ulysses realised that, amongst everything else crammed into the shelf space above Methuselah, was a cathode ray unit. As the doctor began to type sequences of numbers into the machine the screen began to warm up with a rising hum, turning from black to a glowing green.

After a few more minutes there was another gasp from the absorbed doctor.

"Where did you get these hairs?" Methuselah asked,

unable to hide the astonishment and excitement in his voice.

"You know better than to ask that doctor," Ulysses chided.

Methuselah grunted and muttered something that Ulysses strongly suspected was either blasphemous or a personal slight against him.

There was now an image on the difference engine's view screen. Ulysses assumed it was a magnified cross-section of what Methuselah could see through his microscope. Streams of data scrolled up the side of the screen in a repeating pattern. Knowing a little about the science of biology he recognised what he was seeing in the flickering emerald lines as cells. To understand anymore he would need the expert to explain it to him.

"If we extrapolate the data back to the original source," the doctor said, thinking aloud rather than addressing Ulysses directly, "and if my hypothesis is correct," the doctor tapped something into the difference engine's brass-faced keypad, a series of confusing images now being relayed by the screen, "... we find... Yes!" he declared triumphantly. "An exact match!"

"With what, doctor?"

"Hmm?" Methuselah seemed to have become absorbed in his work to the point of practically forgetting that Ulysses was still there. "What?"

"An exact match with what?"

"Oh, an exact match with human DNA of course."

A feeling of self-satisfied vindication settled like a warm mist over Ulysses. "I love it when I'm right," he said, smiling to himself. He couldn't say he was surprised; it was what he had suspected ever since he had visited the scene of the crime and heard of the disappearance of Professor Galapagos. He had just needed someone with the scientific knowledge to prove that his hunch had been more than just that. He still had no idea, though, what could have caused such a degeneration in the evolutionary biologist.

"Doctor, I appreciate your candour but if you can see to putting what you have discovered into layman's terms. And start at the beginning."

Methuselah sighed in irritation at the thought of having to dumb down his findings for this dandy.

"Take a look at this," the doctor said in a weary tone, nodding at the thinking machine's monitor. He typed something else into the Babbage engine and the magnified image of cells appeared on the screen again. "What you are looking at here is one of the hairs you brought me but at the cellular level."

"I realise that, doctor. But what is it that they have revealed to you?"

"If you let me finish I could tell you."

"Of course, doctor. I am sorry. Please continue."

"Very well," Methuselah said, almost grudgingly. "These are hair cells from a member of the primate family. There is nothing particularly remarkable about that until we observe them at a molecular level."

The image on the screen flickered and blurred, reforming to show Ulysses something he had never seen before in his life.

"What am I looking at now?" he asked, staring uncomprehendingly at the spiralling ribbons of bonded molecules.

"This," said Methuselah, unable to hide the tone of smugness from his own voice, "is the stuff of life itself. You are gazing upon the very building blocks of all life on this planet. This is the double helix of deoxyribonucleic acid. DNA."

"That's DNA?" Ulysses uttered incredulously.

"The very same. Chains of only four different nucleotides, combined in an infinite number of ways results in the vast biodiversity we witness on this planet. From snails to whales, from the lumbering leviathans of the Jurassic that are still with us today to the mosquito that feeds on its blood, every living thing is the result of strings of genetically coded information carried by the strands of DNA wrapped up inside its cells."

"But you said that you had found human DNA here and yet now you tell me that these are hairs from some kind of ape." It was not that Ulysses did not believe the doctor; it was just that he wanted to understand more completely what could possibly have happened for this to be the case.

"I was just getting to that. The DNA sample inside these hairs is unstable."

"Unstable? How do you mean?"

"It is unravelling, as it were."

"Doctor, I still don't fully under..."

"How can I put this any more plainly?" Methuselah said, the frustration he felt rising in his voice. "These are now the hairs of a primate but they once belonged to a man, a human being, like you or I. These hairs have somehow devolved into those belonging to one of Man's evolutionary ancestors. And the process is ongoing."

Now Ulysses felt genuine surprise. "It's still happening?"

"The genetic make-up of the sample is steadily reverting to previous evolutionary forms. Imagine it! The very essence of life unravelling, de-evolving, if you will, back into the amino acids and bacteria from which we were first formed. What we are looking at here is a veritable history lesson in the creation of the human race from baser forms of life on this planet. As each layer of history peels away, these cells here are changing into a prior evolutionary form, as the very DNA held inside each of them is continually re-written at a genetic level."

"So when will this metamorphosis reach its conclusion?"

"I won't know for sure without continued observation."

"Humour me. Give me a hypothesis."

"Well, looking at the sample I have here, there's no reason to suggest that it won't stop until it reaches the beginning."

"You might as well be speaking in riddles, doctor."

"I mean at what we understand to be the beginning of all life on this planet. These cells are already beginning to display characteristics of those of a reptile. There is no evidence to suggest that they will not continue to regress until the biological matter under this microscope has dissolved back into the component parts that make up all life on this planet, effectively into a protoplasmic soup."

For a moment neither man spoke as they both digested the import of the doctor's revelation.

"Quicksilver, where is the poor wretch these hairs came from?"

"I wish I knew," Ulysses said with a heartfelt sigh.

"He needs to be studied, quarantined perhaps."

"What, and dissected, doctor?" Ulysses challenged, putting a sarcastic emphasis on the word 'doctor'.

"No, for his own safety."

"Well, when I catch up with him again, I'll be sure to tell him to look you up. Now, what do I owe you for your services?"

Methuselah stared at Ulysses, mouth agape, until the mention of payment reminded him that morals were all very well for men of the cloth but that they didn't cover gambling debts or keep a man in opium. "We'll call it ten guineas – cash."

Ulysses opened his wallet with a flourish, took out the agreed fee and handed it over to the old man, who was watching his every move with the avaricious hunger of a gold prospector.

"Thank you for your time, doctor." Placing his wallet back inside his jacket pocket Ulysses turned to go.

"What about the sample?" Methuselah asked.

"Keep it," Ulysses said, turning at the door to the workroom. "And I'll pay you for any other information you might be able to impart after further observation. I'll see myself out."

Back on the street Ulysses took a moment to clear his lungs of the acrid smell of preserving fluid and savour the honest tarry smell of the London streets. Delving deep into a pocket he pulled out the teak and brass handset of his personal communicator. He flicked it open and extended its aerial. He waited whilst a train clattered by overhead, then keyed in Genevieve's number.

It rang three times before there was the click of a receiver being lifted at the other end and he heard Genevieve's voice. "Hello?" was all she said, but even that one simple response made Ulysses' stomach flutter with a frisson of excitement. He surprised himself with such a psychosomatic reaction. He hadn't realised how sorry he had been to cause her so much distress only hours before and how unhappy he had felt at the abruptness of their parting.

"Genevieve, it's Ulysses. Please don't hang up."

"I have nothing to say to you."

"But I have more news," he gabbled.

There was no response from the other end of the line. Was she still there? "Genevieve?"

"What news?" Her tone was flat with suppressed emotion.

"I'd rather not discuss it over the phone. Let's meet up."

Again there was a pause. "Where?"

Ulysses thought fast. His mind was awhirl with their last encounter among the prehistoric exhibits and Dr Methuselah's talk of DNA and evolutionary genetic heritage. One place came immediately to mind, but he thought it best to avoid the Natural History Museum for the time being. He didn't want Scotland Yard getting in the way of his private business again and somewhere public and open was always best if you wanted to avoid arousing suspicion.

"London Zoo," he said, "the Challenger Enclosure. Then I can share with you what I have discovered."

"Very well." Her tone had softened. "I'll meet you there at ten o' clock tomorrow morning." The connection went dead.

Ulysses closed the communicator and stowed it back in his pocket. Soon he would have to convince Genevieve of the horrifying truth regarding her father's disappearance and no doubt batter her emotions once more.

CHAPTER SEVEN

Terrible Lizards

"Thank you for agreeing to meet with me," Ulysses said.

Breaking eye contact Genevieve redirected her gaze at the floor, demonstrating the same demure tendencies she had shown on their first meeting. "Well seeing as how I am your client and I am paying you to assist me in this matter it would be foolish not to. You said you had some news."

"That's right."

"I was surprised to hear from you so soon," she admitted. "In fact, I was surprised to hear from you again at all."

"Why? What do you mean?"

"After the way I... overreacted. I was overly emotional."

"That's hardly surprising when you consider all that you have experienced. I should have been more tactful."

"I may not have known you for very long, Mr Quicksilver, but I already know that you are a hopeless liar."

"Is that so?" The disarming smile came easily to Ulysses' lips.

Genevieve returned the expression, also returning the soul-searching gaze of her rich russet eyes to his.

"You are a champion of the truth. And no matter how painful that truth might be, it should be known and faced up to."

"But perhaps I did not choose the best moment to impart all I suspected, particularly without the evidence to back it up."

"But you have that evidence now." It wasn't a question. Genevieve Galapagos was no fool. The previous night's adventure had convinced Ulysses of that much.

"Walk with me," Ulysses said.

As she took his arm he caught the scent of her again carried on the warm breeze; the scent of jasmine flowers. For a moment he was transported back to Tibet and the Gardens of Sanctuary at Shangri-La. Then, in silence, the two of them joined the other promenaders in their wanderings of the Challenger Enclosure.

The Regent's Park menagerie was always popular with the leisured classes and it was busy now, the zoo having been open for over an hour. Chaperoned courting couples were making their promenade of the dinosaur pens. There were ladies at leisure carrying parasols against the glaring sun, and nannies pushing perambulators whilst trying to keep their slightly older and yet more unruly charges under control.

Genevieve had been late. Ulysses had waited half an hour, with only the lowing and farting of the goliath animals and the clattering of the Bakerloo line above him for company, before trying her again on his personal communicator. The phone had rung and rung without anyone answering. After an hour, and with the crowds steadily increasing, he had begun to wonder if she would come at all and whether he shouldn't just give up on the distraught Miss Galapagos and continue with his investigation.

And then she had appeared between the crowds of sauntering zoo-goers, dressed in a long green velvet coat with her luxurious auburn hair done up in a bun under a top hat, an anxious searching look in her eyes.

They joined the ambling throng of the general public as if enjoying the wonders of the Challenger Enclosure like any other curious couple, for a moment all their worries and the pressure of the mission put to one side. As they walked they caught snippets of conversation.

"In the wild they graze the low-growing vegetation of their savannah homes but here at the zoo they do just as well on a diet of hay and fresh fruit and vegetables," a keeper was explaining to an interested party of parvenus, describing the dietary habits of the stegosaurus. "Mabel here is particularly fond of bananas, aren't you girl?"

"Are they not dangerous?" a young woman asked.

"Only if they're frightened and you get in the way of a stampede. They're quite placid really. They're only really dangerous during the mating season when the males fight for the females' attention but old George over there is a bit past that sort of thing these days. He can only really manage a bit of bellowing now. But then we don't have any other younger males here at the zoo to threaten his position as top dog, as it were."

They moved on to where a party of school children were completely ignoring what their harassed teacher was trying to tell them about the styracosaurs they were supposed to be studying. "They produce as many as eight eggs in a clutch," the schoolmistress was saying. "Gregory Pike, will you stop that at once!"

"But what's to stop the animals escaping?" a concerned portly woman wearing a garish ostrich-feather hat was asking another attendant whilst her hunched and hen-pecked husband gazed distractedly at a younger man's more comely companion.

"Don't worry, madam," the zookeeper reassured her jovially. "Every pen is either surrounded by a moat or ditch, like this one here, so that the animals can't climb out, or they are kept behind six-inch thick reinforced steel bars, like the carnivores in the 'Prehistoric Killers' section. And if that weren't enough the fences are also electrified."

"Goodness me. Did you hear that, Stanley?" the woman asked her husband.

"What was that, my dear?" he replied distractedly, as though enjoying some lovely private dream.

"The fences are electricityfied. Oh I do wish you would listen!"

"Yes dear."

"So you have nothing to fear, madam. You are perfectly safe, as is the rest of London," the keeper said with a chuckle.

They walked on, leaving the herbivore pens behind, moving into the area the keeper had referred to as the 'Prehistoric Killers' section.

"Why, they're just like birds," a chinless fop with a monocle and an oiled moustache was saying to impress an equally inbred-looking pug-nosed girl.

"And of course the work we're doing here has an environmental aspect to it as well," a zoo employee dressed more like a clerk than a keeper was explaining to a group of broad-waisted businessmen venture capitalists. "In the wild these animals are either being hunted to extinction for sport or their natural environment is being steadily destroyed as a result of Man's continued, and utterly thoughtless, pillaging of the planet. Either to provide farmland to grow crops to feed an ever-increasing population, or to be strip mined in the incessant quest for coal for the monstrous machines on which we have all so come to depend. So you see, gentlemen, your investment is of vital importance to our continued good work here."

They passed a large domed enclosure that looked not unlike a giant birdcage, for that was effectively what it was. Perched on the branches of trees growing inside were a flock of leathery-winged pterosaurs.

"Look, Templeton Trench brought this specimen back from the Congo as an egg," a tanned, older man with a huge white handlebar moustache was bellowing to the two simpering girls hanging off his arms – both young enough to be his nieces but of no apparent familial connection. They ooh-ed and ah-ed and giggled in all the right places as he continued his monologue, casting only half-interested glances in the direction of the monstrous, red-skinned allosaurus devouring a pig's carcass in front of them.

"Of course the Megasaurus Rex is our finest specimen." The party of businessmen and their fund-raising guide had moved along with Genevieve and Ulysses. "A true king of the megasaurs, although of course ours is a female. The keepers call her Glenda. She eats up to three cows a day."

"How horrible!" Genevieve suddenly exclaimed and Ulysses felt her squeeze his arm more tightly. In the shade of a magnolia tree she pulled him to a halt. "You said you had some news." Suddenly he was abruptly back in the real world with all its attendant worries and inconclusive problems.

Ulysses looked Genevieve squarely in the eyes. He could have let himself drown in those limpid pools. "What was your father doing? What did his most recent work entail?"

An expression of guilt flickered across her face for a moment and she turned her eyes away. The croaking cries of the dinosaurs filled the silence.

"The truth is, I don't know," Genevieve admitted at last. "I hadn't actually seen him for some time. He had become totally absorbed by his work, whatever it was. And you think that whatever it was he was working on caused him to…"

"Change?" Ulysses finished for her. "Yes, I do."

Then she was staring intently into his eyes again with that imploring look of hers and Ulysses felt his heart leap inside his chest. "Help me find my father," she said, "I beg of you. Help me." There was a hand on his shoulder now, the other slipped from his arm around his waist. Above them an Overground train whistled as it approached the aerial platform of Albany Street station four storeys above.

She was beautiful, of that there was no doubt – her body athletically slim, accentuated with curves in all the right places – and she was no mean markswoman either. What more could a man look for in a girl?

But he was becoming distracted. Another part of his mind was musing upon the matter of where a rogue apeman would hide in London, if not the Natural History Museum or London Zoo? Except that the sample he had taken to the old curmudgeon Methuselah was now showing signs of turning into something more akin to lizard scales, so the supposition was that Professor Galapagos would be undergoing the same unspeakable transformation. So the question wasn't so much, where would an apeman hide in the overrun capital as, where would a lizard make its lair? And then, by extension, how on Earth would Ulysses Quicksilver, dandy adventurer and detecting intellect for hire, find it?

All the while that other part of his mind, the part ensnared by Genevieve's lustrous gaze, her cherry bud lips, her jasmine blossom aroma and the warmth of her breath on his cheek, was aware of how close the two of them were to one another now. He took her in his arms, lowering his head to meet hers. Her glistening lips parted to meet his.

Then another, almost subconscious part of his mind,

took over as his sixth sense screamed for his attention. And what it screamed was 'Danger!'

The thunderous roar of the explosion tore through the peace of the morning promenaders, the force of its shockwave throwing many to the ground. Ulysses instinctively threw himself on top of Genevieve as the two of them were bowled off their feet by the blast. Pieces of twisted metal and other debris rained down around them. One man went down with blood pouring from his head. Another cried out as a buckled spar speared his torso and then fell silent.

Ulysses turned to look up at the Overground line that crossed the sky above the zoo, his body taut, ready. Thick black smoke shot through with greasy orange flames, rose into the sky over Regent's Park from a fifty foot wide span of the Bakerloo line. As Ulysses watched, with a tortured metal scream, a section of track broke free from a cast iron stanchion and fell, cantilevering under its own great weight. To Ulysses' adrenalin-heightened senses it seemed that the track was falling in slow motion, trailing oily smoke and charcoal-blackened railway sleepers as it swung down towards the crowded Challenger Enclosure. People were screaming. Some were running in an attempt to escape the catastrophe unfolding around them.

The descending track crashed into the side of the stegosaurus pit, crushing a keeper and the panicking woman he was trying to save as the pen wall crumbled. Other pieces of debris continued to rain down from the devastation of the Bakerloo Line above. Ulysses could hear the schoolmistress screaming hysterically, her wailing charges suddenly desperate to obey her instructions.

The animals were in uproar. Herbivores hooting and bellowing in fear. Carnivores paced their cages roaring, smelling the pheromone fear of their natural prey. The musky scent was sending them into a frustrated frenzy, desperate to get to the panicking animals – and desperate humans.

Keepers were running from other parts of the zoo, along with huddles of zoo-goers, eager to witness the escalating drama within the Challenger Enclosure as much as to aid those at the forefront of the disaster.

But it seemed that Ulysses alone realised that this was only the beginning and that a more terrible disaster was about to strike. The Overground was running still, the drivers of the trains on the Bakerloo Line as yet unaware of the accident, or act of sabotage, whatever it might be. And there was a train coming now.

There was the shriek of brakes being applied as the driver saw first the roiling column of smoke and then the gaping hole in the track, but with the train still travelling at speed there was no hope of it stopping in time. Instead, the fully laden passenger train careered off the broken span, following the track down into the zoo, the carriages being pulled violently off the rails as the lead engine hurtled down into the Challenger Enclosure. The engine hit the tarmac with deadly force, its boiler casing rupturing and its smokestack exploding into flame. Those within ten yards, not crushed beneath the falling train, were scalded to death by the superheated steam rushing from the broken boiler or burned alive in the fiery inferno that followed.

But the train did not stop there. It ploughed on through the enclosure, carried forward under its own momentum as well as being shunted from behind by the ten carriages that clattered after it. Walls crumbled to dust before the hurtling comet of the burning engine, bars of cages crumpling and steel tearing like paper. Yet still the train hurtled on, sparks flying from the pathways and plazas, carriages keeled over onto their sides, the passengers trapped within screaming as fires took hold throughout the body of the wreck. Dinosaur pens were breached, carnivore cages torn down and the pterosaur enclosure smashed open.

Finally the devastated engine broke through into the apatasaurs' lake enclosure, killing a young female as the train wreck smashed through the electric barrier and into the animal's flank, ploughing a great furrow into the turf leading to the shore of the herd's watering hole. Carriages piled into the back of the engine, several breaking free at last. Ulysses watched as one of the carriages – its side scraped bare of its coat of paint – barrelled through the air over him and Genevieve. He momentarily glimpsed the faces of the carriage's terrified occupants pressed against the shattered windows as it spun in its hurtling airborne path. Then it crashed down into the high perimeter wall of the zoo and smashed through, breaching the one barrier that remained between the prehistoric bubble of the Challenger Enclosure and the outside world in a cloud of mortar and brick dust. Ulysses – his heart pounding from their dramatic escape – heard the blaring of car horns, the screech of more brakes and the inevitable collisions as the carriage ploughed onto the thoroughfare beyond the boundary of the zoo.

People fled in panic as did the zoo's most prized exhibits, the dinosaurs breaking free of their long incarceration. There was a sobbing shout from one of the keepers that the electric fence was down.

"We have to get out of here!" Ulysses yelled at Genevieve over the screams of the fleeing crowd and the bellowing of the dinosaurs, pulling her to her feet. Genevieve was too shocked to answer but merely stumbled after Ulysses through the chaos as he pulled her onward, his hand in hers, the force of his desperate grip crushing her fingers.

Already a pack of velociraptors were running through the enclosure, instinct taking over, seizing the opportunity to hunt amidst the confusion of the crowd. Out of the corner of his eye Ulysses saw one of the lithe reptiles leap from the top of an ice-cream kiosk onto a nurse, snatching the child she was desperately clinging onto with its razor sharp jaws. Genevieve whimpered beside him.

They ran on. If they made it to the exit Ulysses knew Nimrod would be there waiting for them, ready to carry them clear of this present danger.

Then Ulysses stumbled as he heard a crunching thud behind him that he felt ripple through the ground beneath his feet. Genevieve tripped and, as she went down, her hand slipped from Ulysses' sweaty grip. He stumbled to a halt, turning in time to see the terrifying form of the zoo's Megasaurus Rex bearing down on them both.

It was as tall as a house, its bipedal saurian form built of slabs of muscle. Its hind legs were two massive pistons of bone and muscle, powerful enough to carry it at a speed of twenty-five miles an hour under the right conditions. By contrast its forelimbs were little more than tiny, grasping claws. But then the monster had little need for anything more when one considered its over-sized jaws, filled with teeth the size and sharpness of butchering hooks. Its eyes were tiny black orbs of pitiless, primeval savagery, and they were fixed on the fallen Genevieve.

Even as its head came down, its jaws hinging open, Ulysses grabbed Genevieve around the waist and pulled her clear as the megasaur's teeth snapped shut, the weight of its hard-nosed skull cracking the skin of the tarmac where Genevieve had been scant moments before.

And then they were running again, their legs given a

new burst of energy by fear.

The zoo's ornately gated entrance appeared before them as they barged through the stumbling masses, Nimrod blaring the horn of the Silver Phantom even as he revved the engine, ready to make a speedy getaway. They hurdled the turnstiles as a pod of apatasaurs barged through the breach in the wall made by the crumpled carriage that now blocked the road outside.

Then, in the merest blinking of an eye, he caught sight of a face in the crowd ahead of him – an unpleasantly familiar face that made his blood boil in fury – and suddenly he understood what had happened here.

Ulysses slammed into the side of the car and pulled open the back door. "We ran into a little trouble," he panted, pushing Genevieve onto the back seat.

"Evidently, sir," Nimrod managed with barely any hint of emotion, despite their current predicament.

"And I think I know who's responsible."

Ulysses slammed the car door shut.

"What are you doing, sir?" Nimrod called through the open passenger window.

"Ulysses, get in the car!" Genevieve screamed.

Ulysses looked back into the fleeing crowd. One man stood still as an island amidst the panicked flow. Dressed all in black like a navvy, bald-headed, roguishly unshaven, his darkly handsome features twisted by the livid purple scar that bisected his face. The figure stared back at Ulysses, his expression set in a tight-lipped scowl, his narrowed eyes filled with a depthless hatred. It was a face from his past, one that he had believed he would never see again, that belonged to an enemy he thought he had put an end to long ago. It was Jago Kane: agitator, revolutionary, terrorist.

Then, as if suddenly shamed by what he had done under

Ulysses' righteous glare, the reactionary turned and fled, running for the Albany Street stop elevator pillar.

"Nimrod, get Miss Galapagos out of here," Ulysses commanded.

"But what about you, sir?"

"Please, get in the car!" Genevieve was begging, pushing the rear door open.

"I can't, Genevieve," he said, flashing her a manic grin. "There's an old friend from the past who I really must catch up with."

"Now?"

"Well, there's no time like the present," he laughed mirthlessly, slamming the car door again. "Now, Nimrod, drive!"

With a screech of tyres the Silver Phantom hared away along Prince Albert Road leaving a cloud of burnt rubber in its wake. Ulysses sprinted across the road – men, women and children running, screaming in disarray all around him – towards the Overground pillar, and after Jago Kane.

CHAPTER EIGHT

Overground

Ulysses burst out of the elevator carriage and onto the Bakerloo Line aerial platform. The platform was packed, the people there milling around in confusion. Some were crying in fear, many were trying to barge past Ulysses and into the lift, while just as many were pushing their way towards the end of the platform to his left. Ulysses craned his head that way, trying to see over the heads of the crowd.

He could see the smoking void left by the explosion and the resultant train crash. The end of one carriage still poked above the visible portion of track. Overground staff and altruistic members of the public were helping shaken passengers out of the back door of the last carriage and onto the vertiginous track. Just as many were merely interested in peering over the edge of the precipice in morbid fascination at the devastation below. To his right the platform ended at a barrier another thirty yards away. What he could not see, in either direction, was his quarry, Jago Kane.

"Going up," came the tinny voice of the automaton lift attendant behind him. Ulysses turned and pushed his way urgently back into the box-cage of the elevator. "Next stop, Bakerloo Line southbound." Kane must have gone on up to the next level, another two storeys above the city streets. But of course, Ulysses inwardly chided himself, why would as experienced an agitator as Jago Kane leave himself trapped on the line he had already put out of action? He would already have his escape route planned. If he were planning to ironically escape via the

Overground he would be heading for the southbound route.

"Here, what do you think you're doing?" a red-faced man protested as Ulysses pushed him out of the way to get inside the elevator.

"Careful, sir. Only twelve passengers are allowed to travel at any one time," the lift-droid told Ulysses.

"Yes, and I was here first, you blaggard," the red-faced man continued to complain officiously.

Cursing in frustration Ulysses pulled the leather cardholder from his jacket pocket. "You, scan that," he instructed the droid. "You," he said, turning to the protesting beetroot, "this is a matter of national security. If you don't get out of my way now the Lord High Chancellor himself will have you up on a charge of treason. Now, piss off!"

He had been back in London for less than forty-eight hours and already the red tape of its bureaucrats and the petty mindedness of its citizens was obstructing him for the second time in as many days.

"Well I never," Ulysses' challenger blustered, staggering back out of the lift. Several other passengers, having half-heard what Ulysses had said, followed him.

Ulysses turned back to the lift attendant. "Now, take this lift up to the next level or I'll see you melted down for scrap."

"Right away, sir," the automaton's synthesised voice said cheerily.

"Do you know what's going on down there?" another man was demanding of anyone who would listen. "The dinosaurs are loose! It's every man for himself." Men cursed in disbelief. Women gasped and one even swooned, her partner catching her in his arms.

It had been cramped enough inside the carriage to the

first level as it filled with people already attempting to escape the confusion that had taken hold around the zoo. Kane had made it into a lift ahead of Ulysses, its doors shutting in his face, the carriage sailing up into the shaft of the Overground pillar, leaving him cursing in frustration.

For a second he had considered taking the maintenance stairs in the pillar to the next level, exhausting as that would have been. But then almost immediately the second elevator opened at ground level. Ulysses made sure that he was onboard, and readied himself to make a swift exit at the next level. But of course Kane had not stopped there.

Ulysses was sure that Kane had had a hand in the chaos that had been unleashed on the capital. It had all the hallmarks of his indiscriminate terrorism and revolutionary philosophy, whereby whatever warped end he was trying to achieve always justified the means, no matter how many innocent people died as a result. In fact, considering Ulysses' encounters with Kane in the past, it seemed quite possible that the more innocent victims who died the more effectively he felt he had made his reactionary point to the ruling classes of Magna Britannia and the supporters of the British throne.

Several people were now demanding to be let out of the ascending elevator, rumour and half-accurate information working its bewildering magic on them, as they started to believe that it was now as unsafe on the higher levels of the Overground as it was down on the streets with the dinosaurs.

The elevator clanked to a stop. "Alight here for Bakerloo Line southbound," the attendant announced jovially. The gate concertinaed open and Ulysses burst from the carriage onto the platform. Up here the Overground was level with the rooftops of the grand townhouses that lined the streets adjoining Regent's Park. However, the aerial railways were still dwarfed by the tallest skyscrapers at the heart of the City financial district further to the south.

Incredibly, the Bakerloo Line was still running. But then again, the train crash, the breakout from the zoo and Ulysses' subsequent pursuit of his old enemy had all taken place in less than five minutes. A train was waiting at the station, steam hissing from its wheel-pistons. Those who had just alighted looked in dazed confusion at the smoke rising from the ruined track below, or peered over the safety railings at the chaos unfolding beneath them on Prince Albert Road.

A whistle sounded. The train was ready to depart and then Ulysses saw his quarry dashing on board some three carriage lengths further down the platform.

"Stop!" Ulysses yelled just as the whistle sounded again and the train's driver released a great hissing cloud of steam from the boiler. He shouted again but only those travellers nearest him took any notice, looking at him in annoyance. The aural receptors of the automata station porters were deaf to his cries, his desperate shouts drowned out by the furious noise of the train itself. The flag was waved and the train began to pull away.

Barging startled travellers aside, Ulysses ran down the platform after the departing train, dodging his way through the obstructing masses to get at his quarry. He suddenly found himself unavoidably bowling into a large, matronly woman carrying two heavy bags and could only manage a snatched, "Pardon, madame!" as he sent the poor woman tumbling onto her well-padded behind, her shopping spilling out all around her.

Then he was past the last of the travellers, the platform

a clear stretch of iron and concrete ahead of him as the distance between him and the train widened. With the matron's tirade haranguing the insolent fop – as she called him – Ulysses put on a turn of speed, the adrenalin still racing through his system as he sprinted after the Overground train.

The last carriage was still just parallel with the end of the platform as Ulysses caught up. Then it was past him and, without hesitation, Ulysses hurled himself at the train.

He hit the rear carriage, his feet finding purchase on the backplate as he grabbed hold of the bars either side of the door. Cane still in hand, he tugged open the door and swung himself into the train to be greeted by startled gasps and exclamations of surprise.

"Excuse me, ladies and gentlemen," he said, making his way between the seated passengers. "There's absolutely nothing to worry about but if you'd just like to clear the way, your compliance would be much appreciated."

He hustled his way through the passengers as the train got up to speed. He knew that Kane was at least three carriages closer to the front. At the far end of the carriage Ulysses reached forwards and opened the door into the next passenger compartment, the wind tugging at his hair and jacket. Making sure he maintained contact with at least one of the carriages at all times he stepped across the divide.

On reaching the end of the third carriage in this way, cane in hand and with the upper floors of tall apartment buildings speeding past beyond the train's windows, he paused with his hand on the handle of the next access door. Packed in with the rest of the passengers he saw Kane's unmistakable profile ahead of him

Ulysses pressed on, now even more determined to catch up with his old enemy. Bursting into Kane's carriage he shouted, "Seize that man!"

Kane's head snapped round, his eyes locked onto Ulysses and gave him a sour look, pure hatred. Reacting immediately, Kane began forging his way through the throng. "Stop him!" Ulysses shouted.

His sixth sense suddenly flared and he ducked even as Kane swung round, gun in hand. The shot was painfully loud in the confines of the packed carriage. The passengers flinched as one as the glass pane in the door behind Ulysses exploded.

Then Kane was pushing his way through the carriage again, his progress less hindered by the people who whimpered as they strove to get out of his way. Not one of the passengers tried to stop him. *The great British public*, Ulysses thought, *as reliable as ever.*

His own pistol was in its holster beneath his jacket but he didn't want to risk using it in the packed train. He doubted he would be able to get a clear shot anyway and the continual jolting of the train as it sped over the high-rise tracks ruled out such rash behaviour altogether. It was one thing for uncaring revolutionary terrorists to carelessly gun down innocent members of the public, but it wasn't behaviour becoming of an agent of the throne of Magna Britannia. Besides, he wanted to finish this up close and personal. Kane had got away before. Ulysses was not about to let him do that again.

Although the terrified passengers were doing their level best to evade Kane's fury they were still slowing his progress and Ulysses was beginning to catch up. Kane reached the door to the next carriage as Ulysses reached the mid-section doors. Ulysses considered pulling the emergency cord, to get the driver to stop the train, but decided that such an action might merely aid the terrorist's escape.

And then Kane was gone anyway, not into the next carriage but up the ladder bolted to the end and onto the roof. Ulysses hurried to the banging door as the train sped on through the Upper City. In a matter of seconds he too was on the ladder, clambering up towards the roof of the hurtling train.

The hobnail heel of a boot came down on the top rung where Ulysses' fingers should have been, just as he had anticipated. Lurking one rung lower, he athletically pulled himself up in a sudden spring as his feet kicked off from their footing below. With one hand still on the ladder Ulysses swung with his cane at Kane's other leg, as his premature stamp unbalanced him for a moment. The ebony cane struck home as the train bumped over a join in the rails. Kane crashed down onto the roof of the carriage, landing hard on his backside. It was all Ulysses needed to finally make it onto the roof himself, no longer threatened.

He braced his legs against the rocking motion of the train as Kane slid himself backwards out of reach. Ulysses now stood between Kane and the front of the train, smoke from the engine stack whipping back over the carriage roofs around them like escaping wisps of cloud.

"I should have known you would cheat death. I just don't know how you managed it," Ulysses said, taking in the long scar that bisected Kane's face.

"You just can't keep a good man down," the revolutionary sneered, the scar twisting his lips into a grotesque sneer. Kane's educated accent seemed as at odds with his appearance as with his revolutionary politics.

"This little debacle we find ourselves caught up in has all the hallmarks of a Kane mutiny," Ulysses said, the words dripping with venomous bile.

"Prove it!" Kane spat back.

"And what do you know about the disappearance of one Professor Galapagos from the Natural History Museum?"

"More than you will ever know and more than I will ever tell you!"

"Oh, I'm so glad," Ulysses said with a cruel smile. Just for a moment doubt flickered in the terrorist's dark eyes. Ulysses smoothly pulled the sword blade from the sheath of his cane, the action culminating with a grandiose flourish. "Because that means I don't have to worry about bringing you in alive for questioning. So I rather feel that this concludes our brief reunion. You and I have nothing more to say to one another," Ulysses pronounced.

"Nothing you would want to hear, I'll warrant, fascist!" the revolutionary spat – his gun suddenly in his hand again – and fired.

Nimrod pulled the steering wheel hard to the right as another apatasaur lumbered into the path of the Silver Phantom, throwing Genevieve across the padded white leather upholstery. Horns blared as he crossed onto the other side of the road, narrowly avoiding an omnibus heading straight towards them, and then they heard the shattering crunch of collision as the double-decker collided with the column of the leviathan's pillar-like leg.

Beyond the comparative safety of the car the streets of Marylebone were in chaos as the unleashed dinosaurs stampeded down Portland Place.

"What are you doing?" Genevieve yelled at him, her hands gripping the back of the driver's seat. "Ulysses told you to get me out of here!"

"Yes, ma'am," Nimrod calmly agreed, swerving to avoid a man who had stumbled into the road to avoid a lumbering ankylosaur. "That is what I am attempting to do." He peered upwards at the distant winding course of the Bakerloo Line high above and the train speeding on its way towards the next station. This stretch of the Bakerloo Line followed the streets beneath quite closely and, despite the stampeding dinosaurs and the chaos they left in their wake, Nimrod was managing to keep up with Ulysses' progress above.

He brought the Phantom back onto the left side of the road. Genevieve yelped in surprise and Nimrod shot a glance out of the passenger window to see a velociraptor running along the pavement beside them, keeping pace with the car. For a moment the terrible lizard returned Nimrod's gaze with its cold-blooded reptilian stare. Its ophidian pupil dilated as if, in that moment, it recognised the car's occupants as potential prey. The tone of the car's engine rose as Nimrod floored the accelerator and the Silver Phantom powered away from the sprinting raptor.

They sped through Langham Place into Regent Street, Nimrod bouncing the vehicle over the corner of a pavement, pedestrians scattering before them. "Where did you learn to drive?" Genevieve gasped.

"On the streets of Calcutta," he replied, flatly. "It might be wise to fasten your seatbelt, ma'am."

There was the screech of brakes and a delivery van shot past them, colliding with another running dinosaur and sending the creature smashing through the plate glass window of a jewellers.

They were now right in the thick of the stampede as the city streets funnelled the animals into the bottleneck of Regent Street, towards Oxford Circus. Despite the alien nature of their surroundings, some of the dinosaurs were reverting to their natural instinctive behaviour. Apatasaurs charged past startled shoppers, crushing the unwary beneath their elephantine feet, running in fear of the pursuing carnivores.

Still some way ahead of Nimrod and Genevieve, the Megasaurus Rex turned into a packed Piccadilly Circus. A startled omnibus driver spun his steering wheel to avoid the prehistoric obstacle. The bus lurched violently to one side and into the path of a steam-belching hansom cab. The two vehicles collided with a dreadful inevitability, the bus toppling onto its side. The Megasaur put a huge clawed foot on top of the stricken omnibus, as though claiming its kill, and snapped the driver from his cab.

An old battle-scarred bull triceratops ran amok through Langham Place, dragging torn shop awnings behind it as its tiny, enraged brain translated every obstacle in front of it as a potential challenger to its position as alpha male. It didn't stop even when it hurtled into the front of the Langham Hilton Hotel, shattering the glass revolving doors with its battering ram horns.

The police had mobilised, the emergency services having been notified of the unfolding disaster, no doubt by the embarrassed zoo authorities. A pair of squad cars were now racing up the road towards Nimrod and Genevieve, blue lights flashing, sirens wailing.

With a metal buckling *crump* a clawed fiend landed on the bonnet of the Silver Phantom. Nimrod's first instinct was to brake, but the furiously working rational part of his brain told him that if he did that chances were that the Phantom would be crushed beneath the hooves of the stampeding creatures behind it.

For a split second Nimrod looked up through the windscreen into the ophidian eyes of a velociraptor and, in that moment, was convinced that it was the same creature that had kept pace with the car only seconds before. The monster opened its terribly fanged jaws

– giving Nimrod a clear view right down its throat – screeching as it butted the glass of the windscreen, trying to get at the people within.

Nimrod worked the steering wheel, trying to unbalance the raptor whilst still remaining in control. The creature scrabbled for purchase on the automobile's bonnet, trying to hook its deadly talons into the thin metal. Nimrod gave a sharper pull on the wheel and the raptor was gone, tumbling onto the road and into the path of a police car. The squad car slammed into it, its radiator grille buckling, the whole vehicle bouncing over the top of the fatally injured predator. A smoke-belching coal-lorry hit the raptor's carcass after it and turned over into the path of the apatasaurs. One of the leviathan herbivores tripped, its front legs becoming entangled within the wreckage of the steam-lorry. As its forelegs buckled its momentum carried it forwards and the apatasaur came crashing down just metres from the Silver Phantom. The car sped on, leaving behind it the sounds of shop windows shattering, people screaming and one vehicle after another smashing into the stampeding dinosaurs.

A horse-drawn carriage suddenly came face to face with a hunting allosaurus. The horses whinnied in panic and reared. Then the carnivore was on them, crushing one of the terrified beasts under a massive clawed foot and ripping the head from the other with its steel-trap jaws.

Elsewhere Peeler-drones had surrounded an ankylosaur. One of the automata advanced confidently towards the tank-like brute, giving its default, "'Ello, 'ello, 'ello, what's going on 'ere then?" The ankylosaur gave a guttural bovine moan, feeling threatened by the Bobbies that were steadily tightening their cordon around it. Then the creature decided that it had had enough. With one deadly accurate swipe of its heavily armoured tail it took off the head of one advancing drone and sent another three tumbling like bowling pins. It would take more than Scotland Yard's finest to bring this situation to a satisfactory conclusion. At this rate, the authorities were going to have to call in the army.

Leaning forwards against the steering wheel, Nimrod looked up again at the top of the canyon formed by the buildings either side of Regents Street, moving a momentarily misplaced flick of hair out of his eyes as he did so. He had lost sight of the train he had been certain Ulysses was on, as the Bakerloo Line was replaced by the Victoria branch of the Overground. A family group of five pterosaurs flapped past above the rooftops, keeping clear of the carnage consuming the city streets below. Nimrod could only hope that his employer was having more success than they at evading danger.

Ahead of them lay Oxford Circus, beyond that the teeming hunting ground of Piccadilly Circus, and nothing that could stop the frenzied dinosaurs and the world of carnage that was surely to come.

Ulysses arched back, pulling his exposed midriff out of the path of Kane's bowie knife as the anarchist slashed at him. Kane pressed forwards, following up with a backhanded swipe.

The two combatants so far appeared to be evenly matched. Neither had managed to draw blood, although Ulysses had managed to lay a punch against Kane's chin, Kane in response having kicked Ulysses painfully in the shins. Incredibly both had managed to maintain their balance on the roof of the speeding train, in spite of its irregular rolling motion. Ulysses thanks, in part, to the skills the monks of Shangri-La had imparted to him. Kane through sheer luck or stubbornness. Yet both were putting their all into the duel and the energy they were expending was beginning to weary them.

But now, as Kane pressed home his attack with an angry snarl, Ulysses saw a way to break the exhausting impasse. He had to concede ground to escape the blade but did so by spinning on one heel and turning himself at a right angle, placing himself very close to the cambered edge of the carriage roof and with his back to the precipitous drop beyond the edge of the aerial railway. As Kane's blade nicked the lapel of Ulysses' jacket, Ulysses grabbed hold of his opponent's over-reaching arm and pulled him forwards with all the strength he had in his left arm, the rapier blade of his sword-cane still held tightly in his right.

The revolutionary stumbled forwards, losing his balance at last, sprawling onto his hands and knees on the roof of the rattling carriage. Ulysses didn't waste a moment. But Kane was fast too. As Ulysses brought down his blade in what would otherwise have been a killing stroke, Kane twisted round, stopping the rapier with his bowie knife. Ulysses' blade slid free, turned by the knife, and as he tried to bring his weapon back under control, and not lose his own footing, he managed to snag its tip in Kane's wrist. The felon cried out in pain and astonishment, unable to stop his hand spasming, the knife falling from his open fingers onto the roof of the carriage.

Ulysses rocked backwards as the train clattered over an intersection. Kane, seeming to ignore his new injury, lunged after the knife. His fingertips scraped the carved horn handle, only for the motion of the train to send the knife over the edge. The weapon clattered down between the sleepers of the aerial track, to plummet towards the distant streets below.

Kane shot a savage look of pure hatred over his shoulder as Ulysses bore down on him. Then the sneer became a grin, more disconcerting than anything Ulysses had seen in a long time. Before he could stop the anarchist, Kane pulled himself forwards and threw himself off the edge of the train.

Ulysses made a grab for him, landing heavily on his stomach, his head and shoulders over the edge of the roof, one arm outstretched. He could not bear to lose Kane again now. From this position Ulysses was treated to a clear view of the fate of his enemy. Kane dropped, arms and legs flung out, his body flat, freefalling for a good twenty feet. Then, incredibly, the northbound Bakerloo train hurtled by beneath him and he landed on its roof, snatched from a certain death on the rails below. Ulysses watched, stunned, as Kane was carried away.

Without hesitation Ulysses swung down onto the side of the carriage, still clinging onto the lip of the roof with one hand and, breathing deeply, watched the carriages passing on the track below him, carefully timing his jump.

But the moment passed. The train was gone taking Jago Kane with it. His heart sank.

The ringing from his pocket took him completely by surprise.

He extracted his personal communicator and flipped it open. "Yes?" he barked into the handset.

"Sorry to trouble you, sir," his manservant's cultured tones came through. "I hope this isn't a bad time."

"No, now is fine," Ulysses said, his voice relaxing even as he did so. The train's passengers watched him through the windows in appalled fascination as he calmly conducted his call whilst clinging to the exterior of the carriage.

"I'm pleased to hear it, sir. I wish the same could be said of down here but we have a situation developing."

In his desperate determination to corner and finish his old adversary, Jago Kane, Ulysses had momentarily put from his mind the breakout from the zoo. Now, high above the city streets, the wind roaring in his ears, he was only too aware of the dinosaurs rampaging through the streets a hundred feet below.

"What's happened?" was all he could think to say. "Is Genevieve all right?"

"Yes sir, Miss Galapagos is with me."

Ulysses heard a muffled scream through his communicator accompanied by a primeval reptilian roar.

"What was that?"

"That was the situation I was telling you about, sir. It would appear that there is a Megasaurus Rex running amok down the Mall. It is all most perturbing. Something needs to be done, sir."

Ulysses looked beyond the engine ahead of him, trying to ascertain the train's precise location within the capital, peering at the architecture of the Upper City through the smoke belching from the chimneystack. Slowly he began to recognise particular buildings – the Regent Palace Hotel, the Criterion Theatre.

He was somewhere over Piccadilly. Distant guttural bellowing, hooting car horns and shrill human screams rose to his ears from the streets below. Ahead the Bakerloo Line curved round as it passed over Trafalgar Square.

"Where is the beast now?" Ulysses said into the communicator.

"It's passing under the Admiralty Arch. It's now moved

into Trafalgar Square itself."

"Don't worry, Nimrod, I'm on it."

Quickly and carefully he stowed the communicator.

Peering over the edge of the blurred track speeding past a few feet below him he saw the domed roof of the National Gallery and the towering pillar of Nelson's Column as the Bakerloo Line began to descend towards the station at Trafalgar Square.

And then he saw the terror-inducing form of the colossal carnivore. People fled in waves of panic before the titan as it claimed dominion of its new territory.

His heart in his mouth, Ulysses judged that he would pass over Trafalgar Square as the Megasaurus lumbered under this stretch of the Overground.

He took a deep breath to steady his nerves, checking his grip on the roof of the train and adjusting his hold on his sword. Ulysses was about to attempt either the bravest or the most stupid stunt in his life.

"Well, here goes nothing," he said to himself.

And jumped.

CHAPTER NINE

Evolution Expects

Ulysses dropped, the wind whipping through his hair and pummelling his face. Just as he was beginning to wonder whether he had misjudged his fall and that he would not stop until he collided with the flagstones of Trafalgar Square, he came to an abrupt halt as he slammed onto the back of the dinosaur. He started to slide but then managed to get a grip on the knobbly exterior of the dinosaur's hide. Its scales were rough as sandpaper and one cheek was grazed from his collision with the creature.

But it seemed to Ulysses that as far as the Megasaurus Rex was concerned he might as well not be there at all. It continued to stalk between the leonine statues of the square and Ulysses took a moment to recover himself, feeling the creature's body moving beneath him, the curious texture of the dinosaur's hide uncomfortable against his skin. His cheek stung from the graze, but it was not the only part of his body now telling him that it was suffering. His fight with the revolutionary Kane had taken its toll more greatly than he had realised, so focused had he been on thwarting his foe, his bloodstream flooded with adrenalin. On top of the dramatic drop he had just made onto a surface almost as hard and resistant as tarmac, all his old injuries had come back to haunt him. The calf of his left leg ached, but that would pass and certainly wasn't debilitating. However, he knew for a fact that he had strained his shoulder again, and he had added a whole host of bruises to his battered body. The ribs of his left side in particular were protesting forcefully, wincing stabs of pains reacquainting him with past battles. But there would be time enough to worry about that later. For back in the present he had to see to bringing the matter in hand to conclusion.

Fortunately – incredibly even – he had managed to maintain his hold on his sword-cane. He also had his personal communicator about his person, as well as his Brabinger pistol.

He raised his head, all the while keeping the rest of his body flat, lest he dislodge himself from his precarious position. They were in the middle of Trafalgar Square. Lord Admiral Nelson and his attendant pigeons watched with, on one side, stony disinterest and, on the other, dumb avian curiosity as the Megasaur scattered the crowds. But still there were those who could not get out of the way in time, the monster scooping them up with its dredging jaws, gulping them down to satisfy its newly acquired appetite for human flesh.

"What did I think I was doing?" Ulysses asked himself aloud as the rational part of his brain took over, his gung-ho, thrill-seeking side evaporating in a cloud of logic.

But what he was doing now on the back of the dinosaur was academic. The more pressing question was, now that he was lying between the heaving shoulder blades of the dinosaur, how was he going to bring its bloodthirsty rampage to an end?

He felt the weight of his gun in its holster against his aching ribs. "That has to be the way, surely," he told himself, but he didn't sound too convinced, even to his own ears. But if he were going to be able to take a shot, he would have to get into a better position than the one he was in now. Somehow he was going to need to get up onto his feet, or at least his knees.

Pushing himself up with his left hand, his fingers

clenched around a protruding scale, he was able to bring his sword to bear. With one powerful downward thrust, he plunged the tip of the blade into the creature's hide. It sank up to fully half its length. Now he knew for sure that he had got the monster's attention.

The dinosaur let out a primeval roar, redolent with pain and savage fury. Its jaws opened wide as it threw its head back in agony, the megasaur leaving the pram and its occupant that it was about to consume, the infant never knowing how close it had come to an early death.

The megasaur bucked. Ulysses kept a tight hold of his half-buried sword, riding the beast like some American rodeo rider. And then the enraged beast was off. With its massive piston legs of muscle and bone covering five yards with every bounding stride, the megasaur left off hunting the tiny, shrieking mammals and abandoned the abattoir it had made of Trafalgar Square, haring off at speed along Whitehall.

As he clung on to the hilt of his rapier-blade, his legs braced against the rolling gait of the running carnivore, Ulysses pulled his gun from its holster. There was no time to check the load, and certainly no way of reloading here and now. It was all he could do to maintain his position on the creature's back; it was like trying to keep his balance in a storm-tossed boat. He pointed the muzzle at the creature's heaving sides and let off five shots in quick succession.

The beast bellowed again and careered in front of a steam-driven omnibus – Ulysses was dimly aware of further cries of horror and surprise rising from the street, the screech of brakes and the dull crumps of collisions – but the megasaur showed no signs of slowing, let alone of actually dropping down dead.

The Admiralty passed by to the left in a blur. The

plume-helmed guardsmen on sentry duty outside Horse Guards Parade were thrown into disarray, one terrified horse throwing its rider, the other galloping away back in the direction of Trafalgar Square.

It had been nothing more than dumb hope that had made Ulysses try shooting the creature, he realised now. If he had been able to get into a position whereby he was close enough to shoot the megasaur through the eye, at point-blank range then he might have been able to bring it down with a single shot. But chances were that he would die before he even managed to take aim, either eaten alive by the brute or by having his brains smashed out on the tarmac of Whitehall as he was thrown from his curious steed.

The megasaur sprinted past the entrance to Downing Street, a rattling fusillade of gunshots chasing after it from the armed sentries on duty there. Their bullets did nothing to stop the monster and fortunately missed the startled Ulysses as well.

"Bloody hell!" he swore as they swept past the Cenotaph.

The momentum of the charging beast beneath him swung Ulysses to the left so that he could see the pavement clearly beneath him, as the dinosaur cracked the dressed stones beneath its massive, pile-driving feet, forcing him to pull on the embedded sword. The megasaur roared again as the blade cut deeper into its flesh.

And then the jumble of desperate thoughts crowding Ulysses' mind resolved into something resembling a logical idea. The orbits of the eye were not the only weak point in an animal's skull; something as thin as a rapier blade thrust into the base of the skull, where it joined the neck, could find a way between vertebrae and sever the spinal cord, or even pierce the monster's diminutive brain.

"All very well in theory," Ulysses addressed himself again. Achieving such a feat would be another matter altogether. But there was no longer any time to think about how such a thing could be achieved. There was only time for action. The Palace of Westminster and the looming tower of Big Ben lay ahead. This had to stop now.

In one deft movement Ulysses pulled the sword-cane clear of the beast's flesh even as he used it to steady himself as he scaled the ridge of the megasaur's back. He flung himself forwards, bringing the sword in a high arc as he did so. As he landed on the neck of the creature so he landed his blow, the devilishly sharp tip of the rapier blade split scales as Ulysses put all his weight behind it, plunging the sword beneath vertebrae the size of ale casks, cutting cleanly through the cable-thick spinal cord they shielded and into the monster's cerebellum.

All muscle activity within the creature ceased. Its legs gave way beneath it and the dinosaur crashed to the ground, its massive jaw ploughing a trench through the scrubby grass in the middle of Parliament Square. Its glassy eyes closed and its jaws slammed shut, half severing the monster's huge purple tongue that lolled from the side of its mouth. The megasaur was dead.

Ulysses gratefully slid down from the back of the beast, stumbling to regain his balance now that he was back on terra firma after his hair-raising ride. He was bruised and battered, bloody from numerous cuts and grazes. The joint of his right shoulder had gone beyond pain to a dull throb that told him he had probably dislocated it.

Slowly, the sound of a city in heightened panic seeped its way back into his beleaguered senses. The megasaur's desperate charge and subsequent death had brought the streets around Parliament Square to a standstill. An expectant host of Londoners surrounded the square. Confident that the megasaur was dead, some of the bolder members of the public were approaching the fallen monster and the dino-killer, their faces slack with bewilderment, making them look like weird wandering lost souls as they tried to make sense of what had just happened. There were robo-Bobbies among the crowd too. The Northern Line branch of the Overground trundled on its way overhead as if nothing out of the ordinary had happened at all.

A stupefied tramp, sporting a filthy white beard and clutching a crumpled brown paper bag to his chest, cautiously approached the equally stunned Ulysses, an outstretched hand offering comfort. "Are you all right, son?" the old codger asked.

"A-Am I?" Ulysses stammered. "That's a very good question. Give me a swig of whatever you've got wrapped in that paper bag and I'll tell you."

As Ulysses put the fumy bottle to his lips, and felt the bite of the alcohol on his tongue, he saw the sleek silver shape of the Mark IV Phantom ease its way through the gathering crowd as Big Ben struck noon.

A discordant wail, like a hundred foghorns sounding in jarring synchronicity, suddenly filled the square. The crowd tensed and Ulysses, despite the sharp pain in his shoulder, tried to cover his ears.

With an epileptic flickering the kinema-sized broadcast screens around Parliament Square hummed into life. But rather than the usual propaganda messages or mega-corporation advertisements, grainy static soon resolved into the image of a rippling New Union Jack. Only rather than bearing the encircled silhouette of Britannia herself at the centre there was the silhouette of a dinosaur's skull.

"People of Britain and Londinium Maximum!" The voice boomed from the loudspeakers. No one could ignore it. Suddenly all eyes were drawn hypnotically to the massive broadcast screens. "This is the voice of the Darwinian Dawn!

"The British Empire of Magna Britannia is a dinosaur of a previous age and should have perished long ago. Our cities are over-populated and none more so than the jewel of the Empire that is Londinium Maximum. The filthy slums overflow with the poor, the unemployed, the destitute, and the downtrodden."

As the condemning voice continued in its tirade, like that of some vengeful deity passing judgement on the British Empire, the image of the defaced flag faded to be replaced by a relentless moving montage culled from newsreel footage and who knew what other media sources. There were starving, malnourished children begging in gutters clogged with filth. The automata armies of Magna Britannia marching against unarmed Indian villagers. Factories the size of towns pumping clouds of polluting toxins into the atmosphere from colossal chimney stacks. A pox-ridden prostitute kicked to death by a gang of thugs. Swathes of rainforest being cut down by monstrous harvesting machines to feed the hungry furnaces of the workshop of the world. Livestock being reared in appalling conditions in cathedral-sized factory barns to feed the rapacious appetites of the decadent elite while the poor starved only streets away in the same cities. But no matter what the image being broadcast – whether war, famine, poverty, moral decline or the heedless raping of the Earth's natural resources – they all had one thing in common; each and every image was a condemnation of the world-dominating super-power of Magna Britannia, the rapacious, world-devouring monster that was the British Empire in the dying days of the twentieth century.

"We have become slaves to the machine," the voice was saying now. "The workshop of the world has become the most heinous pillager of the planet. And now, the rulers of this Empire are prepared to make the same mistakes beneath the oceans and on other worlds beyond our own, condemning the rest of the solar system to death."

The images being broadcast changed accordingly, now including scenes from the lunar cities and the colonies on Mars.

"Every minute of every hour of every day, the Empire commits the most heinous crimes against the planet and its own people. The upper classes hunt animals they do not intend to eat whilst children starve on our own doorsteps. Magna Britannia is the most technologically advanced nation on the planet and yet disease is still rife among the abused lower classes.

"And what are these crimes perpetrated in aid of, in an endless cycle of abuse of this planet and its soon-to-be endangered indigenous species?"

At this point a picture of Victoria Regina, from her heyday during the last century, appeared on the multiple screens, and flames began to lick hungrily at the sepia-tint photograph.

"To maintain the intrinsically corrupt status quo. Magna Britannia is morally and ethically moribund. After 160 years under the yoke of the corrupt, bloated ogre that is the British Empire, it is time for a change, in order to beat the social and moral stagnation and corruption that has infested this nation like a life-stealing cancer, and to welcome in a new age of freedom from the shackles of industrialism and Imperial rule. The old must make way for the new, so that social evolution can pursue its natural course."

The last scraps of the photograph of the Queen burnt away to reveal a new flag that was entirely black other than for the white-stencilled dinosaur skull at its centre. This too was ultimately consumed by the flames.

The protests and even occasional cheers from the crowd could not drown out the voice of condemnation that damned a nation and a whole, world-spanning way of life. The voice blasted from every street corner across the capital, and could be heard throughout the cities of the United Kingdom, wherever the propaganda screens of Magna Britannia stood, so that every citizen of the British Empire – man, woman or child – who laboured under the dominion of the Empire might hear the Darwinian Dawn's brutal message of savage hope.

Ulysses Quicksilver, his manservant Nimrod and Genevieve Galapagos – emerging from the back of the battered Silver Phantom – simply stared dumbfounded at the burning screens before them.

"The time for change is now. We are the agents of that change, the Darwinian Dawn. It is time for the old way of life to be made extinct. Our terms are simple. We demand that the Queen abdicates her throne immediately and that the bloated glutton that is Magna Britannia be dissolved. Until such time as our demands are met we vow that such incidents as have been witnessed today will continue to escalate, and anarchy will reign."

As the booming echoes of the voice of the Darwinian Dawn died away two words – one simple alliterative phrase – swam into clarity on the screens amidst the crackling flames of anarchy, until they dominated every screen visible around the city and beyond. And in case any could not read the words, the same voice of thunder uttered the phrase over and over.

"Evolution expects!

"*Evolution expects!*

"EVOLUTION EXPECTS!"

ACT TWO
SURVIVAL OF THE FITTEST
MAY 1997

CHAPTER TEN

Wormwood

Uriah Wormwood stepped into the Members' Lobby, beyond the Commons Chamber of the Palace of Westminster, and allowed himself a smile. His speech on the occasion of being elected to the position of Leader of the Conservative Party, and thereby Prime Minister of Her Majesty's government, had been particularly rousing.

Minister for Internal Affairs to leader of the Tories and First Lord of the Treasury in a few simple, yet cunning, moves that seemed to have taken everyone else, including the leader of the opposition and his own predecessor, totally by surprise. But then he was a chess player of grandmaster level, so the Machiavellian manoeuvrings and machinations of the British Parliament were easy enough for him to negotiate and twist to suit his own agenda.

His predecessor discredited, following the recent terror attacks on the capital, he was now the single most powerful politician in Magna Britannia and hence, effectively, the world. In light of his predecessor's perceived ineffectual action in the wake of the terrorist atrocities perpetrated by the Darwinian Dawn there had been no way that he could keep his position as head of the government. George Castlemayne had been forced to resign in the face of further terror attacks on the city. Following the Overground disaster at London Zoo, and the subsequent release of the dinosaurs from the Challenger Enclosure, there had been bombings at Marble Arch, Charing Cross and even during a concert at the Royal Albert Hall. All had resulted in loss of life and the Overground had been forced to close. It was still closed now and the situation was having a crippling effect on the city's economy.

"What we need now is a man of action as well as words, who will see Londinium Maximum, and hence this nation, put back on track. And Her Imperial Majesty's jubilee will not only be a celebration of 160 years of her noble reign and wise rule but will act as a starting point for a new Imperial age the like of which the world has never seen, as we approach the dawning of a new millennium." That bit in particular had made him smile wryly to himself.

He had made all the usual vapid promises – an end to poverty, jobs for all, better health care, a clearing of the slums, open formal discussions with the Martian Separatists – fully aware of the fact that if any such things ever did actually come to pass that it would, in reality, spell the end of the Empire. And that wasn't what he had in mind at all. No, not at all. He smiled his chilling crocodilian smile again at the thought.

"But how can you seriously countenance the idea of Her Majesty's jubilee celebrations going ahead at this time, in this climate of terror watched over by the spectre of the threat of violence? Would you, newly elected as First Lord, really make your first action to put our beloved monarch in mortal danger?"

"My Honourable Friend is labouring under a serious misapprehension," Wormwood had said, to chuckles from the commons benches behind him. "Of course not, but Magna Britannia will not kowtow to terrorists. This glorious Empire, of which I am proud to be a part, has endured for over one and a half centuries. It is the strongest and most profitable it has ever been. Fully two-thirds of the world's population, and two-thirds of its landmass, are fortunate enough to fall under the benevolent shadow of this great nation, enlightened by both its knowledge and power. We rule on land, and sea, and below it, and the skies are ours to command.

"No, I make my declaration now that the celebrations intended to mark Queen Victoria's 160th jubilee, along with the unveiling of the nearly-completed statue of Britannia in Hyde Park, will go ahead as planned, come hell or high water. And to ensure that this all comes to pass, as it should, I would take this opportunity to urge each and every honourable member here present to vote in favour of the new Anti-Terrorism Bill."

There were shouts of "Here, here!" from his own party and childish mutterings from the other side of the House.

"It will mean more police on the streets with more effective powers, tighter controls on those passing through our borders and, most importantly, a safe home for the good people of Britain. Britannia rules the waves – above and below – the land, the air. Even the worlds beyond our own submit to British rule. Britons never, never, shall be slaves!"

At that a great cheer had gone up from the Conservative benches and his rhetoric had even stirred some members of the opposition to raise their voices in support, before they realised what they had been duped into doing by his powerful oration. The public gallery had gone wild.

But it was all just words, telling his fellows what they wanted to hear. And yet Uriah Wormwood never underestimated the power of words. With armies, fleets and factories a man could rule all the peoples of the world. But with words you could own their thoughts, their hopes, their desires, their very souls. Magna Britannia's armies could bring a nation to its knees! Words could make those same nations give themselves willingly to the rapacious monster that was the British Empire without a single shot ever having to be fired. No, he never underestimated the power of words. The man who controlled them could reshape the world as he saw fit.

The Bill Against the Predations of Terrorism – devised by Wormwood himself – was as good as passed, he was sure of it. When the House of Commons voted in its favour there was no way, in light of the current situation, that the Lords would dare contest it. For the peers almost all had a vested interest in keeping London free from terror attacks. As well as having personal palatial residences within the capital, many of them were feeling the aftershock of the effects on the nation's economy, having great portions of their own fortunes tied to the success of various businesses throughout London and beyond. The sooner the Overground was open and running the sooner a number of the lords would see the money stop draining from their accounts.

And with the Anti-Terror Bill in place Wormwood would be in a position to personally do something about the current climate of fear and dread of imminent, and bloody, disaster. For, amongst other measures, such as allowing the police to arrest anyone suspected of terrorist activity, the bill would give the First Lord of the Treasury the power to declare martial law in cases of extreme emergency. Then all the resources of Magna Britannia would truly be at his disposal, to be used to reshape the Empire as he saw fit.

Wormwood made his way through the corridors of power – the civil servants he encountered on his way all bowing or congratulating him on his recent rise to power – until he reached his office.

He pushed open the door into the outer office where his personal secretary was rearranging the papers on her desk in a state of some agitation. She had only been with him for the last two weeks and was still having to adjust to his draconian ways.

"Oh, sir, thank goodness you're back."

"What is it, Blythe?" Wormwood demanded, his eyes narrowing and the unnatural smile disappearing from his lips.

"Y-you have a guest, Prime Minister."

"Where?"

"Well, that's the thing. He is waiting for you in your office."

Wormwood's face darkened to a scowl as he strode towards his private chambers, without waiting to hear any more.

"He said his name was Mr..." The rest of the sentence was lost as Wormwood flung open the door.

"Good afternoon, Prime Minister," came a voice from the high backed leather-upholstered chair in front of his desk. "Congratulations on your recent promotion."

"Quicksilver. What are you doing here?"

"Can't a friend drop by to congratulate you on your recent success? You've got it all now, haven't you?"

Wormwood rounded the desk and sat down. Ulysses Quicksilver grinned at him, glass of cognac in hand.

"I hope you don't mind. I helped myself," he said, raising the glass as if in a toast. "Anyway, here's to you."

"What do you want?"

"Like I said, I just wanted to come by now that I'm up and about again, pat you on the back and say well done! Perhaps you'll get a nicer office now. One with a little more natural light. A view of the river, maybe. By the way, when do you move into Number 10?"

"Quicksilver," Wormwood said, arching his fingers in front of his face, elbows on the edge of the desk, "my patience is like the spare time I have to conduct impromptu meetings such as this one, there is very little of it."

He stared into the smiling face before him. Ulysses looked a mess, despite his otherwise smartly turned out appearance. His cheek was grazed, there were the scabs and scratches across his forehead and he was still sporting the yellow and purple bruise of a black eye.

"I thought you might like an update, seeing as how I am currently engaged on a mission on behalf of the British throne."

"Then why not arrange a meeting at the usual venue, as protocol and good sense would dictate?"

"My time is precious too. I decided direct action would be the best approach. You are a man of action, aren't you, as well as words?"

"Why are you really here? Why risk exposing our unique... relationship."

"Very well," Ulysses said, putting the glass down on the desk, the smile vanishing from his own swollen lips. "I want some answers."

"So am I to take it that your mission is still ongoing, that you have not reached any conclusions? The murder remains unsolved, the item stolen from the museum... missing?"

"Indeed. That would be a fair assumption to make."

For a moment, Magna Britannia's new First Minister said nothing. Then he eased himself stiffly back in his chair. His face remained an impassive mask, his lips pursed.

"Then I shall do my best to answer your questions, if it means that you will then be able to pursue your mission without further assistance and you will leave me in peace."

"Very well. Why did you send me to investigate the incident at the Natural History Museum in the first place? Am I to take it that Internal Affairs was already aware of the work of one Professor Galapagos?"

"That might have been the case. I couldn't possibly comment."

"But what possible interest could it be to Whitehall?"

"Naturally everything that might be a threat to the security of this nation and its people is of interest to the powers that be."

"So what you're saying is that Galapagos was developing a biological weapon?"

"I am saying no such thing. That is an assumption that you have managed to come to all by yourself. You know what was taken from the museum?"

"You might choose to make that assumption."

"I see. Very well." Wormwood breathed in sharply. "But you have not rounded up a suspect?"

"Again, you might choose to assume that, but I have my suspicions." Ulysses picked up the glass and took another sip of the warming spirit. "Did you know that Jago Kane is back in town?"

A nervous tic tugged at the left side of Wormwood's face.

"Didn't you claim that he was dead?"

"It would seem that appearances can be deceiving. I think I recall reporting that he was missing, *presumed* dead. Happens all the time."

"And now you are claiming to have seen him again?"

"I've done more than that. I fought him, up close and personal. There's no doubt it was him."

"And you believe he was involved in the robbery at the museum?"

"I wouldn't be surprised, but I think he's up to his neck in more than just that."

"I assume you are talking about the attacks by the group calling themselves the... Darwinian Dawn?"

"You know I am. Couldn't have come at a better time for you either, could it?"

"I hope you are not suggesting that I would use the occasion of such a tragic loss of human life to further my own ends?" Wormwood snarled, rising to the bait despite himself.

"You might think that, I couldn't possibly comment," Ulysses said with a smile. "And, while we're about it, how did the Darwinian Dawn manage to take control of every broadcast screen in the capital?"

"That is being looked into."

"By whom?"

"All you need to know is that the matter is already being investigated."

"And Kane?"

"You can leave that matter with me as well. It too will be looked into. Do not worry about Kane. You already have a job to do. Focus on finding this Professor Galapagos."

"Did I say that he was missing?"

"Now, Quicksilver, you have tried my patience enough today. Do not come here again, do you understand?"

"Oh, I understand."

"Then this meeting is over. Good day to you."

Taking his cue, Ulysses rose stiffly from the chair and put the glass back on the desk. "Good day, minister," he said, turning towards the door. Then he paused, glancing back at the scowling Wormwood. "Sorry... Prime Minister."

Then he was gone.

CHAPTER ELEVEN

The Missing Link

From the shadows on the other side of the street Ulysses looked up at the façade of the town house. It looked as decrepit as its neighbours – all crumbling brickwork and paint-flaking window frames. It looked like the kind of place you might find an Oriental's opium den, or a back street abortionist's, rather than the home of an eminent professor of evolutionary biology.

After the Challenger Incident – as it was being referred to in the popular press – and the surfacing of the Darwinian Dawn, both the trails he had been pursuing had gone cold. Following the train-top battle and Kane's escape from his clutches, there had been no sign of the revolutionary. It would take all of Ulysses' underworld contacts for there to be any chance of him getting even a sniff of the anarchist's whereabouts. The Darwinian Dawn were a new group that, apparently, no one had ever heard of before, which would make tracking them down ever harder. And besides, Wormwood had made it plain that Ulysses was not to pursue that particular line of investigation any further.

With regard to the missing Galapagos, as far as Ulysses was aware there had been neither hide nor hair seen of the apeman since the de-evolving professor's breakout from the Natural History Museum weeks before. London was a big place after all, a vast teeming metropolis, one of the largest cities – if not *the* largest city – in the world. It had a population that numbered in the millions and covered an area of hundreds of square miles, operating on several towering levels within that vast expanse of space. And in such a large warren of a city there were an uncountable number of places to disappear, if one had a mind to.

It was always possible that Galapagos was already dead, of course, having met his end in any one of a thousand ways – under the wheels of a train, drowned in the Thames, or even as a result of the morphological change taking place within his body. However, a niggling instinct, that wasn't often proved wrong, told Ulysses that this was not the case. He was almost certain that Professor Ignatius Galapagos was still at large, somewhere within the capital.

So it was that Ulysses and his trusty manservant now found themselves on a dilapidated street in Southwark, the Overground line that ran above its length holding it in almost perpetual shadow.

Both of the men were attired in dark, practical clothes, a world away from the sort of flamboyant attire Ulysses usually favoured. With their black roll-neck jumpers, and woollen hats – Ulysses lacking his trademark bloodstone cane – the two of them looked like a pair of cat burglars.

"Not much to look at is it, Nimrod?" Ulysses said.

"No, sir."

"Are we sure this is the right place?" Ulysses had managed to wheedle Professor Galapagos' address from a rather staid secretary at the Museum who at first had been wholly unhelpful, until Ulysses had confronted her with his irresistible charm.

"Quite sure, sir."

"Then we had better get on with it, hadn't we?"

"If I might be so bold sir?"

"Why of course, Nimrod. Be as bold as you like."

"Why didn't Miss Galapagos mention this place, sir?"

"I don't know, Nimrod. I don't know."

"How do you suggest we gain access, sir?"

"I thought I would leave you to solve that problem, Nimrod," Ulysses said, flashing his flunkey a devilish grin, "what with it being your area of expertise and all."

"Then follow me, sir," Nimrod said, his plummy accent never slipping for a second.

There did not seem to be anyone about at this time of the morning to see what they were about as the two of them strolled nonchalantly across the road, passed the front of the house without showing anything other than a passing awareness of it, and then ducked sharply down the narrow alley next to it.

It was dark and cold in the alleyway, the narrow space between the terraces being out of reach of the sun for all but about fifteen minutes a day. The only ones to observe their dubious actions, as Nimrod forced open a grimy window, was a pair of rats that were more interested in devouring the distinctly inedible-looking detritus of the alley. With no little amount of grunting and groaning, the two of them eventually managed to scramble through the window and into the near total darkness of the house.

Inside, Professor Galapagos' home festered under a pall of perpetual gloom. Every shutter and blind or curtain in the place must have been closed. What was it that Galapagos had been wanting to hide? What atrocities had been committed here in the name of evolutionary biology and scientific advancement?

The only sound was the slow, dull ticking of a grandfather clock in the hall.

Ulysses' skin crawled. The house felt empty, hollow – dead. What had gone on here? It was certainly not the sort of place he would have expected the delicate Genevieve to have had anything to do with. But then she had confessed that she had not seen her father for some time. Ulysses wondered how long 'some time' really meant.

"I don't mind telling you, Nimrod old chap," Ulysses hissed in barely more than a whisper, "that this place gives me the willies."

"I know what you mean sir," Nimrod replied, smacking the hooked end of a crowbar into the palm of his glove. "Where now?"

"I'll check this floor. You check upstairs," Ulysses instructed, and the two of them went their separate ways. Creeping like cats they tried not to make a sound as they moved over the creaking floorboards.

Ulysses found a drawing room darkened by heavy velvet drapes. It looked like any other drawing room, with a potted aspidistra on a plant stand and portraits of the professor's family above the fireplace. All of the pictures seemed to be of the older branches of the Galapagos family tree. The room had the air of a chamber that was never used, except on the most rare and formal of occasions.

Next he came across a dining room, similarly formal in its layout and similarly infrequently used. Everything was in order, if a somewhat clinical, dispassionate order. The only thing that gave the rooms any reflection of their owner's character were sinister stuffed birds and animals, masterpieces of the taxidermist's art. Hawks glared down from the tops of bookcases – which in turn contained the usual classics, most showing no signs of having been read at all – foxes snarled from beneath occasional tables and an owl, with wings outstretched menacingly, looked as if it might launch itself from the top of the grandfather clock at any moment.

When was the last time anyone had even been here?

The house felt like it had been unlived in for some time, possibly even before the Professor's disappearance. When *was* the last time Genevieve had visited her father?

In the kitchen Ulysses found a mess of unwashed plates and mouldering food. The room was thick with flies. They congregated in a black mass against the grimy panes of a window that looked out over a featureless back yard. Although this room was clearly the most lived in, no one had been here for a while either.

Ulysses and his manservant met again in the hall at the foot of the stairs. "Anything?" Ulysses asked.

"Nothing of note, sir, apart from one attic room that appears to have been used for the practice of taxidermy. The rest are just bedrooms. Most have dated décor and have probably not been used in years. The master bedroom shows no sign of having been used recently."

"As I suspected," Ulysses confided.

"So where do we go from here, sir?"

Ulysses nodded towards the door to the basement. "The only way we can go, down."

Ulysses led the way, cautiously. Neither of them had any idea what they might find in the stygian depths below.

What they found was what had evidently been Galapagos' workroom. Ulysses boldly flicked a switch and electric lamps around the walls crackled into life, casting jaundiced pools of light around the room. A little natural light crept uncomfortably into the long room from grime-obscured windows positioned at pavement level, adding its own insipid grey haze to the room.

There was a sharp intake of breath from Ulysses. "This could be the missing piece of the puzzle."

The basement ran the length of the house and had been divided into clearly defined sections. First there was the professor's workspace. This part of the room had been fitted in the style of a gentleman's study. There was a desk, bulging bookshelves and a small grate, set into one wall. Walnut-framed lithograph studies of animals had been tacked up, along with an authentic nineteenth century map of the Galapagos Islands and a watercolour of Darwin's exploratory vessel *The Beagle*. A pair of stuffed finches, frozen in the moment of taking wing from a branch, sat on the narrow mantelpiece above the cast iron hearth.

Curiously, the desk and tables were clear of papers. It looked like someone had gone to some deal of trouble to clear up thoroughly before leaving. As he looked with more care Ulysses also saw that there were gaps, distinct gaps, within the bookshelves. He moved to the grate. The charred, fire-eaten remains of leather-bound notebooks and other papers lay in the cold hearth. He picked a few scraps of blackened paper out of the fireplace but was unable to read anything more than the odd word. Disparate snatches of scientific jargon, written in a well-formed copperplate, that made little or no sense to him anyway and were certainly nothing more than nonsense, their context destroyed by the illiterate flames.

"He was here," Ulysses thought out loud.

"I'm sorry, sir. By 'he' do you mean Professor Galapagos?"

"Indeed I do, Nimrod. These notes, they've been burnt. And there are no signs of anyone having been here before us. I think Galapagos burnt his notes himself and then left here to return to the museum."

"You think he was trying to wipe out any traces of his work?"

"Do I think he was trying to reverse what he had done? Yes, I do."

"But what has been done cannot be undone, sir."

"Yes, I know. However, it would appear that Professor Galapagos chose to ignore that particular metaphysical fact, in a moment of irrational desperation no doubt. And inventions cannot be uninvented, discoveries cannot be undiscovered again. And now it would appear that he fell foul of whatever he had been developing himself."

Ulysses had moved into the next part of the room. A series of scrubbed oak tables were covered with pieces of glass and brass apparatus – including crucibles, condensers and various Bunsen burners connected to the house gas supply – which formed a complex chemical still. A little liquid remained in some of the blown glass vessels and a furry grey coating of dust covered everything. Again, this equipment hadn't been touched for some time. Cruelly large syringes lay on the table, as well as neatly arranged scalpels and other operating tools.

Ulysses sniffed. There was the faintest trace of a lingering odour amidst the acrid aftertaste of burning that had been trapped in the airless basement. It spoke to his subconscious. It was said that the human sense of smell was the strongest trigger for memory, but Ulysses couldn't quite recollect where or when he had last come across the bittersweet aroma.

"And what have we here?"

Beyond the Heath Robinson laboratory were several rows of shelving racks. Filling the shelves, held suspended in glass jars of various shapes and sizes, was Professor Galapagos's private collection of biological specimens.

There were the usual subjects anyone might have expected to find in the lab of an obsessively driven evolutionary biologist such as deep sea angler fish, octopi, an aborted elephant foetus, a calf's head. But then there were other things as well, less identifiable things, all preserved in the same urine-coloured formaldehyde.

They were amorphous with barely recognisable protrusions of pallid malformed anatomy here and there; a vestigial limb, a lidless staring eye, half a dozen teeth where there was no mouth, flippers, fish-like tails. Whichever way Ulysses looked at it they were grotesque abominations that were an affront to God and Nature, half-evolved, or perhaps de-evolved, foetal things that should never have been brought into existence and that could never have naturally been given life. All were dead, floating in their preserving jars like the corpses of fish in a polluted river. Some looked like they had been partially dissected and then returned to their containers. What had the eminent professor been up to in this house of the macabre?

Beyond the shelves of abominations, at the other end of the basement room was a heavy iron door, set into a sturdy frame in the bare stone of the unlimed wall. There was a key in the lock.

"Shall we go on, sir?" Nimrod asked.

"Well we've come this far, haven't we," Ulysses said, smiling grimly. "And after this morbid museum I have to confess that I am curious as to what could possibly lie beyond an iron door in an evolutionary biologist's house."

"Very good, sir. Shall I do the honours?"

"Why, thank you, Nimrod."

"Not at all, sir." The manservant turned the key and held the door open so that Ulysses could pass through.

A flight of stone steps had been cut into the foundations of the Southwark house descending to a narrow sub-basement corridor. Light filtered through another pavement-level slit, enough for Ulysses to see where he was going. The walls ran with moisture and there were patches of moss growing between the joins. There was a strong earthy smell, mixed with the tang of ammonia and damp straw.

The corridor ran off from the foot of the slime-slick steps and soon led to a T-junction. To the left was another iron door. To the right the stygian passageway opened out into a larger subterranean chamber.

"Flashlights on, I think," Ulysses said, taking out his own torch.

The door to the left had been locked from the outside and the key left in the lock. Ulysses turned the key and opened the door. Only then did his uncanny sixth sense alert him to danger. Instinctively he leapt backwards, away from the open door, the stink of ordure assaulting his senses in a potent wave, whilst the spot-beam of his torch pierced the lightless cell beyond.

"Careful now, old chap," Ulysses warned. "We're not alone."

There was a shuffling movement, the sound of straw rustling underfoot as something moved out of the way of the light. Nimrod and Ulysses both stood before the cell, flashlights penetrating the darkness. There was a whimper from inside and both men were rendered speechless by what they saw before them.

Pressed into the corner of the tiny stone walled cell was a hulking brute of a creature. It might well have been a good head taller than Ulysses but it held that head low, its posture that of an ape. It was naked apart from a loincloth. Its skin was pallid, its body heavily muscled, its head covered with lank hair that hung down to its shoulders. It had flung its hands in front of its face, blinded by the sudden invasion of torchlight. The heavy line of its brow and the blunt shape of its snout suggested that this creature was closer to Man's ape ancestors than *Homo sapiens*.

"Get down, sir!" Nimrod shouted, pushing Ulysses out of the way. The manservant barged into the cell, crowbar in hand. The creature flinched. Raising the improvised weapon above his head, Nimrod stared into the face of the half-human creature in front of him. Wholly human eyes looked back into his, welling with a deep sadness.

Nimrod hesitated. It was all the time Ulysses needed. He had seen the look in the cowering creature's eyes as well.

"Nimrod, old chap, thanks for your concern for my well-being, but I don't think you'll be needing to use that crowbar."

"But it's the apeman, sir."

Keeping his manservant at bay with one hand, Ulysses slowly but deliberately moved between Nimrod and the creature. Despite such an action of disarming trust his body remained tensed, ready to fight if he had to.

"Correction, old chap. It's *an* apeman, not *the* apeman, not Professor Galapagos." Boldly Ulysses took another step, his nose inadvertently wrinkling against the smell. He had seen its like before. "In fact I rather think it's an *Homo neanderthalensis*."

"A what, sir?"

"A Neanderthal, Nimrod. An evolutionary dead-end but an ancestor of the human race nonetheless. I rather think that *this* is our missing link, so to speak."

"But it could still be dangerous, sir."

Ulysses took another step, lowering his torch and holding out a hand towards the creature. Slowly the Neanderthal lowered its hands from its face and reciprocated the gesture, reaching towards Ulysses with one meaty paw.

"It doesn't look like it so far, does it? Besides, have you not noticed the manacle around its ankle chaining it to the wall? I know it's a cliché – and this fellow here could probably snap both our necks like twigs – but I think he's more scared of us than we are of him."

For a moment their fingertips touched and Ulysses sensed a common ancestry – a shared humanity with the captive Neanderthal. At the back of his mind he wondered how someone who had sired such a magnanimous wonder as Genevieve Galapagos could have been so cruel to this creature. The Neanderthal was not so much the Professor's pet as the result of some inhuman and immoral experiment.

"Nimrod, pick the lock on that manacle."

"Are you sure, sir?"

"Trust me."

His sense of duty overcoming the persuasive voice of doubt in his mind, Nimrod approached the creature. It jerked away from him, Nimrod's immediate reaction being to do the same. But slowly, with ever such cautious movements, the creature allowed Nimrod to free it from its chains.

A terrible reptilian roar rang through the echoing darkness of the cellar space, a crocodilian bellow of defiance and savage prehistoric fury. It was a roar redolent with the promise of a cruel death.

The Neanderthal howled in abject fear. Ulysses' blood ran cold.

"Now what was *that*?"

In the black hole of the basement chamber opposite the cell, stabbing their torch beams into the stygian gloom as if trying to drive it back into the bowels of the underworld, they found a single cast iron manhole cover.

The reptilian roar echoed through the chamber, emanating from beneath them through the slits in the iron plate. Was it the cry of some rogue saurian, still loose after the break out from London Zoo, or did it belong to something infinitely worse?

As the echoes died away the sound of running water could be heard coming up from below and a gust of foul air rose with it. Whatever had given voice to that terrible sound was lurking somewhere below, in the noxious labyrinth of the city's sewer system. So that was where Ulysses Quicksilver would have to go too. Destiny called. Whether the creature realised it or not, it was waiting for him.

CHAPTER TWELVE

Going Underground

The winding, low-roofed tunnels stank, which was unsurprising considering Ulysses and Nimrod now found themselves exploring one of the largest sewer systems in the world. The stench of human waste filled the sewers with its miasmic stink, as foetid brown water swirled around their ankles, and sometimes up to their knees, soaking through their trousers and boots as they trudged through the filth. Ulysses breathed in through his nose as much as he could, so as to avoid tasting the foul stench, concentrating hard on not letting his gorge rise. Nimrod simply advanced through the tunnels with a permanent, nose-wrinkled scowl distorting his aquiline features. They could feel solid lumps of waste swirling around their legs with every step; every time they placed a sodden boot down they felt the filth shift and ooze underfoot.

From the shaft leading down into the sewers the two explorers had found themselves in a cramped, brick-lined tunnel that ran away ahead and behind. Their torch beams illuminated about twenty yards of the tunnel in any one direction and revealed walls coated with glistening slime whilst unspeakable things slipped past them in the insistent current of the waste channel.

They trudged on, any efforts at stealth thwarted. Every dredging step they took sloshed in the filthy current, every word spoken – even whispered – was amplified into uncomfortable clarity by the cavern-like acoustics of the place. Ulysses found himself wondering whether any of Professor Galapagos' aborted experiments had ended up down here. Although it looked like he had kept everything he had ever created in his unholy laboratory, perhaps other degenerate things had survived and escaped into the sewers beneath the city. There were certainly all manner of urban myths regarding what was living, hidden and undisturbed in the sewers of the Empire's largest city, from giant albino salamanders and ancient crocodiles to more far-fetched rumours of a tribe of cannibalistic troglodytes. It was not so far-fetched to believe that there could be other things living down there too, things like the offspring of an obsessive scientist's experiments.

They had left the maltreated Neanderthal in the basement room. It had appeared unwilling to follow them into the sewer; perhaps it knew what was waiting for them down there even if it couldn't communicate that fact to them directly.

At every junction they waited in anxious anticipation. Never quite sure of what they might meet. Ulysses waited either for his sixth sense to give him an inkling as to which direction they should head or for another reptilian roar to guide them to its source.

Sometimes the roars sounded like they were coming from just around the next corner in the twisting tunnels and at other times they sounded more distant again. Then they would not hear anything at all for as much as a quarter of an hour.

Was the reptile or dinosaur, or whatever it was, hunting them, scenting their blood even over the overwhelming stink of the sewers? And there was another nagging thought at the back of Ulysses' mind that he almost didn't want to even consider. Were they in fact hunting the transformed Professor Galapagos altered even further, changed into a totally inhuman form by whatever degenerative disease he had contracted?

Then, at last, the tunnel began to widen, the roof becoming higher, so that they could walk two abreast without having to stoop. Another thirty yards further on and a walkway, raised from the stream of filth, appeared on the left hand side. It was a relief for them to get their feet out of the stinking sludge.

Ulysses paused at another parting of the ways. Four tunnels met at an intersection, the current becoming stronger at the confluence as three of the sewer passages emptied into the fourth – and largest. The roar of water suggested that a little way down this last tunnel the depth of the sewer increased, the current being carried over a precipitous waterfall into the even more unsavoury depths of the sewer network.

But Ulysses was not interested in any of these new tunnels, at least not for the time being. He was shining his torch down at the narrow walkway they were now on.

"What is it, sir?" Nimrod asked. "What have you found?"

"Something's last meal," Ulysses said, studying the half-eaten remains of a rat. It was missing its hindquarters, the spill of its pallid intestines a greasy purple-grey in the light of his torch.

"And here's another one." Something had clearly taken a bite out of the middle of this rodent. The rat's head, tail and legs were all intact but the flesh of its middle was completely gone, only a few stringy bits of gristle remaining attached to its gnawed spine. "Watch where you're stepping, old chap."

"Sir?" Nimrod's voice floated back up the tunnel. "I think you should see this."

Ulysses turned and looked back down the tunnel. His manservant had stopped a few yards behind on the walkway. He had his torch beam pointed down at the side of the ledge.

"What is it?" Ulysses asked, joining Nimrod where he was crouched at the channel's edge.

Whatever it was, it looked like a swatch of leather, discoloured almost beyond recognition by the filth of the effluent half-filling the tunnel. It had caught on a rusted pipe jutting out from the stonework. Nimrod pulled it free and carefully laid it out on the mouldering pathway.

Now that it was out of the muck both men could see quite clearly that the material was covered in coarse hair and had gathered in folds. In the light of the torches Nimrod began to tease out the folds, separating them in an attempt to stretch the object out.

"My God!" Ulysses gasped, as the shape of the object became unquestionable. The thing Nimrod had recovered from the sewer was undoubtedly a skin. It was not complete but both men could see arms, the outline of legs and a face.

"How vexing," Nimrod said, without any apparent emotion. "It would appear that something has eaten the wretched Professor Galapagos."

"I don't think so, old chap," Ulysses corrected, running his torch up and down, the ape-skin. "I don't think that the errant professor has been skinned and eaten. These ruptures here don't look like talon marks, they look more like tears to me. There's no subcutaneous fat, blood and general mess on the skin. It's relatively clean, if you choose to ignore the fact that it's been soaking in sewer filth. I think that Professor Galapagos has shed his skin."

"I am no naturalist, sir, but as far as I am aware, mammalian species do not shed their skin."

"No, they don't, do they?"

"So," Nimrod said, seeking a better understanding so

that he was clear as to what the two of them could expect to face down in the stinking darkness, "you believe that the cry we heard was not made by the professor's killer but by whatever he might have become."

"Something like that, yes."

A sense like precognition sent shockwaves skittering along tingling nerve endings. Ulysses threw himself backwards against the wall of the tunnel as the effluent stream exploded, showering the two men with filthy water. A hulking shape hurled itself at the crouching men. A sweeping claw struck the edge of the walkway, the rotten brickwork crumbling under the blow.

Mastering their shock at the abrupt appearance of the monster, Ulysses and Nimrod turned their torches on the creature. The thing roared in fury, its reptilian voice brimming with anger, and threw its arms up in front of its face. Its eyes had become used to the fetid darkness and so it was now blinded by the sudden sharp light of the torches.

It had used other senses to track the two hunters which, as well as a heightened sense of hearing and smell, included the ability to sense a creature by body heat alone.

The creature had found it easy to hunt the rats, the scrawny rodents appearing as scampering blurs of hot orange and yellow against the dull black of the bone-numbing slurry water. Then it had chanced upon the two men, sensing the heat of their bodies in the darkness, feeling an animal thrill of satisfaction that here at last were some more satisfying prey with which it could sate its ravenous hunger. It was only Ulysses' precognitive sense that had saved him from an instant death at the claws of the lizard man.

In the split second in which it was rendered incapable

by the light of the torches, Ulysses' heightened mind took in every detail of the creature's unnatural anatomy. The trunk of its body was like that of a muscular human but covered with scales instead of skin. The scales of its belly were pale, the colour of ivory, but on the rest of its body the creature's rough hide became more like the colour and texture of tree bark. Its arms were again humanoid in form, but corded with muscles like ship's cables and ending in sharp-clawed talons.

The monster's face and head had lost all vestiges of its original form, showing no signs of its human origins. It looked more like that of a lizard. It was completely hairless and had a short crocodilian snout, strong jaws bristling with needle-sharp teeth, its tongue a stabbing spear of black muscle. But its eyes were the most chilling aspect of all; they had lost any sign of the humanity that might have once lingered within. Around the scales of its neck – so tight that it was cutting into the saurian flesh beneath – was a silvered chain and the curiously shaped locket Ulysses had seen before around the neck of the apeman in the Natural History Museum. There could be no doubt now as to the identity of the mutated half-lizard thing.

"Professor Galapagos, I presume."

The creature responded by issuing another blood-curdling roar from between gaping jaws, large enough to remove a man's head from his shoulders with a single bite.

The change that had come upon the professor was obviously not as straightforward as him simply transforming into other ancestral life forms as his body regressed. With every change he underwent his body maintained its overall human proportions as if he was actually becoming a hybrid of a human being and whatever other evolutionary form he might be regressing into. It was as if the damned Professor was creating new species, or sub-species, with every transformation. The form he was in right now the academics would give the name *homo lizardus* or *lizardus sapiens*. That was his divine punishment for the hubris he had demonstrated in meddling with the secrets of evolution, for cracking the Darwin Code. God alone knew what he would turn into next. It seemed to Ulysses that Galapagos's regression was accelerating.

The monster howled, its saurian voice like the shriek of a circular saw. It lashed out again, this time catching Ulysses' flashlight, smashing the torch from his hand and shattering the bulb. The light died, but with Nimrod's torch still dazzling the creature Ulysses sought a way to defend himself.

Before the pistol was even in his hand, the lizard-thing hurled itself back into the brown slurry and vanished beneath the surface.

Ulysses trained his gun on the spot where the lizardman had disappeared but it failed to resurface. "Come on, we can't let it get away!" He shouted, recklessly leaping into the sewer channel again.

"But which way, sir?" Nimrod asked, shining his torch after Ulysses.

Ulysses scoured the sewer intersection for any sign of where the Galapagos-lizard had gone, whether that sign be sight or sound of the lizardman or some precognitive clue from that extra-sensory part of his subconscious.

"This way," he declared, pointing into the pipe into which all the other channels emptied, and began dragging his legs through the water with heroic strides.

"Sir, wait!" Nimrod called after his reckless employer, but Ulysses' blood was up and he would not be held back.

Entering the gaping mouth of the main tunnel Ulysses instantly felt the pull of the stronger current. Only a few yards ahead the sewer passage emptied over the edge of an abyssal drop, the sound of the water a thunderous roar.

"Sir!"

Ulysses heard his flunkey's warning as his heightened sixth sense cut through the adrenalin. He spun round to see the monstrous saurian shadow rise behind him, filthy brown water running from its rugged hide.

He had been ready for the monster but turning cost him precious fractions of a second. Something lashed out of the darkness, whipping him across the forearm, smacking the gun from his hand and opening up the flesh of his wrist.

"A tail! A bloody tail!" Ulysses gasped, clutching a hand to the gash in his arm. Galapagos had become even more like one of humankind's prehistoric reptilian forebears than Ulysses had at first realised.

As the creature bore down on him, Ulysses realised that he had no choice but to fight the creature hand-to-hand. And then the time for calm, reasoned thought was gone and there was only time for brutal, instinctive action.

The lizardman reached for Ulysses with taloned hands and Ulysses grabbed hold of both the creature's wrists, feeling the scales scrape against the softer skin of his palms. The Galapagos-lizard was taller than he and had the greater body mass. But Ulysses was lithely strong too, more so than might at first have appeared to the casual observer. And in his months away from the rest of civilisation he had learnt how to use an opponent's own strength and weight against itself. He did so now, pulling the lizardman towards him whilst deftly sidestepping. As the scaly creature stumbled past him, Ulysses delivered a strong, straight-legged kick into the base of the lizard's spine.

The beast stumbled but retained its balance, the taloned claws of its feet anchoring it to the floor of the tunnel beneath the rushing effluent. Without even looking back over its shoulder, the Galapagos-lizard delivered another unavoidable whip-cracking stinging blow with its tail, this time catching Ulysses across the chest. He stumbled backwards, desperate to keep his balance, fearing what might happen should he become submerged.

Then the beast was on him, Ulysses and the lizardman wrestling one another at the very edge of the subterranean waterfall.

Ulysses looked up into the elongated face of what had once been Genevieve Galapagos' father and into the eyes of what had become *Lacerta erectus*. Those eyes were now a chilling ophidian yellow, the pupils cruel crescent slits. The monster stared back, nictitating eyelids blinking rapidly.

There was the crack of a pistol shot and a bullet buried itself in the wall of the tunnel next to them.

"Try to hold it still, sir!" Nimrod called over the roar of the lizard and the furious crashing of the cascading sewage.

Ulysses felt his shoulder cry out as he tried to resist the weight of the beast bearing down on top of him.

"All right," Ulysses spluttered, closing his eyes against the torch beam as it swept into his eyes, "and while I'm at it, I'll ask the dear Professor Galapagos to pose for his portrait for the National Geographic Magazine"

Nimrod's aim was compromised by the disorienting shadows cast by his small torch and also by the fact that he did not want to hit Ulysses. To kill one's own employer would not look good on his curriculum vitae should he have to look for other gainful employment following this incident.

There was another crack and this time the lizardman cried out in pained surprise. For a moment it turned, as if considering this new threat.

"A hit, Nimrod, a very palpable hit!"

"Thank you, sir!"

"Not that it seems to have made any difference," Ulysses added to himself.

Driven on by its rage at having been shot, the lizardman grappled with Ulysses, snapping at him with its alligator mouth, forcing him closer and closer towards the edge of the pitch-black precipice. Ulysses lashed out with kicks and punches, but the creature's hide protected it from his pummelling. Where he landed punches with his fists he winced as he took the skin off his knuckles.

There was a splash as Nimrod entered the channel after them. The manservant's torch beam wavered as he did his best to run to the aid of his master. "Watch out, sir! I'll get the blighter!"

There were two more pistol shots. It sounded like one of them spanged off the bony ridges of the lizard's back. The other hit home.

The creature roared, enraged by the manservant's constant goading. It spun round savagely, delivering Ulysses a reeling blow to the head with one club-like fist as it did so.

For a moment grey supernovae exploded across Ulysses' vision. He reeled backwards, grabbing out at anything that might arrest his fall. His fingers closed around something small, sharp and hard. There was the ping of a chain snapping and then the mighty pendulum weight of the monster's tail connected with the back of his legs.

There was no way he could have avoided the tail attack.

His legs swept out from under him, his feet slipping in the rancid silt covering the floor of the sewer passage, Ulysses felt the surging current catch him and pull him with it into the void.

The flickering light of Nimrod's torch illuminating the circular mouth of the tunnel disappeared rapidly upwards, receding gunshots echoing from the sewer pipe.

He could feel nothing but air beneath him, his ears deaf to all but the roar of the effluent-fall. And the hungry darkness of the sewer swallowed him up.

CHAPTER THIRTEEN

His Waterloo

Ulysses surfaced, coughing violently, the surging current of the sewer channel bringing him to a stone ledge in the septic darkness. He scrabbled for a hold, trying to pull himself out of the vile water. His stomach heaved and before he was fully aware of what was happening he vomited, his body's reaction to the presence of the noxious effluent that had suddenly flooded his digestive system. He spluttered, spitting in an attempt to rid his mouth of the ordure, and his stomach heaved again.

Eventually Ulysses managed to pull himself onto the ledge and then could do nothing but sit with his head hung low, weakened by the experience and disorientated by his plunge into the deeper sewer tunnels. Taking in heaving lungfuls of air he retched again, unable to rid himself of the nauseous taste. This time nothing more came up; there was nothing left inside him. There was a dull throbbing ache in his skull from the resounding blow the lizardman had laid against him during their struggle.

As he sat there, leaning over the sewer channel in the darkness, he became uncomfortably aware of his own ragged breathing. Ears straining to hear anything else, he searched for any clues as to his surroundings using sound alone. Down there in the darkness, soaked to the skin in malodorous sewer water, without a light source to see by and minus his gun, Ulysses felt horribly vulnerable.

He could hear the ever-present gurgle of the steady stream coursing through the sewer pipe. There was also the slow drip of moisture from the ceiling and the small plashes of the drips falling into puddles collecting on the pitted stone of the ledge. And then there was the occasional scampering patter of tiny feet as the rats went about their disgusting business.

He could see nothing and smell far too much. It was as if the fetid stench had taken on physical form and was trying to smother him as well as take away his sight.

Ulysses couldn't hear the sound of gunfire anymore, but then he wasn't sure how far he had been carried following his plunge. He wondered what had become of the ever-loyal Nimrod. Had he bested the lizardman or had he simply become Professor Galapagos' latest victim? There was no time for mourning now, though. Besides, he had no idea really as to his manservant's fate one way or the other – Nimrod had been armed, as had the lizard in its own way. His priority was to get out of the sewers alive so that he could pursue his investigation to its conclusion, and if that meant avenging Nimrod's death, then so be it.

Ulysses could still feel the professor's curious locket gripped tightly in his fist. Incredibly, he had managed to hold onto it after his fall and all the time he was being carried along through the miasmic dark.

He couldn't hear anything that might hint at the approach of the inhuman lizard-thing – either the sound of something breaking the surface or surging towards him through the foul water – but then he had barely been given any warning the last time that the monster had attacked. Was the lizardman hunting him even now through the cloying, fetid darkness? Or was its corpse floating through the tunnels, on its way to the Thames, shot dead by his butler?

As he sat there in the gloom, the nausea slowly subsiding, he realised that he was not actually in total darkness. As his eyes adjusted to the gloom, eking every scrap of light from his surroundings, he saw that the curved walls and ceiling of the brick-built tunnel were covered with patches of luminescent moss that appeared to thrive in the putrid, methane-rich atmosphere.

It was as nothing in comparison to having a halogen beam or storm lantern but it was enough to help him discern one shadowy form from another. It was enough for him to make his way without braining himself against a low arch or stepping off the edge of a precipice, but he would still need to proceed with caution. The darkness could still hide a hundred hazards.

Rising to his feet carefully, using the crumbling, slime-encrusted wall for support, Ulysses set off, following the same course as the brackish water through this stinking subterranean world. He saw little point in trying to return to where he had begun his frightful journey. He didn't fancy his chances of trying to scale the precipice he had been thrown from. And besides, the water in the tunnel would ultimately end up pouring into the Thames and lead him to a way out.

So, in almost total darkness, save for the dull green glow of the bioluminescent vegetation, feeling weak and nauseous, as well as wet and cold, with barely any awareness of time passing, Ulysses Quicksilver continued to navigate the labyrinthine tunnels, every sense straining to make sense of this disorientating world.

He had no idea for how long he had been exploring the dark tunnels. His watch had a luminous dial but it had rather uncharacteristically stopped working. He suspected that his dunking hadn't done the usually reliable timepiece much good. It hadn't done much for his communicator either.

Steadily, through the nigh on impenetrable black murk, the broken edges of a patch of deeper darkness could be discerned in the gloom. It was ahead of Ulysses and slightly to the right. Cautiously he made this his focus and approached the hole in the darkness. As he neared the space his straining eyes were able to discern depth to the darkness too. Reaching out a hand, he ran his fingers over the broken, angular edges of bricks. Something in the past had caused part of the sewer wall to collapse. The current diverged at this juncture. Most of the stinking water continued on its way along the brick pipe, but some swirled out through the hole mixing with a second subterranean watercourse.

Ulysses paused, listening. At first he could hear nothing beyond the rush and churn of the sewer and the ripple of water lapping against the wall. There was an echoing quality to the watery sounds coming from the other side of the hole, suggesting that the dimensions of the space beyond were of more cavernous proportions than the tunnel in which he now stood.

Then he heard another sound, muffled by distance. It sounded like the clanking of machinery, a rhythmic tattoo, the beating of a mechanical heart.

For a moment Ulysses considered the sewer passage ahead of him but then felt compelled to enter the larger tunnel, beyond the hole, and follow the sound to its source. With no other beacon to direct his way through the fetid darkness, Ulysses concentrated on the distant, echoed clanking.

Clambering through the half-submerged rupture in the tunnel wall, Ulysses immediately felt the floor drop away beneath him and started treading water. The water filling this new tunnel was just as bone numbing as that of the sewer but, although it smelt old and brackish, it was like the scent of roses compared to the stench that he had just had to wade through.

Ulysses let his senses adjust to this new space, hearing the rippling waves his swimming sent out rebound from a barrier only a matter of a few feet away. Light-excreting blankets of moss grew in irregular patches on the curving walls and ceiling here too, so that gradually Ulysses was able to make sense of the puzzle and realised that the space he was in now was much larger, but just as tube-like, as the sewer passage he had emerged from.

The tunnel was flooded but the water here was more or less still; there was no restless current pulling him one way or another. Instead he directed himself towards the distant, rhythmic clanking that sounded like the echoing hubbub of a factory production line. He moved with a strong breaststroke. Ulysses followed the gradual bend of the tunnel, the sounds of the relentless machinery becoming clearer and being joined by other noises now – the wheeze of steam being released under pressure, the regular *thud-thud-thud* of a hammer, the wail of a klaxon, even human voices.

The sounds were so clear now that Ulysses felt that he was on the verge of making out recognisable words, snatches of conversation, between the loud thumping, pounding and rattling of the hidden production line. As he rounded the bend, the architecture of the tunnel changed, as the roof seemed to rise away above Ulysses' head, an oblong shape emerged from the gloom to his left. At the same time his feet kicked against the bottom of the tunnel floor. His foot slipped on a submerged obstruction. It felt like the floor was cut with grooved channels or... set with rails.

Then the pieces of the puzzle finally fell into place.

The oblong was a ledged walkway. He pushed his way through the sludgy water and there hauled himself out of the chill, oily lake. He sat for a moment listening to the *clank-clunk* that seemed to come from above as well as beyond now, feeling the slight tremor of a vibration pass through the stone beneath him.

Ulysses reached out a hand to the wall. The surface his fingertips came into contact with was cold and slick with moisture, but it was smooth. In fact it felt like glazed ceramic.

"Tiles," Ulysses said to himself. Leaving the collapsed sewer he had entered the flooded tunnels of the old, abandoned Underground railway system. It explained much – the increased size of the tunnel, the materials from which it had been constructed. He was sitting on a station platform.

The Underground had been abandoned for more than sixty years, ever since the Kingdom Incident, as it had since become known. The capital's subterranean rail network had been replaced by the far superior Overground in the intervening years. Ulysses had believed most of the Tube tunnels to be completely flooded, but it would appear from the evidence of his own eyes that this was only partly the case.

He got to his feet. Fetid water ran from his body and clothes, pooling on the slime-coated platform under the soles of his sodden shoes. Taking a moment to gather himself, he pushed his wet hair out of his face, slicking it down with a greasy palm.

He was lost within the forgotten tunnels of the London Underground which had once been the pride of the nation, having been thwarted by the lizard-beast that the missing – not to mention, evolutionarily-degenerating

– Professor Galapagos had become. Whatever awaited him within the supposedly abandoned labyrinth of the subterranean railway system could not possibly surprise him – not now. It was all in a day's work for Ulysses Quicksilver, dandy adventurer and servant of the crown.

"You couldn't make it up," he said to himself, smiling inwardly, despite the dire state of his personal attire and the nature of his current predicament.

Further along the platform he found himself at the opening of a side passage, which connected to a flight of steps. A flickering orange glow came from above, illuminating the top of the steps. Ulysses blinked, his eyes taking a moment to adjust. Then, taking a firm hold of the rusted handrail next to him, he began to ascend.

Pressing himself flat against the smooth tiled wall, Ulysses took several measured breaths and then peered warily around the edge of the archway.

The place might once have been the warren of gleaming tiled tunnels that made up an Underground station concourse but it had now been filled with machinery and transformed into an underground factory. Ulysses was looking down on a veritable production line, which would not have been out of place in one of the steam-driven mills of the Black Country. The whole place lay under a fug of steam and coal smoke, whilst caged sodium lights pierced the smoggy murk, looking like fog-distorted ship's lanterns. The factory was also pervaded by the noise and vibration of the working machinery.

To Ulysses' left, at the far end of the concourse, massive machines – all spinning flywheels, thumping hammers and crushing compressors – produced shell-like spherical steel cases, from which protruded sea urchin-like spines.

Steam and clockwork powered automata-drudges separated each steel globe into two equal halves, and half of these hemispherical cases were then heaved onto a rattling conveyor system. These shell casings then passed along the production line to have other components fitted inside them by other robot-drones. The air reeked of lubricating oil and hot metal, accompanied by an all-pervading acrid chemical smell.

To the far right, in the shadow of a broad archway at the end of the relentless production line, yet more drones put the two halves of the metal spheres back together and from there they were ferried away into the darkness of a side passage on great wheeled frames.

On the wall above it all, through the smoke and steam, Ulysses could make out the rusted Underground sign that signified which station it was he now found himself in. The name on the banner read: Waterloo. It somehow seemed apt.

There was no doubt in Ulysses' mind that this place was a bomb factory. But how long had production been in operation on this spot, hidden from the prying eyes of the world above?

Carrying out all manner of unskilled labouring jobs around the automatons, so that the man-machines might complete their work without hindrance, were the kind of dregs of society that made the beggars on the city streets above look fortunate. These troglodyte workers might once have been human but they were now barely more than warped wretches, their bodies afflicted by all manner of hideous mutations.

They all wore the same, shapeless, grubby overalls and shambled about the place with their ankles shackled together. They were prisoners here, as much as they were workers, employed to do the jobs deemed too lowly even for the automated workforce. Not one of them would have looked out of place in a circus freak show. They all looked like they could be descendants of Joseph Merrick, the Elephant Man. These people – if they could still be referred to as people – were either losing their hair, or their teeth, no doubt as a result of the terrible conditions in which they were forced to work, their faces and bodies misshapen by hideous growths of pallid, purple-veined flesh. In some cases, their disfigurements were so extreme that it was impossible for Ulysses to determine the gender of the limping creatures that had been enslaved to the production of the evil devices.

It was these same wretches who were spooning a noxious, bubbling green gunk from a crusted iron vat into each of the shell casings. Wisps of malodorous vapour rose from the patently toxic goo. Ulysses' eyes stung and he was in no doubt that it was as a result of this poisonous stuff diffusing through the atmosphere of the factory.

Watching over the production line from gantry walkways and the openings of side passages were armed men, dressed in plain black uniforms. The only distinguishing marks on any of them was the insignia of their clandestine organisation that until, only a few weeks ago, Ulysses had never even known existed. They each wore the badge of an encircled dinosaur skull on their arms. Each of them was armed with a sub-automatic machine pistol, their faces hidden by the rubber snouts of gas masks.

Ulysses' rage at witnessing first-hand the fate that had been forced upon the poor mutant work force seethed and simmered just beneath the surface, ready to explode with volcanic fury. He would dearly have liked to vent that fury against any one of the armed guards but such recourse would merely lead to his own demise. He was still unarmed, and no matter how skilled he might be, in unarmed combat the odds did not appear to be in his favour.

No, he would have to bide his time and wait, and perhaps then a more practical course of action would present itself to him.

Watching the factory floor, Ulysses saw a figure unlike any other he had so far seen. He was wearing a grubby lab coat that might once have been white. His eyes were hidden by a pair of thick goggles. His hair was matted and spiked with filth. His hands were encased within heavy rubber gloves. He grasped a stained clipboard on which he was scrawling notes as he monitored progress on the production line. He was followed by a gaggle of similarly garbed assistants, but there was no doubt that this tech-engineer scientist was their senior.

Ulysses watched the scientist as he made his way through the converted station concourse. There was little he could do directly to counteract whatever the Darwinian Dawn were doing here, but if he stealthily shadowed this individual he might be able to get one step closer to the heart of the group's operations. They were obviously planning a bombing campaign on a scale undreamt of before by those in power in Whitehall. Quietly, Ulysses ducked out from behind the pillar and in two long strides was hunkered down behind one of the supports that held up the clanking conveyor.

He was suddenly distracted by a shout from the other side of the factory. He glanced to his left, peering between cast iron spars and his heart was suddenly in his mouth.

A figure, dressed in practical black clothes had emerged from a passageway on the other side of the concourse, accompanied by two of the armed guards. It was Kane

– Jago Kane – here! He was instantly recognisable, thanks to the distinguishing mark of the livid scar that bisected his face. It was all Ulysses could do to stop himself gasping in surprise. So the blackguard *was* at the centre of the Darwinian Dawn's operations. Ulysses had *known* it!

The vile revolutionary joined the scientist-supervisor and his lackeys on the factory floor. The two of them immediately engaged in what appeared to be an intense discussion. If only Ulysses could discover what it was they were talking about, the information he could then provide to his masters in Whitehall would be all the more valuable, but to achieve such a thing he would have to get closer.

Keeping himself crouched down behind the conveyor production line, obscured by the steam, any sound he might make drowned out by the roar of the bomb-making construction, Ulysses crept towards the plotters' position, at the same time assiduously avoiding the human slaves and their masked overseers. Gradually he began to pick up snippets of conversation.

The scientist was assuring Kane that they would be ready, as planned, and on schedule. Kane pressed on about having the devices in position by... but then Ulysses missed the rest as an automatic valve released a burst of steam from a pipe above his head.

The snatches of conversation didn't make any real sense out of context, and merely added to Ulysses' frustration and determination to find out more.

Concentrating intently he pressed on. Kane seemed almost close enough for Ulysses to reach out and touch. Ulysses was concentrating so hard that he only became aware of the tingling at the back of his brain at the last second, when it was too late to do anything to save himself.

With a sharp jab, the cold metal of a rifle muzzle was shoved against the back of his neck. He had been in such a hurry to catch up with his nemesis that he had thrown all caution to the wind and acted like some reckless youth.

"Don't get up," came a gruff, uncultured voice from behind him, "unless you want me to put a bullet through the back of your skull."

He was prodded in the ribs by a second gun muzzle and another voice declared, "At this time of social civil war you can consider yourself a hostage of the Darwinian Dawn."

CHAPTER FOURTEEN

A Bad Day to Die

"So, Ulysses Quicksilver, we meet again."

Ulysses looked up into the sneering scowl that was Jago Kane's face. Ulysses had been roughly searched, dragged in front of his nemesis and the scientist and then forced to kneel before them, his hands behind his head. "The pleasure's all yours."

The punch snapped Ulysses' head sharply to the right.

"Always there with the snappy, oh-so-clever retorts and hilarious one-liners," Kane snarled.

Before Ulysses could come back at the revolutionary with another of his trademark verbal ripostes, Kane's fist descended again. Something cracked and Ulysses spat a gobbet of bloody saliva from between bruised lips. His head sagged.

"Not so quick with the witty ripostes now, are you?"

"I see falling from a train hasn't dampened your eternally optimistic spirit, more's the pity."

Fury seething in his eyes Kane said nothing, simply delivering a sharp kick to Ulysses midriff. Ulysses could not stop himself howling in pain and doubled up, his forehead practically touching the floor.

"I won't ask how you stumbled upon our operation or how you got past the guards."

"What, aren't you even a little bit interested?" Ulysses managed between agonised gasps.

"No. Such details are irrelevant now because you're never going to get out of here alive."

Eyes watering from the pain of the kick to his stomach Ulysses nonetheless managed to raise himself enough to fix the terrorist with a withering stare.

"I know exactly what's been going on down here, you traitorous bastard." His voice was a strained snarl of contempt. "And when the authorities pick up my message..."

"Again, irrelevant. You're never going to get the chance to report back to those self-serving idiots who so desperately hang on to the failing status quo. You're too late."

"Too late?" Ulysses coughed. "I would think that a handful of Special Forces strike teams are on their way down here as we speak."

"But your masters in Whitehall have no idea what is right beneath their feet."

"Oh no?" Ulysses purred. "Before your goons here picked me up I sent a coded message to those in the know."

"What on this?" Kane held out a hand. One of those same goons who had searched Ulysses passed the terrorist his waterlogged personal communicator.

"I doubt very much that this is working after its dunking in God knows what."

At least they hadn't found where he had hidden Galapagos' locket.

"Well, it was worth a try."

Kane hit him again.

"Will you stop doing that?" Ulysses screamed, his nerve suddenly snapping.

Kane looked down at him, eyes narrowing.

"No one's coming down here to look for you. There are no strike teams on their way. And there is nothing to stop us proceeding according to schedule. But what should we do with you?"

"I expect your mother asks the same question on a daily basis," Ulysses threw back.

"What shall we do with him, Mr Tesla? Any ideas?" Kane mused, feigning indecision.

"We could use him as a test subject, Agent Kane," the goggled scientist suggested. "Strap him to one of the devices, set it off in one of the lower tunnels. See what happens."

"Hmm, fun as that sounds I don't think so. It would be a waste of resources. No, but I do like the sound of the lower tunnels. Bring the bastard with you and follow me," Kane said addressing the two guards, "and bring some rope as well."

Ulysses was dragged back down the steps by which he had entered and back to the flooded Underground tunnels. The two guards heaved him into the numbing, fetid water and, at Kane's direction, forced him down into the chill subterranean canal. But he was not prepared to go willingly to his doom. In desperation he struggled to free himself until, eventually, Kane put an end to his thrashing by giving him a kick to the head.

Barely conscious, Ulysses could do nothing as the guards tied both his hands and feet to the rusted rails submerged beneath the water, leaving only his head above the filmy surface. Once he was secured Kane crouched at the edge of the platform and looked down at his prisoner, shining a flashlight into Ulysses' eyes.

"You want to know something interesting about these tunnels?" he said with a dark smile. "The water that fills this flooded labyrinth comes straight from the Thames, and just as the Thames is a tidal river, so these channels too are tidal. Only, because the water's forced into such constricted passageways, as the river rises the water level in these tunnels can change dramatically. The water in here can come right up to the top of those stairs we came down by and the tide's on the turn. I'll let you work the rest of it out for yourself."

Kane rose, ignoring Ulysses – who made to shift the ropes by pulling with his arms and trying to bring his knees up – and spoke to his fellow conspirators. "Fun's over. Get back to work. The clock is ticking. The new dawn is coming."

As the scientist and guards left, Kane hung back, looking down at the futilely struggling Ulysses once more. "Any last words? Any snappy retorts? A last clever one-liner by which you would like to be remembered?"

"I hope you burn in the hell of your own making!"

"Oh yes, very witty. Very clever. Say hello to eternity for me."

With that Jago Kane turned on his heel and left.

Alone in the cold and the dark Ulysses contemplated his fate. If he could loosen his bonds even just a little he might be able to create enough friction between them and the rusted rails to break through. Muscles bunching he pulled, feeling the rough hemp of the rope rubbing the flesh of his wrists raw. Similar agonies were being suffered by his ankles.

Was it his imagination or was the water level in the tunnel already beginning to rise? As Ulysses thrashed against his bonds, his head aching from the cruel blows he had received, the water splashed against his face and he spluttered to keep it out of his mouth.

Ulysses did not consider himself a particularly godly man but now seemed like an ideal occasion to become better acquainted with the Almighty before they actually met face-to-face. Closing his eyes, arms and legs still straining, he prayed for a miracle.

His constant struggling was beginning to take its toll. The throbbing in his head was worsening and white-hot pokers of lightning pain shot through his muscles. Gritting his teeth he let out a great howl of rage, frustration and exhaustion. Filthy black water poured into his mouth. Ulysses coughed, gagging on the brackish liquid, and cleared it from his mouth with a gob of oily phlegm.

For a moment he stopped struggling, submerged up to his neck, muscles straining to keep his head back out of the water. It was in that moment that he heard a tiny splash – little more than a ripple – as something lithe and sinuous broke the surface of the water.

In the meagre luminosity of the moss patches Ulysses could not see what it was that was approaching him, but he could see it in his mind's eye all too clearly. His desperate sixth sense, scratching furiously at the inside of his skull, wailed at him from his subconscious.

Something touched his leg and Ulysses kicked out. A wall of water suddenly rose out of the murky flood in front of him. Then, as it cascaded away, the hulking, hideously changed shape was revealed to him, a dark shadow that glistened in the near-impenetrable gloom. Ulysses could make out the outline of its broad, curving shoulders, muscular arms and barrel-like torso. But there was something else, the impression of an equally broad toad-like head, a wide mouth bristling with needle-like teeth. Smooth skin glistened. A hand – fingers more like sucker-tipped tentacles than shredding talons – reached out and stroked Ulysses face, the languid touch making him shudder in revulsion. He felt the caress of a finned tail against his legs.

Part of Ulysses' subconscious mind, disconnected by the horror and desperation of the moment, reasoned that Professor Galapagos had tracked him down at last, and yet that this was not the same Professor Galapagos he had battled at the edge of the sewer precipice. The damned biologist had changed again, into something soft-bodied, amphibian, newt-like.

But no matter what the truth of the weird science behind it all, Ulysses knew that he was still going to die and resigned himself to his fate.

However, God had clearly decided that it was not yet time for his meeting with the dandy, for it was then that the longed-for miracle came.

A shot rang out through the flooded tunnel, the unreal acoustics of the place giving its echo a strange, otherworldly quality. The amphibian-Galapagos turned, distracted.

There was a second shot. The creature howled – a grotesque wailing hiss, a grisly parody of a voice – and suddenly the Underground station was filled with the noise of splashing, human shouts and half-human yelping.

Something bounded out of the darkness, leaping through the water towards Ulysses, yowling as it did so, all pallid flesh and lank hair flapping around its shoulders. This new arrival sounded like it was trying to scare the amphibian away, and it was working. The amphibian recoiled, hissing in annoyed retaliation. Then the Neanderthal was on top of it, fists flailing. The toad-creature fought back but the proto-human soon proved itself to be stronger. The Galapagos-amphibian freed itself from the Neanderthal's clutches and, as its attacker lunged again, the apeman determined to trap the huge newt in a crushing bear hug, the creature slipped back under the water and was gone.

Torchlight flickered across the tunnel walls. There was more splashing as another figure strode through the water towards Ulysses.

"Sir," came an acutely cultured voice, the sound of

which filled Ulysses with unadulterated relief. "It looks like you could do with a hand."

Ulysses opened his mouth to speak but water rushed in before he could say a word. The tide was still rising.

His faithful manservant reached him in four more strides and, attempting to haul him up out of the water, immediately made an accurate assessment of the situation. It took Nimrod no time at all to take a knife to the knots and free his master, lifting him under his arms and up onto the station platform.

"Just in the nick of time, eh, Nimrod?" Ulysses managed before his body was wracked again by hacking coughs.

"It is a batman's duty, sir. After all, look what happens when you're left to your own devices," Nimrod added, rolling Ulysses onto his side on the cold, wet platform.

The last of the oily water dribbled from the side of Ulysses' mouth. He lay there for a moment, gathering his reserves of strength. "Are you alright Nimrod?"

"Apart from smelling like a blocked drain," the manservant replied, his nose wrinkling, "I suppose so." Nimrod looked as dishevelled and unkempt as Ulysses felt, quite a contrast to his usual impeccable appearance. "A few more shots from my pistol soon sent that despicable lizard-thing running for cover."

"They've got a factory down here, Nimrod. A bloody bomb factory!" Ulysses spluttered between hacking coughs, as his body expelled the rancid water from his lungs, trying to push himself up on his hands. "We've got to shut it down."

"All in good time, sir. You've just narrowly escaped drowning."

Ulysses gave in to the coughing fit seizing his body, and closed his eyes against the pain for a moment. Nimrod was right. The Waterloo operation could wait five minutes. Kane and the Darwinian Dawn wouldn't be going anywhere in a hurry.

There was more splashing and Ulysses opened his eyes to be greeted by a guttural grunt and the lumpen face of the Neanderthal peering at him from the edge of the water channel. He blinked. Its face a gormless mask, the proto-human blinked earnestly back.

"Nimrod," Ulysses croaked, "you appear to have found yourself a friend."

"Yes, sir." Nimrod glanced at the Neanderthal, making no effort to hide his expression of disdain. "It would appear that he – it – followed us down into the sewers after all. I bumped into him – *it!* – again after driving off the saurian, sir. Couldn't get rid of the bally thing after that, and believe me, I tried."

"Why didn't you shoot it then?" Ulysses said, managing a tired smile.

"It would seem that I simply hadn't the heart, sir."

"Fortunately for me, as it would transpire."

"As you say, sir, fortunately for you. It was the brute that tracked you down here. I think it somehow managed to follow your scent, despite the hellish stench of these tunnels."

"And now he's saved me from poor Professor Galapagos' attentions again. Did you see what he's become now, Nimrod?"

"Barely, sir."

"He looks like a ruddy great toad, or a newt or something. There can't be much further for him to travel back down the evolutionary ladder before he's just pond slime."

"So it would seem, sir."

"But anyway," Ulysses said, sitting up and starting to rise to his feet, "back to more pressing matters. The bomb factory."

"Very well, sir."

By the time Ulysses had led Nimrod back to the station concourse and its wheezing, rattling production line, there was no longer any sign of Jago Kane or the scientist-engineer, Tesla.

"What now, sir?" Nimrod whispered as the two of them peered around a tiled pillar.

"The devices come off that conveyor over there," he said, pointing through the clouds of filthy steam. "If we can find where they're storing them, I think from that point on it would be a relatively straightforward thing to bring an end to this terrorist facility."

"What did you have in mind, sir?" Nimrod asked guardedly.

"Just a few fireworks. Nothing spectacular."

"And how do you suggest we achieve the initial part of your plan?"

"Oh, you know me, Nimrod. I'm making this up as I go along. We need a distraction. Something that will keep those guards off our backs."

There was a grunt from the shadows behind them. The Neanderthal knuckled over to the two men.

"By Jove, Nimrod, I think this fellow here's got the right idea. I think he understands just what we've got in mind."

"You think he can understand more than a few simple phrases?"

"You shouldn't have such low expectations of your new

friend. He's not a dog, you know? What do you say, boy?" Ulysses said, turning to the Neanderthal. "Do you think you could cause a bit of a rumpus in there for us?"

The hulking subhuman nodded excitedly, his tongue lolling from his mouth like that of a happy hound.

"Off you go then."

Scampering forwards on all fours the Neanderthal disappeared into the obscuring smog of the factory floor.

"And good luck, eh, old chap?"

It was only a matter of moments before startled shouts of surprise came to their ears followed rapidly by the chatter of sub-automatic gunfire as the Neanderthal swung out of the roiling smoke right into the midst of the Dawn's guards, only to disappear back into the obscuring clouds a moment later.

It was exactly what Ulysses had hoped for.

"Come on, Nimrod. Let's get this party going with a bang!"

"Are you sure this is a good idea, sir?" Nimrod asked, with the tone of a disapproving schoolmaster, as Ulysses ran his hands over the explosive device on the gurney in front of him. Its hard metal body was a full metre in diameter.

"Don't worry, Nimrod," Ulysses said, flashing a devilish grin. "Remember, I've seen how these things were constructed. Now if I turn this knob here, and then depress this switch here..."

The bomb on the rack in front of him had been silent all the while Ulysses had been examining it. But with the depression of the button an ominous ticking commenced somewhere inside the spiked steel ball.

"Ah, I think it's time we weren't here, Nimrod." Ulysses jumped to his feet.

"I couldn't agree more, sir."

The two men sprinted out of the side passage and back across the concourse, not caring now whether they were seen or not.

Explosions ripped through the station, shaking its very foundations, as one detonation after another tore through the factory, bringing the great conveyor production line to a standstill before blasting the machinery to smithereens. The wreckage of monstrous steam presses was hurled about, along with the shattered remains of automata-workers. The mutant workforce died or fled in panic, Darwinian Dawn troopers and scientists suddenly made equal by the threat of sudden, violent death.

"This way!" Ulysses yelled over the sounds of destruction ringing in their ears. They ran hell-for-leather across the concourse and through the archway underneath the Waterloo sign. They found themselves in a broader exit tunnel. There was another concussive blast behind them and dust and fractured tiles fell from the roof.

It was then that Ulysses' sixth sense screamed a warning. He skidded to a halt. "Nimrod, back!" he shouted. "The roof's about to–" before he could finish his warning, with a yawning heave the roof of the tunnel came down ahead of them.

The two men turned tail, running back the way they had come, back towards the inferno that had taken hold of the factory.

"Bloody hellfire!" Ulysses exclaimed. "Now where?"

"Over there, sir!" Nimrod shouted, pointing back to the archway through which they had entered the factory. The Neanderthal was hunched there, its body smeared with soot, blood running from a number of gashes, but otherwise alive.

Ulysses didn't need any further encouragement. The dandy gentleman investigator and his manservant legged it back across the concourse – dodging falling masonry, throwing up their arms to protect their faces from the fierce heat and flying shrapnel of shattered machines.

As Nimrod joined the Neanderthal beyond the archway, Ulysses stumbled, his foot catching against a fallen scientist. In one hand the man – who was either dead or unconscious – clutched a clipboard, the notes it held sullied with stone dust and soot.

"What have we here?" Ulysses wondered.

"Sir, you must hurry!" Nimrod shouted back over the thunderous rumble of destruction.

"Don't worry about me," he called back, snatching up the clipboard in one hand, "you get yourselves out. I'm right behind you."

And then the three of them – master, servant and Neanderthal – were stumbling back down the steps to the flooded station platform. Their feet splashed into several inches of water, the tidal Thames having risen the level as Jago Kane had said it would. Had the Neanderthal not tracked him down here, Ulysses would have drowned in that same stinking tunnel.

There was another shuddering blast and a fireball of intense ferocity rushed down the stairs after them.

"Into the water!" Ulysses screamed, throwing himself forwards, pushing the subhuman and his manservant into the water ahead of him.

As the water closed over their heads, the flames ignited the pollutant film on its surface.

Ulysses surfaced again, some way further down the tunnel, amidst patches of flame. Nimrod and the Neanderthal both surfaced nearby.

"Nimrod, are you alright?"

His manservant gave him a wet, disgruntled look. "Again, apart from being soaked to the skin and smelling like a petrol sump, yes, sir."

A strong rubbery hand grabbed hold of Ulysses' leg and yanked him sharply back under the water. Lit by the burning pollution on its surface, through the filthy murk Ulysses could see the fish-like features of the amphibian-Galapagos. The professor was persistent, he'd give him that.

For a moment his eyes met the lidless jellied orbs of the altered thing and a startled cry escaped his mouth in a rush of bubbles. Then he was kicking furiously at the creature. He planted a foot squarely between the fish-thing's eyes and the creature's grip went slack.

Ulysses surfaced again, gasping for air, followed almost immediately by the Galapagos thing, breaking the surface in an impressive salmon leap. The monster landed on top of him. Nimrod was shouting behind him, the Neanderthal splashing through the water towards him too, but Ulysses had the creature by the throat now. The tables had been turned.

Another explosion ripped through the tunnel and a fiery wind swept over the water's surface. Shielded from the blast by the creature in front of him, Ulysses witnessed something the like of which he had never known despite all he had seen in his curious life.

With a hideous gulping gasp, like a fishy death-sigh, the creature stopped fighting him and went limp. He could feel his hands sinking into its unnatural flesh as it went soft around them. It felt like he was putting his hands into buckets of cold semolina pudding. And then, quite simply, Professor Galapagos's body collapsed in on itself, the flesh dissolved into slime. Its fish-face mere inches from his own, Ulysses stared into its horrible liquid eyes, unable to tear his gaze away, as those same eyes melted like hot wax.

In mere moments all that was left of the transformed professor were strings of glutinous protoplasmic slime, cooking like frogspawn amidst the burning residue all around them.

Professor Galapagos – or rather the evolutionary-regressing freak that he had become – was gone.

CHAPTER FIFTEEN

On Evolution and the Modern Man

"So, doctor," Ulysses said, entering the hallway of the old man's house, "how are you?"

Doctor Methuselah blinked myopically from behind the bottle-bottom lenses of his spectacles. Despite having obviously made a supreme effort to uphold his usual high standards of dress, being attired in a crushed blue velvet frock coat, moss green satin waistcoat and lilac cravat, with charcoal grey moleskin trousers, the gentleman adventurer did not seem to be quite the same man who had visited him the previous month. He appeared drawn and tired, his cheeks hollow, his eyes sunken and grey. His skin had a waxy sheen to it.

"Better than you, by the looks of things."

The old man shuffled off along the hallway towards the back of the crumbling house, as decrepit in appearance as its badly aging owner. Ulysses followed. After his sojourn in the sewers he was barely even aware of the malingering odour of stale tobacco smoke. Half the time he still thought he could smell the cesspit-stink of the effluent tunnels.

He might look like death warmed up but it was better than *feeling* like death, which was precisely how he had felt for the last week. His days and nights had been spent vomiting every few hours, reduced to a shaking wreck following relentless barrages of diarrhoea. For all the mental training and physical healing he had received in the highlands of the Himalayas, they did nothing to alleviate the gut-knotting agony this bout of sickness brought. There was nothing he had been able to do but wait it out.

On top of that it had taken half a dozen baths since returning to his Mayfair home, scrubbing himself with industrial cleaner to rid himself of the stink of the sewers, and even now he could still sometimes catch the acrid, bile-taste of the chem-polluted water in the back of his throat.

But on this morning he had actually managed to get out of bed and so, having carried out his ablutions and dressed to impress, bloodstone cane in hand, he had set out to pay a visit to the curmudgeonly Dr Methuselah. And although he didn't want to admit it – least of all to himself – even that simple effort had weakened him.

"So enough of this small talk, what news?"

"I take it you mean the sample."

"Of course." Ulysses tapped the end of his cane impatiently against an overburdened worktable.

"That was a very interesting little project you set me," Methuselah said, powering up his difference engine. There was a hum as the cathode ray tube came to life. "Look at this." He pointed at the grainy, green and black image coming into focus on the screen.

Ulysses realised that there was a Petri dish already in place under the magnifying lenses of Methuselah's brass microscope. The image on the screen was obviously a significantly enlarged image of the contents of that dish. At his last visit Ulysses had at least been able to determine that he was looking at the image of cells projected on the screen. This time, however, he couldn't make out a thing.

"What am I supposed to be looking at, doctor? I can't see anything."

"Precisely."

"What do you mean?"

"There's nothing there to look at."

"But isn't that the sample I gave you?"

"Yes, but that's the point."

"What's the point?" Ulysses suddenly felt incredibly weary. The effort of being up and about was taking its toll more that he had expected. "Doctor, I am tired. Please explain."

The old man grunted, hawking phlegm into the back of his mouth, and pushed his glasses back up his nose with an index finger ingrained with dirt.

"It's like this. I maintained close observation of the tissue sample, as requested. And my initial hypothesis proved, in time, to be correct. What started out as a few hairs first took on the qualities of lizard scales, then the cells mutated into those I would expect to find in an amphibian – the Central American axolotl was the closest match I could find. Towards the end of my observations it became apparent that the process of cellular degradation was accelerating. The sample briefly exhibited piscine characteristics and then it simply dissolved into slime. Look."

Methuselah removed the Petri dish from beneath the microscope and passed it to Ulysses. Where there had once been three reddish-brown hairs there was now what looked like nothing more than a blob of snot.

"What you're looking at is now just so much biological detritus. The only cells in there belong to the bacteria no doubt feasting on that gunk. It's not even protoplasmic slime anymore. Total cellular collapse."

"Do you know what could have caused it?"

"Why, yes." Ulysses looked at the doctor in excited anticipation. "Acute genetic-regression. And I would extrapolate that precisely the same thing happened to the subject the original sample came from. Is that not the case?"

"Evolution and the modern man, eh?"

"You're sure you don't want to tell me where these came from?"

"You know better than to ask," Ulysses chided, remaining tight-lipped. Professor Galapagos might now be dead, having literally turned to slime in Ulysses' hands but this case still qualified as one that was a potential threat to national security.

"Have it your way," Methuselah grumbled. "So, what happened to you? Did you find the errant professor?"

"How do you know about that?" Ulysses said sharply, alarm bells ringing in his mind, suddenly suspicious.

"Don't get your knickers in a twist. You're not the only one with contacts, you know. So, did you?"

"After a fashion."

"What was it like? How did it happen?" Methuselah said, almost slavering at the prospect, his interest having been piqued, his eyes alight with eager, almost boyish, excitement.

Ulysses paused, considering his next words very carefully.

"It was... messy."

"Is that all you're going to give me?"

"That's probably more than I should have told you already," Ulysses muttered, unable to get the image of the overgrown trout-face bearing down on him before turning to milky frogspawn out of his mind. "Now," he said, reaching into a coat pocket and pulling out the curious barbed locket he had recovered from the Galapagos-lizard, "what can you tell me about this?"

Genevieve Galapagos was standing in the shadow cast by the gleaming golden Albert Memorial. Ulysses realised, with momentary surprise, that she was wearing a full-length dress, pale cream with a lilac flowery pattern. It was the first time he had ever seen her wear anything other than trousers or jodhpurs. Her luxuriant auburn tresses were gathered together beneath a small bonnet. He felt a rush of warm adrenalin in his chest and let out a sigh. She was strikingly beautiful. And then her eyes met his. She looked so... womanly. Not that she had not looked so before, but her appearance now leant her a vulnerable, feminine quality.

"Ulysses!" she gasped and, despite the restricting nature of the dress, trotted over and flung her arms around him, trapping him in a heartfelt hug. "It's wonderful to see you again." She squeezed him again and then, as if suddenly remembering herself, held him back at arm's length. "Um, I did call but your butler sent me away."

"Yes he did say. I was sorry not to be able to see you, my dear," Ulysses felt an earnest need to apologise, "but I was... indisposed."

"So I understand. Nimrod said that you had been through quite an ordeal."

"Yes, you could say that. But it's in the hands of the police now."

Much as he resented having to pass the operation into the hands of Inspector Allardyce, Ulysses knew when a situation demanded more than merely he was capable of. He was still intermittently suffering from the dysentery that he had picked up following his foray into London's murky underworld. But the escapade had brought its own benefits as well; the paperwork he had been able to salvage from the clipboard he had rescued from the burning factory, for one thing.

It was amazing that he had been able to salvage anything at all, considering that the papers had been scorched and then submerged in water as Ulysses, Nimrod and the Neanderthal had made their escape from the flooded Underground, which had necessitated allowing themselves to be sucked through an overflow pipe that ejected them into the Thames.

After some careful scrutiny, the documents had revealed a crucial part of the terrible plan the Darwinian Dawn had for the capital. They had been intending to use the old Underground network to position the deadly explosive devices they had been developing throughout the city. Had they succeeded in completing their task the cost to the city in terms of collateral damage, as well as the cost in human life, would have been catastrophic. The death toll could easily have been in the thousands, if not the tens of thousands.

But thanks to Ulysses' timely discovery, their plans had been irrevocably set back and even though it was suspected that a number of the devices had already been put in place, so far none had detonated. With the authorities now in possession of information as useful as a map, having reluctantly already reported his findings regarding the bomb plot to Inspector Allardyce, Scotland Yard had raced to mount a top priority security operation to recover all of the devices. It looked like matters would be brought to a resolution in time for the Queen's jubilee.

"To think what you went through!" Genevieve exclaimed.

Ulysses smiled. Despite being every inch the ladies' man, there was something innocent and disarming about the genuine affection and concern Genevieve was showing him. It made what he had to tell her all the harder.

"I'm all the better for seeing you. Walk with me?"

"But of course," Genevieve took his proffered arm. "What

is it, Ulysses? Your manner is causing me concern."

The two of them set off, strolling along beneath the beech trees, joining other promenaders, dog-walkers and penny-farthing enthusiasts in their tour of Hyde Park.

"I have news concerning your father."

Genevieve stopped. "I knew you would have. I was too afraid to ask." She looked at him again, her eyes shaded beneath the rim of her parasol. "It's not good news, is it?"

"No, I'm afraid not."

Genevieve's chin dropped and she gave a sob of heartfelt sorrow.

"I'm so sorry, Genevieve, I really am. If there had been anything I could have done I would have, you have to believe that. We found him in..."

"No, don't tell me. I don't want to know. My father died that night at the museum, the night of the robbery. Whatever he had become after that, it was not my father. Not anymore."

And then she gave in to her tears. Ulysses held her close, Genevieve sobbing into the lapel of his frock coat.

It had not been so hard in the end. As Genevieve herself had once told him, he was a champion of the truth and no matter how painful the truth might be, it should be known so that it could be faced up to.

Neither of them cared that the eyes of half the promenaders in the park were on them. For them there was only their shared grief. Genevieve mourning the loss of the father she had never really known, and for Ulysses the knowledge that he had been responsible for causing her such heart-rending sadness.

Eventually she eased herself away from him, blinking the tears from her reddened, puffy eyes. She could not look him in the face.

"Here," he said, putting his hand into his coat and removing something from a pocket. "I have this for you."

He opened his hand. There lay the locket Genevieve had told him she had once given to her father as a gift. A smile of incongruous delight broke through her sorrow-spoiled features. Her bottom lip started to quiver as she took the silvered object, clean now of the muck that had tarnished it on its journey through the sewers.

She reached up, putting a soft hand to Ulysses' face, caressing his cheek with delicate fingers. "Thank you," she whispered.

And then, before Ulysses really knew it, they were closer than they had ever been before, her lips only inches from his, her breath warm on his face. The air was heady with the scent of jasmine flowers, the ground beneath their feet dappled with the golden light filtering through the leafy branches, despite the ever-present smog over the city.

He held that moment in his head, that perfect moment when nothing else but the anticipation of the kiss to come mattered.

"We aren't close to any Overground lines here are we? Or dinosaurs?"

Genevieve smiled, her tear-stained cheeks flushed red, and she pulled him closer.

"Now, now, Mr Quicksilver," she chided. "Do you always put work before pleasure?"

And then they kissed.

CHAPTER SIXTEEN

A Night at the Opera

"So, do you think you'll see this woman again?" Bartholomew Quicksilver asked, tucking into his plate of roast pheasant with such gusto that it rather implied that this was the first decent meal he had enjoyed for some time.

"I don't know," Ulysses mused, looking up from his plate. "I would certainly like to, at least I think I would, but I rather suspect that the ball, as they say, is now in her court. But enough about me. How have you been since I last saw you, dear brother?" This last acerbic comment did not sound quite like the enquiry after his brother's health as the wording of it might have suggested.

"About that," Bartholomew said, his face reddening.

"And what would *that* be?"

"Look don't make this harder than it already is."

"Why not? You were certainly planning on making it quite hard for me, all things considered."

"Look, you have to believe me. I didn't know you were still alive."

"Patently."

There was silence between the two of them for a minute.

"Go on then. With your excuse, I mean." Ulysses had to admit that part of him was enjoying watching his brother squirm.

For a moment Bartholomew struggled to find the words he needed to express himself. The hubbub of the Savoy rushed in to fill the vacuum left by his reticence.

The dining room was a sea of hazy lamplight, interspersed with the circular tables of the diners. For a moment Ulysses could almost believe that he had returned to his former life of evening revels and outrageous parties.

He shook the memory from his mind. That seemed a lifetime away now. Besides, he felt an ambivalent mix of rival emotions, both purposeful resolve and nervous anticipation at the same time. Resolve at needing to confront his brother and nervous as to the effect the rich food in front of him might have on his body. It was the first full meal he had eaten since rising from his sick bed.

"Look, I acted too hastily. I know that now. But you have to realise that there had been no word from you or any sign of you for eighteen months. I thought you were dead. The *world* thought you were dead. Would you have had me wait indefinitely for you to return?"

"And what would you say if I answered your obviously rhetorical question with a 'yes'?"

"I'd say you were being pig-headed, just like you always were when we were boys and Nanny wouldn't let you get your own way."

For a moment both of them sat in seething silence again.

"But look, let's put all that in the past now, shall we?' Bartholomew ventured, at last facing up to the fact that it was going to have to be up to him to proffer the olive branch. For all the grovelling he was being made to do, Bartholomew might as well have been eating humble pie rather than roast pheasant. Taking up his wine glass, he gestured as if to make a toast.

"To you, eh, Ulysses? No hard feelings?"

Almost reluctantly Ulysses picked up his own glass.

"No, to us, Barty, heirs to the Quicksilver name," he

said, and knocked back the last of the Pinot Grigio.

The hubbub of the Savoy returned and the two brothers finished the rest of their main course in a tolerable silence.

"How's business?" the younger asked at last.

"Oh, you know, a matter of life and death on a daily basis. How's the world of profit and loss, and fund management?"

Bartholomew eyed his elder brother coldly. 'Fund management' was a coy euphemism for a compulsive gambling habit of which Ulysses was fully aware. He also knew what sort of situations his brother had gambled himself into over the years, which was why he guarded the rest of his family's fortune with such care.

Ulysses met the younger man's stare, his brother quickly wilting under the sun-fierce gaze and suddenly finding something to occupy his attention on the tablecloth in front of him.

"Well?"

"Oh, you know how it is."

"Yes, I rather think I do. Still planning on leaving the capital, or even the planet, anytime soon?"

"Hmm. Funds won't stretch that far."

"Now why doesn't that surprise me I wonder," Ulysses said witheringly, shaking his head in disappointment at his feckless brother's mismanagement of his share of their father's legacy.

"I wasn't going to bring it up," Barty said, an uncomfortably familiar wheedling whine entering his voice, "but as you've seen fit to raise the matter yourself, if you could shout me some cash – consider it a loan – I could purchase my passage on a lunar liner and be out of your way at last, dear brother."

"And what would you do once you got to the moon?"

"I've got a few job prospects lined up there, one out at Serenity, another couple of possibles in Luna Prime. You know, friend of a friend kind of things."

"Yes, I know the kind of thing. And I know the sort of people you curiously choose to call friends."

"Now, don't start, Ulysses."

"Well, you said it. If you're not going to look out for yourself, who else will, if not me?"

"You're not father, you know."

Ulysses was quiet for a moment, as if wrong-footed by his brother's riposte. "Yes, I know."

"How's your dinner?" Bartholomew said, obviously uncomfortable and trying to change the topic.

"Well, the warm roasted wood pigeon salad with black truffle sauce was barely warm and the pigeon not as tender as I would have liked. The wine is not to my palate, the company tolerable. Let's hope the dessert is something more worthy of writing home about. Although, whatever the final outcome of this entire dining experience, I rather suspect that I'll be made to suffer for my excess in the morning."

"I'm sorry I asked," Barty said miserably.

The awkward silence returned.

Neither of them said anything as a waiter cleared their plates away, topped up their wine glasses and then brought them their desserts. Ulysses' chocolate torte was more to his liking, although even as he savoured the last mouthful he rather regretted such a rich choice of dessert.

He put down his fork and looked at his forlorn brother. Despite being the younger of the two of them, and despite all that Ulysses had been through, Barty looked to be the more harassed and careworn by life. A curl of hair had come free and hung in front of his eyes. His shoulders looked bowed as if the weight of the world rested upon them. His skin had an unhealthy pallor to it and his red-rimmed eyes belied a lack of sleep. "When was the last time you ate a meal like that? Come to think of it, when did you last get a decent night's sleep?" he asked.

"What do you care?" Barty riled at his brother's condescending tone.

"Of course I care, you ungrateful wretch," Ulysses sighed. "Anyway, this dinner was supposed to be a reconciliation. Let's not fight anymore. I have enough enemies in this world without my brother being one of them. What's done is done, and there's been no real harm as a result either. Pax?"

Ulysses offered his hand across the table. Bartholomew maintained his grumpy demeanour for a few moments more before relenting.

"Pax," he agreed and the two brothers shook.

"Now let's settle up here or we're going to be late for curtain up."

Ulysses summoned a waiter. "Can I get you anything else, sir? Coffee? Liqueurs?"

"Just the bill," Ulysses said.

"Ah, about that too."

Ulysses gave his brother a withering look. "It's on me, as usual," Bartholomew visibly relaxed, "as is tonight's performance of Puccini. Now let's get out of here."

Dinner paid for, the Quicksilver brothers left the Savoy and made their way to the Covent Garden Opera House, there to join the expectant throng awaiting that night's performance of Madame Butterfly. The opera lasted a barely tolerable three hours, at the end of which the two brothers departed the auditorium, with a feeling akin to what it must be like to be released from a stay in prison.

"How did you find it?" Barty asked as the two of them made their way across the cobbled forecourt in front of the Opera House.

"About as good as the meal beforehand," Ulysses said cuttingly.

"That bad?" Bartholomew laughed. He appeared significantly more relaxed than he had during dinner. The two double whiskys during the interval had helped, of course.

"Perhaps not that bad. Although, to my mind, the character of a nubile, teenage Japanese *geisha* girl should not really be played by a middle-aged soprano with a figure like a circus wrestler, and the body hair to match."

His brother laughed heartily. "I know what you mean. And the dashing young lieutenant looked like he'd be out of breath dashing for an omnibus!"

"You're right there, Barty, old chap."

"Is one supposed to *enjoy* opera?"

"No, I don't think so. It's just one of those tiresome things one must be seen to do if one is to be received into polite society – rather like plucking one's eyebrows or visiting the dentist. I only partake myself because it is part of the social high life and it is good for one to be seen to be doing such things. I just wanted to go – having not been for so long – to confirm to myself how bad it is. And, of course, the ladies love it! Now then, back to mine for a nightcap? Nimrod should have the Phantom parked around here somewhere."

"Yes, why not?"

The subconscious warning came like a burst of lightning in his brain even as the shot rang out, echoing like a thunderclap from the close-packed buildings that lined the square. He had no conscious idea of where the threat lay, only that he must move.

Ulysses lurched sideways. There was the report of a second shot. Barty gasped as if he had been plunged into an ice cold bath. He slumped forwards, Ulysses caught him, stopping him from falling flat on his face on the cobbles.

"Barty? Barty!" he cried, easing his brother down onto the ground. He was barely aware of the cries of panic around him.

"I-I've been shot," Bartholomew gasped. "Bloody hell, I've been shot!"

Ulysses carried out a hasty assessment, fully aware of the fact that there was a sniper still scoping their position from somewhere on the rooftops nearby. His brother was shaking whilst blood oozed from the newly made hole in the shoulder of his jacket.

"Try to stay calm," Ulysses said, keeping his voice low so as not to heighten his brother's state of anxiety.

"Stay calm? I've been bloody shot!"

"Look, you're in shock." Ulysses whipped off his jacket and draped it over his brother's prone body.

"Of course I'm in shock. I keep trying to tell you, I've bloody well been shot!"

"If you don't shut up, I'll shoot you myself!"

Ulysses scanned the tops of the surrounding buildings, trying to glimpse anything that might reveal the position of the would-be assassin – the reflection of a streetlamp from a gun barrel, a shudder of movement as the gunman adjusted his position – anything at all.

The bullet had been meant for him, he was sure of it. Of course, when he considered the sort of company his brother kept and factored in the debts he doubtless owed, it was possible that the gunman had really been targeting him but Ulysses' sixth sense had warned him of the danger *he* had been about to face.

Two shots. Anyone attempting an assassination would like as not be using a rifle with two cartridges in the chamber. They would not risk reloading unless they were prepared to give their position away. Right now, the sniper would be putting a previously prepared getaway plan into operation.

There was the sound of someone running across the cobbles towards them. It was Nimrod.

"I heard the gunshots, sir. Are you alright?"

"I am but Barty's been hit. Will you take care of things here?"

"Of course, sir."

"I have a gunman to catch."

As Nimrod rested Bartholomew's head against his knees, Ulysses patted his brother gently on the shoulder. "No hard feelings, eh, Barty?" And with that he hared off across the plaza.

After hearing the second shot, and considering the angle of trajectory of the bullet that had hit Bartholomew, Ulysses judged that the gunman had been hunkered down on the rooftops of the buildings on the south side of the square.

He sprinted across the cobbles, barging past drunken fops and London's social elite making their way home. As he ran, senses straining for any clues as to where the gunman might have gone, Ulysses' mind was awhirl as he considered the identity of the would-be assassin. Who could it be, and how long had the marksman been trailing him? Was it Jago Kane, surfacing again to put paid to his old adversary once and for all? Ulysses had his doubts about that; it wasn't Kane's style. And although Ulysses had made a fair few enemies in his somewhat chequered career as a soldier of fortune and agent of the crown, he was pretty certain that whoever the gunman was, he was like as not working for the Darwinian Dawn. Whether he was an agent of the terrorist organisation or simply a hit man hired to off the dandy adventurer after he had set back their plans, Ulysses was sure of his connection with the enemy.

But in the end, as he ran down an adjoining street towards the Strand, he had to admit that his pursuit was futile. He didn't even know if he *was* pursuing anyone. He could have been haring off in completely the wrong direction. The cowardly gunman had both the city and the night on his side. The two working together to swallow him up and hide him in mundane normality.

Ulysses was aware that his footsteps sounded incongruously loud as they rang from the pavement, passers-by watching his mad dash with incredulous, slack-jawed curiosity. With a snarl of frustration he came to a stop in a pool of wan light cast by a crackling street light. His acute sixth sense was quiet again. The danger had passed, for the time being, but Ulysses knew that it would not be long before jeopardy and peril came calling again.

His blood boiled in his veins, becoming the bitter bile of rage in his stomach. His brother might be a useless, good-for-nothing compulsive gambler with an unlucky streak a mile long, but he was Ulysses' little brother nonetheless, and, as such, his responsibility.

Whoever the secret assassin had been, he had failed in his mission. Ulysses was still alive. And for as long as that was the case there would inevitably be another attempt on his life. He would have to remain vigilant at all times, or pay the ultimate price.

CHAPTER SEVENTEEN

Revelations

"Excuse me, sir, but will there be anything else?"

Ulysses Quicksilver looked up from the copy of *The Times* he was perusing. Nimrod was standing in the doorway to the mahogany-panelled study. Standing there so rigid and so formal. Back in his grey suit, with his sharp, aquiline features he bore all the characteristics of the grandfather clock that was tolling hauntingly in the atrium hallway behind him.

Ulysses glanced at the brandy glass on the desk in front of him, a slosh of the amber fire still in the bottom of it. He checked his pocket watch despite there being the ormolu clock ticking on the mantelpiece behind him.

"No, it's alright, thank you, Nimrod."

"If you don't mind, then sir, I think I shall retire for the night. It feels like it has been a particularly long day."

"I know what you mean, old chap. I know what you mean."

It was not only Ulysses who had been beset by illness following their escapades through the sewers. Although they had both now been given a clean bill of health they had been left fatigued by their bout of sickness. Nimrod was never one to make a fuss about his own state of health but Ulysses could see the weariness in his eyes, even though his posture was as upright and unbending as ever. Of course the faithful family retainer wasn't a young man anymore. In fact, the silver-haired butler had never been a young man in Ulysses' eyes, ever since he was a young boy growing up in the Mayfair townhouse.

"Oh, Nimrod," Ulysses said suddenly, causing his butler to turn. "Is Barty asleep?"

"Yes, sir. I had his old room made up."

"Yes, I think it better that he remain with us for the time being. Just until we sort this mess out. For his own safety, you understand."

"As you wish. Now, if you don't mind, sir?"

"No, not at all, Nimrod. You get off to bed."

Ulysses returned his attention to the broadsheet in front of him. The butler turned to leave again.

"Oh, I meant to ask," Ulysses said, looking up from his paper again. Nimrod paused once more, a nasal sigh escaping his flaring nostrils. "How's Simeon finding the boot room?"

"You mean the apeman, sir?"

"Yes, Nimrod, our guest. Has he stopped eating the shoe polish yet?"

"I've confiscated the last few tins so that I can maintain standards, sir, and keep the footwear in good order. But yes, the monkey has made himself quite at home in the boot room, sir."

"Now now, Nimrod, he's not a monkey. He's merely an ancestor of the human race. The boot room is opposite your room, is it not?"

"Precisely, sir. It would appear that the coach house was not to his liking, despite being a far superior habitat than the one we originally found him in."

"I think you've made a friend there, Nimrod."

"Hmm," Nimrod replied non-committally. "I thought one was supposed to be able to choose one's friends, sir. It's one's family that one has no say in."

"Well I suppose he is family, after a fashion. Think of him as a very distant relation," Ulysses said with a smile.

"Yes, very amusing, sir. Do you know how long our house guests will be staying, sir?"

"For the foreseeable future, I would say."

"Very well, sir," Nimrod conceded morosely. "Might I ask why you insist on calling the apeman Simeon, sir?"

"The name seemed to suit him, that's all. And besides, if he's going to be part of polite society he needs a name, doesn't he. It will help him appear more – what's the word I'm looking for? – civilised."

"I would suggest that he might appear more civilised, sir, if I could persuade him to wear some clothes. Mrs Prufrock has altered an old suit of her husband's especially. Now, if there's nothing else?" Nimrod said tartly.

"No, I don't think so. Sorry to have kept you. You should turn in for the night. I won't be up much longer myself. I just need to wind down after our rather exciting night at the opera."

"I understand, sir. Good night."

"Good night, Nimrod."

The manservant hesitated. He was quite clearly looking at the large portrait hanging above the mantelpiece and yet there was a far away look in his piercing sapphire eyes. Ulysses couldn't remember ever seeing Nimrod look so vulnerable and open.

"Something troubling you, Nimrod?"

"I was just thinking, sir. You look so like your father."

"Indeed, it has been said before."

Nimrod turned and left the study.

Ulysses returned to the papers arrayed before him on the desk. But he was distracted, considering Simeon's nature once again and, by extension, the nature of mankind in an evolutionary context. It was humbling indeed to be in such close proximity to one's ancestors.

Had Simeon always been as he was now, an example of

one of the previously thought lost tribes of proto-humans that had been found to still exist in some of the most remote parts of the world? Or had he been the unfortunate subject of one of Galapagos' sinister experiments, considering what had befallen the evolutionary biologist himself? It appeared that there was no way of knowing and, if the latter was the case, it was highly unlikely that they would ever discover the real identity of the poor wretch who had somehow devolved into the creature that was now Ulysses' house guest. Professor Ignatius Galapagos had turned out to be a very different man to the dedicated scholar and devoted father Ulysses had at first taken him to be. Very different indeed.

The sound of Nimrod's leather heels on the polished floors of the house receded into its shadowy depths. Ulysses listened to the *tap, tap, tapping* of his servant's footfalls whilst the subconscious part of his mind turned over the myriad thoughts that rose from the fathomless depths like great leviathans, immeasurable, terrifying and dark.

Ulysses finished off the last drop of his cognac, closed his eyes and savoured the fumy tang on his tongue before swallowing. Dreamily he opened his eyes, his gaze falling on the pages of *The Times* spread out in front of him. Scattered across the desk, amidst the carefully selected articles, were various pieces of the last few days' post, some as yet unopened. They included a letter from the firm of Mephisto, Fanshaw and Screwtape, an invitation to join the maiden voyage of a new sub-ocean liner, and something from the Cats Protection League asking for his support.

Ulysses ran his eyes over the articles, his attention flitting from one set of column inches to another, as he absent-mindedly ran the blade of his letter-opener under the sealed tab of a crisp, white envelope.

One bold banner headline read, 'Wormwood Wins Terror Debate' and another, 'Anti-Terror Bill Passed'. So, mused Ulysses as he extracted the folded piece of headed paper from the envelope, Wormwood had got his way. The bill that he had championed and pushed through Parliament had been passed by both the Commons and the House of Lords. But, Ulysses wondered, did those who had voted in its favour realise fully the implications of the new law that effectively permitted one man to take charge of not only the government, but also the country and hence the Empire, should a state of emergency arise?

But of course the politicians must have realised. So in that case, what was in it for them? Ulysses was fully cognisant of the Machiavellian workings of the British Government and the nature of those who sought election to that exclusive gentleman's club. They must have good reason to believe that the intentions of the man into whose control that self-same bill would put the whole country were honourable. But then perhaps they didn't know Uriah Wormwood like Ulysses Quicksilver did. Or maybe they did, and their votes had simply been secured by other, uncomplicated means, such as threatening their lives, the lives of their loved ones or by threatening to air their dirty laundry for them in public.

Ulysses glanced at the letter now in his hands. It was another begging letter from the Chelsea branch of the Women's Institute – who were obviously aware of his existence again following his very public David and Goliath struggle with the rampaging megasaur – asking him to speak about his adventures in the Himalayas at one of their forthcoming tea and cake get-togethers.

He turned a few pages of the paper in front of him, skimming them for anything of particular interest. With the Galapagos case tied up, he would have to start looking for another paying job soon. He doubted Wormwood would be in need of his services in quite the same way as he previously had.

The news items he gleaned from the papers gave him a curious snapshot of the capital of the Magna Britannian empire in the dying days of the twentieth century. Apparently some of the escaped dinosaurs from the Challenger Enclosure were still managing to evade capture. A petition had been sent to 10 Downing Street, and copied to Scotland Yard, asking what the new Prime Minister was going to do about the reptilians' anti-social behaviour. Ulysses wondered for a moment whether he should consider branching out into big game hunting, but then quickly dismissed the idea

There was also a piece about the luxury passenger liner *The Neptune*, which would be setting off on its inaugural cruise around the world from Southampton that summer – Ulysses glanced again at the invitation he had been sent, it was the same vessel – and another article regarding the health of the industrialist and amateur naturalist, Josiah Umbridge.

'Jubilee to go ahead as planned' a spokesman for Buckingham Palace had apparently told a reporter. The preparations for the extravaganza appeared to have been upped a notch or two, since Wormwood had come to the office of Prime Minister and following the Darwinian Dawn's terror attacks. Funnily enough, Ulysses thought, with a wry smile, there had been no further broadcasts or public announcements from the terrorist group or any further attacks on London since Ulysses had brought about the destruction of their bomb production plant. Apparently the jubilee celebration and day-long parades were to conclude with a gala dinner, to be held in the re-built Crystal Palace in Hyde Park.

Beneath the article detailing the arrangements for the celebrations, which marked another decade in Victoria's long reign of more than a century and a half, Ulysses' eyes alighted on a much less obvious, almost secondary consideration of an article title. In fact, it was not so much a headline as a question:

'Anti-social behaviour a thing of the past?'

Ulysses read on. Apparently 'an eminent scientist' was conducting 'exciting and ground-breaking experiments' into 'behaviour adjustment' on inmates at London's maximum-security prison, the Tower of London.

"Not another one," Ulysses found himself saying out loud. He was sure that Professor Galapagos' experiments would have been considered 'exciting' and 'ground-breaking' as opposed to 'unnecessary' and 'cruel'. He was certain the moniker 'eminent scientist' would have been used as well, rather than 'malicious misguided genius' or 'sinister sadist'.

There was a box-shaped package amongst the post. Ulysses took up this item now. At the same time his eye caught a small piece at the bottom of the page – his subconscious having made the connection – no more than three column inches. 'Eminent Evolutionary Biologist Still Missing' the title read. There was that word again, 'eminent'. It appeared that the reporters at *The Times* were in need of a new thesaurus.

The package was approximately eight inches along every vertex and wrapped in unassuming brown paper. His name and address had been written on one face but there was no stamp. It must have been hand delivered. He would have to ask Nimrod who had delivered that morning.

Ulysses gave the box a gentle shake. There was a muffled rattle inside. The weight of it in his hands made him think that the enclosed object must be made of metal. Placing the package carefully back on top of his desk he began to undo the brown paper, glancing back to the article as his fingers worked on the package.

The piece reported that Professor Ignatius Galapagos had been missing since his office at the Natural History Museum had been broken into and ransacked weeks ago. It also mentioned – without shedding any more light on the true extent of his work – that he had been carrying out research into the evolutionary path that connected man with his distant, primitive forebears.

The article reported some of the facts but, Ulysses thought – a wry smile on his lips as he did so – it didn't report the whole story. One day he would have to write his memoirs chronicling his weird and wonderful adventures, revealing the truth behind dozens of allegedly 'unsolved' mysteries. It would be a best seller, if anyone were prepared to believe that the stories he had to tell were true. Would any editor ever believe half of what he had experienced? Perhaps it would be better to publicise his tales as a work of fiction, just in case. But some of the people Ulysses worked for might not appreciate such candour from one of their employees. He wondered how much more his clandestine masters in Whitehall knew than he did himself.

Ulysses folded back a flap of paper. A card had been slipped in between the folds of the package. The message on it had been written in a delicate, feminine hand. Ulysses' cheeks reddened as he read the four simple words.

'From Genevieve, with love.'

Carefully, he put the card to one side. As he did so, his eyes momentarily focused on a particular sentence towards the bottom of the article about the 'missing' professor.

In the event of confirmation of Galapagos's death, his estate will be sold and the monies raised given to trustees of the Natural History Museum, that his ground-breaking work might continue, Galapagos being unmarried and having no heirs to follow after him.

He was suddenly sharply aware of the ticking of the ormolu clock on the mantelpiece behind him. It was answered by a ticking from the package on the desk.

In the moment before the explosion it was as if there was a sudden absence of noise. Then a horrendous cacophony rushed into the vacuum, as the windows at the southeast corner of the house blew out in a hurricane of flame. Curtains were blown outwards by the blast, wooden casements splintered and the ground shook, as millions of tiny shards of glass rained down into the street like diamond shrapnel.

Obscured by the shadows of a darkened alleyway on the opposite side of the road a lone figure watched, unmoving, as the explosion tore through the dandy's study.

As the echoing roar faded it was replaced by the plink of cooling stone, the sound of glass cracking under the heat of the flames and the hungry snarling of the fire itself.

A limousine – no registration and ministerial black – pulled up in the street opposite the alley and the figure stepped out of the shadows. A tress of auburn hair shook loose from the tight bun at the back of her head. A tweed suit that was all the rage amongst London's younger, more daring, fashionable circles, accentuated the curves of a toned, womanly body.

The front passenger door of the car opened and the woman climbed inside, plus fours and suede leather boots giving definition to shapely, athletic legs.

The young woman closed the door. In the darkness of the car's interior she turned to the driver and flashed him her winning smile. Jago Kane smiled back, the bisecting scar turning the expression into a savage sneer.

"Mission accomplished, my dear Genevieve?" a refined voice said from the back seat of the car, oozing self-satisfaction. "Or should I say, Kitty?"

Somewhere, away across London, sirens were sounding. London's fire brigade was already on its way.

Genevieve Galapagos turned round in the leather-upholstered seat and fixed the elder statesman behind her with her striking gaze.

"But of course, Mr Wormwood," she said, her tone flirtatious, soft as velvet, rich as chocolate. "Kitty Hawke always gets her man."

With that the car pulled out into the street and away from the burning town house.

ACT THREE
THEORIES OF DE-EVOLUTION
JUNE 1997

CHAPTER EIGHTEEN

Death of a Dandy

*PHILANTHROPIST ADVENTURER DIES IN HOUSE
FIRE*

*It is with great regret that we report the death of
philanthropist Ulysses Lucian Quicksilver, following
a freak gas explosion at his home on Thursday night.
Quicksilver recently returned to the headlines after
an absence of almost a year and a half following the
catastrophic break-out of prehistoric monsters from the
Challenger Enclosure at London Zoo last May. This the
first in a series of terrorist attacks by the self-styled
evolutionary revolutionaries, the Darwinian Dawn. During
the dinosaur debacle Quicksilver played a significant role
in the suppression of the stampede, bringing down a
fully-grown adult megasaur single-handedly.*

*Ulysses Quicksilver had been missing presumed dead
since October 1995, following his disappearance during
an attempt to cross the Himalayan mountain range by
hot air balloon. Only a few days before the Challenger
Incident, as the authorities have now labelled the first
of the many atrocities perpetrated by the Darwinian
Dawn, Quicksilver turned up alive and well at his London
residence.*

*Sources with connections to Scotland Yard have
reported that Quicksilver had been helping the authorities
with their investigation into the death of a watchman at
the Natural History Museum during the break-in there,
as previously reported by this paper. A spokesman for*

the Metropolitan Police, one Inspector Allardyce, told our reporter that there were no suspicious circumstances surrounding Quicksilver's tragic death and that Scotland Yard do not believe it is in any way connected to the Natural History Museum case. The inspector also said that an inquiry would not be held into the circumstances surrounding the accident.

Quicksilver was at his Mayfair home on Thursday night, having enjoyed dinner at the Savoy earlier that same evening followed by a visit to the Covent Garden Opera House to see Webber's production of Puccini's Madame Butterfly. No one else was injured as a result of the explosion or the subsequent fire, despite there being several other people in the house at the time, including Quicksilver's own brother.

Ulysses Quicksilver, eldest son of the late, great colonial hero Hercules Quicksilver and Lady Amelia Quicksilver, daughter of the Marquis of Malhembury, made regular appearances on the London social scene before his disappearance over the Himalayas and had been connected with many of London society's most eligible heiresses, although he never married.

Quicksilver was educated first at Eton then Oxford University, where he studied social anthropology, following in the footsteps of many of his family before him, including both his father and grandfather. On graduating from Oxford he joined the Royal Dragoons, during which time he saw action in both India and the Crimea, and having completed a three-year Grand Tour of the Solar System he became better known for his socialising and womanising ways than for the heroic deeds of derring-do.

Following the death of his father in 1975 he inherited the entirety of the Quicksilver estate, which, as well as the town house in Mayfair where he met his death, included residences in the Warwickshire countryside, the Highlands of Scotland, and villas in Tuscany and the south of France. He also took on the mantle of philanthropist adventurer and was the most recent in a long line of famous supporters of the British crown from his celebrated family, amongst them his great-great-uncle who was involved in the creation of the Empress Engine.

His many achievements include holding the record for the Paris-Dakar rally for eight years running and re-discovering the lost civilisation of the Kuwato in Indonesia.

Ulysses Quicksilver, who was thirty-seven when he died, leaves no issue and is survived by his brother Bartholomew who stands to inherit the entirety of the substantial Quicksilver estate.

Uriah Wormwood carefully folded the newspaper shut and placed it with precision on the desk in front of him. He sat back in his leather-upholstered chair, steepling his bony fingers before his face, and breathed in sharply through his nose. A languid lizard's smile creased his lips as his eyes took in the décor of his private chambers at Number 10 Downing Street, his thoughts on Quicksilver's untimely demise.

Well at least that was one less fly in the ointment. Quicksilver had started to become an uncomfortable thorn in the newly appointed Prime Minister's side.

Wormwood picked up his whisky, sniffing it with all the finesse of a connoisseur of the finer things in life as he put the rim of the glass to his lips. He glanced down at the paper again.

Towards the bottom of the lead article, regarding the

growing excitement centring on the preparations for the Queen's Jubilee, a source from within the Queen's household had stated that the monarch herself would be making an uncommon public appearance.

The Times had made a great deal of fuss regarding Quicksilver's part in the Challenger Incident. That was one of the things he would put right, as soon as the opportunity arose. He couldn't stand such hero-worship and glory-mongering by the press. *The Times* was supposed to be one of the pillars of British society, along with high tea and cricket, and therefore was one of the benchmarks by which the rest of the world assessed their own achievements. Yet, of late it seemed to Wormwood that it was fast going downmarket, until it was little better than the rest of the gutter press of Fleet Street. But that would all change once the final act in this play of Machiavellian machinations – of which he was playwright, director and principal actor – was put into action.

The aftermath of the Challenger Incident was still lingering within the column inches, like the smell of festering dino-flesh. Some of the smaller saurians released by the Darwinian Dawn's attack were still at large within the capital. The latest press on the matter regarded the breeding colony of pterodactyls that had broken free of the Roxton Aviary. The flying reptiles had since taken to roosting on Tower Bridge and harassing passers-by. Questions had been raised in the House, as well as in the broadsheets, as to what the authorities were going to do about the problem.

It was also reported that it would take months for essential repairs at the zoo to be completed, as many of the animal pens and cages would have to be entirely rebuilt. There were some doom-mongers who were spreading the rumour that the whole debacle would bankrupt the zoo and that it would have to close permanently unless the government baled out its owners. In the meantime many of the animals, including certain prehistoric exhibits, had been moved to other zoological gardens around the country including Whipsnade and Longleat.

There were three precise knocks on Wormwood's office door.

"Come," the Prime Minister said imperiously.

A robotic servant, its metal chassis sculpted and painted to make it look like it was wearing a butler's black suit and starched, white wing-collar shirt, entered at his behest.

"Yes, Harcourt?"

"Your guests have arrived, Mr Wormwood sir," the automaton-flunkey said with a mechanical wheeze.

"Then show them in."

The robo-servant exited again, pulling the door to behind him. Wormwood leant forward in his chair, gripping the arms with his porcelain-fine fingers so that the knuckles showed hard and white. His released his grip, only for a moment, to tuck a stray strand of lank grey hair behind one ear.

The door opened and the servile Harcourt-droid admitted the two visitors.

"Kitty, my dear," Wormwood said. "You are – how can I put this tactfully – late. I do hope that you are not in the habit of being tardy Kane," he nodded at the revolutionary who acknowledged the Prime Minister with a sneer.

Kitty Hawke, until only recently Miss Genevieve Galapagos the imaginary daughter of Professor Ignatius Galapagos, fixed Wormwood with the dark orbs of her eyes, her lips pinching into an aggressive pout. "In case you hadn't noticed from here in your ivory tower, I have been immensely busy making sure that our mutual plans come to fruition," Kitty protested petulantly.

"Small cogs, my dear... mere cogs in the machine. And I would have you show me some respect." Wormwood snarled. "I had enough of that sort of... defiance from that imperious upstart Quicksilver."

"I would have thought that you would have at least been a little more understanding considering that Quicksilver is now dead."

"Don't get me wrong, my dear. I am delighted at the demise of that dandy adventurer. I had grown tired of his insolent attempts at witty repartee. But I cannot forget that, thanks to his meddling, he has forced us to modify our plans at this late stage in... proceedings. Talking of cogs in the machine and being ready in time, how are things progressing at the Tower? Is the good doctor ready to advance to the next stage of the plan?"

"I am pleased to inform you that the formula has been successfully reproduced by the team at the secondary facility," Kitty said, trying to recover some of her lost composure, hoping that the good news she brought might help her save some face following Wormwood's patriarchal chiding, "now that we have been able to access data stored within the late professor's difference engine."

"So, as I understand it, the locket was the key all along," Wormwood said, looking pointedly at the gruff-looking Kane.

Jago Kane, his expression one of disgruntled annoyance, at having his initial failure pointed out to him once again, did not meet the Prime Minister's gaze, instead studying the pattern woven into the carpet that covered the floor of the PM's private chambers. "Yes. It was."

"Then we have something to thank the late Mr

Quicksilver for after all. I wonder how he would feel if he knew that he had inadvertently helped us achieve our goal, despite our initial ... problems."

Kitty Hawke smiled in self-satisfaction at this slight against Kane.

Wormwood could not forget that it was because of Kane's failure to retrieve this item at the beginning of their endeavour that their plans had been forced to change so drastically and had almost been scuppered entirely by the subsequent – yet necessary, as it turned out – involvement of Ulysses Quicksilver. It had been a dangerous hand Wormwood had played, yet one that had seemed to pay off at first, until the somewhat upsetting incident at Waterloo Underground Station.

As a consequence Wormwood could not forgive Kane for his previous failure. Once their scheme had been seen through to its conclusion, the revolutionary would be made to pay for that careless mistake; for his haphazard handling of the simple mission to recover the Galapagos formula from the Natural History Museum.

But there was no doubting the fact that now the professor's difference engine and the locket – in reality the engine's access key – had been reunited. Wormwood's laboratory technicians had been able to open Galapagos's private data files in which was stored the chemical breakdown of his evolution-reversing formula – or his de-evolution formula, as Dr Wilde preferred to call it.

"Dr Wilde is preparing his subjects even as we speak," Kitty went on. "He has assured me that all will be ready in time for the main event."

"Good, good," Wormwood said, nodding approvingly. "You have redeemed yourself, my dear."

"And what of the remaining devices, Mr Kane?"

"Allardyce and his lackeys at Scotland Yard have

unfortunately managed to recover most of them."

"That is indeed unfortunate." Wormwood's knuckles whitened as he took hold of the whisky glass, betraying that which his emotionless tone kept hidden. "Now tell me something that will be more appealing to my ear."

"We are still in possession of a number of the devices, certainly enough to achieve our modified mission objectives."

"Well, that is better news. Have you anything more to further cheer me?"

"They are now at the Limehouse facility being fitted with canisters of the formula. The last phase of the plan is almost ready to be put into action."

"Even better. Then we can progress in a satisfactory manner."

Uriah Wormwood fixed each of his lieutenants with his needling stare, both meeting his intense gaze.

"Miss Hawke, Mr Kane, we are about to make our mark on history." He toasted them with the glass in his hand. "Let us not delay any longer for we have a date with destiny."

CHAPTER NINETEEN

Prisoners of the Tower

"And now gentlemen, we come to the point in our tour where you can see how your money can help us with the good work we do here for, and on behalf of, the Empire," Governor Colesworth said, with some small measure of genuine enthusiasm colouring his voice.

He paused before the solid steel door sunk into the three-foot deep wall behind him. The party of industrialists, steel mill owners, landed gentry and money men, leant forwards in anticipation, tightly-buttoned waistcoats straining against bulging stomachs recently filled from the lavish buffet laid on for their visit. "At this juncture I would like to remind you that you should be aware that a number of the inmates you will encounter here, and some of the techniques that we use to control them, can cause some distress to upstanding, god-fearing men of a sensitive disposition. But do not worry, you are not in any danger yourselves. Orderlies and wardens will be on hand at all times keeping our experimental subjects in their place."

Colesworth turned the large round wheel-handle and with a squeaking groan the heavy vault door swung open. Two orderlies, both armed with electric goads – the associated battery packs needed to power them strapped to their backs – stood to either side of the entrance. The governor proudly ushered his guests into the vaulted space beyond.

It was a huge room at the base of the White Tower, bustling with inmates and orderlies alike, although at first it was hard to tell the two groups apart. The prisoners all wore the same, drab, shapeless coveralls, grey and stained with God alone knew what. The orderlies' uniforms weren't much better. The prison warders looked just as brutal and violent as those they had been tasked with guarding.

The party of visitors was standing at the edge of a balcony that ran around the circumference of the cell-vault. An iron-railed staircase descended to the dungeon floor ten feet below and a second rose up again to the walkway on the far side. Opposite stood another solid iron door. During the early years of Queen Victoria's reign, when the Tower had been open to public visitors, this space had been used to store elaborate displays of weaponry. Now its purpose was more like that for which it had originally been intended.

Several of the governors' guests wrinkled their noses at the fusty damp and ammonia smell of the dungeon but all stared, transfixed by the shambling monstrosities before them. The longer they looked the easier it was for them to tell the incarcerated and incarcerators apart. For one thing, all of the prisoners had at some stage had their heads shaved. Some inmates still bore the nicks and scabs on their pallid white pates of the more recent attentions of a barber.

And there was another distinguishing mark that all the prisoners here bore. Each man had a sturdy iron collar fitted around his neck. These metal braces held their heads up and the more observant amongst the group saw that the thin flesh at the base of the prisoners' skulls was pink and raw. As yet the governor's guests could not see a reason for these devices. Were they some form of punishment, identity markers, or did they serve some other, more sinister, purpose?

Every now and again orderlies turned high-pressure

hoses on the mewling and moaning inmates, dousing them with ice-cold water. This action provoked mixed responses from the party of visitors.

"Is that really necessary?" one woman asked the governor.

"Oh yes, madam," Colesworth replied, matter-of-factly.

"But as far as I could see that poor soaked wretch there hadn't done anything to incur the guard's wrath."

"Madam, if they are imprisoned here at her majesty's pleasure, then they have all done something and deserve whatever punishment is meted out to them. Would you not agree?" There were murmurs and nods of assent from the rest of the party and the busybody said nothing more.

"Besides, a regular dousing reminds the prisoners of their place and of the price they must pay society in recompense for their misdeeds," Colesworth went on, warming to his subject. "These you see before you are amongst some of our most recalcitrant offenders, murderers and rapists – excuse me, ladies! – who, it has been deemed, can never be rehabilitated. It is the judgement of the courts that they should remain here for the rest of their natural lives. Just as it is our penance to care for them for that time." What the investors saw before them now did not look very much like care.

"Excuse me, Governor Colesworth," a haughty-sounding gentleman said, "but might some of these godforsaken souls be classed as retards?"

"Indeed, some of them are," Colesworth agreed, "which is why they have ultimately found themselves here. Gentlemen and ladies, there, but for the grace of God, go us all."

Several of the party crossed themselves and again potential dissenters were hushed.

"And it is the very nature of those incarcerated here that makes them such ideal subjects for Dr Wilde's work." The governor indicated a tall, stick-thin, lab-coated figure striding imperiously through the cavernous space beneath them; very obviously presiding demon lord of this outer circle of hell. Dr Wilde caught the eye of the governor and threw him a jovial salute. He bounded up the stairs to the balcony two at a time. Next to Colesworth he made the governor appear even shorter of stature and wider of girth.

"Ladies and gentlemen, it is with great pleasure that I introduce Dr Cornelius Wilde."

The looming doctor bowed at the middle, looking like a wheat stalk bending in a strong wind, and then sprang back up again. He looked every bit an experimental brain medicine specialist. His thinning blond hair was swept back from a widow's peak and he wore thin-framed round spectacles, which gave his eyes a slightly discomforting magnified appearance. The lengthened features of his face were all the more clearly defined by his gaunt, hungrily thin physique.

"Good afternoon, ladies and gentlemen," he said, with all the manner of a ringmaster about to introduce the star act. "Welcome to what I like to call our little *cirque du freak*." A titter of nervous laughter passed among the investors.

"It is here that Dr Wilde is carrying out some of the most exciting research into behavioural adjustment taking place at this time," Governor Colesworth said proudly, beaming his ingratiating smile at the party. "Would you care to explain the purpose of your work here, Dr Wilde? I'm afraid the science of it baffles me."

"It would be my pleasure," Wilde beamed. "Basically, ladies and gentlemen, here at the Tower of London maximum security prison facility, we have long been involved in finding a way to best rehabilitate those who find themselves on the wrong side of the law. But undeniably, for some, there has never been any hope of rehabilitation within normal, decent human society. That is, until now."

Colesworth looked from the doctor to his guests and back again, simpering all the while. The ringmaster had his audience hooked.

"You see that each of the inmates here is wearing a special collar?" The party nodded. "I am sure that intelligent men and women like yourselves will have wondered what they are for." More nods. "What you see before you is the most exciting advance in social rehabilitation and behavioural improvement this century. Those collars represent a quantum leap forwards in our understanding of the human brain." Here Wilde paused for dramatic effect. "And how it can be controlled."

There were a number of audible gasps from the assembled economic elite.

"At this present time we are carrying out final tests on the patented Wilde Mind Control Collar."

"Can you elaborate as to how the collars work?" an industrialist asked, his eyes twinkling as he imagined the profit to be made from investing in this new project and securing sole manufacturing rights.

"Well, obviously the technical details will only become available to the highest bidder," Wilde smiled, "but the principle of it is really quite simple."

"But then aren't all the best ideas?" Colesworth simpered.

His eyes aglow with unhealthy enthusiasm, Wilde attempted to explain to the group of laymen how the complex collar worked. "Most of what you see locked around each subject's neck is actually a battery power pack. The clever bit, the mould-breaking technical gubbins, is at the back. There an electrode enters the base of the skull, allowing electrical impulses to be sent directly into the cerebral cortex, thereby modifying the subject's behaviour. But I can see that I am losing you. As you said, Governor, the science of it baffles most people so I have prepared a brief demonstration."

"Excellent, excellent."

"If you would care to follow me?"

Wilde led the party around the edge of the chamber to the sturdy door on the opposite side.

A warder armed with an electric prod prepared to open this second door but Wilde paused before it, halting the man's hand on the wheel lock.

"What is it, Dr Wilde?" one of Colesworth's guests asked.

"I should warn you, honoured guests, that some of you – if not all – may find what I am about to reveal a little, how should I put it, unsettling? I would completely understand – and I am sure that Governor Colesworth would as well – if anyone of you felt that they would rather leave the tour at this juncture."

Colesworth looked anxiously from the trailing crocodile of investors to the charismatic doctor and back again, uncertainty writ large upon his face.

The huddle of investors all stared at Wilde, transfixed in nervous, hollow-eyed anticipation, but not one of them asked to leave.

"Very well then. I applaud your courage and tenacity. If you would step this way?"

The party entered a much smaller, white-tiled room. An overpowering clinical smell of disinfectant masked a more deeply ingrained odour of bodily excretions and raw fear.

At the centre of the doctor's lab was an upended steel gurney. Secured to it by thick buckle-locked leather straps so that he was almost vertical, arms held tight to his sides, was an ox of a man. The doctor's latest clinical subject had been stripped to the waist, revealing a torso that was a veritable historical account of his wanton life, a patchwork of livid bruises, tattoos and old scars. The restrained prisoner was being attended to by a pair of lab assistants and watched over by two more of the brutal-looking orderlies.

As soon as Wilde entered the room, the inmate's muscles bulged as he fought against the leather straps and embarked on a blasphemous tirade of expletives that made the more sensitive among the governor's guests gasp in horror. One woman was on the verge of swooning in shock. "I'm going to rip your throat out and eat your heart, Wilde you bastard! Do you hear me?" the inmate screamed in a strong Glaswegian accent.

"Gag him!" the doctor ordered sharply.

As two orderlies pushed a thick padded gag between the prisoner's jaws, the startled investors could quite clearly see that the savage's teeth had been filed to a point so that they looked like sharp arrowhead flints.

"Ladies and gentlemen, let me apologise for our subject's outburst. Unfortunately not all can appreciate the benefits of the good work we do here, least of all those of a criminal bent."

Wilde strode past the captive inmate and, taking the goad from the orderly standing there, rammed the prongs of the device into the prisoner's ribs. The man's whole body jerked violently and the ammonia-stink of urine permeated the close atmosphere of the chamber.

"Honoured guests, let me introduce Ramsey 'The Shark' McCabe. Serial killer, cannibal and downright nasty piece of work. A recalcitrant sociopath, with twenty-six murders, dismemberings and devourings to his name."

The morbidly fascinated group fanned out in front of the gurney, so that all could see more clearly. 'The Shark' McCabe continued to thrash and fight against his restraints, causing the gaggle of investors to flinch and take a step back. But there was no way that he could free himself from the steel slab, and neither was there any chance of any of the party leaving now, for fear of missing what might happen to the brute next.

"As you can quite clearly see, Mr McCabe is a brutal and violent man, who is serving multiple life sentences at this institution, with no chance of a reduction to his sentence and most definitely no chance of a reprieve. Isn't that right, Mr McCabe?"

Wilde stepped up to the restraining table and indicated the collar fitted around the prisoner's neck. As he did so, McCabe twisted his head sideways, veins bulging in his neck as if he would dearly like to bite the doctor's face off.

"You can also see that he has recently been fitted with a collar. Now, ladies and gentlemen, for the purposes of this experiment I am afraid that we must ungag the subject once more. You may want to cover your ears."

Some kind of metal box of tricks, all dials and switches, and sporting a long aerial, had appeared in Wilde's hands.

"Remove the gag," Wilde commanded. The governor's party watched in horrified fascination.

As soon as the gag was off, the tirade began again.

"Wilde, you shit, when I get out of here I'm going to rip off your head and sh..."

Dr Wilde flicked a switch on his handheld device. The

torrent of verbal abuse ceased immediately as McCabe fell silent, the inmate's eyes glazing over and his face taking on a slack-jawed, moronic, almost zombie-like expression. The assembled onlookers gasped.

"Wh-What happened?" someone spluttered in disbelief.

"Ladies and gentlemen," the ringmaster declared, as he came to the highlight of the performance, "the subject is now totally under my control. Isn't that right, Mr McCabe?"

A frown flickered across the prisoner's face and then, his voice as emotionless as his expression, the Shark replied, "Yes, Dr Wilde."

The party gasped again.

"By using this handheld remote I can now coerce Mr McCabe into performing any action I ask of him. It is easier to control less developed brains, of course. Our initial experiments with dogs and monkeys paved the way for developing a mind control device that could be used on humans. Some of our more retarded subjects have proved most susceptible to control, and, believe me, gentlemen, in a place crammed full of backward hoodlums, subnormal rapists and psychotic murderers, we have plenty of those here."

A nervous titter of laughter passed through the assembled group.

"I don't believe it!" a rotund industrialist muttered, jowls quivering as he shook his head in disbelief.

"Believe it, sir," Wilde countered. "In fact, let me prove it to you. What would you like to see Mr McCabe do?"

There was a smattering of 'um's and 'ah's as the gathered voyeurs tried to come up with a suitable test now that the doctor had set his challenge.

"Have him recite *Mary Had a Little Lamb*," a voice

came from the back of the group.

"Very well." The doctor turned to his docile subject. "Mr McCabe, do you know the children's rhyme *Mary Had a Little Lamb*?"

"Yes, Dr Wilde."

"Then recite it for our guests."

"Mary had a little lamb, its fleece was white as snow," McCabe drawled, his Scots accent monotone and lacking any expression whatsoever, "and everywhere that Mary went, the lamb was sure to go."

"Very good, Mr McCabe."

The party of visitors offered a polite round of applause.

"Make him stand on one foot," another man suggested.

"Very well, but we shall have to release him from his restraints first," Wilde pointed out.

There was a hesitant murmur of uncertainty from the group and some of the party took a step back as Wilde directed his assistants to undo the buckled straps.

"Are you sure about this?" Colesworth hissed, suddenly at Wilde's side.

"But of course I am, Governor. Have faith."

Colesworth swallowed hard and took a step back, wringing his hands in anxiety.

One by one the leather restraints were undone. The doctor's assistants moved aside, prison orderlies moving up to take their place, electro-goads ready just in case. McCabe just stood there, a good head taller than anyone else in the room, his great wrestler's form terrifying to behold.

"Mr McCabe," Wilde said, turning a dial on his control box and depressing another switch, "if you would be so kind, stand on one foot."

The prisoner robotically raised one foot so that he remained balanced on the other.

Suggestion followed suggestion from the increasingly impressed investors. They watched as the cannibal serial killer rubbed his stomach whilst patting his head, childishly recited his ABC and the routine ending with a rendition of 'I'm a Little Teapot'. All the while the Shark remained as docile as a kitten.

A spontaneous round of applause erupted from amongst the investors. Colesworth beamed like a Cheshire cat. Dr Wilde, one eyebrow raised in acknowledgement, kept his own counsel.

"Thank you, thank you," Wilde said, taking a bow as he luxuriated in his audience's adulation. "But now, if you will excuse me, I have vital work to attend to."

The show over and Colesworth assured of the investment he had so desperately been seeking, the ringmaster bid the audience of investors farewell. The party filed out of the clinical white laboratory, the governor asking if any of his esteemed guests would be attending the jubilee celebrations in Hyde Park the following day.

Dr Wilde stayed where he was. He turned to one of his assistants.

"Nash, have this one taken back to his cell," he said, throwing a sidelong glance at the subdued psychopath, "shock him hard enough to knock him unconscious and then you can turn this off." He tossed the collar controller to the man.

"Yes, Dr Wilde."

"And remember, Nash, I want the rest of the collars fitted by tonight." His previously crowd-pleasing tone had become pointedly instructional.

"Yes, Dr Wilde," Nash acceded.

Leaving his underlings to put everything into operation

in his absence, Wilde left the lab through another steel door and entered his private office lit by one, lonely, naked light bulb. He shut the door securely behind him and sat down at an unassuming grey metal desk. The only thing remotely interesting about the desk was the teak and brass-finished box that sat on top of it. It looked like a considerably larger version of the control box he had used to demonstrate how the mind control collars worked.

Wilde looked at the clock on the wall and then at his pocket watch, then at the clock again.

Drumming his fingers in distraction on the desktop he gazed out at the smog-laden sky beyond the small barred window. The mauve and mustard clouds were criss-crossed by the sweeping beams of the Tower's searchlights.

The Tower had been many things in its time – a royal palace, a menagerie, a museum, a treasure house and a tourist attraction – but now it was back to being a prison once more. As a prison it had put up many famous 'guests' including queens, kings and traitors. Now it was home to some of the most violent and brutal villains the empire had ever known – murderers, rapists and compulsive criminals the lot of them. In one wing were kept the most dangerous inmates, the clinically deranged psychopaths, the abusers, the schizophrenics, the mentally ill, those who, by rights, should not have been permitted to continue their godless lives. But that would all change soon enough, when the new order was in place. And for the time being, these very wretches were to form the vanguard of the most exciting scientific experiment in the last fifteen years.

A tinny buzzing disturbed the doctor's reverie, forcing him to answer his personal communicator.

"Wilde," he said simply.

"Dr Wilde, the hour is upon us," a voice said at the other end of the line. "The plan is to proceed at the agreed time. Will you be ready?"

"I am ready, Agent Kane," Wilde confirmed.

"The Dawn is coming, brother."

Then the line went dead.

Cornelius Wilde felt a tingling surge of adrenalin and became aware of his heart jumping in his chest.

It was time, the Dawn was coming, and with it a glorious new epoch in the history of human kind. It was time that the social order be overturned and the masters of the sciences given the opportunity to stretch their wings, rather than remain bound to outdated and outmoded scientific principles. The age of steam was coming to an end and ahead lay a glorious era of opportunity. Such an age would need its pioneers, its scientific heroes, its leaders.

The ringmaster smiled. All that had come before was merely the warm-up act, the precursor to the main event. The three-ring finale was about to begin.

"Show time!" Wilde said to himself, as he watched the silhouette-black shapes of ravens clear the barbed wire battlements of the Tower and fly into the storm-dark sky.

CHAPTER TWENTY

The Limehouse Connection

The Silver Phantom Mark IV rolled to a halt in the gathering gloom beside the warehouse, headlamps already doused, its tyres making almost no noise on the harbour side.

Nimrod peered out through the windscreen at the dusk-shadowed buildings of the Limehouse Basin. The smog-clouds, thicker and more cloying thanks to the summer heat, had helped accelerate the onset of night.

This run-down stretch of dockland appeared to be deserted. There was no sign of anyone about but then everyone, from the lowest of the low to the great and the good, would either be taking part in the Queen's jubilee celebrations in person or observing the proceedings as they were relayed via the huge broadcast screens on every street corner and through cathode ray sets in homes across the nation.

"You're sure this is the place, sir?" Nimrod turned to the man sitting in the passenger seat next to him.

"Absolutely," Ulysses Quicksilver assured him, a wicked gleam in his eye, as he checked the scanner he was holding in his lap. A red blip was repeatedly pinging at the centre of a lambently glowing green wire-frame image.

"So that Heath Robinson invention of Dr Methuselah's really works," Nimrod said with a hint of scorn.

"Yes. I have to say I'm rather impressed. Who'd have thought that old Methuselah was as handy with electronic trickery as he is with medical mumbo-jumbo?"

"You think Miss Galapagos is here?"

"Indeed I do," Ulysses said, his face suddenly grim

again. "Genevieve Galapagos, my arse! She and I have unfinished business. The key is certainly here."

Ulysses stared out of the windscreen and back into the night of the explosion, when he had discovered Genevieve's betrayal. One good betrayal deserved another and so he had faked his own death, allowing Genevieve's parting gift to explode with dramatic consequences whilst making sure that he, and anyone else who mattered to him, was out of range of the blast.

With the parcel-bomb counting down the last seconds until destruction, it had been necessary for Ulysses to make a snap decision. He had decided that if he were considered to be dead, it would be much more straightforward for him to discover who was truly behind this conspiracy. Once he was in the grave, as it were, he would have the precious time and anonymity he needed to make a more careful assessment of what was really going on and what needed to be done to put an end to such devilish schemes.

He would be eternally glad that he had asked Dr Methuselah to examine Galapagos' locket before returning it to its allegedly rightful owner. The old curmudgeon had almost instantly identified it as an encoded access key. Seeing as how Ulysses had already worked out that it was a difference engine that had been stolen from the Natural History Museum it did not take a genius to deduce the connection and realise that, whatever it was that Professor Galapagos had created in his lab, the means to recreating it was locked inside that same data storage engine.

It had been Methuselah's idea to fit Galapagos' 'locket' with a tracking device. By means of the accompanying scanner, Ulysses had been able to follow the mysterious and capricious Genevieve Galapagos's movements as she went about her business. Meanwhile Ulysses had put his own spy network into operation through his ever-loyal manservant Nimrod who, himself, had most useful connections to the darker side of the capital.

Since the counterfeit Miss Galapagos had made such an unsubtle attempt on his life, Ulysses had managed to implicate her in the workings of the Darwinian Dawn, which, as it turned out, were not quite as done for as he might have hoped following his own personal Waterloo.

Had it been she who had tried to assassinate him with a bullet earlier on the same night as the explosion? She had certainly demonstrated a marksman's eye on the evening of their first meeting. Ulysses had also managed to uncover her true identity. She was, in reality, Kitty Hawke. Cat burglar, hustler, and consummate actress with her own revolutionary tendencies.

He wondered whether he had found himself his mysterious thief at last and that when she had been so insistent about accompanying him to the Natural History Museum the night they first met, whether she had not, in fact, been returning to the scene of the crime, hoping to bring to a conclusion what she had started by recovering the missing code-key.

It had been a gamble allowing Kitty Hawke and the Darwinian Dawn access to Galapagos's encrypted data files, but he had considered it a calculated risk. He had hoped to bring matters to a halt before they could reach their deadly conclusion.

"What time do you make it, Nimrod?" Ulysses asked, taking out his pocket watch. "Synchronise watches and all that, what?"

"Nine o'clock, sir," his manservant replied, checking the clock built into the automobile's dashboard.

"Good. Dead on. Same as me." Ulysses gazed out at the

purpling sky. "I should think that the great and the good will be sitting down to their aperitifs about now," Ulysses said with a heartfelt sigh.

"Weren't you invited to the Hyde Park celebrations, sir?"

"I would be there right now myself if it weren't for the fact that I'm supposed to be dead. But then I'd have to miss out on all this, wouldn't I?" he said, turning to look over his shoulder into the back of the Phantom. The Neanderthal squatting on the back seat grunted, an amiable grin splitting the lumpen features of his subhuman face. "And besides, now the fun can really start!"

"Sir, I must protest. It should be I who attends you on this escapade. You know what happened the last time I left you to your own devices. You were nearly drowned, blown up and eaten by a de-evolving professor of evolutionary biology."

"But you're my getaway driver," Ulysses said. "You're my Plan B."

"I really don't know why you insisted on bringing him along," Nimrod grumbled.

"Think how useful he proved to be at the Waterloo bomb-making facility," Ulysses pointed out. "I thought he might help to – you know – mix things up a bit. It always pays to walk into a criminal HQ with a bit of muscle and a back-up plan."

Nimrod said nothing more but simply shot his employer a withering look.

"Besides, you've done very well with him. You should be pleased with yourself, Nimrod. I think our friend here looks very dashing in a suit and tie."

"Well..."

"You'll have him drinking Earl Grey out of a cup and not the saucer in no time."

Nimrod sighed tiredly. Ulysses carefully opened his door.

"It's time I returned to the land of the living!" Ulysses declared, with overly exuberant showmanship. "Keep the engine ticking over. We'll be back in a jiffy, just you wait and see."

"Keep behind me and try not to knock into anything," Ulysses told his Neanderthal companion in a hissed whisper.

They were inside the gloomy confines of the warehouse, access gained with the aid of a crowbar through an abandoned foreman's office. The hulking, rusted carcasses of dead machinery surrounded them. According to the blip on the scanner their target was only a matter of a hundred yards further inside.

Simeon looked like a most curious beast, dressed in an altered suit of Mr Prufrock's, buttons pulling against the stitching across the Neanderthal's barrel chest. He crouched behind a rusted iron cargo crane, hairy knuckles dragging on the ground. His feet were bare, his toes gripping the floor almost as fingers might. He was wearing a clean white shirt and one of Nimrod's black ties that the butler had tied for him. His lank dreadlocks had been trimmed and a comb run through his hair before it was slicked down in the same manner that Nimrod favoured.

Ulysses smiled. It looked like Nimrod would soon have an assistant to unburden him of some of his chores about the Quicksilver household.

Ulysses himself had decided to go with flamboyance over subtlety on this occasion. He was wearing a House of Leoparde waistcoat all in chartreuse and crimson thread, his cravat was held in place with a diamond pin, and his bloodstone cane was in his hand. He wanted to make an impact when he returned from the dead for a second time. He had set himself a tough act to follow after his last resurrection from the grave – although at least he had been reported dead this time rather than just having been missing *presumed* dead.

"Ready?" he asked the apeman.

Simeon nodded, his tongue lolling from his mouth like a happy dog.

Cautiously Ulysses led the way through the dead monoliths of the fish-packer's machinery. It might still only be dusk outside but in the warehouse it was dark as night, the skylights above merely grey panes of opacity, their translucence gone with the failing of the light.

Even now that his eyes had become more accustomed to the preternatural darkness, objects merely appeared to Ulysses as amorphous black clots against the only slightly lesser gloom of the warehouse's interior. And although he had a flashlight about his person, he did not want to use it here and draw unwanted attention to their presence.

Simeon didn't seem bothered by the lack of light at all, proving surprisingly nimble at negotiating the various obstacles that the gloom seemed to throw into their path. Ulysses wondered whether there were still some things that the more primitive evolutionary forms were better at coping with than the more sophisticated *Homo sapiens*.

The warehouse smelt dusty and dank, of dirt and mouldering wood. But there was something else – something acrid and unpleasantly familiar – almost subsumed by the smell of old oil and rust-eaten metal. Ulysses suspected that Simeon could smell it too, and probably more clearly than he could himself, for he kept sniffing and then holding back almost nervously after each intense inhalation. What did the aroma remind him of? Where had the Neanderthal experienced the smell before? And where had Ulysses? He could almost taste its sickly sweetness.

Then there were the sounds too. As they advanced across the warehouse they became steadily more distinct – muffled human voices, the rattle and thud of machinery, reminiscent of the Darwinian Dawn's Waterloo Station facility.

Ulysses could feel heat prickling his forehead. Was the closeness of the air and the heat a consequence of the early summer climate or as a result of the industrial processes taking place elsewhere within the warehouse?

The outline of a door became visible ahead of them. The glass pane set into it was so smeared with grime as to be almost entirely blacked out, but for tiny scrapes in the obscuring dirt. Slivers of muted light broke through into the darkness that enveloped them, turning swirls of dust into cascades of golden motes.

Ulysses put a hand to the door and held it there for a moment. Then, with a confident motion, he pulled it open and a waft of something hit him, immediately carrying him back to both Professor Galapagos' ransacked office and the macabre workroom beneath the house in Southwark. It was the lingering odour of meat on the turn and aniseed, like spoiled fennel and beef casserole.

Simeon flinched but the two of them ducked through the door, Ulysses shutting it swiftly behind them. Everything that they had sensed in the outer warehouse space was amplified here – the heat, the noise, the smells – but they still weren't at the heart of operations. Although there was light here and the condition of the machinery told of its recent use, the place was still devoid of any human or even robot presence.

It didn't take long for Ulysses to ascertain the purpose of this part of the complex. It was the still-wet vats, the lengths of glass piping and the all-pervading smell of aniseed and rancid meat that gave it away. Whatever it was that Professor Galapagos had been brewing in his Southwark workshop, the same stuff had been reproduced here but on a noticeably more grand and terrifying scale.

Confident that there was no one to observe their progress Ulysses darted between the distillation tanks and workbenches, always following the lure of the blip on the scanner.

He paused, realising that Simeon was no longer at his heel. Turning he saw the Neanderthal rocking from side to side where he stood between the benches of apparatus. He was whimpering to himself, almost overwhelmed by the now oh-so-familiar and disturbing aroma.

"Come on!" Ulysses hissed. The Neanderthal didn't budge. "Simeon, come here now!"

A grimace of anxiety contorted the primitive's ugly features, obviously torn between his fearful recollections and his desire to please his new master.

"Oh, have it your own way," Ulysses sighed, giving in to exasperation, and continued towards the other side of the workroom, following the thumping of machinery and what sounded like the purr of an engine running up to speed.

Simeon gave a little yelp and then, having overcome his demons – whatever they might have been – knuckled after Ulysses.

It had been a long time since Ulysses had seen anything like it and he froze for a moment in genuine, awestruck wonder. He found recollections of his hair-raising flight over the Himalayas springing to mind, but the balloon on which he had been a passenger was as nothing compared to this Leviathan.

Lit by flickering running lights, the zeppelin was huge – at least two hundred yards from nose to tail. The massive balloon of its inflated gas envelope was barely contained within the converted warehouse-hangar. From the locking clamps and iron cables beneath it hung an armoured gondola, itself as big as two railway carriages strung together. The whole thing was kept anchored in place by sturdy guy ropes.

The rear loading ramp of the dirigible's gondola was down and robot-drudges were loading the last of the Dawn's mine-bombs on board. Close to where Ulysses and the panting Simeon were hunkered down behind the hangar's fuel dump, there had also been discarded the straw-packed crates that had been used to transport the terrorists' surviving devices from the bomb factory. Ulysses had no idea how many the Darwinian Dawn had managed to recover but judging from the amount of robots trudging up the ramp into the bomb bay it was enough to do some serious damage.

And right at that moment, across London, thousands of people were crowded into and around Hyde Park and the newly-reconstructed Crystal Palace for a chance to be a part of Queen Victoria's 160th jubilee celebrations and perhaps even catch a rare glimpse of the monarch herself.

And there was not only the devastation that might be caused by the initial detonation of the devices, considering the level of destruction they had wrought inside the confines of the Waterloo facility. If Ulysses' suspicions were correct – and with all the evidence he had seen with his own eyes within the Limehouse complex, how could they not be? – those remaining devices now carried an added ingredient, an extra surprise for the beleaguered populace of London: Professor Galapagos' de-evolution formula.

Whatever else the Darwinian Dawn might have planned to help the Queen's jubilee go with a bang, Ulysses knew that he had to stop that zeppelin from leaving its warehouse-hangar. But for that he needed a distraction, and time was truly against him.

He cast the Neanderthal an anxious look. "For Queen and country, eh, old boy? You didn't know you were signing up for a suicide mission, did you?" Simeon grinned back amiably, ridiculous in his strangely fitted suit. "That's the spirit."

Ulysses' pistol was out of its underarm holster and in his hand. He snapped off two precisely aimed shots. Two men fell.

There was a burst of furious shouting, a flurry of sudden, instinct-driven activity, as the guards' hours of brainwashed training kicked in and they took up firing positions of their own. A tattoo of gun reports resounded around the warehouse-hangar as the pitch of the airship's engines rose, its pilot preparing the craft for immediate take-off. If a stray bullet ruptured the zeppelin balloon the results could be catastrophic.

A bullet ricocheted from the ground in front of the fuel dump throwing off sparks as it did so. Ulysses was aware of the gentle *whoomph* as a single spark ignited a pool of oil that had collected in the uneven, rutted surface of the concrete floor. He also heard the shout from one of the guards that followed. However much it might gall the terrorists they realised that it they continued to fire on Ulysses' position they risked starting a conflagration, which would in turn jeopardise the safety of the airship.

It soon became apparent to those few armed guards left to oversee the loading of the zeppelin that they were not going to be able to put an end to the interlopers' attack by force of arms alone. Some other means of defence was needed now, something that was no longer required to fulfil any other duties, something entirely dispensable.

The gunfire stopped, rattling into echoing silence. Hearing the clank-clank-clank of pistoning legs and the ringing of metal heels on concrete, Ulysses risked a glance.

The automata-drudges employed by the Darwinian Dawn were running and leaping across the hangar towards the fuel dump behind which Ulysses and Simeon were sheltering. Ulysses counted a dozen, maybe more.

He fired off two more shots, despite knowing that they would make little impact against the droids' armoured chest plates. Perhaps if he had been armed with one of the guards' sub-machine pistols he might have been able to defend himself more effectively.

Something spun over his head and crashed into one of the bounding robots with a resounding clang. A mechanical man was torn off as a heavy engine part collided with it. There was the whickering of more spare parts scything through the air followed by clattering crashes and rattling collisions as Simeon hurled more of his improvised arsenal at the advancing robots. However, although his efforts were making a small difference, they weren't going to be enough to save the two of them for much longer.

Ulysses tugged his communicator from his pocket. "Nimrod!" he shouted into the comm. "It's time for Plan B!"

His voice was drowned out by the roar of the zeppelin's

engines and the rich, gagging stink of exhaust fumes washed over them.

With a loud grinding of gears and the clanking of chains, the panels of the roof above them pulled back, exposing the laden airship to the polluted London skies.

The engines whirring at take-off velocity, the zeppelin, with its deadly payload, lifted off, pulling free of its mooring hawsers, like some great whale rising from the ocean depths.

The robots braving Simeon's barrage were nearly on them now.

Ulysses was abruptly aware of the scream of a revving engine. With a splintering crash, the Silver Phantom smashed through a wall, headlights flaring in the exhaust-smogged gloom of the hangar. It crashed down on the hard floor of the building, bouncing on its tyres and collided with the two robots bearing down on Ulysses and Simeon. The automata-drudges were sent flying, arms and legs windmilling wildly as the automobile skidded to a halt side-on, less than a foot from Ulysses' position.

The front and rear passenger doors flew open. "Get in!" Nimrod shouted from behind the cracked windscreen.

Ulysses didn't need to be told twice. He threw himself into the front of the Phantom as Simeon bounded into the back, slamming the door shut behind him. "Just in the nick of time, eh, Nimrod?"

There was a metallic crash above them and a dent appeared in the roof of the car.

"Get us out of here!" Ulysses commanded, eyes wide with the adrenalin rushing through his system.

Nimrod floored the accelerator. Wheels spun, there was the stink of burning rubber, then the tyres gripped and the Phantom took off like a rocket. The car had suffered a fair amount of damage to its pristine bodywork during the

Challenger Incident, particularly when the velociraptor had crashed onto the bonnet. However, it had since been repaired so that it looked as good as the day it had left the showroom but all that careful work was now being undone in another pulse-pounding escape.

Reaching the far end of the hangar Nimrod swung the car round sharply, dislodging the droid on its roof. The automaton was sent barrelling across the concrete – sparks flying from its steel body – and into a pile of discarded packing boxes. The drudge lay there, like a marionette with its strings cut, flames dancing within the bone-dry tinder around it.

All they could see of the rising airship, through the windscreen of the Phantom, were the swinging ropes and cables of its freed tethers. The abandoned automata, caring nothing for their own well-being, strove to carry out the last command they had been given, dashing and leaping towards the car, their movements jerky and insect-like.

Gunning the engine, Nimrod sent the Phantom hurtling forwards. Droids bounced off the bonnet, were smashed aside by its radiator grill or were sent under its wheels as the automobile's engine flung it forwards with all the force of a steam-hammer.

The fire had now taken over the pile of packing cases and was licking at one wall of the warehouse. A trail of flames slithered across the floor of the hangar behind the Phantom, following the rainbow-sheen of leaked fuel leading back to the fuel dump.

Then the automobile was through the barricade formed by the charging robots and the smoggy dusk beyond the sundered wall of the hangar was beckoning them.

The Silver Phantom, its battered bodywork reflecting the fury of the flames in shimmering crimson and orange, launched through the hole it had made, as the last few barrels of the fuel dump exploded. The car flew through the side of the building chased by a volcanic explosion of greasy smoke and flames as windows blew out above it. The shattered body parts of destroyed automata winnowed through the walls and windows and clattered off the back of the vehicle in a shower of bullet-hard shrapnel. The rear window shattered.

The car crashed down onto the harbour side, Simeon tumbling across the back seat as Nimrod swung into a tight turn, stopping them hurtling into the oily, black waters of the Thames.

Through his window, Ulysses could see the zeppelin rise clear of the Limehouse complex, flood-lit by the conflagration consuming the warehouse-hangar. The airship was turning west, manoeuvring itself in the direction of the centre of the capital, continuing to climb, to soar above the elevated trackways of the Overground.

He turned to Nimrod, his eyes wild. "We have to stop that zeppelin!"

"Yes, sir," his manservant agreed, his expression as stoical as ever, and put the pedal to the metal.

With a screech of tyres and a leonine roar from its engine, the Silver Phantom sped off into the darkening night, leaving the blazing docklands of Limehouse behind.

CHAPTER TWENTY-ONE

Unnatural Selection

The zeppelin plied its way slowly through the smog-bound skies over London. It passed over towering tenement buildings and the spider's web of the Overground network, following the course of the Thames, a darkly glistening amethyst in the last light of dusk and the first hour of darkness. Aero-engines purring at cruising speed, it soared majestically through the encroaching night, caught in the staccato flicker of the city's rainbow display of lights, their ever-changing colours giving the envelope of its balloon the illusion of shimmering scales.

Slung beneath it was the heavily-armoured gondola, looking not-unlike the hull of a battle-cruiser, inside which was carried the vessel's deadly payload, as well as a squad of armed and dangerous Darwinian Dawn guardsmen. These men were fanatics, prepared to lay down their lives for what they believed to be the good of mankind, to bring about a violent social revolution at the very heart of the world-spanning empire of Magna Britannia. Positioned towards the aft of the gondola the twin engines directed the dirigible onwards over the labyrinthine streets beneath, over the crumbling docklands of Limehouse, past Ratcliff, above the thoroughfares of Shadwell, skirting the wharfs of Wapping, and on towards its initial target.

Beneath the great behemoth of the skies, but still a good half a mile behind it, the sleek, darkly gleaming shape of the Mark IV Silver Phantom sped through the celebration-emptied streets, pursuing the dirigible on what its driver hoped would be an interception course.

Dr Cornelius Wilde gazed out over the fenced compound beyond the rooftops of the Waterloo Barracks, past the rolls of razor wire that topped the towers of the Outer Ward and into the deepening darkness to the east.

The air was still and close with the heat of summer, intensified by the smothering layers of pollution-troubled cloud that hung over the city like a funeral shroud. The usual long white lab coat hung from his bony shoulders as if still on its hanger. A large teak and brass-finished mind box was harnessed to his chest and shoulders with leather straps. A deep pocket bulged.

Beneath his lonely position, high on the battlements of the White Tower, his test subjects trudged around the perimeter of the cobbled Inner Ward as they were coerced into enduring yet another hour of enforced exercise, under the ever-attentive optical sensors of the 'Beefeater' model automata-guards.

It was unusual for the inmates to have a drill period when they would normally be back in their cells, doors locked for the night, but then there had been many out of the ordinary arrangements during Dr Wilde's work to develop the mind control collars, that one more aberration was not really that much of a surprise to anyone. As far as the robo-guards were concerned, Dr Wilde's command clearance was second only to that of Governor Colesworth himself. The governor was among the great and the good invited to attend the gala dinner at the recently reconstructed Crystal Palace, to conclude the day's jubilee celebrations. So, as far as the droids were concerned, Dr Wilde's word was the highest-ranking authority left in the complex.

The inmates trudged on round the stark floodlit ward,

begrudging every step but knowing no other life. Any sense of individuality his subjects might have once have had had been stripped from them. Fading blue tattoos, rough scars and other bodily disfigurements, such as broken noses and missing teeth, the only remaining reference to them ever having had a savage and down-trodden life of their own. Their heads were shaved, they all wore the same drab, one-size-fits-none coveralls and each man had his neck trapped in the vice of one of the good doctor's behaviour modification devices.

And then, there it was, a flicker of reflected light from one of the sweeping arc-beams. Peering even harder through his round-rimmed spectacles at the blanket of smog smothering the city, Wilde could make out the piscine shape of the airship as it hove into view over the Thames, framed between the ornamental barbican of Tower Bridge.

His heart leapt in excitement, the dour expression on his face becoming a grin of adrenalin-fuelled excitement. The hour had come.

He could see the running lights as well now. The movement of its tailfin suddenly side on, starkly visible in the sweep of a searchlight, as with a shift of its rudder, the zeppelin angled in over the river, heading directly towards the maximum security prison facility. Wilde could almost make out the distant purr of its engines. It was no distance away at all now, three hundred yards at most. The doctor was not the only one aware of the zeppelin's approach now. The prisoners paused in their tracks, looking up at the great grey belly of the dirigible as it hove into view over the turrets of the White Tower.

Even the Beefeater-drones, their clockwork craniums processing the overwhelming sensory input and calculating that this was a possible threat to the security of the facility, turned their glowing bulb eyes towards the airship – and promptly shutdown.

Wilde smiled, taking his finger off the nondescript brass switch on the control panel in front of him. Command clearance was a wonderful thing.

A klaxon wail began somewhere within the prison compound. Ignoring the clamour and commotion welling up within the cordoned exercise yard, Wilde turned his full attention back to the approaching leviathan. It was preparing to cross the outer curtain wall of the Tower complex, having steadily descended to a height nearing only one hundred feet.

There was a barely-heard whining mechanical noise and the bottom of the steel gondola's hull cracked open, ready to deploy the airship's deadly cargo.

"They're getting ready to deploy!" Ulysses gasped, watching through the windshield as the zeppelin's bomb bay doors eased open. He had assumed that the jubilee celebrations in Hyde Park would be the Darwinian Dawn's target but it seemed that he had been wrong.

The dirigible had moved ahead of them with ease, unimpeded by the need to follow the maze of city streets beneath it, able to travel where it pleased over and among the great canyons of the capital's towering skyscrapers and tenement buildings.

"Don't worry, sir, we're nearly on them," Nimrod said, disregarding a set of traffic lights and steering the speeding automobile over onto the other side of the thoroughfare.

Simeon hooted in wild abandon at the adrenalin-rush of the ride as Nimrod accelerated away from Jamaica Road and onto Tooley Street.

In their journey from the decrepit Limehouse docks they had already crossed the river once at the Rotherhithe Bridge to avoid a road closure, and now they were going to have to do so again if they were to have any chance of catching up with the zeppelin.

The Silver Phantom roared up the road and towards the floodlit bastions of Tower Bridge.

"Oh, I don't bloody believe it!" Ulysses exclaimed.

The bridge was closing to traffic, beginning to rise to allow a steam ship to pass through. Nimrod had to slam on the brakes to stop them from running into the back of the vehicle in front. There was a short queue waiting for the barriers to rise again.

"Don't worry, sir, a little obstacle like this won't stop us," Nimrod declared, pulling out from behind a cab and gunning the throttle. "I have long had a healthy disregard for the rules of the road."

He slammed his foot down. Wheels spun and the stink of burning rubber assailed them. Then the tyres found purchase and the car rocketed forward.

The red and white-painted barrier splintered like matchwood across the front of the Phantom. The front bumper crunched as it hit the rising section of roadway. The automobile hurtled on up the incline. The edge of the bridge section appeared ahead of them – the clear air between it and its counterpart steadily increasing as the bridge continued to rise.

"Nimrod, are you sure we can make it?" Ulysses said, overcome by a sudden moment of doubt.

"Have no fear, sir," Nimrod replied, voice raised over the protesting scream of the engine. "Of course we ca..."

Ulysses' prescient sense flashed like a camera bulb in the darkness. A dark shape swooped at them out of the enclosing night.

"Bloody hellfire," the unflappable butler suddenly exclaimed, "what was that!"

"Pterodactyl I believe, old chap," Ulysses replied, equally startled. "They're getting bold."

The unexpected appearance of the dinosaur had caused Nimrod to swerve instinctively.

And then the car hit the end of the rising bridge-section.

With a clatter the first of the huge spined devices was ejected from the bomb bay of the zeppelin. Looking like some massive steel-skinned sea urchin it dropped like a stone into the drained moat, detonating on impact with the sludgy mud at the bottom of the ditch. The explosion peppered the bastion's outer wall with deadly steel shrapnel that impaled itself in the stonework, smashing windows. Although it had missed the inner curtain wall by only a matter of a few feet, the sudden heat generated by the explosion vaporised the contents of the device's secondary compartment. The steam produced by the exothermic reaction washed across the moat and over the curtain wall of the Tower's original medieval fortifications as a heavy, low-hanging mist.

Alarms bells were set ringing inside the prison, the cacophonous sound of them joining the wailing of sirens, throwing those trapped inside the Tower into a state of panic.

The second bomb smashed through the roof of the hospital block, blowing out every window in the building as it exploded somewhere between the second and first floors, killing or maiming many of those recovering there as they lay helpless in their beds.

A third device – fully four feet in diameter – was

launched into the wailing air and bounced off the north-east turret of the White Tower, crushing the lead-covered cupola and tearing down the seventeenth century weathervane, landing in front of the sturdy, reinforced doors of W block. The solid construction of the stone archway at the entrance to the old barracks directed the force of the blast. It shredded the prison-block doors, hurling what remained of them inwards, chased by a devastating fireball. The concussive force of the blast swept across the courtyard compound, bowling prisoners before it, several men being impaled by the spiny shrapnel of the cruel device.

Inmates were fleeing in all directions, some in panic but just as many having clocked that their robotic guards were failing to react and seizing on the chance to escape, scaling the chain-link fence or throwing themselves through the now unprotected gateways.

Mist was pouring out of the shattered frontage of the hospital block, drifting inexorably across the inner ward and through the chain-link fence surrounding the exercise yard. The choking clouds smothered the desperate prisoners like a thick sea-fog until they could hardly see their own hands in front of their faces, their fellow inmates appearing as blurred grey figures amidst the searchlight-shot whiteout.

There were prison warders amongst them too, unimpeded as their robot counterparts mysteriously appeared to be, but the acrid, obscuring steam took away identities and made one man like another – a new status quo achieved through one simple, violent action – incarcerated and incarcerator truly one at last. The mist smelled unpleasantly of spoiled meat combined with the sickly sweetness of aniseed.

Men were coughing now, choking as they inhaled the

vapour, the mist hot and wet in their throats. Then the wracking coughs gave way to a palsied shaking, the bodies of prisoners and prison guards alike gripped by agonising seizures, hands forming into rigid talons, eyes bulging from faces turned near purple with the strain, veins writhing beneath the skin.

As they struggled for air, drawing in yet more of the poisoned air, a terrifying transformation took hold.

Dr Wilde watched the chaos consuming the Tower of London through the thick lenses of a gas mask.

The walls of London's maximum security prison and correctional facility had been breached and those interred within it were being transformed into a berserk fighting force that would bring the capital to its knees.

"Dr Wilde!" It was Nash, running onto the battlements. "The Tower's under attack."

Wilde turned. "Really?" he said, his voice muffled by the rubber snout of the gas mask.

Nash looked back at him stunned, the assistant's face ashen with fear. "It's a breakout, sir! A full scale prison break!"

"I would call it a liberation."

"What do you mean? Dr Wilde..." but the rest of Nash's words were drowned out by the roar of engines. The appalled young man looked up, his face paling still further as he took in the enormity of the airship above him.

There was the clatter of metal on stone as a rope ladder was dropped down, a black-garbed soldier visible in the open hatchway of the docking port above. As the ladder swept past him, the end of it trailing across the lead panes of the roof, Dr Wilde put one arm between a pair of rungs, a foot on another and held on as the airship moved on over the Tower keep.

With the doctor on board, the zeppelin began to rise. Nash looked on in disbelief as it climbed five, ten, fifteen feet. Then the trailing end of the ladder was in front of him and, without really thinking about what he was doing, he grabbed hold.

"I can't be a party to this!" he screamed into the rushing air over the deafening roar of the engines. Dr Wilde ignored him – probably not even aware of the insane actions of his underling – and continued to climb as the airship rose higher.

Not daring to look down, the downwash of the zeppelin's engines forcing him to narrow his eyes, Nash began to climb. He caught up with Wilde at last and clamped a hand around his ankle.

Then the doctor knew he was there and was not pleased by the discovery. "What are you doing, you idiot?" Wilde shouted through the mask, shaking his leg violently. But Nash would not budge willingly. In fact, now that he had caught up with Wilde, he didn't know what to do next.

Clinging on to the rung before him with both hands, Dr Wilde risked lifting a foot off the ladder. Taking the strain with his arms he kicked out at the poor man beneath him.

"Get off!" he screamed as the heel of his shoe slammed into his assistant's cheek. "Get off!" He struck out again.

Nash's nose broke with a wet crack and he reeled, his vision blurring. His grip on the doctor's ankle slackened.

"Get! Off!"

Wilde's foot slammed down on the fingers of Nash's hand and the man let go. His intentions had been insanely courageous, but ultimately suicidal.

No scream escaped his lips as, only barely conscious,

Abelard Nash dropped one hundred and thirty feet, only just missing the crenulations of the White Tower. The vaporous billows of the Galapagos serum swallowed his body and deadened the sound of his impact on the cobbles below.

Amazingly the fall did not kill the valiant, yet wretched, man instantly. Even as the de-evolved things that had once been the criminal inhabitants of the Tower of London tore his broken body apart, Abelard Nash was already beginning to resemble something less than human himself.

And all the while the bombs continued to fall. Only someone on board the airship was getting his eye in now.

A fourth bomb smashed into the roof of the Bloody Tower checkpoint, obliterating it entirely in a sheet of flame and concussive white noise. A fifth device thudded into the cobbled alleyway of Mint Street and remained there for a moment, buried up to its mid-line in the foundations of the roadway, before detonating seconds later. A sixth bomb demolished the riverside wall of Water Lane.

The seventh device shunted out through the belly of the gondola missed the gatehouse of the Byward Tower but hit the ground in the culvert beneath the bridge connecting the structure to the outer Middle Tower. The explosion brought down part of the bridge and shattered the foundations of Byward, the tower falling in on itself and breaching the outer defences of the facility.

Somewhere in the distance the wails of approaching emergency vehicles could be heard, although what they would be able to do to help now was anybody's guess.

The greatest concentration of emergency services was on standby around Hyde Park and the surrounding streets that night. Those few that would be spared to rush to the beleaguered Tower would be too little and too late to contain the situation.

With a great hooting and caterwauling Dr Wilde's test subjects – no longer men but changed into something more degenerate and primitive – broke free of their prison. The brutal ape-like creatures that emerged from the shattered gatehouse of the Middle Tower wore the garb of prisoners and prison officers alike, burst and torn by the warping bodies trapped within them.

A hairy beast at the front of the brawling pack – stripped to the waist with the faded blue tattoo of a death's-head just visible beneath the thick matting of orange fur covering its torso – rose up on its hind legs and bellowed its savage intent at the sprawling capital. A small red light winking on the iron collar fastened around its neck, with a bellow of primeval fury, the apeman with the shark-like teeth led the rambling degenerate tribe west and into the city.

The Silver Phantom rounded the corner of the Tower and sped away along Byward Road. Having cleared the gap between the separating sections of the bridge and smashed through the barriers on the other side, the car and its three jolted passengers had pulled up outside the Tower as the zeppelin passed over the prison complex.

It had been immediately apparent that there was nothing they could do that would make any real difference to the catastrophe engulfing the prison. Instead they pulled away, Ulysses seizing the opportunity to get ahead and warn the authorities at Hyde Park of the impending danger. Then, suddenly, he had a novel idea.

"Nimrod, stop the car!" he commanded. His manservant reacted in an instant, slamming on the brakes hard.

The Phantom slewed to a halt on Byward Street, west of the Tower, a steam-powered vegetable delivery van honking its horn as Nimrod blocked the road. Ulysses leapt out and ran round to the boot of the car.

"Sir, is this really the time?" Nimrod shouted from the driver's window.

Simeon was bouncing up and down on the back seat in unrestrained excitement.

Ulysses had opened the boot and was rummaging through the eclectic mix of objects that cluttered the back of his car.

"Trying to win us an advantage," Ulysses called back, tugging aside a tarpaulin and rooting around in the compartment next to the spare wheel.

The airship was heading towards their position now, pulling away from the Tower as it continued on its inexorable journey westwards across the capital.

"Sir, I don't think we have anything that can bring down a zeppelin," Nimrod stated with grim finality.

"I'm not planning on bringing it down." He said, and then he found what he was looking for. "Yes! I knew that this was still in here!" he lifted out a heavy metal cylinder.

"Oh no, sir, you don't mean..."

"Look, don't worry about me," Ulysses said, slamming the boot shut and flashing Nimrod a devilish grin. "I've told you before; I'm making this up as I go along. You just worry about getting to Hyde Park before that dirigible does. Find Allardyce, or whoever's in charge there. Warn him. Tell him the Queen is in danger. Here," he said reaching into a jacket pocket and taking out a slim leather card case. "You'll probably need this. Now go!"

Nimrod didn't question the command but, trusting to his employer's instincts, drove off at speed, leaving a fumy cloud of exhaust in his wake.

With Nimrod, Simeon and the Phantom speeding away in the direction of Hyde Park and the festivities being held there, and with the armoured zeppelin of the Darwinian Dawn heading towards him at cruising speed, Ulysses secured his cane in the belt of his trousers before hefting the dull grey barrel of the launcher onto his shoulder. Jerking his shoulders to adjust its position, he sighted the approaching airship.

Ulysses closed his eyes and breathed in deeply. Letting the breath out again in a controlled manner, he focused. It was a conscious effort to slow his heart rate and calm his adrenalin-agitated system, a technique he had learnt from the monks of Shangri-La. All the while his extra-sensory awareness screamed, his heightened fight or flight response setting every nerve ending tingling, trying to prepare him for whatever might befall him next.

Ulysses had the aft section of the airship's gondola caught in the cross hairs.

"Steady," he told himself, letting the dirigible come even closer still. "Steady."

He tracked a spot on the gondola's hull, moving with it, until the airship was directly above him. And only then did he pull the trigger.

With a firework *whoosh* the rocket-grapple launched, the claw hurtling skyward, a high-tensile cable uncoiling from the chamber behind it in a spinning whirl. Through the cross hairs of the launcher's sights, Ulysses watched as the grapple struck the side of the gondola and snagged around an engine mounting, locking shut like a gin-trap.

With the grapple locked tight, the winding mechanism inside the launcher kicked in, motor screaming as it wound in the slack on the cable. Hanging onto the launcher handle, muscles tensed, Ulysses' feet left the ground and the breath was snatched from his lungs as he was carried upwards into the smoggy London night sky. The winch continued to wind him in as the zeppelin continued on its inexorable flight across the capital towards Hyde Park and the downfall of the British Empire.

CHAPTER TWENTY-TWO

State of Emergency

The tornado howl of the engine in his ears, Ulysses clung on as the grapple-winch wound in the last few feet of cable bringing him within reach of one of the gondola's landing struts. Buffeted by the wind, with London spread out below him like an illuminated street map, he reached up with his left hand and grasped hold of the strut. Now, how was he to get inside?

Ulysses looked around him, scanning the exterior of the armoured gondola for an easy access point. An arm's reach away, in front of the undercarriage was an emergency release handle.

Adjusting his grip around the landing strut, his eardrums aching at the pressure of the whirling propeller roar, he released the grapple-launcher and swung himself under the hull of the gondola, grabbing hold of the pull-release. He pulled the handle away from the riveted hull and, with a hiss of escaping air, a panel swung open.

He hung there for a moment, feeling a twinge in his right shoulder, the wind whipping around him, tugging at his jacket, as he considered the precipitous drop beneath him. Then, with a supreme effort, he swung out beneath the gondola, letting go of the landing strut and grasped the lip of the open hatchway. Fingertips scrabbling for a better purchase, he seized hold of a cable bundle, just as the sweaty fingers of his left hand lost their grip on the release handle. He winced, gritting his teeth against the pain flaring in his right shoulder and, for a moment, Ulysses swung from the open hatchway by one arm, the fatal drop waiting below him.

Then, at last, his left hand found a hold and he hauled himself up into the belly of the gondola, puling the hatch shut after him.

Crouched next to the access panel, Ulysses quickly took in the criss-crossing girders ahead and behind him. He was in some kind of service and maintenance sub-deck. Knotted cabling ran the length of the space and the roof was too low for him to stand upright.

Inside the roar of the engines became a background thrumming that he could feel vibrating through his body. The tight space was hot with the smell of rubber glue and oil. To his right a metal ladder led up to a hatch. This, he deduced, must lead into the main body of the airship's gondola carriage. He listened at the hatchway, trying to filter out the background noise of the engines. He could hear nothing out of the ordinary so, pistol in hand, he opened the hatch. Poking his head through he found himself looking at a narrow corridor, with a wheel-locked door at the far end. Without further hesitation, Ulysses pulled himself up and into the main body of the zeppelin.

His sixth sense flared even as he heard the metallic click of a door opening.

Inspector Maurice Allardyce surveyed the great and the good of the empire of Magna Britannia. Minor royalty, nobility, politicians, philosophers, academics, scientists, industrialists, philanthropists and self-made millionaires of one kind or another, all gathered together under the glass roof in the second Crystal Palace.

The Bolshevik in him wanted to rise up and overthrow the bourgeoisie oppressor. This part of him despised them all. In his eyes they had all got to where there were, and continued to enjoy the position they were in, by taking advantage of the downtrodden working classes. Men like that were the bane of his life, just like Ulysses Quicksilver had been. Allardyce prided himself on being a 'common man', rising from a humble working class background, his father a navvy at the cavorite works at Greenwich, to become an Inspector of Her Majesty's Metropolitan Police. He had not taken advantage of anyone to get where he was today.

But cut Maurice Allardyce in half and you would have seen the words 'Royalist' and 'Patriot' running right the way through. Again, it was Allardyce's working class roots that had bred in him a fierce devotion to the crowned head of Magna Britannia. He had been brought up to respect the throne of England and all that it stood for even though, ironically, it was the House of Hanover that had taken advantage of and kept entire nations – and now most of the globe – downtrodden beneath its colossal heel. But then Allardyce's logic gave up long before ever reaching such conclusions. He liked to keep things simple – black and white, right and wrong – which was one of the reasons why he had become a policeman and another reason why he despised men like Ulysses Quicksilver.

As a servant of Her Majesty's police force it was his duty to protect the Queen and all Her Majesty's guests. On this most grand and important of occasions, the responsibility for seeing that the monarch came to no harm had been laid directly upon him. When he had been given the news of this latest assignment he had almost burst with pride.

Pride that he felt now as he looked across the vast expanse of the Crystal Palace's interior. It was bedecked with glittering chandeliers strung with the lights of thousands of candles, and was laid end to end with tables covered with miles of cloth, hundreds of floral arrangements, ice sculptures, and thousands of pieces of cutlery and crockery. All this to feed twelve hundred guests at a gala dinner that was the culmination of a day of empire-wide festivities, parades and celebrations. In London alone these had included a fly-by by Her Majesty's Royal Airship *The Empress*, and the unveiling of the colossal statue of Britannia. Ninety feet tall and wearing draped white robes with her traditional regalia of Corinthian helmet, trident, spear and Union flag-bearing the hoplon shield, this striking statue had been designed by the world-renowned Italian sculptor and artist Eduardo Michelangelo.

As he was checking on the positions of the Peeler-drones and their human counterparts stationed around the perimeter of the palatial dining room, Inspector Allardyce became aware of the commotion halfway down the hall to his right. The guests seated close to this spot were turning round in confusion and annoyance. Swearing like the navvy's son he was Allardyce hurried to intercept the constable-droid now approaching him. The Peeler-drone's black carapace had been polished especially for the occasion to give it that 'just off the production line' look.

"What is going on, Palmerston?" Allardyce demanded.

"Is that Allardyce?" an imposing, grey-haired older man was asking as he pushed his way out from behind the constable-droid. "It is imperative that I speak with you, sir."

"And who the bloody hell is this? Did you let him in here? What's wrong with you? Is your Babbage unit on the blink, you useless piece of scrap?"

"I have a dire warning to impart, Inspector," the man

was insisting. He was wearing an outfit befitting a gentleman's butler.

"How did you get in here?" Allardyce demanded. The butler flipped open a leather cardholder. "You're not sodding Ulysses Quicksilver that's for sure!"

"No, inspector. My name is Nimrod."

"Somebody take that off him at once!" Allardyce snapped. No one had thought to revoke Ulysses' security clearance since his widely reported demise, and the slowly chugging administrative machine was yet to deal with the aberration.

As a Peeler-drone moved to obey, something that looked like a gorilla in a dinner jacket flung out an arm and lifted Constable Palmerston off the ground, one meaty hand gripping the robot's neck.

"And what the bloody hell is *that*?" Allardyce shrieked, pointing at the man-beast lurking at Nimrod's shoulder. Fully half the diners were looking in the direction of the rumpus now.

"*He*," Nimrod stated pointedly, "is my associate, Simeon." Curiously, the Neanderthal didn't look entirely out of place in his black suit, shirt and tie.

"And for the umpteenth time, who exactly are you, Mr Nimrod?"

"I am Mr Quicksilver's personal manservant."

"Well, you are incredibly poorly informed for someone who was once in that dandy's employ. Hadn't you heard? Quicksilver's dead!"

"Look, we haven't got time for this, Inspector. The queen is in terrible danger. There has been a mass breakout from the Tower."

"The Tower? Are you mad as well as stupid? That's a maximum-security facility. The only way anyone could break out of there would be if someone on the outside blasted a hole in the wall."

"Such as someone with a zeppelin carrying a payload of explosives like the ones that you and your men recovered from the Underground, you mean?"

Doubt suddenly seized hold of Allardyce then.

"Mr Nimrod, you are under arrest. Constable Palmerston, would you..."

"Is there a... problem, Inspector?"

Allardyce froze, hearing the icily calm voice behind him. He turned, suddenly flustered. "No, Prime Minister, no problem at all."

Uriah Wormwood peered down his nose at Allardyce from behind steepling, porcelain-fine fingers and arched a quizzical eyebrow in the Neanderthal's direction. "Only her majesty is preparing to address her loyal subjects."

"Yes, Mr Wormwood sir, of course, sir. I was just about to have this felon and his monkey escorted from the premises."

"Very good, Inspector. Carry on."

"Prime Minister!" the belligerent butler suddenly shouted, the carefully judged tone of his voice cutting through the hubbub of the excited diners. "Mr Wormwood, sir! I have a message from Mr Ulysses Quicksilver."

The Prime Minister suddenly froze and then turned quick as a striking snake.

"What message?" he asked in an icy hiss that dropped even a few degrees more.

"Her Majesty is in terrible danger, sir. The Darwinian Dawn are on their way here now in an armoured airship having engineered the release of the maniacs from the Tower of London. They also have a payload of explosives like those used in their earlier bombing campaigns, only ten times more powerful. You have to get the Queen to safety, sir!"

The Prime Minister listened to the butler's outburst with consternation knitting his brow. Then a slow, reptilian smile spread across his face and he leapt onto the dais from which the speeches were to be made, with almost balletic joy. Not once did he question the veracity of the butler's words.

"Your Majesty, honoured guests, lords, ladies and gentlemen," he said into the microphone, his voice reverberating from speakers positioned throughout the Crystal Palace and being relayed to those enjoying the spectacle via the giant broadcast screens around Hyde Park, "I am sorry to interrupt these celebrations but it has come to my attention that those who traitorously seek to overthrow our glorious empire are making one last desperate move at the very heart of our nation, within the capital itself!"

Cries of disbelief erupted from the assembled throng.

"Even as I speak the most violent and dangerous criminals this nation has ever known are running amok through the streets of our capital and all reports suggest that they are bringing their wanton orgy of carnage and destruction to our very gates, whilst the self-styled evolutionary revolutionaries of the Darwinian Dawn are heading this way, intending to depose our most beneficent and dearly loved monarch!"

There were screams now, the clatter and crash of tables overturning as the great and the good rushed to escape the oncoming chaos. Outside, in the shadow of the newly unveiled monolithic statue of Britannia, the crowds of gathered patriots and well wishers panicked, jostling one another to get away from the approaching menace, not caring who they trampled beneath their feet. It was truly every man for himself, as the animal instinct to fight or flee took over.

Back inside the rapidly emptying Crystal Palace Wormwood went on with his address to the nation. "Magna Britannia is facing the greatest threat it has known in over fifty years. And so, by the powers invested in me by the Anti-Terror Bill I declare that this nation is facing a state of emergency and do submit myself to take full control of our proud nation's resources to put down this insurrection and bring an end to this crisis. Londinium Maximum is now under martial law.

"Inspector Allardyce, have your men ready to repel an attack from the ground and the air. And somebody turn off those cameras. This broadcast is over!"

Letting the guard's unconscious body slide to the floor of the corridor, Ulysses paused at the door to the zeppelin's flight deck to check the load of his pistol and unsheathe his sword-cane. It hadn't been hard for him to outwit a bunch of rank amateurs like those employed as guards by the Darwinian Dawn. What they lacked in ability and awareness they made up for in quasi-religious revolutionary zeal.

He paused with his hand on the door. As he was so fond of telling Nimrod, he was really just making this up as he went along. He wasn't sure who or what he would find waiting for him on the other side, or what he was going to do about it once he found out. But in all honesty anything that could be done to slow the approach of the airship or change its flight path would be better than nothing and would give the authorities the time they needed to neutralise the threat the zeppelin and the escaped prisoners posed.

With a bold move he pushed open the door and burst onto the flight deck of the lumbering craft. "Nobody move!" he shouted. "I am taking control of this airship in the name of the empire and Her Majesty Queen Victoria. Anyone who has a problem with that will be the first to get a bullet in the gut. Got that?"

Ulysses Quicksilver panned his outstretched pistol arm across the surprised faces of those on the flight deck. There was the scar-faced blackguard Jago Kane – turning up once again like a very bad penny indeed – an older man wearing a peaked cap and the innocuous plain black uniform of the *Dawn* at the helm whom Ulysses took to be its pilot and a tall, blond-haired gangling figure in lab coat and glasses.

"You're a harder man to kill than I gave you credit for, Quicksilver," Kane said with unsmiling humour.

"Let's hope the same doesn't prove to be the case with you," Ulysses threw back.

Ulysses' attention was momentarily drawn to the conglomeration of lights to the fore and below the still advancing airship. Through the glass bubble at the prow of the zeppelin's gondola he could see Hyde Park spread out beneath them.

"You've failed, Kane. You and your evolutionary revolutionaries," Ulysses sneered, savouring the moment. "It's over. Your little schemes for this great sceptre'd isle have all come to naught."

"Oh, I wouldn't be so sure of that," came a voice like honeyed silk, and suddenly Genevieve Galapagos – or rather Kitty Hawke – was behind him, the cold snub nose of a gun pressed to the back of his head. "And I won't miss this time, lover-boy."

CHAPTER TWENTY-THREE

The Importance of Being Simeon

"Goodbye, lover," Kitty said.

There was a sharp crack. Ulysses flinched whilst Jago Kane gave a stifled groan, his scarred face twisting into an even more ugly grimace as he crumpled to the floor of the flight deck.

Momentarily deafened Ulysses spun round, instinct taking over, bringing both pistol and sword to bear.

"Don't look so shocked," Kitty said, levelling her gun at Ulysses. "He had served his purpose. As have you, Ulysses darling."

In the split second that followed it seemed to Ulysses as if time had slowed and yet, despite his state of heightened awareness, he could not move any more quickly himself. It was like he was trying to run through treacle. He could see Kitty's finger tightening on the trigger of the gun, see the barrel rotating to bring the next chambered round into the breach, see the sinister glint in her eye, the lascivious smile on her perfect rosebud lips. He was aware of the distant chatter of what he thought was gunfire. He could feel the thrumming of the airship's engines through the metal panels of the floor beneath his feet; smell the weird mixture of combusted fuel and hot rubber.

And then time sped up again as an almighty explosion shook the gondola. Kitty's shot went wide, the high velocity round striking one of the floor-to-ceiling windows at the nose of the craft. There was a sharp *plink*. All eyes focused on the perfectly round hole in the glass and Ulysses felt the rush of air being sucked out of the cabin. A spider's web of cracks skittered across the glass and then the window exploded, a sudden strong wind howling through the cockpit.

The airship lurched and its course altered dramatically as the pilot fought to regain control. Then the zeppelin nose-dived, the floor dropping away beneath their feet. Ulysses smacked into the observation bubble at the front of the flight deck, landing facedown on the glass, his cheekbone and jaw receiving a nasty smack. His right shoulder clenched in pain and his ribs felt bruised and sore.

The blond-haired gangling scientist was not so lucky.

Dr Cornelius Wilde felt the rush of air as the window blew out and looked around in frantic panic at the chaos consuming the cockpit. What was going on? Who was the interloper who had just burst onto the flight deck at this crucial moment? And what exactly did he think he was going to achieve? For that matter why were fellow agents of the Darwinian Dawn suddenly shooting at each another?

Before any of his questions could be answered the gondola lurched sharply. The floor dropped away and suddenly he was falling through the cockpit cabin. He flung out an arm to arrest his fall but cried out in pain as it struck the iron girder of an exposed structural beam. And then he was pitched sideways out of the shattered hole where only moments before there had been a floor to ceiling window.

With a shrill scream Dr Cornelius Wilde plunged groundward, dropping through the unresisting air, the cigar of the dirigible seeming to fall away from him into the night sky.

As he hit the ground pain so fierce and shocking, that

it would have taken his breath away even if it had not already been forced from him, seized his body in its bone-wrenching grip. He tried to move but a dislocated part of his mind told him that he had broken both legs, his right arm and probably his back, whilst various ruptured organs were even now filling his internal spaces with blood and other bodily fluids.

He suddenly felt so inexplicably tired that he decided he would just stay where he was and let sleep take him. The police would doubtless pick him up soon – the prospect seemed quite appealing – but until then he would just close his eyes for a few moments...

Hearing a savage grunt, Dr Wilde forced his drooping eyes open again. Standing over him was a colossal brute of a creature. It looked almost like a man in shape and form but there were some distinct differences, which that same detached part of his mind now focused on. The creature had the pronounced brow of a Neanderthal and its bruised and battered features looked like those of the lower orders of primates. Its shoulders were broad, its arms long and muscular and much of its exposed skin was covered with thick, wiry hair. From the waist down it was still wearing its grubby prison fatigues.

Wilde was gripped by a sudden and fearful realisation, just as a glimmer of what could almost have been recognition entered the apeman's eyes. Then he took in the collar clamped around the creature's bulging neck and the improvised club – what looked like part of a drainpipe – clenched in one curled fist.

A low growl issued from deep within the chest of the creature and Wilde felt what little blood there was left in his cheeks drain from them, the perspiration of shock and horror beading on his forehead. His blurring vision was drawn to a smudge of blue ink that was the mark of something on the flesh of the creature's chest under the fur that now covered much of it. The image had been stretched and distorted by the physiological changes that the creature's body had undergone, but it was still recognisable as a death's-head tattoo.

"M-McCabe?"

The apeman growled again, baring sharp yellow teeth in a grimace of simian aggression. Suddenly Wilde found himself surrounded by more of the de-evolved prisoners, all displaying the same stooping gait, arms pent up with furious muscular strength.

Shock forcing any desire for sleep from his mind, Wilde scrabbled for the control box with his shaking left hand. It lay at his side, the leather harness broken. He was dimly aware of buckled metal beneath his fingertips. Then they found purchase on the controls and Wilde furiously flicked at the switches and twisted the dials. But no matter what he did, it made no difference to the behaviour of the creature looming over him now. A high-pitched mewling whimper escaped Wilde's lips as he realised what was going to happen to him.

Wilde's degenerate army of psychotic apemen had reached Hyde Park. And now there was no one capable of controlling them.

The ape-beast that had once been the serial killer and cannibal, Ramsey 'The Shark' McCabe, felt a murmur of something in its primitive brain, an emotion that a more intelligent species might have called satisfaction, a feeling that justice had at last been served. Was there even a hint of something that a creature which could still articulate would have named, 'revenge'? Whatever the truth, it was its own creature again, with a mind of its own – with a mind to kill.

The airship jolted slightly as the shots hit home.

"That was a lucky hit," Nimrod muttered, slighting the Met's efforts.

"Lucky or not we got them!' Allardyce declared with grim triumph. "All units!" he called into his communicator. "Hit them again with everything we've got!"

At his command, the armed officers and droids of the Metropolitan Police Force opened fire once more on the zeppelin, which was even now dropping lower over the park, as if making a final strafing attack run. Truth be told, no one quite knew how they had managed to hit the zeppelin and take out an engine but they were certainly going to try to do the same again.

The zeppelin pulled out of its nose-dive and, hearing a cat-like shriek, Ulysses uncanny prescience flared and he rolled quickly onto his back. Then Kitty Hawke was on him. Carefully manicured nails clawed at his face, drawing blood. Her taut toned thighs gripped him around the waist, painfully squeezing his kidneys.

Pistol and sword abandoned, Ulysses grabbed Kitty's wrists and pushed her back up off him.

"Oh, Mr Quicksilver," she purred, her eyes those of some feral creature, mad and staring beneath the loosened fringe of her auburn hair, "are you always so rough on a first date?"

Swinging from the hips, pushing with his legs and pulling at the same time with his arms, Ulysses rolled onto his side again only this time trapping the coquettish Miss Hawke beneath him.

"First date?" he queried. "I thought this was the break-up!"

The two of them wrestled across the steel plate of the flight deck, the rattle of gunfire besetting the zeppelin and shattering windows around them. Until only recently, the thought of enjoying such vigorous physical contact with the erstwhile Genevieve Galapagos would have brought a twinkle to his eye and a yearning to his loins.

"I bet you never thought Genevieve Galapagos could be so frisky," Kitty teased, as if reading his mind.

Part of Ulysses still couldn't help finding the tousle-haired beauty beneath him attractive, the heave of her bosom in danger of escaping from her low-cut blouse, her lithe legs wrapped tight around his waist, hugging his flat stomach against hers. Only it wasn't Genevieve Galapagos, and although it had been Kitty Hawke's physique he had found arousing, it had been Genevieve's demure vulnerability he had been smitten by.

"Nothing but lies and deception, my dear, that's all it was," Ulysses stated accusingly. "I wanted to believe you. I wanted all my suspicions to be proved wrong. Genevieve Galapagos was such a charming, demure and sensitive young woman, whereas it would appear that Miss Kitty Hawke – streetwalker and gun-for-hire – is another manner of creature altogether. A complete and utter – how shall I put this? – bitch!"

With that Kitty Hawke spat at Ulysses, making him jerk back as the gobbet of saliva hit him squarely in the face. "You bastard!" she snarled.

Ulysses winced as she raised a knee, ramming it into his groin. As his own grip slackened in reaction to the sickening pain, the gorge rising in his throat, Kitty seized her chance. Managing to free one hand from Ulysses' grip, she grabbed his left arm, pulled her head up and sank her teeth into his wrist. Ulysses couldn't help but cry out in pain.

"I don't normally make a habit of hitting women," Ulysses gasped as Kitty hung on with her teeth, "but in your case I think I'll make an exception!"

His own right hand was free now and bunched into a fist. The punch descended, delivering a resounding blow to the side of Kitty's head. Her grip slackened and the hellcat slumped unconscious to the deck.

Wind howled around the cabin-cockpit, smoke boiling in from the burning engine. The remainder of the Darwinian Dawn were dead, unconscious or missing. The pilot lay broken at the helm. There was no one controlling the course of the zeppelin now.

Wrapping a handkerchief around his wrist to stem the flow of blood, Ulysses got rather unsteadily to his feet. He glanced down at the beaten beauty who looked so peaceful and innocent now, as if merely sleeping.

"Consider our relationship over," he said snidely, carefully probing his groin with one hand. And then, to no one in particular, "Now, let's see about stopping this thing."

"What's the situation on the ground, Nimrod?" his employer's voice crackled over the comm.

"In a word, chaos, sir," Nimrod replied matter-of-factly. "It's madness down here. The fugitives from the Tower have reached the park and are going on a bloody rampage. There are hundreds of them, sir and they're all..." Nimrod broke off, suddenly lost for words as he gazed upon the scene of carnage before him.

He stood at one of the entrances to the New Crystal Palace looking out across the darkened lawns of Hyde

Park. Everywhere he saw the public fleeing as the savage subhumans slaughtered policemen and fleeing dinner guests in an orgy of violence.

Simeon loitered at Nimrod's side, rocking from one foot to the other, as if just waiting for the command to join the fray.

The officers of the Met were fighting back but the savage brutes seemed able to sustain endless injuries, some unnatural vigour keeping them going even after they had been shot. The automata-policemen were faring little better, the ape-like creatures tearing them limb-from-robotic-limb, twisting off the droids' heads as if unstoppering bottles of beer.

"Nimrod, please repeat, I missed that last bit," Ulysses' voice came back.

"It's as you feared, sir. They're de-evolving. They're apemen, primitive savages with a taste for blood that delight in killing."

"Just as I suspected. Then I have a solution. Nimrod, get everyone out of the Crystal Palace: the Queen, Prime Minister Wormwood, everyone. And then get the apemen contained within it."

"And how do you suggest I do that, sir?" he asked, letting off a shot from his pistol as a tattooed ape smashed a droid-constable into the ground not ten feet away from him.

"There was some hare-brained scientist fellow on board using some kind of device to control them. He took it with him when he made his unexpected exit from the zeppelin through a window."

"I don't think anyone's controlling them now..." Nimrod broke off again as his eyes focused on the massive brute at the centre of the ape-pack. The creature was bellowing whilst holding something above its head.

"Nimrod? Come again old chap. I lost you again there."

The manservant said nothing as he stared at the mangled, blood-splattered wreckage of what could very well have been the device that Ulysses was talking about. Then the roar of aero-engines filled his ears and he looked up to see the zeppelin bearing down on the New Crystal Palace out of the flickering night's sky.

"Get them inside!" Ulysses was shouting. "I can't keep this thing airborne much longer. Ready or not, I'm coming!"

Nimrod jumped as Simeon gave a great bellowing hoot beside him and then leapt into the fray, barging policemen, party-goers and apemen out of the way as he made for his target.

He might only be a primitive imitation of a man but he understood enough to know that his new masters needed his help and he knew an alpha male of a pack when he saw one too.

Simeon's sudden outburst shook Nimrod into action. Turning, he ran back into the palace behind him. "Your attention ladies and gentlemen, if you would be so good as to make your way to the nearest exit? Everybody out! Move!"

Batting a shambling prisoner-ape aside with a double-fisted swipe, Simeon landed in front of the pack leader, the towering, collared, half-naked creature holding the ruined control box in its massive paws. The ape-thing fixed him with its beady yellow eyes from beneath beetling black brows.

Simeon rose up and then, ripping open his jacket and the shirt beneath, beat a tattoo of challenge upon his chest.

Lips pulled back from yellow teeth as the apeman displayed its response to Simeon's threat. It knew that its position as head of the pack was being challenged. And it seemed that the other apemen sensed it too. With a roar it returned the gesture, hurling the metal box aside. With barely a moment's hesitation, it threw itself at the Neanderthal.

Simeon was braced, ready for the tattooed ape's attack. As the brutal savage grabbed him round the middle, he trapped the brute in a headlock.

Toes gripping the turf beneath its feet the alpha apeman pushed up with its legs. Eyes bulging and face turning purple as Simeon tightened his grip around its neck, the apeman lifted its challenger off the ground. With a guttural, half-choked growl of effort it threw itself backwards, hurling Simeon over its shoulders. The two of them crashed to the ground, the action loosening Simeon's hold. But in the next instant the two battling primitives were on their feet again, a circle clearing around them – as the other apemen moved back or paused to watch – like a pair of roustabout prize-fighters ready for round two.

With mutual roars of aggression the Neanderthal and the apeman threw themselves at each other. Kicking, punching, gouging and biting, the two brute wrestlers fought on. They appeared equally well matched – one a de-evolving serial killer and cannibal, the other the semi-tamed product of a mad professor's dark ambition.

Getting in under Simeon's guard, the apeman sank its teeth into the Neanderthal's side. In response Simeon clubbed the savage around the head with both huge hands locked into one fist. The Neanderthal twisted a red-furred arm behind the monster's back until something snapped, the ape planting a foot into Simeon's midriff and kicked him clear with a roar of shrieking baboon rage.

Simeon crashed to the ground on his rump and felt something sharp dig painfully into his back. He reached behind him, hands closing around the roughly cuboid object, as the apeman, blood streaming from various cuts and grazes, bounded towards Simeon, ready to finish him once and for all.

The Neanderthal brought his arm back round, smacking the ape-savage around the head with the mangled control box. The blow sent the apeman tumbling sideways, stunned. Before it could recover itself, Simeon was on his feet again, the metal box now held in both hands above his head. With one powerful motion he brought the lump of metal and electronics down on top of the apeman's skull. There was a wet crack and the de-evolved convict slumped motionless onto the churned turf, but just to be sure, Simeon did the same again.

Ripping the torn remnants of the soiled shirt from his back, filled with his own feelings of savage satisfaction, Simeon planted one foot on the corpse of the apemen's bested quasi-leader. Howling with barely restrained feral joy he beat his chest again, his bellow ringing across the darkened park. The rest of the ape-pack seemed to freeze and then the regressed fugitives answered Simeon with a hooting cry of their own as they saluted the new leader of their tribe.

With a sweep of his arm Simeon beckoned his tribe towards the glittering structure of the New Crystal Palace.

Ulysses ducked as another pane of glass was blown to smithereens by gunfire. Gripping the wheel tightly in both hands – so tightly in fact that he could feel the nagging pain in his right shoulder grumble again – he braced himself against the floor of the flight deck as the zeppelin closed on the New Crystal Palace.

He felt a sudden tug on his leg and started. It was Jago Kane.

"We're going to die, aren't we?" he gasped, spluttering through bloody lips.

"You might be planning on doing so," Ulysses remarked sourly, "I, however, do not intend to go down with this particular sinking ship."

"Look, I know what you think of me," Kane coughed, bringing up more blood, "and you know what I think of you. You might say that our moral codes are... incompatible."

"Moral code? You?" Ulysses almost laughed.

"Look, just listen you arrogant shit," Kane's voice was as cold and clear as ice. "If you do get out of this alive the one you really want is Uriah Wormwood."

"Wormwood? What do you mean?"

"He's the one behind all this. Who else would have the power and influence to set something like this up, undetected?"

"How can I believe anything you tell me?"

"Can you afford not to?"

"Wormwood," Ulysses mused, half-forgotten suspicions reawakened. "But why are you telling me this now?"

"Because that slimy bastard betrayed me. He sold me out, me and my men, the ones who trusted his intentions." His increasing ire instigated another bout of cruel coughing. "Because if I'm going to die I want him to pay." Kane fixed Ulysses with a steely stare. "Swear it! Swear you'll get the bastard!"

"I... I swear it," Ulysses replied, dumbfounded, the

words feeling strange on his tongue as he swore an oath to the man who had long been his nemesis.

The glittering glasshouse structure now filled the view from the shattered cockpit. There was no doubt that the airship was set on a collision course. Sprinting back up the slope of the flight deck, as the zeppelin dived towards the Crystal Palace, he hurled himself back through the door by which he had entered.

Its one remaining engine emitting a high-pitched whine, the zeppelin hit the Crystal Palace. Iron bracing struts buckled, glass shattered and the flight deck was filled with whickering diamond shards.

The deafening scream of shearing metal and the cacophonous blast of hundreds of panes of glass shattering rang throughout the juddering gondola as Ulysses half-ran and half-fell through the airship as he made his way to the zeppelin's bomb bay.

There, in their steel cradles, hung the last of the Darwinian Dawn's deadly devices. Each carried a portion of Professor Galapagos's deadly regression formula.

Tugging the gas mask from the corpse of a black-clad guard Ulysses put it on, the smell of warm rubber and human sweat assaulting his nostrils.

He pulled hard on the first of a series of large metal levers in front of him. With a yawning groan the bomb bay doors swung open. Looking down, through the hole in the bottom of the airship, Ulysses could see the red-haired ape-things capering about inside the Crystal Palace. Shards of glass had rained down on top of them as the gondola collided with the palace and some lay either dead or mortally wounded as a result. Others were running amok, overturning dining tables and throwing gilt candlesticks, fine bone china and silver-plate cutlery at one another whilst others tried to eat the table decorations.

Ulysses grabbed hold of the second lever and then paused. Keying a number into his personal communicator he put the device to his ear. When the call was picked up he said, "Nimrod, are you clear?"

"Yes, sir. Everyone is out."

"Then keep going. This is one grand finale that's guaranteed to bring the house down."

"Yes, sir. Good luck. Nimrod out."

Ulysses took hold of the lever and pulled hard. Released from its harness the first of the Galapagos-bombs rolled forwards and off the end of the tilting cradle. Locking the lever in place, Ulysses got clear of the bomb bay as the rest of the devices followed the first, dropping towards the half-destroyed palace.

The airship had become wedged within the roof of the Crystal Palace, so that its gondola now hung amidst crumpled roof joists, its dirigible balloon still above it and undamaged outside of the stricken structure. For a moment Ulysses' world was wonderfully still, and then the first of the devices made groundfall.

Sheets of flame burst from the shattered glasshouse, consuming what had, only a matter of hours before, been a grand dining hall in a raging firestorm. The limp bodies of apemen were tossed into the air. The series of detonations rocked the gondola. Then, after the initial explosions, came the transmuting chemical clouds.

Having already been exposed to the weaponised gas of the formula, the Galapagos transformation was accelerated within the bodies of those convict-apemen not killed by the explosions. Stricken by a terrible palsy, their warping bodies spasmed as their entire physiological structure regressed at an unimaginable rate. Savagely snarling ape-features became as fluid as melting wax, mutating into lizard-like visages. Fur fell away to reveal scales or pliable amphibian skin.

Grotesque abominations were born as entire cell structures collapsed under the incessant changes they were being subjected to. Things that were half-mammalian and half-reptilian gurgled and hissed in their death-throes. Things with the blunt snouts of primitive men slithered through the coiling, rancid mists, limbs uncertain as to whether they should be claws or fins. Fish eyes blinked from quivering mounds of amorphous flesh, bones dissolved into the fluid flesh of invertebrates.

The process of accelerated de-evolution continued to a chorus of mewling moans and croaking cries until the warping bodies could no longer support themselves. Every last one of them ultimately collapsed into a morass of protoplasmic ooze that covered the carpeted floor of the New Crystal Palace in sticky mucus-like slime.

And at the far end of the hall, amidst the pooling slime, lay the remains of an altered suit of clothes.

CHAPTER TWENTY-FOUR

Unnatural History

Flinging open the door to the flight deck Ulysses surveyed the devastation. Glass littered the floor in myriad glittering shards. The bodies of the airship's pilot and the guardsmen lay where they had fallen. Kitty Hawke lay unconscious, face down, her body a pincushion for stiletto blade slivers of glass. But Jago Kane was gone.

Ulysses Quicksilver swore. Still his nemesis had managed to evade him. He had more lives than a cat! But wherever the murdering revolutionary had got to, he couldn't have gone far. He wouldn't have been able to make much of a head start with all his injuries. But, if Kane had been telling the truth – and Ulysses' own niggling suspicions made him believe that, incredibly, the terrorist might have been – the real villain of the piece could be making his getaway right now.

Leaning against a buckled strut Ulysses gazed down at the floor of the devastated Crystal Palace. Even through the gas mask he could smell the rancid meat and aniseed stench of the dissipating formula-gas. Amidst the bomb craters and burning piles of debris a thick ooze covered the floor of the building. From it rose wisps of a jaundice-yellow vapour. Nothing was moving down there, other than the occasion pop of a bubble in the seething slime.

Ulysses thought he heard the sound of footfalls. Looking to his left he could just see that where the gondola had come to rest. One of several maintenance walkways was accessible. From there his fugitive could easily make it to the ground and escape. That was the way Kane would doubtless be heading and it was where Ulysses needed to go now. For, even if his old nemesis had evaded him again, somewhere below, amidst all the chaos and confusion, Uriah Wormwood was in danger of getting away.

Wormwood cast fitful glances around whilst striving to maintain an outward appearance of calm, self-assured superiority. He had allowed himself to be evacuated from the dining room, along with the Queen and her dinner guests, and stood now at the side of the contraption-bound monarch, along with Victoria's personal attendants – her ladies-in-waiting and personal physician, the French surgeon Dr Mabuse – the entire party being surrounded by a bodyguard of armed police officers. Fifty yards away stood the smouldering wreckage of the New Crystal Palace, the Darwinian Dawn's airship still locked within its steely embrace.

Wormwood glanced at the ruler of the greatest empire the world had ever known, the merest arching of an eyebrow betraying his true feelings of disgust and distain. She was a far cry from the public image of the noble, determined woman who had ruled a quarter of the world during the greater part of the last century. There was more machine than monarch now, the physical husk the old woman had become was trapped inside the Empress Engine, a Babbage difference unit of the greatest complexity that provided life support and a basic level of steam-powered mobility for the Queen. The Widow of Windsor was just a withered creature kept alive long beyond her natural span and far longer than was good for her deteriorating mind. The scurrilous voice of rumour suggested that the encoded intelligence of the Babbage unit spoke on behalf of Her Majesty these days, mimicking the Queen's own voice by manipulating a bank of sound recordings made when Victoria was still able to speak for herself.

For many people the world over, Queen Victoria, Empress of India, Monarch of Mars and Ruler de facto of the Lunar colonies *was* the empire of Magna Britannia and Wormwood felt that too. She was the perfect embodiment of a decaying, outdated system maintained for much longer than was healthy for the benefit of the privileged few. But all that was about to change. When the sun rose the following morning, it would mark the dawning of a new age for Magna Britannia, its citizens and all the peoples of the world. The age of dinosaurs was over.

Thoughts of the future returned Wormwood to the upheavals taking place in the present. Things had not proceeded exactly according to plan, but he had his state of emergency nonetheless and had been able to put into play the special powers he was granted under the terms of the recently passed Anti-Terror Bill. This could still all turn out to his advantage. He just needed to make sure that he didn't let his mask of calm composure slip.

"Prime Minister, a word!" came a shout from behind him. Wormwood froze, feeling the trickle of ice water down his spine. It was the voice of Ulysses Quicksilver.

There was a gasp of wonderment from the gathered throng as Ulysses approached. Wormwood took a moment to compose himself and then turned to face the approaching dandy.

So it was confirmed. Ulysses had somehow survived Genevieve Galapagos's parting gift but he didn't look any the better for it. His once doubtless impeccable outfit was now in disarray as was the rest of him. His face was a mess of contusions, swollen lips and bleeding gashes. His left forearm was bound with a red-soaked handkerchief and one eye was half shut by a swelling black bruise.

"Greetings, Prime Minister," the rogue said, combing a

hand through the tousled mess of his hair. "I am here to report the successful resolution of the case you yourself charged me with two months ago."

"You are?" Wormwood said warily.

"I am, Prime Minister."

"Did I miss something? Aren't you supposed to be dead?" the astounded Inspector Allardyce interjected, forgetting himself for a moment.

"And good evening to you, Inspector," Quicksilver said with a sideways glance, flashing the bemused trench-coated policeman a wry smile, wincing as he did so. "You just can't keep a good man down I suppose. Aren't you keen to hear my conclusions?" He said, addressing Wormwood again.

"As I understood it that matter had already been brought to a conclusion weeks ago," Wormwood said, a frown of annoyance lining his face.

"Indeed. And that was my own opinion on the matter – although I had some lingering doubts – until you tried to have me blown up."

A gasp passed around the gathered group.

"Are you out of your bloody mind?" Allardyce challenged. It had been a long day and everything had just gone tits up in the most spectacular way possible. He just felt lucky that the Queen herself wasn't dead. "Have you recently received a bang on the head? Cos if you haven't I'll happily give you one if you carry on like this."

"No, Inspector, I am in full command of my faculties, thank you," Ulysses bit back. He was aware of Nimrod joining him at his shoulder.

"Is everything all right, Prime Minister?" the recording-synthesised voice of the monarch herself crackled from the speaker-horn of her mobile throne.

"I do apologise, your majesty," Wormwood said, a quiver of uncertainty entering his voice for the first time. "This will only take a minute. I shall be with you shortly."

"I was about to say the same thing myself, your majesty," Ulysses called out.

Around the park and the streets of the capital beyond, a thousand broadcast screens – that had relayed the apeman attack to the nation as the cameras continued to roll – now relayed the intrigue unfolding before the burning glasshouse ruins to an eager and anxious public.

"Arrest that man," Allardyce ordered a pair of robo-constables. "And turn those bloody cameras off!"

"Hold that order!" Nimrod commanded, stepping in front of the two drones, leather wallet card-case held open in front of their visual sensors.

"On whose authority, sir?" one of the constables asked affably.

"By the authority stated here on this card, Constable Palmerston," Nimrod said, reading the drone's name off the badge on its chestplate.

"I don't bloody believe this," Allardyce fumed, in exasperation. "You're supposed to be under arrest!"

"Inspector, if you would be so kind as to actually do something!" snapped Wormwood.

"Yes, of course, sir." The inspector moved to take hold of Ulysses himself. "I'll have this tosser out of your hair in no time, sir, if you'll pardon my French."

"But aren't you intrigued to know who's been behind the Darwinian Dawn and their attacks on our glorious capital all along, Inspector?" Ulysses asked, turning his attention to Allardyce.

"Scotland Yard are looking into it."

"It was you, wasn't it, *Mr Prime Minister Wormwood*?"

The nation took a sharp collective breath as the dramatic confrontation played out across the empire, courtesy of the Magna Britannia Broadcasting Company's continuous coverage of the jubilee event.

All eyes now turned in startled disbelief to the Prime Minister. Nimrod threw Ulysses an uncertain look as much to say, "Do you realise what you are saying?" Then the merest rumour of a tick rippled across Wormwood's face and Nimrod's moment of doubt was gone; he was convinced. The world held its breath.

"Where's your evidence?" Allardyce demanded.

"Do you want to tell them, Prime Minister, or shall I?"

Wormwood appeared not to have an answer for the dandy, for a moment. That in itself was unusual for the Prime Minister, who was used to verbal sparring on a daily basis in the House of Commons.

"You have wasted enough of my time already," Wormwood said at last and then, changing the subject: "Her majesty must return to Buckingham Palace at once."

"No? Shall I then? It was a dangerous game you were playing, involving me in your schemes. Arrogantly dangerous in fact, but then you had your get out clause planned from the start, didn't you?"

Ulysses began to pace between the frozen constables, making expansive gestures with his hands as if giving an after dinner presentation.

"I don't know what really happened at the Natural History Museum that first fateful night – I suspect only two people really do, and one of them is dead – but I think I have a pretty good idea."

"The Natural History Museum? What's that got to do with anything?" Allardyce asked, incredulously. He was seriously out of his depth now.

"Everything," Ulysses stated simply.

"Would you care to enlighten us then, Mr Quicksilver?" It was Wormwood who spoke now, his voice like the hissing of a viper.

"Inspector, tell me, did you ever discover what was taken the evening the night watchman died?"

"Well..." Ulysses had caught him off guard.

"You must have realised that the late Professor Galapagos' difference engine had been stolen. And who would go to all the trouble of stealing a very specific difference engine from the professor's lab at the museum, other than our mutual friend Jago Kane – eh, Prime Minister? – working on behalf of your good self, of course.

"I can only surmise what happened. Kane broke in but was surprised by the professor who was working late that night. There was a scuffle, things got broken, including a beaker of Galapagos' regression formula, which splashed onto the professor. Kane was untouched and made his getaway but the doomed professor underwent a sudden and violent transformation, becoming the apeman that later escaped from the Museum."

Ulysses was well into his stride now.

"It wasn't the engine itself that you wanted as such, but the formula for the serum that was contained within its data files."

"So who killed the night watchman?" Allardyce asked, having been so sure that it had been the same mysterious thief up until that point.

"Ah, that would be Professor Ignatius Galapagos, or what had once been one of the world's leading evolutionary biologists before the formula changed him. But there's no point looking for him now, he's dead."

"So you said. What happened to him? And how do

you know so much about it?" the bewildered Allardyce pressed on. "Did you kill him, Quicksilver?"

"Oh no, it wasn't me. You might say he was 'hoist by his own petard'."

"You what?"

"He got a taste of his own nasty medicine."

"You've lost me."

"Yes, I rather thought I had."

"But how does all this rumour and supposition allegedly link the Prime Minister with the Darwinian Dawn?" Allardyce threw in, smiling proudly to himself as if he had just played his trump card.

"Because Galapagos' difference engine contained the chemical breakdown of his regression formula, and the man who had that could reproduce as much of the stuff as he needed."

"Needed? For what?"

"For what you witnessed tonight: to create a suitably direct and dramatically devastating attack on the monarch, which would put his newly-introduced Anti-Terror Bill into action, thereby ensuring that he was given total control of the country and, by default, the entire empire. And all this would have been achieved perfectly legally, mind.

"But to access the difference engine's data files first he needed the unit's coded decryption key, and that was where his agent Jago Kane had fouled up. The now transformed Galapagos still had it about his person and that was where I came in, to search for the missing professor.

"If you hadn't given me that particular mission, I would never have stumbled upon the Dawn's secret bomb-making facility, but then you already know about that, don't you, inspector?"

Both Ulysses and Wormwood could see that the resolute Allardyce was wavering. His black and white view of the world was rapidly turning into a messy, confusing grey.

"You would trust the word of a known terrorist over that of your Prime Minister?" Wormwood yelled, his voice rising in pitch, his porcelain-pale skin flushing a deep crimson.

"But I still don't see how this all connects to the Prime Minister!" Allardyce was floundering

"I'm getting to that," Ulysses said darkly. "Two individuals have kept making regular appearances during the course of my investigations, either keeping me on track – giving me new clues, guiding me onwards – or alternatively attempting to frustrate my successful completion of the mission. Your accomplices, Prime Minister. You might call them your partners in crime. Jago Kane and Miss Genevieve Galapagos, the errant professor's lovely daughter."

No one passed comment now. Ulysses had his audience enthralled.

"The former a known terrorist now linked to the Darwinian Dawn, the latter, a fiction. There is no such person as Genevieve Galapagos is there, Prime Minister? This femme fatale goes by another name, does she not? Miss Kitty Hawke, assassin and strumpet extraordinaire!

"And before the good Inspector asks me once again what all this has to do with you, I have the evidence that you have had direct dealings with both these individuals, thanks to hearing it straight from the horse's mouth – the nag in this case being a very ill-humoured and embittered Kane – and secondly because the professor's code-key, which I returned to his oh-so loving 'daughter', was fitted with a tracking device. Wherever your little kitten and her imagined father's locket went, I went too."

Ulysses was interrupted by the abrupt roar of an aero-engine. All attention was diverted away from him and back to the ensnared zeppelin. The craft's remaining engine was firing back into life. Accompanied by a terrible screeching of tortured metal, the airship freed itself from the palace roof.

All eyes in the park watched as the dirigible came about, yawing heavily to port with only one engine still in operation.

There was a sudden shriek from one of the Queen's ladies-in-waiting and a cry of, "Mon dieu!" from Dr Mabuse. Ulysses turned.

"You argue a very convincing case, Quicksilver. Well done, very clever. Consider your mission successfully... concluded."

Wormwood was standing beside the Queen's steam-powered throne, the cold grey muzzle of a gun pushed up against the forehead of the withered old woman smothered beneath her heavily-embroidered mourning clothes.

"Mr Wormwood, we are not amused. What is going on?" an incongruously chiding voice issued from the throne's speaker-horn.

"I am very sorry, Ma'am, but unfortunately it would appear that everything is unravelling around me. The best laid plans, as they say. Consider yourself my... hostage."

A dumbstruck Inspector Allardyce made as if to direct his officers to act.

"And before anybody does anything rash, Inspector, need I point out that a man who was prepared to accept the deaths of hundreds, if not thousands, of innocent Londoners, for the greater good, whose plans have fallen down about his ears and who has nothing at all left to lose, would not hesitate to put a bullet through your dear monarch's head?" Wormwood said.

"Allardyce, stop!" Ulysses commanded. A crocodilian smile spread across Wormwood's lips as he saw a glint of panic in Ulysses eyes. "Just tell me this. Why would a man in your position, with your power, be interested in destabilising the status quo and throw in his lot with a group of zealous, quasi-religious revolutionaries?"

"The Darwinian Dawn? A mere fabrication, an invention of mine. Oh, of course, those who pledged their all to the cause believed it was for real, but it was merely a tool. But the core tenet behind it all is still sound."

"And that is?"

"Look around you, Quicksilver. Are you so blinkered by your own accepted worldview? Can you not see that there is so much wrong with London and, by extension, Magna Britannia itself? I could make it all so much better."

"So the Darwinian Dawn and its actions were merely a means to an end for you?" Ulysses said with growing realisation. "Engineer a suitably threatening state of emergency and then, with the powers granted you by your Anti-Terror bill invoked you would..." Ulysses trailed off.

"Have the power to do what I wanted. To go back to beginning, to start from scratch. I would have brought an end to slum-living, overcrowding and endemic disease and re-built London."

"In your own image."

"I had a great master plan for this city. The greatest advances this nation has ever known have followed times of trial and tribulation, times of enforced evolution, if you will. Consider the Great Fire of 1666. From the ashes rose a greater city, a better city for all. From the ashes of Londinium Maximum a still greater metropolis could have arisen, like a phoenix from the flames.

"And change is always difficult and traumatic, I understand that, but I could have coaxed the nation through that time until it fulfilled its true potential. Magna Britannia is an out-moded dinosaur, a creature of a bygone age that should have become extinct long ago. Just think of me as the agent of evolution."

"By Jingo! Finally I see what all this has been about," Ulysses declared.

"Of course, I have just told you what it is all about you idiot!" Wormwood said.

"Well yes, but you have given us the politician's answer. It is when we read between the lines that we see the truth. This is all about power. That's all it's ever been about from the start. Absolute power... corrupts absolutely."

"The opinion of fearful fools."

"You would have effectively re-written history according to your own warped view of how you think the world should be, your own unnatural history of the British Empire. But history is written by the victors. And you just lost!"

"Sir!"

Ulysses heard his manservant's shout at the same time as he became aware of the swelling sound of the zeppelin's straining engine and felt the howling gale of its downwash tugging at his clothes and hair.

Nose angled towards the ground, the zeppelin powered across the spoiled lawns of the park on an apparent collision course with the royal party. Gunfire chattered and ricocheted from the body of the armoured shell of the airship as Victoria's personal guard opened fire.

And then the dirigible was passing directly over them. Something swung out of the darkness beneath it. Ulysses ducked, the rattling rope ladder sweeping past him. As Ulysses rose again, following the airship's passing, his sixth sense flashing him a warning, he already knew what was going to happen. Time seeming to slow around him, he reacted without thinking, operating on instinct alone.

Then the zeppelin was rising and the Queen stood alone again, Wormwood scrambling up the ladder as the airship climbed to move out of range of fire.

Ulysses sprinted across the grass, paying no heed to how Allardyce and his robo-Bobbies might react, and then the last rung of the ladder soared away out of reach. The moment had passed. He had missed that vital window of opportunity.

Prescience flared again and one of the craft's mooring cables swung out of the darkness behind him. Suddenly fate had presented him with a second chance, and Ulysses leapt.

"Do you think he knows what's he's bloody well doing?" Allardyce asked the manservant.

"Oh, I expect he's making it up as he goes along, sir. That's his usual strategy," Nimrod replied.

Arms and legs aching, lungs heaving, heart pounding fit to burst, Uriah Wormwood staggered onto the flight deck of the airship. Air howled in through the shattered hemisphere of the gondola's burst glass bubble.

Amidst the wreckage of the cockpit Kitty Hawke, clothes and skin cut by splinters of glass, clung to the ship's wheel, her half-leaning stance making it hard to discern whether she was struggling to maintain control of the craft or whether she was clinging tightly to the steering mechanism to hold herself up.

Wormwood joined the young woman at the controls. Kitty turned, glaring at him in petulant, frustrated fury. Her hair hung down about her shoulders, in a wind-swept mess. Her perfectly-sculptured features were criss-crossed by the surgeon-fine red lines of myriad glass cuts and a bruise darkened the flesh above her right cheekbone.

"We failed," she said, the fire suddenly gone from her.

"No, my dear. This is not a failure. It is merely a... setback," Wormwood said, pulling himself up tall, staring into the distance. "We have merely lost the battle, not the war. I am not done with Londinium Maximum yet. No, this is not the end. The world has not heard the last of Uriah Wormwood. Or Kitty Hawke." Stiffly the elder statesman stretched out an arm and placed a hand on Kitty's shoulder.

"No, father."

Wormwood continued to stare out of the shattered cockpit, eyes narrowing against the rush of air. Below them the Victoria Embankment gave way to the rippling black mirror of the Thames, glistening with the lights of the sleepless city.

"We appear to be losing height, my dear," he said at last, as the floodlit barbican of Tower Bridge filled more and more of his field of vision.

"It's the balloon," Kitty said, sounding exhausted. "We've taken too much damage. I've lost rudder control and we're going down."

"How vexing. Then it is time to take evasive action, my dear, would you not agree?"

"Yes, father, only I think it might be too late for that."

"It's never too late, my dear. Remember that. It's never too late."

Ulysses clung on. His arms ached, his right shoulder numb with pain. He only wished he knew what he was supposed to do next. All he could do, it seemed, was hold on and hope to finally catch up with the errant Prime Minister when the airship finally came to ground, wherever that might be. But it seemed that the craft might be making its descent sooner rather than later.

Tower Bridge loomed before it and, rather than rising to pass over the rather obvious obstacle the edifice presented, the zeppelin was dropping towards it. A hundred feet below the dark waters of the Thames swept on towards the sea.

Ulysses considered his options and soon surmised that he didn't really have any. A fall into those turgid waters from this height would like as not prove just as fatal as a collision with the stone pylons of the bridge.

Let go or hang on. "Damned if you do and damned if you don't," he found himself pondering aloud. "Come on, Quicksilver, you've got out of worse scrapes than this in the past." His mind suddenly rushed back to his plummeting descent through the freezing air over Mount Manaslu. He had escaped death then – thanks to the fickle whim of fate and the beneficent monks of Shangri-La – but could he again? Had he finally run out of last chances?

And then the decision was taken out of his hands.

The nose of the zeppelin struck the north tower of the bridge and crumpled. Moments later the gondola collided with the crenulated turret tops. There was the sound of metal scraping against ornately carved stonework as chunks of masonry came away from the towers. Then there was a spark.

The balloon erupted into flame, a series of explosions blowing it apart as one gas compartment ignited after another. The zeppelin's final blaze of glory lit the City district and the tenements of Southwark for miles in every direction.

Ulysses fell, the rope suddenly slack in his hands, eyebrows scorched by the explosion, the blazing carcass of the dirigible dropping after him.

Then there was a stabbing pain in his right shoulder, as talons seized hold of him. The thump of leathery wings beat the air and Ulysses was suddenly pulled away over the water, away from the plummeting zeppelin.

Ulysses looked up. Above him the pterodactyl that had decided that he would make a tasty snack was struggling to maintain height itself. A moment longer, Ulysses realised, and the flying reptile would let go again, abandoning him to his original fate.

Now it was Ulysses' turn to hang on, grabbing hold of the pterodactyl's scaly legs even as it released its grip on his protesting shoulder. Ulysses' descent continued, only now in a more bizarrely controlled manner. It was only when his feet were practically dragging through the muddy waters of the river that Ulysses let go, the pterodactyl flapping away, back to its roost on the bridge.

He pulled himself from the river and climbed the iron rungs set into the embankment as the battered Silver Phantom pulled up on the road adjacent.

"It would appear that you have prevailed once again, sir," his butler said stoically as he emerged from the car and opened the rear passenger door.

"Indeed," Ulysses replied.

"If you don't mind me remarking, sir, you appear to be a little worse for wear."

"There's nothing quite like a night-time dip in the Thames is there Nimrod?"

"I wouldn't know, sir."

Nimrod shut the door after him and got back into the driver's seat. Ulysses gazed out through the darkened window.

"How is her majesty?"

"Returning to Buckingham Palace as we speak, sir."

"Good. Then the status quo is maintained. Everything is as it should be."

"I wouldn't say that, sir."

"No, I suppose you're right, now you mention it. Wormwood has made a change after all," he said, watching the burning wreckage of the zeppelin slowly being carried away on the surface of the restless river. "It is how those of us who are left deal with it that will make all the difference."

"Yes, sir."

"But we can worry about that later. Magna Britannia will still be there, waiting for us, in the morning won't it, old chap?"

"Thanks to you, sir."

"Bully for me."

And with that, the Silver Phantom slid away into the remains of the night and towards the dawning of a new day.

EPILOGUE

"Her majesty will see you now," a lady-in-waiting said and Ulysses Quicksilver was admitted to the high-ceilinged Throne Room.

Ulysses kept his head bowed as he approached the dais at the end of the ornately decorated audience chamber. Everything gleamed or sparkled, the crystalline light of the Throne Room's magnificent chandeliers reflecting from the gold leafed surfaces and polished marble.

The top tier of the dais, from where Queen Victoria had once received royal guests in person was now cordoned off from the rest of the room, surrounded by a curtain of scarlet velvet drapes.

There was a hazy quality to the air of the chamber and an all-pervading smell of pomanders and lubricating oil. Flunkies stood to either side of the dais, each of the automata-drones decked out in a footman's finery.

Ulysses looked up at the dais. The lady in waiting ushered him forwards and then disappeared behind the curtains herself, before emerging again and returning to Ulysses' side without saying a word.

Ulysses waited, standing to attention. He certainly didn't look out of place in top hat and tails, the sombre tones of the suit set off by a striking gold silk cravat embellished with a diamond pin and a red carnation buttonhole. In his right hand he held his bloodstone cane. His left arm was held tight to his chest in a black satin sling.

He cleared his throat nervously, recalling the last time he had met his monarch. A week had passed since the dramatic events surrounding the celebrations to mark the Queen's 160th jubilee year. If a week was a long time in politics, the political world had never known a week like the one just passed. Despite the Thames being trawled Jago Kane's body had not yet been recovered and he appeared to have disappeared from the face of the planet once again. At least the breakout from the Tower of London had been contained and work crews were already affecting repairs to the aging prison facility.

"Good morning, Mr Quicksilver," a voice like an old gramophone recording crackled from speakers standing either side of the drapes.

"Good morning, your majesty," he replied.

"Mr Quicksilver, we are informed that we have you to thank for the happy resolution of Prime Minister Wormwood's disgraceful rebellion."

Ulysses considered the hundreds who had died during the course of the Queen's jubilee and the terror attacks on the capital leading up to it. He would hardly have called it a happy resolution himself. But, "Thank you, Ma'am," was all he said.

"It would appear that you are following in a long-established family tradition, keeping the realm and the monarch safe from the predations of those who would see Magna Britannia fall."

"Just doing my bit, Ma'am."

"Well you are to be congratulated for your sterling work, and rewarded."

With a hiss of compressed steam one of the flunkies suddenly lurched into life. As it strode up to him, Ulysses saw that it was bearing a small tasselled cushion before it. Resting on the cushion was a piece of crimson ribbon, attached to a gunmetal-cast cross, bearing the motif of a crown surmounted by a lion, and the inscription 'FOR VALOUR'.

"We are awarding you the Victoria Cross for the valour and gallantry you demonstrated in selfless devotion to your Queen and Country, in the face of seemingly insurmountable odds." The Queen's lady-in-waiting stepped forward and, taking the medal from its cushion, pinned it to the lapel of Ulysses' jacket. "Congratulations, Mr Quicksilver."

"Thank you, Ma'am. I am deeply honoured."

There was a moment's silence, Ulysses waiting to see what else the monarch might have to say for herself, not certain whether it would be decorous to say anything himself without being spoken to first.

There was a crackle of static and Queen Victoria addressed him again. "That is all. You may go now."

"The Victoria Cross, very nice. I bet that would be worth a bob or two," Bartholomew Quicksilver said, eyeing up the medal as Ulysses descended the palace steps to the waiting Phantom.

"Yes, I expect it would. But it's not for sale," Ulysses said, smiling grimly at his incorrigible younger brother.

"Congratulations, sir," Nimrod said, beaming with paternal pride.

"Thank you, Nimrod."

"So, what did she say?" Barty pestered.

"Not a lot really."

"Not a lot? You have an audience with Queen Victoria herself..."

"After a fashion."

"... a privilege very few ever receive, and when asked what her royal highness said, all you can say is 'Not a lot really'? I would have thought you would have memorised every word, every syllable."

"You perhaps, Barty. It was quite underwhelming really."

"Well, I suppose anything would be after what you've been through recently."

Barty was much more his old self now. He was making

a good recovery from the bullet wound he had received thanks to Kitty Hawke's botched assassination attempt. His near death experience had apparently given him a new lease of life.

"Look, I'll tell you all about it over luncheon," Ulysses sighed with mock weariness, giving his sibling an affectionate slap on the back. "What I need right now is a stiff drink. My last dose of painkillers is starting to wear off and I simply can't face another day of press interruptions and well-wishers without being at least a little bit tipsy. Nimrod, the Ritz, if you would be so kind?"

"Yes, sir. The Ritz it is."

As the two brothers settled themselves in the back of the automobile Barty turned to Ulysses. "Now that you're by royal appointment, as it were, think of the future, Ulysses!"

"That great unwritten adventure you mean?"

"Absolutely!"

"Well, when I was plummeting towards the dark waters of the Thames a week ago I didn't even think I had a future. So I'm living for the now. Here's to the present! The future can wait."

Elsewhere, behind closed shutters and heavy drapes, in an inconspicuous room in an equally inconspicuous building within the comforting anonymity of shadowy gloom, the Star Chamber met.

"I call this meeting of the Star Chamber to order," said a voice almost smothered by the enshrouding semi-darkness, a commanding baritone in the mote-shot quiet of the hidden chamber.

The warm gloom was permeated by the gentle ticking of a clock, accompanied by the gurgle and splash of a cup of tea being poured.

"So, Wormwood failed," said a second voice, this one a rich claret, smooth and well rounded with age.

"Does that matter?" asked a third, crisper in tone and more pernicious, like the bark of a snapping terrier.

"No, it is enough that he tried. The Empire has become complacent," the first replied. "If it is to survive it must be tested, it must be challenged."

"And Quicksilver has a further part to play in this?" asked a fourth, aristocratic and sharp as a rapier's blade.

"You should know the answer to that better than most," said the second.

"Indeed."

There was the *ching* of a silver teaspoon ringing against the finest bone china and the sound of tea being stirred.

"So what is next in store for Mr Quicksilver, our agent of destruction?" asked the second.

There was the slurp of hot Earl Grey being supped. "Time will tell, gentlemen," said the fatherly tones of the first. "Time will tell. But rest assured we will be there, watching, every step of the way. After all history needs a helping hand every now and again, does it not?"

"Indeed it does," agreed the fourth, with a heavy sigh.

There were murmurs of assent.

"Then, for the time being, we are done, gentlemen," declared the first. "Let us be about our business elsewhere. I declare this meeting of the Star Chamber at an end."

Dusty silence returned to the room, other than for the rattle of a cup being returned to its saucer and history resumed its predetermined path.

THE END

Jonathan Green has been a freelance writer for the last fourteen years. In that time he has written *Sonic the Hedgehog* and *Fighting Fantasy* gamebooks – including the much-anticipated *Bloodbones* – atmospheric colour text for a variety of Games Workshop products, and numerous short stories for the Black Library's *Inferno!* magazine. To date he has written six novels set in the worlds of *Warhammer* and *Warhammer 40,000*, which have been translated into five languages. The co-creator of the world of *Pax Britannia, Unnatural History* is his first novel for Abaddon Books. He lives in West London, with his wife and two young children, where he spends his nights behind a computer keyboard and his days working as a teacher.

coming
June
2007...

Now read the Prologue from the second book
in the exciting *Pax Britannia* series...

PAX BRITANNIA

EL SOMBRA

Al Ewing

COMING JUNE 2007 (UK)
AUGUST 2007 (US)

ISBN 13: 978-1-905437-34-X
ISBN 10: 1-905437-34-4

£6.99 (UK)/ $7.99 (US)

W W W . A B A D D O N B O O K S . C O M

PROLOGUE

The Man and The Desert

The man walked across the desert.

And the desert destroyed the man.

The sun was a dragon that breathed fire on his neck and his back. Each grain of sand beneath his feet was a branding iron. He wanted to cry, but the desert had stolen his tears. Instead, his eyes wept blood.

In his left hand he clutched a sash of silk, red stained black with spattered gore. His right hand gripped a sword. The knuckles on both hands were white and straining, almost bulging through the burned skin. He couldn't have opened his hands if he'd wanted to. But he didn't want to.

All the man wanted to do was die.

The wedding had been three days before.

And oh, what a wedding it had been!

The groom had passed the bride the thirteen coins and the rosary lasso was placed around their shoulders and then Father Santiago had blessed the couple – and when they kissed, you should have heard the noise! The whole town cheered and stamped their feet for joy! Everyone from old Gilberto, who'd crafted a pair of wedding ducks, to little Carina, the *madrina de ramo*, nine years old and too shy to do anything other than giggle and punch the dashing *madrina de laso* on the arm. The cheer rang until the mariachis struck up their lively wedding march and Heraclio led Maria – his Maria! – to his magnificent white horse, Santo. The noble beast stood quietly as his new mistress was lifted onto his back and then bore her with all the grace his old horse body could muster to the Great Square. Heraclio gave the venerable beast a gentle pat on the muzzle and fed him a lump of sugar from his wedding-coat as the townspeople followed behind, led by the mariachi band, for dancing and laughter and food and good wine.

It was all the little town of Pasito had been talking of for months. The day when Heraclio, the handsome guardsman who rode through the town on his white horse and gave sugar-drops to the children from the pocket of his coat, would marry his Maria, perhaps the most beautiful girl the little Mexican town had ever yet produced and certainly the very finest dancer. To see her laugh and smile atop the gently pacing Santo was to catch a brief glimpse of what life could offer a man. Miguel the baker, forty-three years old and fat as his own loaves, drank her in with his eyes, and then turned those green eyes to his wife, whom he had not shared a bed with in more than a decade – and did those laughing green eyes not now have a certain sparkle that said: *Come, mi amor! Let us forget the passing of years and find ourselves again under the desert stars!*

Little Hector, the *madrina de laso,* who carried the coins and the lasso, all of twelve years old and looking very handsome in his miniature version of Heraclio's red wedding sash, looked at Maria as though he had never seen her before, never seen anyone before... and this time, when little Carina punched him in his arm, he grinned a cocky grin at her and said, "One day I'm gonna marry you!" Poor Carina, she blushed as red as that wedding sash, and ran to hide behind her father, the chubby jailer Rafael, who chuckled and murmured to his neighbour in the crowd – "That boy, he's *muy caballero!* Like a little Heraclio, hey? In ten years we'll be going to his wedding!"

"Ah, not if you can catch him first!" chuckled Isidoro the schoolteacher, and Carina blushed even redder – but smiled secretly at Hector from the safety of her father's legs.

The only one who could look at Maria and not feel as though life was worth living was the poet Djego. Thin as a rake and soft as dough, with a mane of lank, black hair and a tiny pencil moustache, he might have been considered handsome – even debonair – if not for the air of misery and sorrow that he had carefully crafted to hang around himself like a funeral shroud. He was generally tolerated, occasionally even humoured, but there was not a soul in the town who could possibly understand how Djego and Heraclio could be brothers.

The wise old women of the town nodded sagely in their rocking chairs when the question was put to them, and the reply was always the same. "Sometimes, a mother and a father put so much into that first child, that it takes a little out of the womb and the balls, and after that they don't work so good. So the first son is like a god, or maybe they have a princess for a daughter. And after that..." At this point in the telling Djego would strut past with his nose in the air, frowning as though there was nothing to be enjoyed on a sunny day but his own secret and special pain. And the old wise women would chuckle. "After that... *blehhh*."

And that was the reaction when Djego walked through the town, composing his awful poems, never turning his hand to anything of value, never allowing his heavy, leaden, rhymeless, metreless verse to breathe or represent something of beauty or worth.

Blehhh.

His brother looked after him, as he always had since their parents had died, because he felt sorry for him. "Djego is an idiot," he would say, "but he is my brother.

And one day he will be able to laugh with me."

All of this is not to say that Djego could resist Maria's charms – quite the opposite. But when most men would see the most beautiful girl in Pasito and want to go out and live life, dance, sing, make great plans for themselves – Djego looked upon her and only wished to be transformed into stone.

The reason for this was simple. Djego had been hopelessly in love with Maria since the first moment his brother had brought her home.

The man in the desert fell to his knees and then fell forward onto his face.

Each breath was agony now. His throat was numb and his lips were swollen with the lack of moisture. His skin was like cracked parchment, burnt red. Blisters covered his feet from the red–hot sand that now seared his body.

In front of him there was a small cactus, no larger than his head. His eyes could barely focus on it, but some switch in his mind triggered the thought that here was water. If you could question his conscious mind on the matter, he would tell you vehemently that he wanted no water, he wanted nothing but to die, and die soon. But his fingers crept forward, scrabbling at the spines of the cactus, drawing blood, then reaching for the hilt of the sword.

The conscious mind was all but dead. The brave desire to walk himself to death had boiled away in the furnace of the desert sun. All that was left was the instinct to survive. The sword flashed, carving the cactus open, the dry, cracked mouth making a terrible noise of despair and rage as a precious drop of moisture was lost to the sand. Then he was leaning forward to drink in what little moisture there was, eating the pulpy, wet flesh, swallowing and sucking it down, tearing at it with his teeth, breaking away the spines so he could devour the skin of the cactus itself.

When he began to choke on the cactus, he rolled to his side and slumped on the sand, unable to move, the pulpy meat of the cactus resting in his arid mouth as the sun beat mercilessly down.

The cactus was of the *Trichocereus* variety. Originally from Ecuador, it had slowly migrated north through Central America, mutating as it went to survive the greenhouse effect brought down on the planet by Magna Britannia's runaway industrialism. Originally, the *Trichocereus* was used by tribal shaman to provide them with intense, often terrifying visions. Those botanists who had discovered this new variety termed it *Trichocereus Validus*.

This was because its psychotropic qualities were hundreds, perhaps thousands of times more powerful.

The man's eyes bulged. He began to convulse. Foam ran from his lips as from a rabid dog.

He could no longer recall his name, but he remembered very vividly that three days before he had been punched in the face by a woman, for the first and the last time in his life.

The procession had reached the great square, and there the dancing began. Heraclio danced with his beautiful bride to the strains of the mariachi band, and all around him, the whole town danced in the shape of a heart, as was tradition. Had there ever been a happier moment in the whole time that the town of Pasito had stood? Certainly no-one could remember, although occasionally a husband would turn to a wife and squeeze their hand a little tighter, the glimmer in their eyes seeming to say: *Yes, I remember it well.*

And then the great circle broke up, and every man in the town took their turn to dance with the lovely Maria, and the women queued to be whirled around by the manly Heraclio, who danced well, but not as well as with Maria, and danced with consideration, slowing his pace where necessary – even when gently escorting the 95-year-old Consuela Vasquez, the town's oldest resident, from one end of the square to the other.

Occasionally, Maria would sit herself down in her magnificent white dress, and pass time with the old men and women who, unlike the beloved and venerable Consuela, were unable to dance – either through advanced age, physical disorder or, in the case of Toraidio DeMario, several bottles of good wine. She would also flash her stunning smile at Elbanco the singer and the rest of his band, who would not fail to play whatever song she requested. Even those they did not know, they would do their very best to attempt, plucking the words from the air and making up a tune which fit them. A song called The Dark Side Of The Moon, for example, had been the talk of London some ten or twenty years previously. It was a melancholy ballad with subtle undertones of laudanum abuse, and had become so famous that word of it had managed to spread as far as El Pasito. In the hands of Elbanco's band it because a quick, jolly tune about a cuckold painting his wife's bottom black to discourage the many suitors who came running when she waved it out of the window. Maria laughed and danced to it regardless, and thanked each of the band with another sparkling smile, which they considered ample payment for their labours.

And so, when Djego finally deigned to take the floor and dance, Elbanco and his cohorts were busily attempting to perform an apparently famous European ditty called The Dancing Queen which allegedly went something like:

"No le gusta caminar, no puede montar a caballo!
Como se puede bailar? Es un escandolo!"

Eyebrows were raised – the venerable Conseula gave a gasp of shock which was a rare event as she had, it was believed, seen it all. Djego the poet, who was above all petty enjoyments, was moving to dance for the first time! It was scarcely believable. To her credit, Maria acknowledged the rarity of the event, and took him gently in her arms to start a waltz about the floor. Heraclio watched with a proud smile. Djego had never told him his feelings on any matter, and so he assumed he was simply watching his shy younger brother finally coming out of the thick shell he had so painstakingly built for himself. He accepted the hand of the chief bridesmaid, and led her into a stately twirl as Elbanco waved his guitarist into a spirited solo.

Of course, he had no way of knowing what was truly on Djego's mind.

Maria's green eyes sparkled as she looked into his, and the smile on her face held a hint of mischief. "So you've finally decided to enjoy yourself, hah? Is this the start of a trend or a momentary bout of insanity?"

Djego smiled stiffly in response. "I... would like it to be the start of something."

She raised an eyebrow. "A new career as a lady-killer? Well, in that case, you'll have to stop these hands shaking. Let me lead a little." She began to gently guide him around the floor, and soon they were moving almost gracefully, with Djego even managing a little smile. "There! Isn't this nice? Djego, if you can keep this up, I promise I will dance at your wedding. Come on, smile! You look handsome when you smile, my brother-in-law. You should do it more. Where's the harm? It might bring your wedding day closer, hah?"

Djego's smile faltered. "I do not see that I will ever get married now, Maria."

Maria laughed, and the laugh was strong and sure. "Oh, there's time yet. Look at your brother when I first met him! Remember how he used to spit out of windows? And then he hit poor Father Santiago in the eye!" She laughed again, but Djego's attempt at a smile was nervous. His hands were shaking again. Maria sighed. "Djego, if you keep this up I'm going to abandon you to Consuela. She'll teach you a few more things than dancing, I warn you. You've not seen how she has her eye on you?"

Djego shuddered, but not because of Maria's mental image. He swallowed hard, then spoke softly, barely heard above the music.

"Maria... do you remember the poems that Heraclio sent you?"

She blinked at him, continuing to lead the dance more by reflex than anything else, cocking her head slightly to look at him. "How do you know about those? He showed them to you to get a second opinion, right?"

Djego shook his head. "I wrote those, Maria. Those were *my* words to you."

Maria said nothing, but she stopped the dance.

"Those poems I wrote to you – I gave them to Heraclio because I didn't think I was worthy. But those are *my* feelings, Maria. The poems that won your heart, that made you his – they were mine." He swallowed, searching her eyes. Her expression was unreadable, but he pressed on. "This... this should be my wedding day." His eyes welled. The sadness was almost too great for him to contain. "I... I know I've waited too long... but... perhaps one day..."

This was the moment that Maria pulled away from him, swung around and slammed one of her fists into his jaw, sending him tumbling onto the ground in a cloud of dust.

"Estupido!" she yelled, and kicked him in the ribs. Elbanco and his band stopped playing. The venerable Consuela gave another gasp of shock. It was doubtful whether her heart would be able to stand any more unthinkable happenings that day. Little Hector put his hand over his mouth, turning ashen – his juvenile meditations on the power of manhood shattered in an instant. Carina only grinned.

Heraclio stood dumbfounded, then found his voice. "Djego, what have you done now?"

Maria spat venom as she grabbed the lapels of Djego's black shirt and hauled him up.

"You honestly think you can walk up to me on my wedding day and say such things? Those poems were terrible, Djego! They were *desgraciado*! It was nice that Heraclio thought of reading me poems, but in the end I used them as kindling for the fire! You cannot write, *tonto!*"

Djego sniffled, reaching to wipe the blood from his nose, looking at the blazing Maria with wide eyes.

"Seriously, *idiota*, what was your big plan, hah? Would this be like one of those stupid books you read? Was I going to be the unattainable great love you pined away for for the rest of your life? Were we supposed to swap charged glances over the dinner table? Well guess what..."

Her foot slammed into his groin. Hard. Djego gasped, crumpled and then began to retch, throwing up a puddle of half-digested wine onto the ground.

"I fell in love with a man. Not a bunch of stupid poems. So crawl off and hide away for a while, hah? You're no longer welcome at my wedding party. Get the hell out!"

Silence rolled across the great square. All eyes were on the sobbing Djego as he lay there, weeping openly. And had there been a more awkward moment in Pasito's long history than this? It was certainly the most public embarrassment anyone had suffered. Shocked, helpless eyes turned to each other, then to Heraclio who shrugged as if to say: *What can I do? She's right!* Not even the venerable Consuela could see a means of rescuing the occasion.

So in many ways it was a mercy when the stage exploded in a gout of fire and shrapnel, tearing Elbanco and his band into bloody shreds.

Djego convulsed on the sand as the sun fried his flesh like dough. The memories seemed so clear. He could feel Maria's fist as it hammered into his jaw, again, again, again, the shame fracturing him with every impact, breaking him like glass. He could feel his soul filling with bile, hissing black acid that burnt and seared the walls of himself.

The shame. The shame.

His throat burned and he retched. He could feel the vomit, the shame, creeping slowly up his gullet. His eyes were wide, looking down at the glittering sand, and every grain seemed to him like a mountain. The sun was a jewel sparkling on blue cloth and in his ears there was a humming sound, as though he was a string that had been plucked – as though the whole world was a bead dancing on a taut string that had been plucked and now was humming, humming, *humming* and it was *deafening*.

A shadow fell across him, hotter on his back than the heat of the sun. A giant shadow.

A giant.

He turned over and saw everything clearly. Like a mountain.

His brother stood above him. A giant with his brother's face, looming like God. His brother, big as judgement above him, standing and looking down on him. Always. Always.

Djego closed his eyes and tried to breathe. His heart was pounding in his chest, a hot coal resting against his ribcage. Everything in his ears was still *humming*. Humming. His eyes were closed but the scene was the same. His brother, his judgement, looming over him, looking down.

Djego understood that this had always been happening. It would always be happening. His brother would always tower over him, always leave him in shadow, always look down. After what had happened he had no right to expect anything else.

After what had happened. Djego shuddered and retched, more black-bile-memory flooding him, scalding him. He felt something hot on his face. Tears. Or blood. He shook like a child.

The giant's massive hand closed about him and squeezed.

Instantly there came the echo of similar blasts, a tidal wave of fire that seemed to sweep through the town, burning and destroying at random. The courthouse in the north of the town burst like an egg, sending showers of masonry into neighbouring houses, great shards of glass whirling like propellers as they smashed through walls into the cribs of children too young to enjoy the celebration. Then the screaming started.

The crowd scattered, running and trampling in a chaotic mass of bodies, as the crack and clatter of machine-gun fire stabbed through the night air and bullets hit the ground around them. The venerable Consuela's head became a fine mist as a high-velocity round pierced her left eyeball destroying, in an instant, the mind that held so much of the town in the amber of memory. Perhaps she would have died anyway. This was, after all, the third unbelievable event of the day.

A bullet found Isidoro the schoolteacher, and he fell on his face in the dirt before flapping like a hooked fish, looking down at his right leg in horror. Mid-thigh, the flesh had been torn away and he could see bone and the flapping ends of the femoral artery. Isidoro taught biology among his many other subjects and he knew what that meant. But he did not believe. Even when darkness closed over his vision and he toppled backwards, shuddered and went still, he did not believe.

Who could?

Even Santo did not survive. He tried to run to his Master at the first sound of fire, but one of the bullets clipped a leg, shattering it and sending the animal tumbling to the ground. Another shot slammed into his flank, ricocheted off a rib and exited his breast in a fountain of bloody horsemeat that cascaded over the screaming Hector. The boy's screams joined the cacophony from the agonised horse before a third volley of shots silenced them both. Santo's end was merciful. One of the bullets shattered his skull and he died in an instant.

Hector was not so lucky. For the next ten minutes he stared in mute horror at the seeping mass of offal that had toppled from his torn belly.

Maria's blistering anger fell away into confusion and horror. She looked up at the sky, unable to comprehend what could be doing this. And what she saw terrified her beyond measure.

There were men in the sky.

Men in grey uniforms, carrying great black iron guns, with grey helmets and grey expressions. In the sky! On their backs were metal wings, flapping slowly in the air, great gusts of steam shooting from them as they slowly clanked and groaned. *That isn't holding them up*, she thought, madly, unable to comprehend. *Something else must be.* And then one of the men turned his gun on her and she darted forward blindly.

Everything was happening very slowly now. Her feet, moving through thick molasses, hit Djego who was still curled up on the ground, sobbing like a child. Unable to stop herself, she fell forward, landing hard on the ground in her wedding dress. She looked up, winded and spitting dust from her mouth, and then there was a terrible sound and something hit her very very hard.

She couldn't breathe. There was something wet on her dress. It was spoiled. Everything had been spoiled. Somewhere, she could hear Heraclio screaming, but it was very far away. Was he crying? *Don't cry, my love. I'll sort this out for you. I always do.*

The last thing she saw was the insignia on the shoulder of the man who'd shot her. A red cross in a white circle, with broken ends, all the way round. Like four little L-shapes joined up.

Where have I seen that before? Thought Maria.

And that was that.

Heraclio looked up at the flying men and screamed... but that was in the past, wasn't it? Djego felt himself resting on sand, on the giant's palm. He could feel the flesh through the sand. He saw now the truth of it. Heraclio was looking down at him and his mouth opened in hungry anticipation.

The mouth of the giant hung wide open, then closed, and between the teeth were the bones of Djego's ankles, snapping, cracking like chicken-bone, bitten through. Djego screamed. He was going to die. He was going to be eaten bite by bite. Eaten by the giant, the giant judgement, the giant *reputation*. The reputation he always had to live up to.

When they had been children Djego had often been pushed over and beaten and his books taken and trampled in the mud. The boys in the village thought he was fat and doughy and pasty, and they kicked him sometimes until he pissed blood. And that was happening now. He was a child again. He was crying again. His brother was coming to rescue him again, wild swinging fists and shouts. Heraclio always came in the end, running and punching and kicking the bullies until finally the attacks stopped. Nobody picked on Heraclio's brother. Nobody. Djego heard his brother's confident shout again from the giant, the wind of it rushing in his hair.

And Djego felt shame again. Black bile. Again, his brother had done what he could not. His handsome brother, his popular brother who fought where Djego could only cower and weep. He had fought so hard. Never harder than that day, that day it had all ended between them. Heraclio had no brother now.

Djego hated him, and the hate brought more self-disgust that cut him open like a knife.

The giant bit deep. One of Djego's legs was torn from the pelvis, crunched and swallowed whole.

He looked up at the giant's eyes and screamed.

Heraclio looked up at the flying men and screamed.

"*¡Conchas!* Get down here! Get down here and face me!"

The sight of his beloved lying on the ground – the look in her eyes, the *anger* that was there – filled his vision with red mist. He gripped his sword in white knuckles, waving it at the sky-soldiers as they fired, bullets cascading on the ground all around him. Heraclio seemed a vision of bloody vengeance. Righteous and pure.

One of the soldiers took notice.

He had been barking orders to his fellows, but now he handed command to a subordinate and swooped down, landing in the dust of the great square. As the soldier slowly removed his helmet, Heraclio's streaming eyes burned into him, as if seeking to destroy him with a gaze.

The soldier smiled. He was tall and blonde, barely nineteen, with sharp blue eyes that returned Heraclio's burning look with an audacious twinkle of his own. Heraclio was handsome but this newcomer was beautiful. Beautiful in the way that men can be. That dangerous, tempting perfection that can be found in ancient Greek statues. Or the rebellious teenagers in films who break all the rules, the wild ones.

An angel's face with a devil's eyes.

He smiled, and the smile promised terrible things.

And then he drew the sword from his scabbard.

Heraclio was not in the mood for niceties. He screamed and lunged, the point of the sword aimed at the heart of his enemy. The soldier, smiling softly, stepped back and swept his sword in a short arc, deflecting Heraclio's wild thrust easily before transforming the fluid motion into a strike. The point of his sword slashed across Heraclio's cheek, leaving a deep cut.

"Is that all you can manage?" purred the angel-face.

Heraclio screamed. His face was contorted in a fury nobody had ever seen there before, and yet his movements were precise now, as though the rage boiling in his belly was giving him focus. Djego, cowering on the ground, looked up at him through tears, and saw perhaps the greatest display of sword fighting he had ever seen. In Heraclio's white knuckles, the blade flashed and darted like a living thing, seeking those gaps in the defence of his foe that would allow him to plunge the blade deep into flesh.

It found none. The defence was impregnable. The soldier flashed a mocking grin, the blades clanging as he parried each blow without effort.

Above them the flying men circled like vultures, firing when necessary to herd the crowd into position, then landing and screaming orders at them in a foreign tongue.

Pasito had only one guardsman, and he was busy.

The swords flashed and struck. Sweat poured into Heraclio's eyes and he blinked, the sword jerking, leaving him wide open for the killing strike. But it did not come. In that heartbeat, the handsome young soldier looked straight into Heraclio's eyes. Heraclio blinked again. The pause seemed to stretch on forever, and the implication of it made Heraclio's blood turn to ice in his veins.

The soldier was choosing not to kill him... just yet.

The angelic face smiled again. He had seen the realisation strike home, the fear begin to build, and so he lunged forward, sword flashing, pressing the attack, but keeping within Heraclio's skill. He was forcing Heraclio to work. Toying with him.

"Djego!" Heraclio shouted. "Help me!" The sound chilled Djego's heart. He could not move.

The angelic soldier pushed forward a little further, enjoying the fear. This was the moment when his foe realised that there was no hope of survival, that he was outclassed and outmatched. The sight of that knowledge blooming in Heraclio's eyes made his heart sing. Soon, there would come that other moment he savoured. The sweet moment of surrender, when the enemy knew he could no longer fight against his own death. He licked his lips in anticipation as his sword flashed, carving a line across his enemy's chest, then striking his blade through the muscle at the shoulder. Two quick strikes, designed to remove all hope. The end would come soon.

"Herr Oberst!" One of the other soldiers called over. "Wir haben die Verarbeitung beendet."

The angel-faced soldier nodded briskly. "Ich bin dort in einer Sekunde."

And then he moved very quickly, lunging and flicking with the tip of his sword. The blade carved deep into Heraclio's belly, slicing up, opening out the guts, sending a tide of blood and offal and filth spattering onto the ground. Heraclio's eyes went wide, and then he looked down and he saw. And the look of disgust on his face at his own body, so exposed and revealed for what it was – such a look was sweeter for the soldier than the look of surrender could have been. It was perfect.

"Eine vollkommene Tötung." Murmured the angel-face. And then he simply walked away.

Heraclio collapsed into his own offal, giving shuddering gasps punctuated by hacking coughs that sprayed more blood into the dirt.

Djego stumbled to his feet and ran forward to cradle his brother. "Oh God... *Dios Mio*... Heraclio, you have to keep still..." He tried to remove the red wedding sash, to use it as a bandage, but Heraclio gave a sharp twist, snarling like a dog, blood and spit dripping from his chin as he looked at his own brother with the same hate he'd had for the soldiers. The sash was left hanging in Djego's hand.

"Bastard."

Djego recoiled as if he'd been slapped, but Heraclio reached to grip his wrist, pulling him back, spitting blood with every word.

"*Corbarde.* Spineless coward. You... you cower in the

dirt while your brother is cut to shreds... while Maria, my wife, is murdered! Maria, who you make a big scene over, who you say you love – but you didn't love her enough to protect her, did you? A dog would have done that! But not you! You *bastardo asqueroso!*"

"Heraclio, please! I can get help..."

Heraclio gripped his sword and thrust the handle towards his brother. "It's too late to help, *mierda*. Go ahead and run. Run away like the bastard coward you are!"

"I... I won't run..." stammered Djego, taking the sword, horrified at the blood that coated the handle, that coated his hands, that flowed into the sand like a torrent and soaked his wedding–suit.

"You will. *Inmundicia*. My brother the shit. You will run away as you always do... but never far enough. Never far enough."

"Heraclio, *Please*..."

Heraclio looked up then, and fixed his brother Djego with a terrible stare. A look which would never fade.

"No matter how far you run Djego, my blood will always be on you. My ghost will always be with you. You can run from your home, your family, your responsibilities but you can never, never run from me. That is my curse upon you, brother. I will be with you until the day that you die."

Djego opened his mouth to speak, to plead, tears streaming down his face – but it was too late. Heraclio's grip relaxed. He slumped backwards, eyes rolling up into his head. Whatever strength had kept him alive long enough to deliver his terrible curse was gone. All that was left was a corpse at his feet.

Djego lifted his eyes, the sword and the sash in his grip, and he saw what was happening. The soldiers had landed and were herding the people through the square

in a great mass, prodding them forward with batons.
Old Gilberto was kneeling over the body of his son,
looking dumbfounded. Two of the soldiers marched to
him in their black boots and almost gently forced him
up and into the march. Then they turned towards Djego,
and a terrible realisation ran through him that poured
ice into his spine.

He would have to fight. He would have to lift his
brother's sword and run towards the soldiers and try
to kill them. Most likely, they would shoot. The bullets
would punch through his chest, his belly, his face and
he would be left dead in the dirt. If he was unlucky,
the baby-faced commander would swoop down and use
Djego for sword fighting practice. Cut him up like meat
and leave his guts hanging out for the vultures.

Djego swallowed and took a step forward, tears
streaming down his face, the sword a blur in front of
him. He had to fight. It was the only thing left to do. If
he didn't fight then what did that make him?

The soldiers raised their guns with a chuckle, then a
laugh – laughing at the man in the dirty black clothes,
doughy and pathetic and lank-haired, with his wobbling
sword and his streaming crybaby eyes.

The sound was enough to break Djego. He turned and
ran, bullets kicking up the dirt at his feet.

He didn't stop running until he reached the desert
and his breath gave out, and then he forced himself to
keep walking as the town receded in the distance behind
him.

The sword and the sash were clutched in his hands,
his knuckles were white with the strain and he could
no longer see through the tears, but he kept stumbling
forward, breath ragged, one foot in front of the other.
He was walking in search of death.

He walked for three days.

The teeth of the giant bit through Djego's, severing his spine. Heraclio's perfect teeth. His perfect, handsome face. Crunching down into his chest. Djego understood then, as every piece of him was bitten away and crushed, how small and pathetic he had been. How meaningless. How futile and ridiculous. It was a pleasure to let go, to let 'Djego' be eaten and swallowed bite by bite, to let his ugly soul fracture and split into infinite pieces. Swallowed into something larger than he was.

He no longer felt pain, but something itched at him, at the back of his skull. The face. The face on the giant. He thought it was Heraclio's, but it had never been. The face on the giant was his own.

He heard laughter from his own throat, deep and rich, booming across the sands, a wonderful, joyous laugh of triumph and confidence. Whose laugh was that? Not Djego. He was dead and gone and he never laughed. But if not Djego... then who?

Who was lying in the sand?

He shuddered, convulsed once more, every muscle rigid. The eyes in his head rolled back. He gripped the sword and the sash tighter, until they seemed to pulse with a life of their own.

And then his heart stopped.

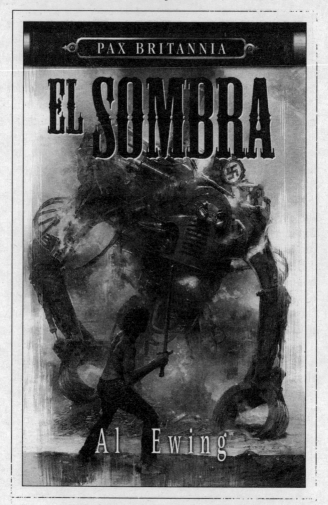

JNUE 2007 Price: £6.99 ★ ISBN: 1-905437-34-X

AUGUST 2007 Price: $7.99 ★ ISBN 13: 978-1-905437-34-4

THE AFTERBLIGHT CHRONICLES

KILL OR CURE

Rebecca Levene

APRIL 2007 Price: £6.99 ★ ISBN: 1-905437-32-3

JUNE 2007 Price: $7.99 ★ ISBN 13: 978-1-905437-32-0

TOMES *of the* DEAD

THE **WORDS** OF THEIR **ROARING**

Matthew Smith

MAY 2007 Price: £6.99 ★ ISBN: 1-905437-33-1

JULY 2007 Price: $7.99 ★ ISBN 13: 978-1-905437-33-7

Dreams of Inan

A KIND OF PEACE

Andy Boot

Price: £6.99 ★ ISBN: 1-905437-02-1

Price: $7.99 ★ ISBN 13: 978-1-905437-02-3

Dreams of Inan
STEALING LIFE

Antony Johnston

Price: £6.99 ★ ISBN: 1-905437-12-9

Price: $7.99 ★ ISBN 13: 978-1-905437-12-2

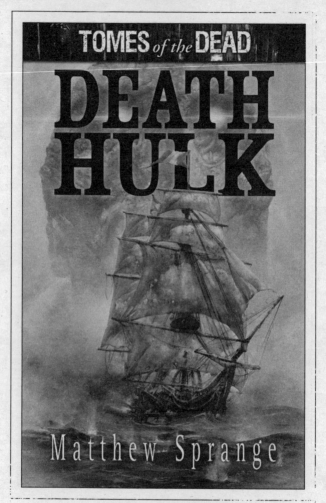

TOMES *of the* DEAD
DEATH HULK

Matthew Sprange

Price: £6.99 ★ ISBN: 1-905437-03-X

Price: $7.99 ★ ISBN 13: 978-1-905437-03-0

Price: £6.99 ★ ISBN: 1-905437-04-8

Price: $7.99 ★ ISBN 13: 978-1-905437-04-7

Abaddon Books